Catalyst

A Novel

Catalyst

A Novel

Dustin Taylor

Emerald Inkwell
Eugene
2020

Published by Emerald Inkwell

Written and published in Oregon.
Printed in the United States of America.
Published 2020.

First Edition

ISBN: 978-0-9965382-2-0

Cover art by Dustin Taylor

For the people who pushed me to start,
the people who kicked me in the ass to keep going,
and the people who were there when I finished.

A very special thank-you to my 7th grade teacher, Mrs. Jean London, who instilled in me a passion for crafting sentences. This book wouldn't flow without you.

"Travel changes you. As you move through this life and this world you change things slightly, you leave marks behind, however small. And in return, life – and travel – leaves marks on you. Most of the time, those marks – on your body or on your heart – are beautiful. Often, though, they hurt."

—Anthony Bourdain, *The Nasty Bits*

<u>Prologue</u>

Jack Porter lay cold and lifeless in a rich, walnut casket lined with white satin. Candles flickered around him, but the warmth I had once known no longer filled his face. His soft features had tightened, and the rosy cheer had been replaced with sallow severity. He was nearly unrecognizable, and it left an uneasy feeling in my stomach. I reached into my inside pocket and pulled out a black-and-white photo of a younger Jack and his wife, sliding it gently beneath his clasped hands. "Say 'hi' to Marci for me."

I took a step back and broadened my focus to take in the main altar of the church. The mass of black marble columns and white marble sculptures topped with a golden cross cast an eerie shadow over an already dark day. With one last look at Jack, I turned to leave. It was a small funeral, mostly made up of family sitting in the front row of pews. His two daughters wore black dresses with black veils over their faces, and their husbands wore black suits with white shirts and black neckties. I nodded solemnly at them to say *Thank you for inviting me.* They nodded back, trying to smile, appreciation peeking out of tear-soaked eyes.

Beyond Jack's family sat a scattering of several other guests. He lived a more isolated life in his later years and had few close friends then. Those he had early on were either dead or couldn't make the trip.

My footfalls echoed in the high, vaulted ceiling as I made my way down the center aisle toward the entrance, but my feet didn't seem to be making the sounds. I knew I was moving, but I felt no sensation when my feet touched the stone floor. Glancing from side to side, I observed those who had come to pay their respects. Some prayed, some cried, some comforted those who cried. The rest sat with a glazed-over expression that was either due to a slow realization or because they handled funerals that way. I saw a couple of familiar faces, but when our eyes connected and I opened my mouth to speak, no words would come out.

I reached the entrance to the church and looked back at Jack's casket one last time. Silence had closed around me so that I heard nothing but my own heartbeat. Then, I took a deep breath, turned up the collar of my wool overcoat, and stepped out into the icy air. A few yards from the church, I sat on the cold steps next to a frozen fountain and pulled my flask from my inside pocket. Tipping it back, I let the whiskey warm my body all the way through. "It's colder than a well-digger's ass out here," I muttered to myself as I pulled my coat tighter around me and began the frigid walk back to my hotel.

Chapter 1

Two years earlier…

I think about this shit way too often. A frigid gust of air sent my hair into a frenzy and set the shorter hairs on my neck on end. I looked down at my feet, balanced side by side on the rail, then past them to the dark turbulence below. The bitter cold and poisonous thoughts sent shivers through my body, and I decided it would be best if I left my perch. I stepped down to the concrete below and lit a cigarette.

It feels terrible to want to kill yourself. The sunken feeling that seeps through your entire body, through your soul. The sudden awareness that all it would take is a step. One step to end everything. Your pain and euphoria, your sorrow and happiness. Any future you once had, good or bad, would be gone. At that moment, your life is in your hands and your hands only. When that feeling shows up while you're standing on a bridge, it's as if God arranged a field trip through Hell and personally signed your permission slip.

That's exactly how I felt that night, as well as many others over the past few months when I found myself on the footbridge behind Autzen Stadium. The air bit at my face and ears, punishing me for not wearing my hood. I ignored it and took another drag from the cigarette dangling from my lips. I didn't smoke often, only when I really felt the weight of life on my shoulders. Five stamped-out cigarette butts at my feet served as evidence that life weighed heavily on me that night.

The smoke warmed my body as I inhaled, and the menthol soothed me. My arm dangled at my side, the cigarette held loosely between my thumb and forefinger as I stared off at the distant lights of downtown Eugene, wondering who was in the lit windows and what they were doing. *Whatever they're doing, I bet they don't feel this way*, I thought. I'd had bouts of mild depression in the past, but never had they been so intense. Never had I thought so much about what would happen if I took that step.

I knew I would never take it. Too many people meant too much to me. I'd seen what happens when someone leaves everything and everyone behind, and I would never do that to the people I loved. Nevertheless, the desire was strong. I couldn't even fully explain where the hell such darkness came from. I'd always been such a happy and ambitious kid, but where was that now? The confusion of wondering that did nothing to help my state of mind. I flicked the rest of the cigarette toward the river below, watching the crimson glow disappear, then lit another.

"Bum one?"

"Jesus!" I jerked out of whatever trance I had been in and saw my friend Ben walking up with a smile. I pulled a cigarette from the pack and handed it to him.

"You scared the shit out of me, man." I flipped open my silver Zippo lighter and held the flame to the end of the cigarette hanging from his mouth. "How'd you know I was here?"

He laughed and took a drag. "My bad. You're usually much more observant. I texted you and didn't hear back, so I figured I'd see if you were down here.

"Oh, shit." I pulled my phone from my pocket and saw the text message notification from a half hour earlier. "Sorry about that. How was work?"

"The usual. Shitty. What's going on? You look like you've seen better days."

"Haven't we all?" I took another long drag. "I'm just tired of it all. Tired of the bullshit at work, tired of everything in my life and not knowing how to get it moving again. Plus, it doesn't help that I keep getting hit with memories of Liz, nearly every night now. Naturally, it's when I'm trying to go to bed, so I really haven't been sleeping."

"Really? I thought you'd been over that for a while."

"I had been. I don't know what's going on. I think that hole in my life is just becoming more noticeable again, and she's the last person who filled it. I'm at that point where it's gotten lonely to keep doing things alone."

"That makes sense. You guys were together for quite a while. It'll pass, eventually. Just gotta keep your mind occupied in the meantime. Write!"

"It's not as easy as it sounds. And if I write, it'll probably all wind up being about her." I dropped the remaining half of my cigarette and rubbed it out with my toe. "Too many of those tonight. Too many of those this week. This is the third night in a row I've been out here and smoked just as many." I didn't say anything about my adventures on the handrail.

Ben looked down at my feet. "I guess! You want to go get a beer? I'm buyin'."

"I appreciate it, but I'm gonna take a rain check. I'm kind of tired."

"Wooow, not a single word about *me* offering to buy beer? You *must* be in a bad place."

I attempted a smile. Ben joked, but I sensed the air of concern in his voice.

"No worries," he said. "I should probably get home myself."

I took one last look at the city lights in the distance, sparkling on the surface of the river, before walking with Ben back down the path to the parking lot. "Don't worry about writing about Liz. If you're writing, it's good. It might hurt a little—or a lot—but it's words on paper." "True…" "Give me a call if you need to talk or anything, man." "Will do. Thanks." I got in my car and drove off.

I arrived at my apartment complex to find an early-90s Honda Civic with an enormous spoiler and chrome rims parked so poorly in my space that I couldn't even take the next spot over. "Douchebag," I muttered. I drove a little farther down to the guest parking area and pulled into the last open space. *Fantastic,* I thought, glowering at the clock on my dashboard. *The parties are just starting.* I walked indifferently through several groups of college kids huddled outside various apartments, smoking and drinking from red party cups, just as they had last Friday and the Friday before that, and as they would Saturday night and the Saturday after that. Pot smoke hovered in the air near some of the groups. A trio of attractive girls—all wearing precariously high heels, low-cut tops, and skirts that made no sense in mid-January—stumbled drunkenly past me toward one of the apartments, laughing and talking loudly.

Watching them enter the apartment, I couldn't help but feel a little jealous of whatever guys they were going to hang out with. Then, I unlocked my door and stepped into my dark apartment, glad to realize I had left the wall heater on when I'd gone out earlier. Without bothering to turn on a light, I tossed my keys and wallet on the kitchen counter and pulled a short rocks glass from the cupboard. In the glow of the floodlights coming through the kitchen window, I poured three fingers of Jameson into the glass and tossed in a couple of ice cubes for good measure. I took a long drink, welcoming the warmth in my body, then refilled the glass and sat on the couch. I kicked off my shoes and propped my feet on the coffee table.

Nothing good was on TV, just the same movies that somehow wound up on the cable channels over and over again. *Why do you even pay for this shit?* I asked myself for the umpteenth time. I loaded Netflix and searched through the available TV shows until I settled on an episode of one of my favorite shows about four friends who own a failing bar in Philadelphia. I honestly didn't really care what I watched. Any distraction would be good, but I had no real faith in anything to distract me that night.

The suburbia-sitcom theme music that usually brought at least a small smile to my face played through, barely catching my attention. Fifteen minutes of the show passed, and I had forgotten which episode I was even watching. My glass was empty except for two half-melted ice cubes. I went to the kitchen, tossed in another ice cube, and refilled my glass about as full as I had before.

Chapter 2

The next morning, I woke hanging halfway off the edge of my couch. My TV screen was adorned with a question from Netflix: "Are you still watching?" Condensation from my glass had formed a puddle on the coffee table. *I really was tired,* I thought.

My watch said it was nine-thirty on Saturday morning. Cold air had come through the open kitchen window all night and left the apartment chilly, despite the wall heater having been left on. I heard the padding of difficult, bare footsteps outside and glanced through the blinds to see one of the trio of girls taking the walk of shame through the complex in the direction of the bus stop. She was carrying her high heels in one hand and nursing a headache with the other.

I turned off the TV, went to the bathroom to relieve myself, and stripped down to my boxer briefs before falling onto my bed. Pulling the blankets around me, I curled up and allowed myself to fall asleep once more. It was Saturday, and by some rare luck, I had the day off.

I woke next at the sound of the generic ringtone of my cell phone. I reached off the side of my bed to where my phone lay connected to the charger and, without bothering to check the on-screen caller ID, slid my finger across the screen to answer.

Groggily, I answered, "Hello?"

"Did you just wake up?"

"Maybe… Who is this?"

"Ryan. Who did you think it was? What're you doing today?"

"Absolutely nothing."

"Tom and I are going to get brunch at Studio One. Come with."

"Alright, let me shower and I'll head over."

I pushed the "End" button on my phone and dropped it back to the floor. Forcing myself from the warmth of my bed, I stumbled out of my boxers and into the bathroom, turned the shower water on as hot as I could handle, and stepped into the steam.

When I got to Ryan's place, he was already outside and bundled up in a sweatshirt and a heavy snowboarding jacket. He motioned for me to park and made a walking motion with his index and middle fingers. I locked my Jeep and pulled my hood over my head. "Are we meeting Tom there?"

"Yeah. I figured it'd be easier. If he's late like he always is, we can at least get *our* food going."

"Good call."

It was a cold, dry walk to Studio One from Ryan's house on the east side of campus. Ryan said he'd been up since seven-thirty and had already gone for a run and gone grocery shopping. I didn't know how he could get up so early most weekends. I was irritated he'd woken me up at ten.

Tom was already outside the restaurant, waiting among all the college kids who were there to cure their hangovers. "Hey, guys. I got our name on the list about ten minutes ago. Should only be a few more."

Ryan and I grabbed cups of coffee from the table outside the door and rejoined Tom. The hot coffee sent instant warmth through my entire body as it went down. It was hard not to drink it all at once.

"So, what'd you and that girl do last night?" Ryan asked Tom.

A mischievous smile crept across Tom's face. "I think 'What *didn't* you do last night?' might be the more appropriate question."

"Okay, what *didn't* you end up doing last night?"

Tom sighed heavily. "I'm not gonna lie. We watched *The Lego Movie*. When it was over, we started making out, but then she passed out. So…nothing. We did nothing."

Amid my and Ryan's fits of laughter, I managed to spit out, "You watched *The Lego Movie*—to *completion*—and *then* started making out? You mean your little theory about how it's the perfect movie to watch with a girl when you want to hook up instead, that's bullshit? Who knew."

Ryan was still laughing, and Tom looked ashamed.

"I know, I know. I had no idea it was her favorite movie. She knew every fucking line! But it's worked every other time."

"Sure it has," said Ryan.

"I'm seeing her again tonight, so who knows."

"Maybe you should try *The Lorax* this time. Beanie swears by it." Beanie was another friend we'd known for the last five years or so, yet none of us could pinpoint what his real name was. Somehow, he stayed off the radar—Google searches didn't even bring anything up—and we didn't know his family, so we stuck with "Beanie" and he never seemed to mind.

A waitress came out and called Tom's name. She led us across the deck in front of the building to an outside table just under the carport roof. Studio One Café was built in an old house on campus, without much remodeling, so it had a cozy, homey feel inside and out. They were known for their French toast, and not without reason. It came covered in almond custard, creamy Romanov sauce, and berry compote, and every time, it was the most delicious French toast I'd ever eaten. That morning, however, I ordered Eggs Benedict. The other two ordered the French toast, and we all ordered mimosas and more coffee.

Ryan and Tom had invited me to go out with them the night before, but I told them I wasn't feeling well and was calling it an early night. It was partially true; I just went to the bridge first. They recounted the tale of how Tom met Lego Lisa, as we decided to call her.

They'd met up with Beanie and some of our other friends at the downtown bars—the Barmuda Triangle, as the area was known. Over the last couple of years, we'd learned the name to be accurate. Several times, we lost friends there after a long night of drinking, not to hear from them for a couple of days. Lisa and her friends were sitting on the couches at the Starlight Lounge, their eyes beckoning Ryan and the rest of the group. Naturally, the guys went over to them and struck up conversation. The group paired off into separate chats for a while before they all decided to go down to the pizza place on the corner. At some point during that journey, Tom and Lisa snuck off and went back to Tom's place.

"I swear to God there was a gleam in her eye when I asked if she wanted to watch *The Lego Movie*," Tom said. "I just figured that gleam meant she wanted to get laid."

Ryan laughed. "It would have appeared that way. She really seemed into you."

Our food came, and we all dug in ravenously. That was the thing about Studio One: you might wait a while to get seated and to eat, but it was always satisfying and well worth it.

The other two kept talking as we ate, but it wasn't until our plates were empty that I realized I had no idea what they'd been talking about.

"You here, Michael?"

"Huh?"

Ryan took a drink of his full mimosa; apparently we'd ordered a second round at some point. "You haven't said a word for twenty minutes."

"Yeah, what's up man? You've kinda just been eating and looking through us."

"Sorry, guys. I didn't sleep well last night, so I guess I'm still a little tired."

"Ah," said Ryan. "Well, wake up, bud. That coffee should be doing something by now."

"It's making *me* have to shit."

"No one's surprised by that, Tom."

I cracked a small smile and chuckled. "Hey, sorry to bail, but I have a lot I still need to do today, so I should probably head out." I pulled some cash out of my wallet and handed it to Ryan to cover my meal. "Thanks for the invite, guys. I'll talk to you later."

They both seemed a little caught off guard but said goodbye and didn't ask any questions. I could feel their eyes watching me as I walked down 19th Avenue to where I had parked.

Back at home, I stripped down to my boxers once more and crawled into my bed, curling up in the blankets. Lying on my side, I stared at the wall and found myself picking out shapes in the paint texture.

I stayed in bed all afternoon, occasionally dozing off, getting up once to go to the bathroom. My phone rang a couple of times and chimed three times with text messages, so I eventually switched it to silent mode, not even bothering to check to see who was trying to get in touch with me. I didn't put a movie on my laptop, listen to music, read, or do anything else. I just lay there, wrapped up in my own discouraging thoughts.

What am I doing? I thought. Not just in that moment, but in life in general. The awkward flight from Studio One wasn't my first such incident in recent memory. I'd been that way a lot over the last few months since summer. And that was on the rare occasion that I even agreed to go out and do anything with people. Frequently I'd be out with my friends, all of them having a good time, but I felt removed. I couldn't stay focused on the conversations, couldn't get into whatever we were all doing. I constantly made excuses to leave. Most of the time, I ended up either going home and flopping on my bed or the couch, or going to the bridge first and then home. I don't know what it was about that bridge. It was such a beautiful place. I loved it during the spring and summer, despite the influx of spiders that spun their webs along the railing. But it was also the place that called to me when I felt like there was no point to anything else. It was my best friend and my worst temptation.

Chapter 3

I woke Sunday morning to several text messages and three missed calls. Resolving to respond later, I lay in bed for a few more minutes, allowing my eyes to adjust. I didn't understand how I could have slept so long; I'd only gotten out of bed to go to the bathroom a couple of times since the previous afternoon. Finally, I sat up, stretched, and went out to the living room to turn on the wall heater. In the kitchen, I filled a large glass with water from the filter pitcher in the refrigerator and emptied it in a matter of seconds. I refilled the glass and drank it a little slower the second time. Staring out the kitchen window, I grimaced at the rain and at the fact that I'd spent the rest of the previous day the way I had. My day was free of commitments until work in the evening, so I started a pot of coffee and a slice of toast and ate a banana while they finished.

When I had a full, hot cup and had greedily eaten my toast, I lay down on the couch with pillows behind my head on one end and picked up the book I'd been reading. It was about a twentysomething from Orange County who found himself vagabonding through Los Angeles after his grandmother's death, fueled by booze, cocaine, and women who were just as lost as he was. I saw so much of myself in the main character, not in the heavy debauchery but in his hopeless stagnancy and having no idea how to crawl out of it. It was his first book, but the author painted an extraordinary picture of the desperation with which we often cling to any shred of hope we can find, no matter how unlikely it may be to save us.

After reading for about an hour and making a sizeable dent in the book, its pale-yellow cover curled back from three previous readthroughs, I replaced the bookmark on the current page and put the book back on the coffee table. I forced myself off the couch, put on my bathrobe and slippers, and refilled my coffee cup before going out and sitting in the chair on my small back patio. The roof extended just far enough over me that I was protected from the gentle rain outside. It was chilly, but the combination of coffee and a soft, thick robe kept me warm enough. Soon, to my delight, Carrie came down the sidewalk.

Carrie was a gorgeous nursing student who lived a few apartments down from me. She was extremely fit and health-conscious, always out running or riding her bike. I hated running any time of year, so I couldn't fathom what would compel someone to run outside during the rainy Oregon winter.

"Hey, Michael! How are you this morning? That robe looks cozy!" She walked up and waited for my smile and nod of approval before sitting in the other chair. True to form, she'd just finished a run. Her face was red, and her chest heaved under a neon-pink Nike running jacket.

"Oh, it is. I'm doing alright. You?"

"I'm great! Just had a really good run. The rain is so exhilarating!" She pulled off her hair tie and shook out her long, silky, blond hair.

I was always impressed by, and somewhat envious of, Carrie's constantly high energy. I'm sure it was attributed to her active lifestyle and eating healthier than Panda Express on a regular basis. That was a difference between us that I had quickly accepted.

"Can I get you a cup? I have plenty inside."

"Thank you so much, but no. I can't stay. Some girlfriends and I are going for brunch, so I need to get home and shower real quick. Actually, do you want to join us? We're going to that new place on Coburg Road."

The offer caught me off guard and I took a too-quick drink of hot coffee, scalding my throat as it went down. I closed my eyes tightly in a wince, then said, "I appreciate the offer, but I have quite a bit to get done before work today."

"Okay, well let me know if you change your mind. You have my number, right?"

I smiled and nodded.

"Great! It was nice talking to you!" She leaned over and hugged me briefly before standing up. "I hope you have a good day!"

I lifted my mug in farewell. "You too. See ya, Carrie."

Carrie walked quickly down the sidewalk to her apartment, her fit form accentuated in tight, black running pants. I didn't have her number; she'd never given it to me. Occasionally when we talked, she'd invite me along to whatever she was doing. I just always assumed it was a pity invite and made up excuses as to why I couldn't go, maybe also in part because I had no idea how I'd interact with a girl as hot as Carrie and her friends, who I assumed were just as attractive. Carrie talked about so many different plans and parties and events and slung so many names through our brief conversations, I doubted she had the word "alone" in her vocabulary. I don't know how she even remembered all the names. Every once in a while, I told myself she *had* to be making shit up.

I'd considered asking her out in the past, just casually, but I assumed she would probably prefer a guy as fit as her, and a fit guy I was not. I was surprisingly content being graced with her occasional presence, when she would stop by before or after a run or a bike ride and chat for a few minutes. The fact alone that a girl *that* attractive would take the time to sit and talk to me made me feel good, and Carrie had a way of clearing my fog, if only for a moment. I figured I shouldn't risk losing that. I watched the rain while I finished my coffee and then went back inside.

I turned on my shower, hung my robe on the back of the bathroom door, and stepped in when steam had started to fill the room. I loved mornings when I had no timely commitments and I could just stand in the shower and let the hot water run over me without worrying about getting out and getting ready for the day. If Carrie didn't live in the same complex, maybe I would have offered her use of my shower. That was another recurring fantasy of mine that I quickly pushed out of my head.

After standing under the heavy stream of water for about twenty minutes, I finally decided to shampoo and wash. *I should probably do something with my day before work,* I thought. I dried off quickly, brushed my teeth, and threw on a pair of jeans and a T-shirt. Layering a sweatshirt under my rain jacket, I grabbed a granola bar from the cupboard and locked the door behind me.

In the car, I let the engine warm up for a few minutes with the warm air and the heated seat on "high." Despite wearing more clothes than I had been earlier, I was freezing. I didn't really know where I was going to go; I literally had nothing to do, no errands to run. I didn't feel like spending time with anyone, so I didn't bother looking through the contacts in my phone. Finally, I backed out of my parking space and drove off down the street past Autzen Stadium, with no real destination in mind. I grabbed a caramel macchiato from Starbucks and decided to drive to the top of Skinner Butte.

There were several other cars in the parking lot, a few of them fogged up for one reason or another. A handful of people braved the cold, morning rain with their hoods up and stood on the lookout point by the flagpole. I was happy within the comfort of my warm vehicle and climbed through to the back, putting my feet up between the two front seats. Then, I watched and listened to the rain and tried to enjoy my solitude. I turned the music application on my phone to a radio station based on one of my favorite acoustic singer-songwriters. The mellow, melancholic music played nicely with the raindrops. Guitar strings plunked, piano keys plinked, raindrops plopped.

During the hour that I sat up there, several fogged-up cars were replaced by other fogged-up cars. I supposed it *was* a good day for a cozy hilltop hookup, or a hotbox if that was your thing. A few health nuts in their cold-weather running gear came up through the field next to the parking lot, which first made me shake my head in admiration at their dedication and then brought Carrie to my mind. Suddenly, my thoughts were full of the desire to have the warmth and companionship of a pretty girl next to me, and I was irritated with everyone around me on the butte who had that. I awkwardly scooted back to the driver's seat and drove down the hill.

Just past the Ferry Street Bridge, I hit the freeway onramp that would take me east through Springfield to Thurston. The light rain turned to mist, something that is an *actual* distinction if you live in Oregon, so I rolled my window down and blasted the heat. It took me back to the days when Ryan and I would drive around in the winter with the top down on his convertible, hoods up, "feet heat on high." I smiled when I thought of the time we were doing just that, driving up the McKenzie Highway—the same road I was now on—to see a friend of ours, when a semi-truck passed us going the opposite direction, and there just *happened* to be an enormous puddle from the rain earlier in the day. The semi hit the puddle, spraying us fully in the faces. Damn, it was cold! But we laughed about it and kept cruising with the top down. *Things were so much simpler, then,* I thought. It was nice to have such happy memories, but I knew relying on them for happiness would only impede my forward movement in life.

I passed the small gas station-convenience store and drove over Hendrick's Bridge. Next to the bridge on the McKenzie River sits a wayside that is, during the summer, a hot spot for launching boats and families out for a day of swimming. In the winter, it was desolate, and the water was high.

On the far end of the bridge, Herrick Farms was closed. Herrick's is a local favorite for fresh produce throughout the warmer months, and when fall comes, they make some of the best apple cider in the area and offer autumnal decorations, hayrides, and an expansive pumpkin patch. Before closing for the winter, they sell pre-cut Christmas trees. Two years earlier, I'd started a personal tradition of driving up Camp Creek Road to where it meets the McKenzie Highway and going a little farther upriver before coming back down to Herrick's and picking up a jug or two of their cider. The timing had to be just right, though. I waited until the leaves had started to change colors and were a crisp variety of reds, yellows, and oranges. It had become something I looked forward to every year, though that year, after Liz and I had ended, I never made it.

I continued up the McKenzie Highway through Walterville and turned on Holden Creek Lane, taking the bridge across the river toward Deerhorn Road. I decided to stop at the park at the end of the bridge and stretch my legs.

As a born-and-bred Oregonian, I generally don't mind the rain, but I was glad that the mist had gone away as I'd driven farther upriver. It was cold enough that moisture just annoyed me at that point. I pulled my hood up to keep my ears warm and locked the Jeep. Then,

I made my way down the driveway that led to the boat ramp, taking care not to slip on the wet leaves that covered the pavement.

I had many happy memories of time spent with family and friends by the river over the years. Burying my hands in my pockets to keep the feeling in my fingers, I stood on the bank and recalled the times we jumped off the large rock in the river and all the small rocks we threw from the bank, trying to get them into the softball-sized hole in the side of it. I removed my hands briefly from the warmth and threw several rocks; they grouped decently around the hole, but none made it in. I watched the river swirl by for a few more minutes until my nose started running a little and decided I should probably get back to the warmth of my Jeep, for the sake of my health. Inside with the engine on, I blasted the heat and held my hands right up to the vents to bring feeling back to my fingers. "God *damn*, it's cold!" I said to the silence.

When I could once again grip the steering wheel, I backed out of the poorly graveled lot and drove up to Deerhorn Road, which is a beautiful route to take any time of year. It twists and turns past a small residential area that eventually thins out into bigger houses with larger plots of land around them before turning into a hybrid country-mountain road. The river follows it closely the whole way. I drove as one often does on an empty country road: fast and across both lanes. As long as there were no other cars near me, I felt no need to follow every curve, especially when it was wet out. I also felt recklessly indifferent on the road, as I often did in a variety of situations those days. Crossing the street, for instance. As long as I wasn't putting others in harm's way, I often found that I didn't really care what happened to me.

Nothing happened to me on Deerhorn that day, nor on the freeway, nor on the streets leading to my apartment. I supposed I was thankful, but slight disappointment clouded my mind. I parked in front of my apartment and, instead of going inside, put my hood on and walked down the street and around the corner to the small bar in the center of the six apartment complexes along that road.

The clock above the liquor bottles said it was one-thirty. Other than a table of four enjoying a late brunch, I was the only person there, so I sat at the bar counter and ordered a porter.

"You eating?" the bartender asked as she placed the dark beer, thick with foam, on a coaster in front of me. "Brunch ends at two."

"No, thanks. I'm alright."

Without a word, she left me to my beer and went to the kitchen to chat with the cook.

I sipped the porter and licked the thin layer of foam from my lips. *Mmm... Nothing like a dark beer on a cold, rainy day,* I thought. My eyes drifted to the big-screen TV on the wall behind the bar, which was showing whatever NFL game was on that day.

Figuring I probably shouldn't go to work drunk, I gave the bartender my debit card at beer number three. It was four o'clock, and the bar had gained a few customers since I'd arrived. Three of them sat at the bar near me. The football game was over, the TV now showing reruns of a 90s sitcom. I wasn't sure how I'd missed all the transition.

I finished my beer quickly and headed out. The rain had ceased, but a heavy fog had settled in its place. I could barely see the apartment complex across the street. The brisk walk home hardly warmed me, so I stripped down and climbed into bed, burying myself in blankets. I had an hour and a half before work, so I set my alarm for an hour and closed my eyes.

Chapter 4

My stomach woke me before my alarm, reminding me that I hadn't eaten since the morning. I showered quickly and dressed in my black slacks and a stiff, blue oxford emblazoned with the company logo: a fork and knife crossed beneath a green, tree-covered hill and several buildings of the city skyline. Between the landscape and the cutlery, the name of the restaurant—"The Hillside"—was stitched in blocky, yellow lettering. A roll of the eyes at the logo in the mirror had become a regular occurrence when getting ready for work. I grabbed my keys, put on my jacket, and began the short drive to another miserable shift. My commute was spent wondering how the hell I'd gotten to a point of feeling so stuck.

The job hadn't started out bad. It was my first job when I was sixteen, and I was good at it. I'd been quickly cross-trained and utilized in every position at the restaurant, excelling in all, but eventually settling in the bar area. Though I'd always dreamed of flipping bottles and tins like Tom Cruise in *Cocktail*, the restaurant only served beer and wine. It wasn't always terrible. I really enjoyed a few of the people I worked with, and we had a lot of fun during and after work. However, shift after shift of working toward nothing had gotten old.

After bartending for a year, I was offered a management position. I was nineteen. My innovative thinking and strong work ethic stood out to my boss since I started, but a position had not previously been available. Because I was going to school full time and had big plans for my life once I graduated with a business degree, I declined the offer. I didn't want to commit to the additional responsibility and wind up stuck.

Irony struck, and I quit school two years later because I was wasting my time and money to learn nothing useful. When I revisited the possibility of management with James, the general manager, the position was no longer available. Yet they hadn't hired anyone else instead, in the entire two years since they'd originally offered it. I tried not to take it personally, but James was the kind of guy who, if he didn't get his way, would make you feel it indefinitely. I knew dead horses that had been beaten less than James's issues. Rumor had it he once tried to hook up with one of the hostesses after work, but she rejected him. Instead of simply firing her to assuage his ego like a normal asshole, he allowed her to work there for two more months, making every second hell for her, and *then* fired her for some bullshit reason unknown to anyone. We all wondered why she didn't just quit before he fired her. She was incredibly attractive, so we figured someone would hire her for that reason if not for anything else. Nevertheless, she hung on for those two months. Who knows how long she would have gone on working at The Hillside if James hadn't fired her.

As I drove around the bend in the road that led up the hill to the restaurant, the glaring, new sign broke through the fog in all its brightly lit, yellow glory, nearly blinding me as it came into view. The sign was a giant version of the logo stitched on my shirt with the same block letters and was, in all honesty, a poor choice in signage for the restaurant. Customers even talked about how gaudy it was for such an understated restaurant, and the longtime regulars complained about the movement away from the old vibe, but their feedback fell on deaf ears. The owners were too proud to admit it didn't fit the atmosphere. Besides, the neon atrocity had cost them a fortune. There was no way they'd incur the expense of taking it down and having a new sign designed, fabricated, and mounted.

I pulled my Jeep to the side of the building where employees were required to park and sat in the warmth for a few minutes before releasing a heavy sigh and going inside to start my shift.

"Hey, Mikey," Alicia said from her podium inside the front door.

"Hey, Alicia."

Alicia was one of the few people I allowed to call me "Mikey," mostly because she was damn beautiful and her voice was soothing like a mountain lake lapping against its shoreline. Alicia could call me whatever the hell she wanted. Occasionally, she'd catch me gazing at her from behind the bar and give me one of her wide, pearly smiles. My favorite shifts were with her; our flirting back and forth made even the most stressful dinner rush bearable.

"How was your day?" she asked.

"Nothing special. How's it been around here?"

"It's been *so* slow. We haven't had anyone new in over an hour."

"Thrilling." I looked past her toward the near-empty main dining room, wondering what the point was of me even being there. "Who's all on tonight?"

"Umm… Eli, Nick, and Darren in the kitchen, Hayley and Tracy on the floor. And…Craig is in the office right now." Alicia said the last name cautiously, watching my face. I rolled my eyes and sighed as she had likely expected.

"*Shit.*"

"I know, I'm sorry." She gently rubbed her hand up and down my arm, which gave me a moment of surprising peace.

"No worries. Just another day in paradise." I forced a smile—

which she returned—and headed back-of-house to hang up my jacket and get my schedule for the next couple of weeks from the bulletin board. It wasn't posted yet.

"Mike! What's up, man?" Darren called from the kitchen. I turned to see him and Eli poking their heads around the corner.

"Hey, guys. Not much. I hear it's been quiet today."

"You have no idea. Here, look what we created between orders."

Intrigued as I always was when they said some sort of variation of "Check this out," I followed them into the kitchen and watched as they pulled out a platter holding a delicious-looking take on a baked potato.

"It's a Philly cheesesteak twice-baked potato," Eli said proudly.

"It looks like a heart attack," I said. "Give me a fork."

Eli obliged, and I speared a piece of steak, slices of onion and green pepper, and a chunk of potato, dragged it around in the gooey, yellow cheese sauce on the side of the platter, and ate the entire sample in one bite. "Ohmygod."

"Delightful, right?" Darren looked at me eagerly, waiting for a thumbs-up, a smile, some sort of affirmation.

My mouth still full, I nodded and asked, "Where the hell did you get Cheez Whiz?"

"Brought it from home," Eli said. "I've been thinking about this one for a while."

"Well, bravo, sir. That's fantastic. You should pitch it to James."

"You think?" Eli looked at Darren and shrugged. "Maybe we will."

"I better get to slingin'," I told them. I went over to the time-clock computer station and entered my code, hit "Time In," and headed up to the bar. Hayley was leaning against the rear counter, drying glasses.

"Hi, Michael."

"Hey. Thanks for doing that. I can take over now if you want."

She shook a few rogue strands of auburn hair away from her face. "I don't mind. It's not like there's anything else to do. Poor Tracy wound up with a real peach over there against the windows."

I leaned over the bar and looked out into the main dining room and saw a thirtysomething couple with two young children sitting by the windows. The couple was sitting, anyway. The kids, on the other hand, were scrambling around, playing tag between the tables and chairs, laughing and screaming at each other when they were caught.

I leaned back and rolled my eyes. "I know we're not busy, but what happened to basic parenting?"

"That's not even the half of it." Tracy joined Hayley and I at the bar, looking incredibly vexed. "Each of their kids is allergic to thirty different things, and the mom is on a gluten-free, vegan diet but still wanted to order from the regular menu, so she's got all sorts of substitutions. She asked to see every single label for the ingredients in her meal. Dad apparently had a really bad experience the last *three* times he's been in, so he made sure to let me know that it better not happen again. Taking their order took me almost half an hour." She pulled her dirty-blond hair out of its ponytail and ran her fingers through a few times before putting the hair tie back on.

"Why didn't they just eat at home then? Especially if it's been *so* bad three other times."

"Your guess is as good as mine. I told Eli and Darren to fuck with their stuff." She noticed my raised eyebrows. "Not the allergies, don't worry. Just to, you know, *forget* to substitute out the steak strips and put in extra instead. And they're gonna overcook the dad's chicken until it's drier than the turkey on *Christmas Vacation*."

Hayley snorted, spraying the soda she'd been drinking all over the counter.

I stifled my laughter as best I could. "I hope Nick didn't hear you.

You *know* he'll tell James."

"He didn't. I waited a few minutes before I put their order in, until Nick had gone out for a smoke break."

"Good."

Nick was a nice guy and all, but his only loyalty was to himself, and he'd do whatever he needed to get ahead. He'd blown the whistle on lesser things in the past.

"Order up!"

Tracy looked at her watch and gave us a mischievous smile. "Thirty-five minutes. Perfect." She skipped off to the order counter to pick up the food.

I chuckled. "No way they're coming back after this one."

"Not if they have any sort of sense." Suddenly, Hayley went stone-faced. "Oh, great…"

"Hey, guys!" Craig sauntered up to us, entirely too jovial for such a cold, rainy, foggy Sunday.

"How's it going, Craig?" I shot Hayley daggers with my eyes as she simply walked away to avoid talking to him.

"Great! Hey, I finished the schedule, so I'll post it in a second."

"I wondered about that, thanks. Wait, *you* finished it?"

"Yep. James is letting me write the next few schedules. He thought the extra responsibility would be good for me."

Shouldn't you be able to do your normal job before taking on anything extra? I thought. "Oh, I thought that had been a one-time thing. Well cool. Don't go cuttin' my hours," I joked dryly.

"Ha! No worries, buddy. You'll still have plenty of hours."

"Good. Do you mind if I take a look? I'll pin it to the board when I'm done."

"Sure." Craig handed me the printed spreadsheet. "I'm gonna go check in with the cooks."

"Sounds good." I watched him head toward the kitchen before looking at the schedule. I scoffed. He hadn't cut my hours down at all, but he had scheduled Alicia and I on completely different shifts so that we didn't ever overlap for even a half hour. He'd done the same thing on the last schedule. He'd had an obvious crush on her for as long as she'd worked there, and he *hated* that she and I flirted so much. As much as I enjoyed working with Alicia, it was more for Craig's benefit that I swapped all my shifts with the other bartender, Nicole, who had been scheduled with Alicia. Alicia quickly noticed what I was doing and winked at me each time he showed up and saw us both there.

Pulling out my cell phone, I snapped a quick picture of the schedule and sent it to Nicole with a short message—*Swap again?*—and waited. A minute later she sent me a reply: *Sure!* I didn't feel bad asking it of her; she had another job that was her focus, so she gave up shifts frequently anyway. I sent a quick thank-you and put my phone back in my pocket.

As I filled drink orders for the two tables that had been seated while I was talking to Craig, I wondered, as I often had, what would have happened if I'd accepted the management position when it was offered.

Craig had been given the position two weeks after I'd asked James about it again, the position that was "no longer available." He was the son of a local hotshot investor who had his hand in just about everything in town, everything except The Hillside. Hiring Craig in the first place had been a favor, an attempt at forming a relationship with his father that might result in some sort of revamp for the restaurant. Promoting him and putting him in charge of people had been a severe lapse in judgment, meant partly as a slap in the face to me and partly as a next step toward an investment that never came. Now, we were stuck with a guy who had no mind for management whatsoever, evident on every shift he worked, and a general manager who was too proud to rectify his mistake. We all dealt with Craig alright, but it was still annoying to have to answer to him.

The night was as slow and uneventful as expected, with the exception of Craig getting chewed out by the father from the table whose order had been butchered. I was right, they *wouldn't* be coming back again. Craig, in turn, chewed out Eli and Darren, because *of course* Nick couldn't have had anything to do with it. They didn't mind; Craig wasn't intimidating in the slightest, and no one had any real sort of respect for him. Especially when he went back to being entirely buddy-buddy with them as soon as he had wrapped up his attempt to rip them two new assholes.

Even though I hadn't taken the promotion offered to me, the rest of the staff still had a high level of respect for me and openly took my direction, which I offered in limited situations. The rest of the management team trusted me enough to leave me in charge under various circumstances. Even James acted in a way that said he was apologetic for the way things had gone down, of course without explicitly saying so. I just made sure not to be insubordinate or step on any toes—Craig's included.

"Have a good night, everyone," I said as I held the back door open for the other staff to file through. Clouds of breath filled the air around us as we hurried to our cars. It was ten-thirty, and the night had grown foggier and colder than the forecast said.

"Bye, Michael."

"See ya, man! You sure you don't want to follow me and Darren downtown for beers?"

"I'm sure. Thanks, though. Have fun."

Craig had all but stormed out to his car without a word to anyone; Alicia and I had found ourselves working closely while taking care of our closing duties, and he'd come up front from the office at all the best times.

"See you Tuesday, Mikey."

Only after hearing that did Craig stop for a split second outside his Camaro before getting in, slamming the door, and peeling out into the night.

Alicia and I looked at each other, amused.

"Wow," I said. "Hope he doesn't hit anyone going down the hill."

"Seriously!"

"Well, see you Tuesday. Have a good night."

"You too."

I watched her walk to her car to make sure she was in and safe. She smiled and waved before closing the door. I held my hands in front of the vents in my Jeep for several minutes before gripping the frozen steering wheel and making my way carefully through the fog and down the hill toward home.

Chapter 5

I didn't go home. Back on the bridge, I took a swig from the small bottle of Jameson I kept in the glovebox for special occasions, interrupted frequently by a quick drag from another cigarette. I suppose the occasion wasn't exactly special, since I'd spent several recent nights in the same manner, sans whiskey. Nothing specific had prompted me to bring out the bottle. I just remembered I had it and decided it was a good night for a nip or two. I couldn't help thinking for a moment how pleasant the combination of whiskey and cigarettes was, but the feeling was immediately replaced by the melancholy that had been there seconds before.

Lately, I often found myself wondering what it would feel like to force a couple dozen pills down my throat or thrust a razor blade into my wrist or kick a chair out from under me once I was certain the rope was securely around my neck. That night, as I stared out at the distant city lights, I formed a gun with my hand and put the tips of my middle and index fingers to the side of my head, twitching my ring finger on an imaginary trigger, trying my hardest to imagine it as a real gun. Feeling disgusted with myself for even having the thought, I finished the rest of the bottle, dropped the cigarette butt in it, and threw it as far as I could into the river ahead of me. I lit another cigarette.

"You alright, kid?"

Jesus, I really need to stay more alert when I'm out here, I thought as I jolted, dropping the fresh cigarette on the ground. Lighting another and holding the pack to the stranger who'd crept up beside me before I even looked at him, I said, "Yeah, thanks. Just one of those nights."

"Heh, whatever you say! Holding a gun to your head on a bridge on a dark, winter night while pounding whiskey and cigs doesn't quite fall under 'alright' in my book. Even if the gun *is* nothing more than your frozen digits." He burst into a fit of laughter as he took a cigarette from the pack and leaned in so I could light it.

I chuckled out of amusement as I lit the cigarette and took my first real look at my new companion. The glow from the cigarette between his lips cast a glow over his scraggly beard and sunken eyes, and a quick breeze carried an un-showered scent to my nose. *Fuck, he's homeless. What do I have to complain about?*

Every once in a while, when I was heavy with despair, I reminded myself it could be worse. My friends told me it could be worse. I knew they were right, to a point, but I convinced myself that they could never *really* understand and that my situation was unique. It was a selfish, idealist justification, but it made sense to me, and that's all that really mattered then.

I turned toward the raggedly dressed man and leaned on the rail on one elbow. "What brings you out here at this time of night?"

He laughed. "You mean out from under the bush whence I came?"

"Uh...I guess? Or...wherever you live...?" I hoped I didn't offend him somehow, but the way he had responded caught me off guard.

"Ah, sometimes I like to go for a walk—rain, shine, snow, or sleet—once all the folks are home for the night. It lets me enjoy where we live without the passing gauntlet of judgmental eyes. There's beauty here all year round, you know."

I nodded. "On that we agree." For me, the beauty had all but lost its edge, but I knew he was right. I loved Eugene, and it really did have so much to offer, if I only paid attention. I'd lost sight of that. Not much was beautiful to me then.

We stared at the downtown lights without conversation, our cigarettes sizzling quietly as we took a drag every few moments. Then, he broke the silence.

"Well, I think it's about time for me to head back to my bush. Thank you for sharing your smokes with a grungy fella like me."

"It's my pleasure, sir. Thank *you* for the company." I pulled my free hand from my pocket and extended it to him.

He looked at it for a second before extending his own and shaking mine. "*That* is my pleasure." He turned to walk off the bridge to wherever he was staying. Without turning to face me again, he called, "Stay off that rail, kid!" With that, he was gone into the fog at the far end of the bridge.

I'm not entirely sure where the spur came from, but I immediately dropped the rest of my cigarette on the ground and walked quickly back to my Jeep. Back at home, I poured some whiskey in a glass, sat at my desk, and opened a blank document on my laptop. I started writing a story about a homeless man who wandered around Alton Baker Park and the footbridge, seemingly unaffected by his own circumstances, with only the desire to help other people driving him. So many people only saw him as a nuisance and a blemish, and only the "worthy" gave him the time of day and discovered his truth. The story took the form of several different interactions of a variety of people who crossed paths with the man over the course of a single day: a girl out for a jog, a couple on a walk with their young son, two suited businessmen walking during their lunch hour, three male college students playing disc golf and drinking their way through a case of cheap beer, and a depressed, twentysomething loner. Sixteen pages later at one in the morning, the story ended with the disc-golfers drunkenly beating the homeless man under the cover of night because he had interrupted their game earlier in the day, simply to have a conversation. It was unclear if the man was still alive or not. I tipped the last of my whiskey into my mouth, turned off my desk lamp, and fell onto my bed. As exhausted as I was, mentally and physically, it was another hour before I fell asleep. I couldn't get the real-life homeless man off my mind.

The next morning, I made coffee and sat back at my laptop to read over the story I'd written. As I read, I added another few pages that gave some insight as to why the man was the way he was. As it turned out, he had made some choices that ruined his life and those of his loved ones, who then cut themselves off from him. When he found himself at rock bottom, he began spending his life striving to atone for all he had done. When I finished rereading it, tears trickled down my face. At the top of the first page, I titled it "Forgiven" and saved it to the folder of short stories on my hard drive.

Looking over the list of files in the folder, I realized it was the first thing I'd written since before Liz and I had broken up. I was thrilled about the story, though sorry it had ended so sadly. But at least I was *writing*. I spent the morning rereading some of the fragments I'd written and saved, wondering why I'd left some of them alone, wondering how others were such shitty shows of writing.

Inspired by my newly finished story, I made a short list of some of the stories in my file that I wanted to develop further and pinned it to the bulletin board above my desk. I figured that if I was seeing these every day, I might be more likely to continue working on them and make a habit of it.

Chapter 6

I worked an early shift the following day, which was a nice break from closing as I had been all winter long. The lunch hour was usually slow in the early part of the week with the exception of several regulars who came in either every day or every week on the same day at the same time. They were the only reason the place was able to open any earlier than dinner most of the time. The lucky few of us who ever worked on the skeleton crew during the day were grateful for their business. We would have been bored out of our minds, otherwise. Some of us, maybe even out of work. During the day, I acted as host and server in addition to my normal bar duties. And when it was slow enough and the right managers were on duty—or the wrong managers weren't around to see—I helped out in the kitchen with some of the less complicated orders.

The usual Monday crowd came through that day: the local Lions chapter in the private dining room, the ladies' Bible study in the corner by the windows, a few local businessmen in the bar area, and a few retired, married couples I'd gotten to know during my time at the restaurant.

Sometimes, I preferred the day shifts because I usually knew about what I could expect, and I didn't have to deal with as many people as I might in the evenings. Craig didn't work many days, so that helped, but the few people I really enjoyed working with rarely worked during the day. I was efficient at my job and often found myself with a lot of free time and difficulty figuring out what to do with it. I'd eventually begun bringing my pocket-sized Moleskine notebook in with me and keeping it next to my register in the bar so that I'd be able to write when the creativity struck. It didn't strike often, but I was still glad I had the notebook. Just in case.

The restaurant was nearly empty by early afternoon. I'd cleaned everything that made sense to clean, so I pulled out the notebook and thought back to the list of stories I'd made the night before. About twenty minutes later, I had several pages of notes on a couple of pieces from the list as well as a new idea that hit me out of nowhere.

"Hey, Michael."

My pen hand jolted, scratching a line across my page. I looked up quickly. "Shit, sorry, Brian. How's it going?"

"I haven't been here long," Brian said, laughing. "I'm good, how are you?"

"Living the dream." I bookmarked the Moleskine with my pen and strapped it shut with the elastic band attached to it. "It's a quiet afternoon, at least. What'll you have?"

Brian leaned on the bar and glanced at the tap handles, brushing his disheveled, brown hair off his forehead. "You know what? Give me a Ninkasi IPA."

"Strong beer for one-thirty on a Monday. Long day already?"

"Ha, no, but I have a feeling it's about to be. I'm meeting with James in a bit to go over his ideas for the revamp. I figure a pre-meeting beer will give me a little more...flexibility...with his ideas."

I smirked. James had a penchant for kitsch and fluff, and most of the staff felt that the restaurant was held back from its potential by his ideas. The Hillside's history and the view from the main dining room were perfect for a classier establishment, but casual and family-friendly it was and would remain.

Brian paid me for his beer and left a buck on the counter as a tip.

"Thanks, man. Good luck."

"Cheers," he said, taking a drink so that it wouldn't slosh over the sides. Then, he took up his place on the other side of the dining room next to the window and pulled out his laptop.

I poured myself a Coke and watched Brian for a minute. I always enjoyed when he came in. We usually spent some good time chatting before or after his meetings. He was the restaurant's webmaster and digital media guy, independently contracted, so he showed up a few times a month to get the lowdown on any specials or events that might be coming up. Sometimes, he'd be at an event to take pictures, but mostly he asked a few of us on staff to take some pictures with our phones and email them to him. He charged a solid hourly rate and got discounts on food on top of that. I often found myself envious of Brian. He did the same thing with businesses all over town. The way he talked, no day was ever exactly the same for him. Sure, he had to deal with the shit that comes from someone else's whim, but he made decent money doing it, wrote his own schedule, and ultimately decided who he dealt with. He'd been coming in a lot more over the last couple of weeks, ever since James decided the website needed a makeover. To be fair, James wasn't wrong. The website was complete shit. I just hoped Brian had some good ideas that would distract James from his own.

A few more guests came in that afternoon, giving me a little to do for a while, but it was empty again, except for Brian, when James came in at three. He greeted the staff breezily, went to the office to check in with Sarah—the manager on duty, who I'd seen all of fifteen minutes in my five hours there that day—and then joined Brian at the table by the window. I couldn't help but watch them between guests and orders.

The evening crew started showing up an hour and a half later, and I covered the bar while Nicole restocked and checked everything for the night. I saw Brian pack up his laptop and shake hands with James, who went back to the office. On his way out, Brian stopped at the bar.

"How'd it go?"

"Not as bad as I thought. He actually liked a couple of the ideas I showed him. He kept changing the subject, though, so who knows. I'm just gonna roll with it, and if he has a problem later, that's just more time he's paying me for."

"You've got a good point," I said, laughing.

"Hey, you write...right?"

"Yeah, why?"

"Send me something. I'd love to read your stuff." Brian handed me his business card.

"Uh, yeah, sure. I don't have a lot, but I'm sure I can find something. What makes you ask?"

"Oh, I just finished *The Sun Also Rises*. Hearing you talk about it before made me want to read it again. You've got good taste. I figured you might be interesting to read, too."

No one had ever said that to me before. In fact, I didn't remember the last time someone besides Ben had asked to read anything I'd written, which was good since I hadn't written much over the last few months anyway.

"Well, hey, thanks, Brian. I appreciate that. I'll send you something tonight." I slid his card in my back pocket.

"Cool. See you next time."

"Have a good night."

I finished handing the shift off to Nicole and headed out a few minutes early. Beanie had sent me a text message about seeing a movie in a couple of hours, so I said I'd meet him at the theater, and then went home to take a quick shower and change.

After I changed, I opened my laptop and skimmed through my folder of stories. I didn't really know what Brian would want to read, so I sent him "Forgiven" and another story I'd written after a weekend at the coast in Newport with Liz. I couldn't help feeling a little nervous upon hitting "Send," and still very curious, too. Brian had seemed almost lost in thought, but not distracted, when he asked me about my writing. I looked at the time and, since I still had about an hour to go before meeting Beanie, decided to go to the Starbucks on Coburg Road for a pick-me-up and an attempt at writing. Slow days at the restaurant were often just as tiring as the busy ones, and I was drowsy. Besides, a cozy coffee shop was always heaven on a cold night.

Chapter 7

The pretty blond girl behind the counter carefully pulled two shots of espresso and poured them over frothed milk in a cup, finishing the drink off with a heavy drizzle of caramel.

She must have noticed me watching her reflection in the window, because she simply placed the caramel macchiato on the counter and smiled in my direction.

I stood up from my stool and went to pick up my drink. "Thank you," I said, smiling and feeling slightly red in the face.

"Anytime." She had a beautiful, reassuring smile that seemed to say, *Don't be embarrassed. I was watching you, too.*

I took a sip of the hot, delicious coffee and looked down at the page of my notebook. In the forty-five minutes I'd been there, I had written two measly sentences. I absolutely hated at least one of them and couldn't decide how I felt about the other. I picked up my pen and began to write about the biker gang gathered outside in the cold, drinking their sweet, creamy espresso drinks. It was an odd sight: twenty leather-clad, bearded and tattooed men and women who I had distinctly overheard ordering extra whipped cream and skinny soy lattes with extra vanilla. There might have been one black coffee ordered in the bunch. I found the irony amusing.

Thick fog settled in, and the coffee shop filled with people looking for something hot to warm them up. A girl with wavy, brown hair just past her shoulders came through the door and surveyed the few available seats. Her grey, crew-neck sweatshirt, black yoga pants, and UGG boots were typical of college student in winter, but her face carried an air of intrigue typical of nothing. I figured she would probably remain a mystery to me because I wouldn't gather the courage to say hi. As I went back to my notebook, I noticed out of the corner of my eye that she was walking toward me. My heartbeat picked up speed.

She nodded at the stool next to me. "Is anyone sitting here?" Her voice was gently confident. My gaze was immediately drawn to the soft, caramel eyes peeking out from behind narrow, black-rimmed glasses.

"Not anymore." *Nice one, Michael,* I thought proudly as I pulled the stool out for her, shocked that I'd been so quick on my feet.

The girl laughed, looking back into my eyes. "Thank you." She placed her backpack on the stool and went to the counter to order. I was surprised by how gracefully she carried herself. When she came back with her coffee, she pulled two thick packets of paper and a fat, yellow highlighter from her backpack. The packets looked like the study guides my professors used to enjoy handing out three at a time.

I nodded at the papers in front of her. "I do *not* envy you."

"Oh, my God! They're the worst, aren't they?"

"They might have been my least favorite part of college."

She took a sip of her coffee and smiled when she tasted how good it was. "Did you go to the U of O?"

"For a couple of years, yeah. I wanted to get a degree in marketing, but I felt like most of the classes I had to take to even get *into* the business school were a waste of time."

"I know what you mean. It's been a struggle for me, too, but my major requires a lot of variety, so it's all at least going toward the same thing."

"What're you studying? Sorry if that's cheesy." I halfway smiled, feeling self-conscious.

She giggled. "It's okay. I like cheesy."

Thank God, I thought.

"Education. I want to teach elementary school."

"That's really cool. What made you want to get into that?"

"I want to be able to give kids a good impression of school early on. So many kids have such a hatred for it, and I've never understood that. I *loved* school."

"You were one of those girls who carried all her textbooks around in her backpack and showed up early for class, weren't you?" I smiled.

She tucked a loose strand of hair behind her ear, her cheeks growing rosy. "Maybe..."

"We need more teachers like you, especially at that age. My favorite teachers were really good at making learning a fun experience. I can't say I loved school like you did, but I didn't hate it either, thanks to them. I guess I was kind of indifferent about it, but I did alright." I realized I was rambling and forced myself to stop and take a sip of coffee. She smiled and did the same.

"So, what made you sign up for an art history class?" I pointed at the black-and-white photo of Istanbul's enormous basilica, the Hagia Sophia. "I took that same class. In fact, I think I had to do this same packet. Seems a bit beyond fifth-grade curriculum."

Her eyes widened. "I *love* architecture and sculpture, especially in Europe. Just how time seems to blend in the cities over there. It's amazing how everything is so..."

"Seamless?"

"Exactly! Buildings like the Pantheon just coexist with more modern buildings like two people who have known each other for years.

I've never been there, but…someday." She said all that in a way that made me want to hear her talk about everything else she was passionate about as we sat side by side on a flight to Paris.

"And we're learning about all these amazing paintings and sculptures! I completely agree with you about all the bullshit prerequisites"—she broke eye contact for a split second—"but there are a few random classes I've really enjoyed taking. Like this one." She held up the packet with a pearly grin.

"I enjoyed that class a lot, too. I wish I'd had more like it to keep me going. Working and going to school full time just got to be too much. I never had the time or energy to even *think* about my writing."

"Ooh, you're a writer? Why didn't you lead with that?" Her pretty eyes smiled through her glasses as she took another sip of coffee.

"I don't usually think of it as something that might impress people, but I suppose it's a better lead-in than 'college dropout.'"

She laughed. "I don't think less of you for dropping out, if that's what you're worried about, but that's so cool that you write. I'm curious, though. If that's what you're passionate about, why not just switch majors to Journalism or Creative Writing or something like that?"

"All my friends ask me the same question."

"And what do you tell *them*?"

"A lot of the same prerequisites. And I feel like there's not much I could learn about writing in school that I couldn't learn online, without spending eight grand a year. Besides, it'll be a *long* time before my writing pays the bills – if it ever does – so I still have to make sure I've got a good paycheck, however I can. That was where the marketing degree came in. Now, it means spending less time in school, more time working, and writing when I'm not."

"That makes a lot of sense. I don't think college is a must for everyone, no matter what anyone says. Some things are just learned better through immersion and experience." She smiled and took another careful sip of her coffee. "What do you write? Anything I might have read?"

Laughing, I said, "No, I haven't been published. Whatever I can. Mostly fiction, though. I've got a couple of different book ideas I've been trying to work out, and a few short stories. I'm also really interested in travel writing. I suppose a degree would help with getting my foot in *that* door, but oh well. I can still get my name out there in other ways. I just have to produce, which is the struggle. In the meantime, I bartend at the restaurant over on the side of Skinner Butte, The Hillside."

"Aptly named," she said, drawing another smile from me. "A writer *and* a bartender? You're just winning 'Most Interesting Man in the World,' aren't you?"

"You're funny. Trust me, it's not all flipping bottles and flaming shots. Actually, for me, it's not like that at all. I don't know why I even call myself a bartender, really. We only serve beer and wine. The owners don't want it to become 'that kind of place.' It's pretty tame, but I still make decent tips, especially during the summer. We host a lot of class reunions, and older women *love* being asked for their IDs."

This sent the girl into a fit of laughter, which included a light snort that caused me to laugh, too. She covered her mouth with her hand, blushing again, and her smile gleamed through her eyes.

"Horrible, I know, but it gets the tip jar overflowing. I've seen one-dollar bills become tens over the course of an evening."

It had only been ten minutes, but I knew I hadn't enjoyed talking to a girl so much in a long, long time. I couldn't help but notice how delicately she drank, how gingerly she held her cup with both hands. She seemed almost afraid to crush it, yet afraid to let it go. Her small fingers looked as though they'd fit perfectly between mine.

She was well-rounded, too. In addition to her love for European architecture, she was an avid Oregon Duck football fan, enjoyed most kinds of music and movies, and liked to do pretty much anything in the outdoors. While she hadn't yet traveled abroad, her near-obsessive longing to go to Europe reminded me of the same yearning I'd had before I went there when I graduated high school. If she was anything like me, that longing would only become more obsessive after spending even a few hours there.

As we talked, I surprised myself with how well I held up my end of the conversation, and I appreciated how freely she spoke about anything that came up and anything I asked about. She said just enough to make it clear she was enjoying the conversation and still retain an air of mystery. I found myself wondering what things she *wasn't* telling me and, as innocent as they may be, *why* she wasn't saying them. Obviously, I was a complete stranger, so that was more than likely the reason. But she'd already shared some things one might not typically share with a random guy in a coffee shop, so I had a hard time believing that could be the reason. Maybe she, like me, didn't want to risk telling all in the off chance that our meeting might become something more, something long-lasting, something in which we would have all the time in the world to talk about things. Whatever her intention, she had me hooked.

We talked for another twenty minutes or so before, out of the corner of my eye, I noticed four text message notifications on my cell phone, which I hadn't given a second thought since she'd walked through the door.

Hey man, you comin'?

Movie starts soon. Hurry up!

Dude

Don't be a jerk, bro, I already bought the tickets

"Shit," I said under my breath.

"What?" The girl looked worried.

"Sorry," I said quickly. "I didn't realize what time it was. I told a friend I'd meet him for a movie that starts soon."

She laughed. "Don't apologize. You'd better hurry up!" Her face said genuinely that she wasn't the slightest bit offended by either my swearing or my sudden departure.

"I feel bad rushing off. I've really enjoyed talking to you."

Her soft eyes twinkled. "So have I. But I suppose I should *probably* be doing some homework." I was happy that she didn't seem to mind having been distracted.

I put on my coat and slipped my Moleskine into the inside pocket. "Good luck with your study guides." I winked and smiled.

She giggled and gave a playful sigh of exasperation. "Thank you. Enjoy your movie!"

As I opened the door to head out into the icy air, glancing at my phone just long enough to type a message to Beanie – *On my way* – I noticed the girl's reflection in the glass when it angled just right. She was watching me leave, chin resting thoughtfully in her hand.

"So, when are you gonna text her?" Beanie and I sat in the theater, drinking six-dollar sodas. It turned out he had misread the movie times, so it wouldn't be starting for another fifteen minutes. Needless to say, I was a little peeved that his mistake had forced me to cut short a wonderful conversation with a *very* pretty girl.

I looked at him sheepishly without a word.

"You didn't get her number?"

"Are you really that surprised?"

"Come to think of it, no. Well, what's her name? Find her on Facebook."

My eyes widened, my heart stopped, and my jaw dropped. "Shit." *I didn't even get her name.* "Goddamn it!"

Beanie tossed a few pieces of popcorn into his mouth as he appraised my face. It wasn't difficult for him to put two and two together. "Wow, man. You need a wingman with you twenty-four-seven if *this* is how you're gonna play the game."

By that point, I was leaning forward, elbows on knees, halfway to yanking my hair out.

"I can't believe this. I guess I got so lost in the conversation that I didn't even think about it. Talking to her was so easy, I felt like I already knew her."

"Yeah, you fucked yourself royally on this one. She sounds like she was perfect for you. Shut up, the previews are starting."

I took a long drink of my soda as the theater lights dimmed. I was too busy beating myself up over the massive social failure that had taken place a short while before to notice what movies were coming soon. An on-screen explosion snapped me back to reality.

"That was such a cool movie! I can't believe that final fight." Beanie walked excitedly out of the theater toward our cars in the parking lot.

I strolled sullenly behind him. "Yeah, that was pretty sweet," I said, still lost in thought.

"Dude, what's up with you? Still thinking about that chick?"

"Well, you were right. She *did* feel perfect for me. I've never felt a connection like that from one conversation before. And I blew it." *As usual.*

"Yeah, you kind of failed. But don't sweat it. You know how

many smart, beautiful girls are out there just waiting for you to start a boring, intellectual conversation with them? Too many for my taste, but for some reason they eat up what you've got. Just find another one and tell *her* some interesting facts."

I laughed at Beanie's form of reassurance, but I knew he was right. There was no point in dwelling on something like that. I hate platitudes, but there *are* plenty of fish in the sea.

"Just promise me one thing, Mike? Don't look for her on Craigslist. It still creeps me out that you've done that."

I smirked. "I can't make any promises."

"Do you *not* remember the last girl? The one from, like, Sweet Home or whatever? You said her and her house both smelled weird. And she was wearing"—he cringed— "*Juicy* sweats."

"Yeah, you're probably right. That one didn't work out so well. Fine, I promise I'll put my best effort into *not* looking for her on Craigslist."

We made plans to hang out again soon and parted ways for the night. On my way home, I stopped at the nearest convenience store and grabbed a six-pack of Ninkasi IPA. Not my typical beer, but it was good on a cold night, and it hit harder, which is what I was really going for after the debacle with the coffee shop girl. My stomach was empty, too, so I got some food from Taco Bell and took it home.

I made it through three beers before I even touched a chalupa. By then, my appetite was gone, and I preferred my buzz anyway. I drank half of a fourth beer and decided to call it a night.

Before I went to my room, I opened my laptop and went to the Eugene Craigslist website. Under "Personals," I clicked on "Missed Connections" and went to the page of women looking for men with whom they'd had some sort of contact at some point. Scanning through everything dated for that day, I hoped to see a heading that said "Cute guy at coffee shop" or "We talked about art history, what else?" But, alas, there were no posts that seemed to fit the conversation I'd had earlier that evening. I shut my laptop, turned off the TV, and went to bed. I decided I wouldn't tell Beanie I had looked for the girl on Craigslist. He *did* worry about me, and I'd never hear the end of it.

Chapter 8

I spent the next few days thinking about the art history girl and beating myself up for not asking something as simple and obvious as her name. Nowhere was I safe from thoughts of what I might have missed out on. The couch, my bed, my car, work, the bridge. I couldn't escape her, and that didn't help my current state.

Talking to girls had never come easily to me. Liz had come into my life by way of a mutual friend and an interaction on social media. Before her, I never knew what to do once I made eye contact with a girl at a party, a bar, a coffee shop…anywhere. I felt awkward simply *smiling* once I knew a girl had seen me looking at her, even if she smiled first, which usually resulted in me whipping my head away without a word shared between us. After Liz, I felt just as hopeless, with the addition of my emotional state leaving me with the feeling that I wouldn't be any fun for someone anyway so why bother. I still went out—rarely—and I still took notice of attractive girls, but I no longer entertained even the thought of trying.

The girl at the coffee shop felt different, yet I'd done nothing different. She was a glaringly bright point in the darkness I'd been enveloped in for the last few months, and I'd done nothing to try to sustain that brightness. The best effort I'd promised to Beanie didn't last long; I checked Craigslist for the next three days. I found nothing.

Attempting to distract myself from that particular disappointment, I watched my email inbox religiously, waiting—hoping?—for a response from Brian. Feedback of any kind would be appreciated, confirming one of my two thoughts about my abilities: either I was a great writer, or I was shit. Ben always said I was good, and I trusted his opinion and judgment, but one more would never hurt. On a shift about a week later, I came one step closer to getting that next opinion. I had just gotten behind the bar when Brian came up from the office.

"Hey, Michael. I can't stay and chat—have another meeting to get to—but when are you off tonight?"

"Six. What's up?"

"Want to meet me for a beer?"

"Sure, where?"

"How about the tap house over on 5th?"

"Sounds good to me."

"Great, I'll see you a little after six."

"Alright, see you then."

With a nod, Brian turned around and hurried out of the restaurant. The next seven hours were going to be hell on my mind, but I figured, *At least I have something to look forward to.* That was a rare and precious feeling then.

My shift went by slowly, as is wont to happen when there's something to look forward to at the end of the day. I didn't waste any time passing the shift off to Nicole, nearly forgetting my jacket on the way out the door. Brian was already at the tap house when I got there, and he gestured at me to order a beer on his tab.

"Thanks, Brian," I said as I sat down at the table across from him, breathing in the malty aroma of the pale ale I'd ordered. "How's it going?"

"Good, good. It was a busy day for me. I've been trying to cram more meetings into fewer days so I have more time for other things."

"What other things?"

"Just, like, trying to get out of town more. Take longer weekends more often, you know? I love to travel, but I've been so bogged down in my work lately that I haven't been able to get away. I'm burning myself out." He took a long drink of his beer.

"It's good you're recognizing that at least."

"Mhm. Don't get me wrong, I love my job—most of the time—and I'll never regret making the decision to work for myself, but it's definitely a grind. I'm learning how important it is to take some time away from it before it completely consumes me."

My eyes moved from Brian to my beer as I nodded slowly. It'd been a long time since I really took any time away from my job. My work schedule was pretty flexible, but I had no paid vacation. If I took time off, I wasn't making money, and I had bills to pay. That left only time for day trips, which are plentiful from Eugene, but I hadn't even taken any of those over the past several months because I was too busy sulking in my apartment.

"You have anything on the horizon? I know you've talked a lot when I've been in about wanting to get back to Europe."

"Yeah, I know. It's just so damn expensive, and I don't have a whole lot of extra money lying around. I'd like to…but probably not for a while."

"You should make it sooner than later, just saying. Start setting a little aside specifically earmarked for it. Travel is *always* a worthwhile investment."

"Cheers to that." I raised my glass toward him, he followed, they clinked, and we drank.

"In the meantime, at least try to get away more. On your days off, hit the coast or the mountains or Portland, even somewhere in between. I'll do the same, and we can hold each other accountable. Maybe you'll even find something to write about out there. Oh! Speaking of…" Brian rummaged in his laptop bag and pulled out a packet of paper, waving it in front of him. "*This* is incredible, Michael."

Amid the movement of the papers, I was able to make out "Forgiven" at the top of the page. "Really?" I asked, caught between relief to finally get some feedback on the story I'd sent him and shock that he was so enthusiastic about it.

"Yeah! I liked the other one, too, but this one kept me awake afterward. I printed it out so I could read it again later, and it's been just as good the next two or three times. It's dark, and certainly thought-provoking. How the hell'd you come up with it?"

"Honestly, I was having a kind of rough night a while back and went for a walk by the river, and this homeless guy comes up to me and has a little heart-to-heart with me, which oddly left me feeling a little better. When he was gone, I immediately wondered what his story was, what he does during the day, if he talks to anyone else. Then I went home and started writing. I must've been up till two in the morning finishing it." I took a breath and a drink. "You really like it?"

"Love it. Write more like it. It's inspired me to finally try writing again, too. That's part of why I want to get out of here more often. I know there are plenty of stories I could tell around here, but I feel like putting myself in a fresh, foreign situation would really help open my eyes to things."

I nodded. "You're probably right. I always feel like writing about my day-to-day would be boring, both for me and for anyone who reads it. I know that's not necessarily true, and that there's probably some sort of worthwhile story I could tell about a guy who goes to a dead-end job every day and drinks by the river afterward, but I'd rather write something else, you know? Something I'm not actually living every day. *What*, I'm not sure."

"Right there with ya. Well, keep working on it. Like I said, I'll keep you accountable if you'll do the same for me. Send me whatever you're writing when you feel like it. I want to read anything you'll throw my way."

"Will do. You do the same. It would probably help me stay motivated and inspired to read someone else's work more often. What do they say about writers who don't read?"

"Probably that they're useless."

We laughed and decided to get another round. Another hour or so and another couple of beers went by, full of more conversation about travel and writing. Finally, Brian said he needed to get home to work on a project before *he* was completely useless, so we paid our tabs and left the tap house.

"Thanks again, Brian. For the beer and the feedback. I would've been good with feedback either way, but it feels really good that it was so positive."

"Hey, you earned it. Like I said, that was a damn good story. Keep it up. I'll talk to you soon."

"Have a good night." I headed to my car in the parking lot across the street. Back at my apartment, I got ready for bed—something I didn't bother to do very often those days—and went straight to sleep, feeling incredibly high from my conversation with Brian, not realizing that the girl from Starbucks had not once crossed my mind since I'd met him for beers.

Chapter 9

Brian and I were surprisingly good about keeping each other accountable over the next three months. We didn't set tangible goals by any means, but we'd each made a point to get out of town a few times on our respective days off and to write about the experiences we had. Getting out and exploring unfamiliar places sparked a clear change in my mood, and I even came away with a couple of complete short stories and a few promising beginnings. Brian had taken to writing some essays based around the history of the places he went, and we frequently shared what we wrote with each other. I was inclined toward fiction, so it was good for me to read something different as I developed my writing. It made me think about settings and general details a little differently, and my writing, I felt, was better for it.

On the first dry day in April, I decided to take a long walk to the Starbucks on the University of Oregon campus. The sun burned through the clouds as I was getting ready to leave my apartment, so I threw my jacket back on the couch and locked the door behind me. *Good timing*, I thought. I was ready for T-shirt weather.

It was a nice walk past Autzen Stadium and over the footbridge, and the campus was very pretty that time of year. The tall trees were lush and popped vivid green against the brick and stone of the academic buildings. Blossoms bloomed from some of the trees, adding splashes of pink and white to the canvas. I'd spent more of my college years outside appreciating my beautiful surroundings than I had in class, and more recently I had rediscovered the peace I got from simply walking around the campus. It contributed to an overall improvement in my state of living. I wasn't completely out of the darkness, but I was going to bed earlier more often, getting up earlier more often, and doing things besides sitting on my ass in my dark apartment. Compared to the prior months, I felt pretty good.

At Starbucks, I ordered an iced chai latte and sat outside at a table along the sidewalk. In my notebook, I picked up where I'd left off in a short story I'd started writing a couple days earlier. The story followed a recently disabled young man through his stages of coping to his acceptance of his situation, with the help of his girlfriend, his family, and his friends. I had only written three or four pages so far. It had been easy at first and I knew how it would end, but I struggled to find the path the story would take. That's one of the things I love and loath about writing: knowing exactly where you want your story to go but having to figure out how to take it there. While I was abundant in creativity and problem-solving abilities, it could be damn hard to figure it out sometimes.

After adding two pages to the story, reaching a point I knew I could pick up at another time, I closed my notebook and decided to read for a bit. I pulled out my tattered, ever-present copy of *The Sun Also Rises*, opened to a random page in the middle, and began to read. Sometimes I liked to do that. I knew the story well enough at that point that I didn't always feel the need to read it from start to finish. I enjoyed a lot of Hemingway's other work, but it was *Sun* that really reached me and fueled my writer's and traveler's mind.

In addition to my "get out more" agenda, I'd made an effort the last few months to start reading the novels of other classic authors.

Hemingway would always be my favorite, but I'd recently taken to expanding my literary repertoire with Fitzgerald, Steinbeck, and Joyce. As a writer, I desired to understand what it was that made their work so enduring. While I always made a point to write for myself first, my inescapable ego still liked the idea of writing something that people would still be reading and talking about in a hundred years. I kept track of my completed and in-progress stories as well as ideas I had, always looking for something I could see turning into a novel.

I'd only read a couple of pages when my cell phone vibrated on the table next to my condensation-covered cup. It was a text message from my friend Marcus.

Done w classes for the day soon. Beers?

I hadn't seen Marcus in a while, and it was a nice, warm day and a cold beer sounded perfect. I sent a message back.

Sure.

Cool, see you in an hour.

There was no reason to ask where. Marcus only drank at one bar most of the time: the big, old house on Kincaid Street, Rennie's Landing. It was convenient, had a decent beer selection, and the atmosphere was relaxing in the afternoon.

After reading a few more pages, I realized my remaining latte had turned cloudy and melted. I tossed the cup in the trash and decided I should probably get some lunch before it was time to meet Marcus. There was a café with decent sandwiches in the Erb Memorial Union, the building where a lot of students spent time studying, so I headed toward the center of campus.

I chose a sandwich with pesto and turkey and handed a twenty to the clearly stoned cashier. After waiting for him to correct the amount of change he was giving me, I turned to leave. As I pushed open the door, a girl who had been heading in from the side with her eyes glued to her cell phone screen bumped into me, knocking my sandwich to the ground in pieces.

"Shit, I'm sorry. Are you o— Oh, hi, Michael!"

A heavy, tribal drumbeat erupted in my chest. *Shit,* I thought.

"Hey, Liz." I hadn't seen or spoken to her since a few weeks after we'd broken up when I dropped off a bag of things she'd left at my apartment. It had been nearly a year.

"I'm *so* sorry. Please let me buy you a new one."

I figured that was the least she could do, all things considered, so I said, "Sure," and picked up the scattered sandwich pieces and threw them in the trash next to the door.

As we stood in line, I kept my hands in my pockets to stifle my nerves. I didn't really know what to say to her, so I was glad when she spoke up.

"How have you been?"

"Not too bad. I quit school."

"Yeah, that's what Marcus said." Marcus and Liz were both pre-law students and had been in several classes together since we had started dating.

"Well, I realized pretty quickly after getting back into it that it really wasn't what I wanted to be doing with my time. It was a struggle between working and school to find any time to focus on my writing, and school was going nowhere. Didn't make sense to keep paying for it, you know?"

"Oh, yeah, I get that."

Her tone and my knowledge of her told me she didn't. Liz had always been completely career-oriented. Even when we dated and she was first starting college, her time and energy was nearly one-hundred-percent devoted to school and internships that would aid her in her path to becoming a lawyer. To her, school was worth every penny.

I'd always respected—and often envied—her drive, but in retrospect, I realized that it was a good thing we didn't work out. There were too many other things that I wanted to fit into the equilibrium of my life, and that wouldn't have worked with her. Not if we both wanted to be truly happy.

"So, what are you doing now, then? Are you still at the restaurant?"

"Yeah, unfortunately. That's the problem with writing; it's hard to pay the bills with it." I half-chuckled, scratching the scruff of my neck and breaking eye contact with her. "Just trying to figure out what I can do besides the restaurant with no other experience."

"There are a lot of things you can do with writing. I'm sure you'll come up with something. You're a smart guy."

"Thanks, I hope so."

Liz paid for my new sandwich and her salad, and we stepped away from the counter.

"Hey, I hate to run off, but I'm meeting Marcus for beers in a bit. Thank you for the sandwich. You really didn't have to do that."

"Of course I did. I ruined your other one." She smiled at me.

Goddamn it, I miss that smile. I smiled back and shrugged my shoulders since she was right.

"Well, it was really good to see you. I'm glad things are going well."

"Yeah, you too, Liz. Tell your family hi. See ya."

"Bye. I will." She sat at a table by the window and buried her face in a textbook, and I put the sandwich in my bag and headed back out across the quad toward Franklin Boulevard and the footbridge.

Midway across the bridge, I sat on a bench to eat and reflect on what had just happened. The mere thought of running into Liz had been one of the greatest causes of my anxiety in the months after we broke up. There had been times I was at a store or a restaurant that I knew she went to when I would start feeling uncomfortable and clammy. I'd always been unsure how I would handle being in a face-to-face situation with her.

When we broke up, I was heartbroken that she had cheated on me. But I loved her so much and she had become such a big part of my life that I desperately tried to hold on and maintain a friendship with her, telling myself that it was never going to be anything more with the guy she'd cheated with and that I'd never have to face that further. After a couple of weeks, I saw on Facebook that they were in a relationship. I was at home drinking a short glass of whiskey when I read that. That glass was immediately across the room, against the wall, and in shards on the floor. Then, I'd put my fist into the wall. Then, I hated her. That made it even harder, hating her as equally as I had once loved her. It might have been the most painful thing for me at some points. The next day, I had taken the few things she'd left at my place over to her house in a brown-paper grocery bag. Her car was there, but I just left the bag on the porch and walked away. I heard the door open and her voice call my name, but I simply glanced over my shoulder at her, feeling in my eyes the harshest look I'd ever given someone, and kept going. I didn't say a word, and I didn't see her or talk to her again until she knocked my sandwich from my hands less than an hour ago.

Finishing my sandwich, I focused back on the beautiful day I was currently enjoying. People were running and biking and taking a mid-day stroll. The birds were aloft in full force. Seagulls floated on the water while Vs of Canada geese flew overhead. I spotted an osprey perched high atop a dead tree and a great blue heron in the shadow of the enormous oak tree that leaned over the river, each likely scouting out its next meal. It was nice to just relax and observe for a bit. Despite all the human and wildlife activity, the bridge was such a calm, peaceful place on warm spring and summer days. Every once in a while, that day included, I would be enjoying a walk by the river and thinking back to the way I'd been mere months ago. I couldn't imagine how a place so full of life could have been party to some of my darkest moments.

I looked at my watch and realized I had about twenty minutes before I needed to meet Marcus, so I tossed my sandwich wrapper in a nearby trash can and headed back across the bridge toward campus and Rennie's Landing. Marcus was already outside on the patio with a beaded pint of IPA—the only beer he drank—when I arrived. I ordered a Blue Moon and met him outside. He stood up and gave me a hug, patting me on the back.

"How're you doin', man?" I asked.

"Great! Done with class for the day and no work. It's a good day."

"Sounds like it." I took the orange wedge from the glass and squeezed it around the rim and over the beer. Then I took a long, refreshing drink. It was tough to beat a cold Blue Moon on a day like that. The only other drink I'd order then was a Tom Collins, but it was a beer day.

"What've you been up to today?"

"I've got the day off, and it was so nice, I decided to walk over here to Starbucks and try to write for a bit."

"Good, man. It's perfect for it. How's the writing going?"

"Oh, you know, it's here and there. I've actually gotten quite a few short stories started over the last couple of months, but I'm having a tough time getting anything substantial going."

"I can imagine. I've always wanted to try writing, and hearing you talk about it is a great motivator. I just have no idea what I'd write."

"Do what the rest of us do. Write about being a writer."

We both laughed. "That would be the easy thing to do, wouldn't it?" Marcus said.

"You'd think so. Writing what I know might cause me more anxiety than not. Speaking of, I saw Liz earlier when I was grabbing lunch." I took a long drink of my beer, watching Marcus's face for a reaction.

"Shit, how'd that go?"

"About as well as it could have, I suppose. She actually bumped into me and knocked my sandwich out of my hand, so she bought me a new one and we chatted for a few."

"That's the first time you've seen her, isn't it?"

"Yep. It's nice to finally get that out of the way. It's been eating at me, not knowing how I'd handle seeing her. Even though it's way past over." I swirled my beer around in the glass, staring at the spent orange wedge in the middle. Something about my run-in with Liz still bothered me, but I couldn't put my finger on it.

We finished our beers and went inside for a second round.

"I've been thinking about Europe a lot lately," I told Marcus as we each paid the bartender and left a dollar on the counter.

"Like…its politics, its history, its people…?"

"Like *traveling* there again."

"Ha, I knew what you meant. It's hard not to think about that, I know. I've been aching to get back ever since I got back the last time."

"Me too. And that's been stronger than ever lately. It's only been five years since I went, but it feels like ten. And I really just want to get away from everything for a bit."

"Why don't you go, then?"

"I knew you'd say that. Money, man. Always money. And taking the time off. I don't have paid vacation."

"Ah, yeah, I guess that makes it a little difficult. You'll get back there soon. We should go together when you can."

"That'd be cool."

We spent the next hour and another beer reminiscing and retelling our respective European travel stories. Eventually, I felt my sunny-day mood slipping away, so I finished my beer and told Marcus I'd talk to him soon. He decided to stay at Rennie's and wait for another friend of his to meet him for more beers.

The sun felt good on the walk home, but it didn't bring me out of the gloom that had inexplicably settled in again. Back at home, I flopped down on my bed and stared at the ceiling, thinking mostly about my run-in with Liz. It had been casual enough, more so than I had expected. I didn't have any sort of attack like I thought I might. But something about it was still troubling. Then it hit me.

I never knew exactly why she had cheated on me in the first place—I'd never given her the time of day to explain—but for what-ever reason, she had been unhappy with me. Most people would do something with that so that the next time they see that person, the latter is sorry they ever left. Running into Liz, I realized I hadn't done shit. I'd actually stepped *backward* a little by quitting school. I was still in a shitty job that didn't come close to making me happy. I had started writing again, but I really wasn't making anything of that, either.

I didn't know the guy she had left me for. I did know he was nearly done with his MBA; *he* was doing something. I'd felt like a complete idiot standing there and telling Liz I was in the same job and had quit school to focus on writing but had done nothing with my writing. That's what wrecked me about that day. I wasted the next couple of hours sleeping on top of my bedding, but I left the window and cur-tains open, at least, to let the warm breeze blow through.

The evening came along quickly when I finally got up, and the high I'd felt prior to running into Liz had become a distant memory. Dusk settled in, and the grumbling in my stomach told me to eat something, especially since I had developed the idea of drinking through the rest of the evening.

I cooked and devoured a box of Easy Mac, then mixed a tall whiskey and Coke and sat on my back porch. I brought my notebook with me, but it remained closed on the table as I sipped and refilled and sipped and refilled my cocktail. I had a strong buzz by eight o'clock and no real desire to stop there.

Neighbors walked by, some smiling or nodding in greeting when we recognized each other. I gave half a smile and a nod to some and stared through others. At one point, Carrie walked by with some friends and broke away to come say hi.

"Hey, Carrie," I said, correcting my slouch just enough that I wouldn't feel like a complete piece of shit. "What're you up to?" I found myself saying the words as slowly and deliberately as possible, trying to minimize the effects of how much I'd drunk. Even so, I knew it was futile.

"We've been having a picnic by the river. It was *so* nice today!" Her characteristic energy was even more emphatic than usual.

"It has been. That sounds like a fun time." I envied the buzz I could tell she had, one achieved through quality time spent in the company of friends and celebration of a beautiful day. I could feel my own glaring inebriation across my face, impossible to hide in sunken eyes that struggled to find focus on the girl in front of me.

"Are you doing alright, Michael? You seem kind of down." She gave me an encouraging smile and looked at me with kind eyes, filled not with judgment but with compassion and maybe even a little pity. She sat down in my other chair and waited for me to say something.

"I ran into my ex-girlfriend today." And without thinking it through first, I launched into more of a story than Carrie had probably expected to hear in response to her question. My wits were with me just enough to make me feel embarrassed as I spoke, but she listened patiently without interrupting.

"Sorry," I said when I was finished. "I know you probably didn't want to hear all that. It just kind of came out. You should catch up with your friends." My eyes avoided hers and stared into my drink.

Ignoring me, she said, "Michael, I hope you know you're not as worthless as you seem to think you are. I don't know your ex, and I don't know why she cheated on you, but to the small extent that I know you, you seem like a really good guy. So you're having trouble figuring out what to do now that you've gone off on a different path. That doesn't make taking that path a bad decision. It says a lot that you even *made* that decision. Maybe you didn't know what you were taking a chance on yet, but you took that chance because you knew *something* needed to change. Taking control and taking chances is one of the sexiest things a guy can do." She shrugged and smiled at me. "I promise you that it stuck with Liz after you ran into her. And another girl will come along and will recognize and appreciate that about you."

Although I felt as if I was staring right through Carrie as she spoke, I heard and processed every word. At the same time, I couldn't keep my attention from straying to how attractive she looked in a bright-pink hoodie and short, white shorts that made her legs look even tanner than I knew they were. A fleeting thought of inviting her to stay and hang out crossed my mind, but some combination of low self-esteem and reasonable conscience quickly pushed it away. I truly appreciated her taking the time to sit and listen and offer consolation, and I knew asking her to stay would be the first step toward killing her impression of me as a "really good guy." *Don't do it,* I told myself again.

Instead, I said, "Carrie, I really appreciate you listening. You're really nice." I smiled as genuinely as I could, but it felt sloppy. "You should catch up with your friends. I'll be fine, I promise." I straightened my smile as much as I could.

She smiled reassuringly and said, "Anytime. If you ever need to talk, you know where I'm at." She gestured over her shoulder with her thumb in the direction of her apartment. Then, she leaned in and gave me a tight hug and a quick kiss on the cheek. "Go to bed soon."

"I will, thanks again. Have a good night, Carrie."

"You too!" She waved and headed to her apartment. I watched until she was out of sight, then went inside and refilled my drink. It had grown a little chilly outside, so I put on a sweatshirt before returning to my chair.

The next couple of hours were spent scolding myself for even conceiving the idea of asking Carrie to stay. I knew it was my way of trying to take advantage of her kindness in order to bandage my loneliness, and I felt like a piece of shit for it. *Glad to know my conscience is still active, even if it is a little late to the party,* I thought. Carrie was friendly, and gorgeous, but I knew the kiss on the cheek was nothing that should be dwelled upon, that it was just her way of expressing herself and offering comfort. I'd known girls like that over the last several years, and I'd learned to just appreciate it for what it was and not to dig any deeper. I trusted that Carrie was genuine and kindhearted, but I knew it didn't go beyond that and that I should just accept that she would only ever be a friend.

Around midnight, I decided to go inside and, instead of going to bed, refilled my glass yet again, my eyes lingering briefly on the now-empty bottle of whiskey. On the couch, I turned on the TV and switched to the Travel Channel. Bourdain was on—*The Layover*—so

I settled in and watched as he ate *porchetta* and drank Peroni with his Cinquecento-driving tour guide. As Tony toured the city, I found my mind wandering back to my conversations with Brian and Marcus about Europe and traveling in general. It *had* been too long, and I realized I really hadn't been thinking of much else lately, besides the girl from the coffee shop. *I wonder what flights are looking like right now.* Not that I'd be able to go, but I was simply drunk and curious.

I pulled out my laptop, navigated to the Travelocity website, and entered some random dates in September because summer in Rome and Tuscany had been uncomfortably hot on my last trip. The search produced results that I had not expected.

"Less than $1000 *roundtrip*?" *That can't be right.* I reentered my parameters and started the search again. *Wow...*

PDX to Naples with brief stops in Amsterdam and Rome, with a return trip to Portland out of Rome with a two-hour layover in Atlanta: $982, including taxes and fees. I blinked a few times to shake the whiskey from my lids; the number didn't change. Bourdain's voiceover faded to background noise as I stared at my screen. I didn't know *what* I had expected, but it certainly wasn't a price that low.

As if my mind and body had gone on autopilot, I opened a second browser tab and logged into my online banking account. I stared at my account balances for a few minutes, performing the best mental calculations I could in my current state.

If I bought a plane ticket, I'd still have more than enough left in savings to cover the pay I'd miss for taking two weeks off to go to Italy. I could put other travel expenses—hostels, train tickets, whatever—on my credit card and pay them off when I got back. I'd just need to set aside some spending money, mostly for food and drink since I'd done the souvenir thing the first time around and didn't need any more tchotchkes taking up the surfaces in my apartment. That wouldn't be too difficult. There were quite a few class reunions booked at the restaurant over the next month or so, and that always meant great tips for me. I'd just need to be sure to keep the cash under my mattress until it was time to go.

You're drunk. You can't just go spending $1000 on a flight, to what? To go galivanting around Europe? Drinking and sleeping with prostitutes? That's a waste of money and a sin.

Another one of the many reasons I barely ever spoke to my parents anymore: that voice in my head. Not of my own conscience, but of my parents' closemindedness to anything outside their goddamn bubble.

They'd taught me relatively well to save my money, I could give them that. I'd likely not even be able to consider what I was now considering had they not. But our opinions differed greatly about what was worth spending it on. In fact, I had no real idea what they thought *was* worth spending it on, except, maybe, as I later found out, moving somewhere sunny, warm, and slow-moving the second they were no longer legally responsible for me. I had wondered, since I graduated high school, if their pressure on me to save money was the one truly parental thing they did, setting me up to fend for myself so I'd have no reason to rely on them further.

And of course they thought Europe for a young person meant nothing but drinking and hookers. They never read anything but their Bibles, never socialized outside their church friends, and the last time they'd left town had been to pick up my grandma from the Portland airport when she'd gone to visit my mom's sister in the Midwest.

Directing my attention back to my laptop screen and the "Check Out" button below the price, I found myself questioning the decision to take that much of a hit in my savings account, but only for a moment.

"Fuck it."

Chapter 10

"You bought a ticket to *Italy?*"

Chuckling, I took a bite of my Denver omelet and nodded my head, watching Ben try to recover from his initial reaction. He'd nearly choked on a piece of bacon and then washed it down too quickly with fresh coffee. It had been a couple of days since I'd hit "Check Out" and entered my debit card information, and the idea that I was going to be in Italy again in a few short months still felt surreal.

"I thought you were broke."

"I mean, my paychecks don't go too far past rent and bills, but I have a decent amount in savings."

"Yeah, but isn't that the point of 'savings'? *Not* spending it?"

"Sure, but what else is worth spending it on? Besides, it was only a thousand bucks. Not even."

"Do you know how much beer, bacon, and shrimp you could buy with a thousand bucks? I don't but it's an obscene amount, I'm sure. Besides, now you gotta pay for places to stay, food—"

"—and copious amounts of alcohol." I took a drink of coffee. Black, because I was hungover as shit from my excessive whiskey tasting the night before. "I just need to get away, man. Don't get me wrong, I enjoy our nights of ranting over cigarettes on the bridge, but I need to get away."

"Did running into Liz hit you that hard?"

"Look, I know that what happened with Liz is largely to blame for my headlong dive into whatever this"—I gestured wildly around myself with both hands—"is, but running into her made me realize why I've been *staying* in it."

Ben cocked his head to the side, sipping his coffee and waiting for me to elaborate.

"Because I'm not doing *shit*. How long have I worked at the restaurant?"

"Longer than I did. I had to get out of that place. Granted, trying to sell computers to people who don't understand the difference between PCs and Macs is a little disheartening sometimes, but at least I don't have to deal with Craig and James's bullshit anymore."

"Amen to that." We knocked our mugs together. "But my point is: I've hated it there for how long, and I've felt the way I have for how long, and yet done nothing about it? I'm fucking *pathetic,* man."

"Oh, c'mon, you're not pathetic, Mike. You're dealing with some shit. Everyone deals with some shit, they just all deal with it in different ways. You could've easily gone and jumped off a bridge by now, but you haven't.

"Once you get into a rut, it can be really tough to get out. But you've got a lot going for you, man. You just need to figure out how to use it to your advantage." He stabbed a sausage with his fork and pointed it at me. "This trip may be an opportunity to do just that." Then, he bit the sausage in half and sat back in the booth, waiting for revelatory fanfare to start playing and a lightbulb to click on above my head.

"That's what I'm hoping for. It'll be nice just to be there again, but it'd also be nice to figure some things out while I'm there. Maybe even be inspired to write something a little lighter than what I've been writing. I've been putting a surprising amount of words on paper, but it's mostly pretty dark."

"I'm sure something will come to you there. How could it not? I've not been to Europe, but it does have a strong track record of inspiring some great shit."

"That it does. I'm hoping it does the same for me."

We finished our breakfast, talked a little more about our jobs and my trip, and then parted ways. Back at home, I decided I should at least figure out where I'd be staying.

Since buying the ticket, I decided I'd stick to visiting the cities we'd gone to on my previous trip. It was my first time traveling alone, so having some familiarity seemed like a good idea. I mapped out a twelve-day journey from Sorrento on the coast to Montecatini Terme outside of Florence and finally to Rome. That'd give me a variety of sights to see and atmospheres to take in. The first thing I did once I had my itinerary was to purchase a Eurail pass that would make it easy to travel between those places by train. The last thing I wanted to have to worry about was how to get from A to B to C.

Keeping in mind my ill-defined budget, I decided to stay in hostels in Sorrento and Rome since those were the longest portions of my trip, and to splurge on a nicer hotel in Montecatini for a little respite. Not that spending a week on the beach wasn't a respite in itself, but the train trip from Sorrento to Montecatini was going to be a long one and some extra comfort at the end of that trip would be nice.

It wasn't difficult to find an attractive hostel on the coast. A search across a couple of websites produced myriad options, but one stood out very quickly: Seven Hostel. It was in Sant'Agnello, right next to Sorrento on the coastline. Photos on the hostel's website did their job, painting an alluring picture of fun and relaxation all rolled into one. The place had a rooftop bar and lounge, a tanning deck on a higher level of the roof with enormous, round couches and umbrellas, and a central courtyard where there was a restaurant. Both rooftop spaces had 360-degree views of the Gulf of Naples, the coastal towns, and the hills that separated that side of the Sorrentine Peninsula from the other side where the roads led to Positano and Amalfi. At $50 a night for a private room that looked comfortable and safe, I couldn't fathom trying to find something better and immediately booked five nights.

After a quick text-message exchange with Marcus, I tracked down the hostel he'd stayed in on his trip to Rome, a little hole in the wall near the Termini train station. The photos on the website were relatively bland, and the multi-bed dorms had beds that looked like they came straight out of a Dickensian orphanage, so I decided to pay a little more again for what looked like a slightly more comfortable private room. With Marcus's final endorsement—"It was kind of shitty, but the beds were fine"—I went ahead and booked five nights there. During our brief conversation, Marcus also said he'd decided to visit his girlfriend who was going to school in New York, and that he'd try to go around the same time so that we could drive up to Portland together.

Last, I searched for a comfortable, yet reasonably priced, hotel in Montecatini Terme. I wanted to relax for a couple days, but not to starve once I reached Rome. I recalled a large park in the town with the funicular station on one side, which housed the trolleys that took passengers along a track up to the nearby hilltop where the old town was. On the other side of the park, I found a quiet-looking hotel with a rooftop pool: the Golf Hotel Corallo, a four-story, green-shuttered building within walking distance of the *Parco delle Terme,* the funicular station, and Montecatini's *Piazza del Popolo*. I quickly booked two nights in a comfortable-looking room between my Sorrento and Rome dates, and shut my laptop with a satisfying *click*.

The credit card holds I'd racked up within an hour finally gave my upcoming trip some real weight in my mind. It felt more and more real as I told more people about it, including Brian and some of my coworkers. Days passed, then weeks, and I realized I should probably get my request in for time off from the restaurant. *Two weeks without pay.* The thought made me sick to my stomach, but I knew I could pick up as many extra hours as I wanted before and after the trip to make up for some of the lost wages.

"Hey, Michael," Craig said, looking up at the sound of my knocks on the office door. "C'mon in."

"Is James around?"

"No, he already left for the day. What's up?"

"Oh, nothing. I just wanted to talk to him about some time off. I'll just leave it in the book." I nodded at the blue spiralbound scheduling book on the desk next to Craig's elbow.

"Sure, here you go. Where ya goin'?"

Craig knew full well where I was going; he'd been lurking around when I'd talked to Alicia about it a couple of days earlier. Now, his face showed a faint sneer because he didn't like two things: I didn't tell him about it and Alicia had joked that I should take her with me. He hated being left out of the general camaraderie shared by most of us, but he hated when Alicia flirted with me even more.

"Italy. I've been wanting to get back, and I found a really cheap flight, so I figured what the hell. It'll be a nice getaway."

"Hell yeah, dude, that'll be awesome!" I sensed the excessive effort in his voice.

"Yeah, I'm excited. Well, thanks, man. I'll bring this back in a minute." I went and sat at one of the tables by the windows in the main dining room and wrote my request in the next open spot in the book. I double-checked the dates on the September calendar; no one else had requested it off, so it should be no problem. I gave the book back to Craig, who I knew would open it and look at my request when I left, and went up front to get the bar stocked for dinner.

Three days passed before my shift overlapped with James. After the lunch rush one afternoon, I stopped by the office on the way back from the storage room.

"Hey, James, I wanted to make sure you got my vacation request for September."

"Oh, yeah, Michael, I wanted to talk to you about that."

That's never good coming from James, I thought. There couldn't be any issues, though. No one else had requested it off, and I'd checked the reservation calendar for those days—nothing significant was on the books.

"That's a lot of time to take off, Michael."

I did my best to keep my keel and my voice even. "I know, I thought about that. Looks like no one else is off those days, though, and there aren't any huge reservations on the books."

"No, but it's still early. Other vacation requests could come in, and most parties don't book this early anyway. Are you flexible with time at all?"

Only if you're willing to pay to have my flights adjusted. "I mean, I can look at it, but I don't see where flexibility should really be necessary on my end." *Careful, Michael.* My ears felt warm. "The other bartenders have been wanting more hours, and I could even get Hayley trained if you still think there'd be a hole. She's been helping me out a lot lately and really wants to get in there. She'd pick it up quick."

That was true; I wasn't just using Hayley as an excuse.

"Listen, why don't you just think about it and see if there's any way you can make the trip just a little shorter. Maybe seven or eight days? I'd really appreciate it, Michael."

My eyes were locked with his, but I couldn't figure out where the hell his contention was coming from. I felt my jaw cramp from being so clenched. "I'll see what I can do. Thanks, James." *For nothing.*

"Great! Thanks, Mike. Let me know when you decide what dates you're going to take, and we'll get it on the books."

Nice backpedal to diplomacy, I thought as I walked off without another word, my blood boiling.

I'd picked up the evening shift that day, too, so I was there for the long hall. Somehow, James had gotten out of the building without crossing my path again; he was always good at that. Fortunately, it was a pretty slow weeknight, because the anger coursing through me made me jittery and clumsy. I spilled more than a few drinks. Alicia kept glancing over, and the couple of times our eyes met, I could tell she was concerned.

"What's wrong, Michael?" she finally asked as we were cleaning up for the night. "You haven't said much tonight, and you look pissed." She and I and the busser were the last ones there. The closing manager, Kara, had finished up her duties, as had the cooks, so she left me with the keys to lock up.

"James bitched at me about my vacation and is trying to get me to shorten it," I said without looking up from the tray of glasses I was drying.

After she didn't respond, I looked up at her. She was biting her lip and staring down at the counter.

"What?" I asked.

She stared at the counter for a few more seconds before looking up at me. "Craig was saying something yesterday about how it was too bad you weren't going to get to go on your trip. I figured something had come up and you just hadn't told me. Do you think he said something to James?"

Chewing the inside of my lower lip, what-ifs scrolled through my head.

"What could he have said that would make James not give you the time off?"

"I don't know, but…"

"But what?"

"I'm not sure. Come on, let's just finish up and get the hell out of here."

"Okay."

I half-assed the rest of my cleaning, and Alicia, the busser, and I locked all the doors from the inside and left. Using the code Kara had given me, I armed the security system and pulled the door shut behind us until the latch clicked. As the busser got in her car and drove away, I realized I'd forgotten my cell phone inside. "Shit, I need to go back in."

"Do you want me to wait?"

"No, it's fine. Thank you, though."

"Okay, well, try not to worry about this too much, Michael. I'm sure James will come around and approve your whole vacation."

"A big part of me highly doubts that. He takes Craig too seriously, for whatever reason."

"Yeah…"

"But I'll try," I added, trying to appease her concern. "Either way, I'll figure something out."

"Good. Have a good night. I'll see you Saturday."

"Sounds good. You have a good night too, Alicia."

I watched her drive away and then headed back inside, disarming the security system and heading to the bar where I knew my phone was. Now that I was alone again, the anger had resumed its pulse. Thoughts swirled around and around as I tried to figure out what Craig could have said to James that would make him do this. Nothing made any sense. I'd always busted my ass for James, and he'd always shown his gratitude, for the most part. As I grabbed my phone and turned to leave, I noticed the vacation notebook at the end of the counter. Kara must've forgotten to put it away for the night. Opening the notebook, I reread my request a couple of times. There was still nothing else in there after mine.

After another glance at my vacation request, I pulled a frosted glass from the reach-in cooler and poured a cold, foamy pint of Total Domination IPA. Then, I went around the other side of the bar and sat on a stool, the beer and vacation book in front of me. I scrolled through my phone for a few minutes as I drank the beer in the quiet of the dark restaurant, looking at pictures of Italy on Instagram, reading through my flight and hotel confirmations in my email inbox, checking my bank account and credit card balances.

Twenty minutes had passed before I realized I'd set my phone down at some point and was staring through the walls and the cooler, beyond everything I'd grown to know so well over the last several years. Then, I tipped the last third of my beer back in one long gulp, pulled a pen from the cup on the other side of the bar, and wrote "NEVERMIND" in large letters across my request. Unable to *completely* abandon my morals, I took a five-dollar bill from my wallet and set it under my empty beer glass on top of the open notebook, where a ring began to soak through the pages—leftovers from the initial slosh of my beer when I'd first sat down. In a final, somber moment, a blend of reflection and uncertainty, I unbuttoned my stiff, blue oxford and pulled it off, wadded it up, and placed it on the counter next to the notebook and Kara's keys. I typed the code into the security keypad, and the system beeped unceremoniously as I walked out the side door of The Hillside for the last time.

Chapter 11

The days following my abrupt exit from the restaurant were a whirl-wind of texts and Facebook messages, adamant self-doubt, and shaky self-reassurance.

Michael, you quit?!?!

I just heard the news, Mike! What happened man?

Michael, I miss youuuuu!!!!

James had texted and called and texted again. The one voicemail he left was actually somewhat frantic, yet he didn't say a word about my vacation or give any indication that he understood why I'd left. Finally, he texted and asked if I wanted him to mail my final check. I simply typed back, *Yes. Thank you.*

Alicia's text hit me the hardest. It never came.

I was so unsure what to say to her, both because we were close, for coworkers, and because she was the last coworker I'd seen, and she knew exactly what happened. It should've been easy to tell her, to text her right after I walked out, *something*. But I couldn't. I didn't want her to be mad or to think that she could've convinced me to stay. She could've probably talked me into staying a little longer, but that wouldn't have made anything better. Sometimes an abrupt exit is better than no exit at all.

Almost exactly a week later, I was having a drink at the bar at

Applebee's around nine one night and decided to text her.

Hey, I'm sorry I haven't texted you. And I'm sorry I bailed. It just came out of nowhere and I had to do it. I had to get out.

An hour passed with my heart pounding harder and harder. Finally:

I know. I get it. I'm sad you won't be there anymore, but I get it.

Thank you, I'm glad. I'll miss you, too. I'm sure we'll still see each other occasionally :)

:) OK good, I hope so

We will. Have a good night. I'll talk to you soon.

You too. goodnight

I met up with Alicia, Eli, Darren, and a couple of the bussers at the 24-hour diner near the restaurant two times after that, and we all had a good time. After that, we talked sparingly at best, and I'd see some of my old coworkers around town occasionally, but we never got together again. Alicia and I never talked again. It was as unceremonious as the security system beeping on my way out the door.

Panic visited frequently over the next several weeks, even when I thought I'd made peace with my decision and my actions. I had enough money in my account to pay bills for three months after my trip, four if I lived on ramen and water when I got back. That was factoring in enough spending money that I wouldn't worry about where I ate or drank in Italy—without dining at fancy restaurants every night, anyway. Nothing kills a travel high like spending hours searching for the cheapest gelato. I elected to pay for the most basic international phone plan. There was no one I needed to talk to while I was there—it was better if I didn't have easy access, probably—but I figured it would be good to have some data available in an emergency.

If I really felt the need, I could connect to Wi-Fi at my hostel or a café and get in touch with people via Facebook.

Once or twice I thought about getting in touch with James to talk, but then I'd remind myself that it was only a grasp at some level of security. Walking out of The Hillside had been the first truly impulsive decision I'd made in my life, and when I really thought about it, it felt like the right thing every time. Even if a bridge or two had been burned, it felt like the right thing. Rather than falling back on the restaurant, I spent as much time as I could at home and as little money going out as was bearable. I tried to focus on some of my short stories, though the anxiety often hindered my concentration and I wound up binge-watching something on Netflix instead.

As my departure dates got closer, I spent a lot of time reading online articles and blog posts about Italy. I perused a book of common Italian phrases, hoping at the very least to be able to ask how much something cost and where the bathroom was. More than anything, I was trying to occupy my mind so I wouldn't dwell on the fact that I was now jobless with no prospects or on the people I'd been so attached to that I would no longer see on a regular basis. I still had my close friends, and I knew I'd eventually build new relationships with new coworkers, but it still hurt. Finally, before I knew it, the week of my departure had arrived.

Marcus and I had gotten together a few more times, mostly just to drink beer and get excited about our trips. It had worked out well; he was able to get a flight out of PDX a few hours after mine, and he'd be coming back the day before I returned. We decided to drive up together and get a hotel for the night before our flights, and then he'd stay one more night when he got back so we could drive back together when I touched down. Since I was taking my trip alone, I looked forward to at least sharing the initial thrill of going to the airport to head somewhere different and far away. And it'd be nice to get back and weather the jet-lagged, two-hour drive home with a friend.

Marcus picked me up from my apartment around seven o'clock the night before I was to fly out. I threw my luggage in the trunk of his Nissan, and we hit the freeway toward Portland. The car's custom muffler purred loudly the whole way as we rapped along to hip-hop songs from our high school days and talked about our journeys.

Since Marcus drove like a maniac and raced several other cars on the way up, we made the trip in record time and cut east toward the airport before getting into Portland proper. Our hotel was just down the road from PDX next to the enormous, blue IKEA store, and we were checked in quickly at the front desk. After claiming our beds, we decided we should get some food and beers.

"Hooters?" I asked.

"You know it. Where's it at?"

"Jantzen Beach. Right before the bridge into Vancouver."

"That was quick."

"I know my Hooters. Let's go."

Half an hour and several wrong turns later, we were sitting at a high table with two tall, frosty mugs of beer. A plate heaped with Buffalo wings came shortly after, delivered by our beautiful server, Tina, who whipped her long, dark hair over her shoulder as she left. We'd both been to Hooters restaurants before, but the appeal of attractive waitresses in short shorts and tight, white tank tops had not yet jaded us. As we ate, we watched another waitress stand on a nearby table and pour beer into several mugs as she kept a hula hoop going with her gyrating hips. The guys at the table, a bunch of younger businessmen, whistled and shouted and high-fived each other like a group of frat brothers.

After enough beer and hot wings to know that we would sleep well in between trips to the bathroom, I paid the bill to thank Marcus for driving to Portland, and we headed back to the hotel. We fell onto our beds and put some stupid buddy comedy on TV before deciding we should probably get some sleep. Marcus didn't fly out until the next evening, but my flight left at ten in the morning.

Showered and dressed by seven, we ate a quick breakfast in the hotel restaurant and drove to the airport. I figured out where my gate was, and Marcus suggested that we hole up in the restaurant outside the security checkpoint and have a sendoff beverage. Since it was a tiki-themed restaurant, breakfast time, and we were on vacation, we decided it would be appropriate to order the fruitiest cocktails on the menu. Rum and fruit juices fueled our laughter and our hopes for our trips.

When it was time for me to head through security, Marcus paid for the drinks, gave me a hug, and said, "You better get laid over there. You need it."

I laughed. "Man, I'll be happy just drinking wine with a view in the company of a pretty girl."

"Classic Michael. You've got to be willing to approach them first. Just have a good time, bud. I look forward to hearing about it."

"I'll try to come back with some stories." I winked and thanked him again for the drink and for coming up to Portland with me. "Enjoy New York. I know it'll be good to see her. She'll love the surprise."

"I will, man, thanks."

Marcus gave me a pat on the back and watched me through the security line before he headed out of the airport.

Through security, I found my gate and, realizing I still had a little while before boarding, sat at the bar just down the concourse and ordered a Johnnie Walker Black on the rocks. I wasn't the only one with that idea, which made me feel a little better about drinking scotch before ten in the morning. I nursed my drink and took in all the other travelers hurrying back and forth in the concourse. Families, couples, businessmen and -women, all going one of hundreds of places for one of hundreds of reasons. Travel intoxicated me no matter the reason behind it. The fact that I was doing it alone for the first time, internationally at that, was almost sobering. Back at the gate, it finally came my section's turn to board, so I made sure I had everything, stood in line, and presented my boarding pass when it was time.

Settled into my seat—by the window, thank God—I pulled out my earphones, plugged them into my iPhone, and turned on a relaxing, acoustic playlist. My only seatmate was a Spaniard who was very friendly but smelled as though he hadn't showered in a few days. After an unusually smooth takeoff, I requested two mini bottles of Jack Daniels, a can of ginger ale, and a cup of ice from the woman pushing the drink cart. I hoped that a strong double would ward off any anxiety that might pop up, and maybe even make me forget about the smell sitting next to me. It was about to be a long flight: no East-Coast stopover, but direct to Schiphol in Amsterdam and then to FCO in Rome before finally hitting Naples. I couldn't wait to get down to the warm, sunny Italian coast to forget about every care I had in the world.

Chapter 12

After twenty hours of navigating security, watching in-flight movies, and finding my next gate during my brief layovers, the small Naples airport was a welcome—albeit shabby—sight. The combination of old, fluorescent lighting, worn tiles, and years of cigarette smoke on the walls gave the entire place a very jaundiced appearance. I made my way as quickly as possible through the airport to the front doors and stepped out into the hot *Napoli* afternoon.

I've always felt that being pickpocketed, mugged, misled, or even just blindly ripped off is an inevitability for a traveler; at some point in life, at least one of those things is bound to happen. Accepting that fact rather than expecting each second of every trip to be perfect makes all the difference in the overall experience. That said, I knew it would be cheaper to find the train station and get a ticket to Sorrento than to take a cab there, but I had no idea where the station was. I was exhausted from nearly a full day of travel, and the line of Italian cabbies gathered along the sidewalk looked refreshingly convenient and worth getting the rip-off out of the way early in the trip.

"*Quanto costa a Sant'Agnello?*" I asked the nearest driver, looking him directly in the eye to let him know I wanted a straight answer.

The short, balding man pulled the cigarette out of his mouth and called over to the other cabbies. "*A Sant'Agnello?*"

The group deliberated quietly before calling back to him. I didn't understand the response, but I knew it wasn't a number.

The man turned back to me and said, "One hundred-twenty euros."

"Seriously?" I shook my head. "I'll find another way. *Grazie.*"

The old man muttered something under his breath, replaced his cigarette in his mouth and rejoined the other cabbies. I didn't get the feeling he really cared that I'd turned down his offer; he seemed less than interested in doing his job.

While I thought quickly about a plan B, I heard the group of drivers talking amongst themselves and saw them looking at me. Then, a driver far younger than most of the others, probably no older than twenty-five, walked over to me. He wore designer jeans and an ornately decorated, bright purple collared shirt. "You want to go to Sant'Agnello? I can take you for eighty euros." I guessed that he would take whatever job came up if it meant maintaining his expensive wardrobe. Weighing my lack of energy against the time it could take to find the train station, I realized this was that moment when I could get being ripped off out of the way early. "I'll take it," I said to the driver. He smiled and grabbed my bag, hurriedly putting it in the trunk of his car. I got in the back seat, rolled the window down, and leaned my head back against the head rest. As he navigated his way to the freeway toward Sant'Agnello and Sorrento, I realized how much I appreciated the quiet solitude of a cab ride after a full day of pushing my way through crowds. Giovanni, as the cab driver had introduced himself, seemed to sense that I wasn't in the mood for conversation, and I was grateful he was respectful of that. He drove in silence, except when he would yell obscenities at other drivers.

I tried to relax, but I was too concerned with Giovanni's weaving in and out of other cars on the freeway during what seemed like rush hour. Try as I might to get comfortable, my knuckles quickly paled as I gripped the oh-shit handle above the window.

Traffic in Italy is like a food chain in reverse. The smallest vehicles seem to have the most power. The smaller the car, the more ballsy the driver; the more ballsy the driver, the smaller the spaces they'll pass through. Giovanni's Fiat Bravo put him high in the food chain, third only to Smart cars and *motorini*. As we got closer to Sant'Agnello and the road snaked nearer the sea, hills rose on the other side. This created a very narrow passage with some uncomfortably tight corners. In a fashion exactly opposite of most Oregonians, who often slow down to nearly nothing on a corner, this seemed to be a highly desired stage for Italian drivers to showcase their talents. Giovanni was no exception.

More than once, I was tempted to send text-message goodbyes to my closest friends as Gio—the nickname he'd asked me to use—cut into the opposite lane on a blind corner to pass someone who, I felt, was going a rather respectable speed considering the road, only to swerve back into our lane as his side mirrors tickled those of cars in oncoming traffic. The only things passing Gio were the motorini. At one point, an especially courageous driver on a bright blue *motorino* passed Gio in the shoulder on the other side of the road as Gio passed a small work truck in the wrong lane.

My grip on the oh-shit handle loosened when traffic was forced to slow down through the neighboring municipalities of *Vico Equense* and *Meta*, and I allowed myself to sit back in my seat and let out a long, slow breath. So many people walked along and across the road here that drivers didn't have much choice but to lower their speed and stay in their lanes. It also gave me a good chance to enjoy the scenery; I hadn't had much opportunity to do so in the hustle and bustle of making my way through airports and finding transportation.

The first thing I noticed was the smell. There was the inevitable odor of vehicle exhaust that comes with a high-traffic road like the *Strada Statale della Penisola Sorrentina,* but beyond that, a combination of salty sea air and citrus trees wafted under my nose. I immediately fell in love with the area all over again. We passed several cafés just off the highway where locals and tourists sat and watched the cars go by as they sipped an afternoon *aperitivo* or *birra.* In the shade of several tall trees behind one of the cafés, I caught a glimpse of a group of older men playing a game of *bocce.* I took a deep breath and closed my eyes. The air was just so damn intoxicating. I couldn't believe I was finally there again.

We finally passed through *Piano di Sorrento,* which is where the *Strada* turns into the *Corso Italia,* the main road that goes through Sant'Agnello and Sorrento. A few more minutes and we turned right onto *Via Iomella Grande.* Gio drove for a little under a mile and pulled over to the side of the road in front of what appeared to be an old, nondescript church.

"Here we are!" He looked back at me with a wide smile that said he had not been nearly as terrified on the journey as I had been.

I almost asked if he was sure we were at the right place. It looked nothing like a building I would expect to house the sort of accommodations pictured on the hostel's website. But then I saw a square, grey sign to the left of an entryway, sporting a modern, red "7H" logo.

"Perfect." I pulled out my wallet and handed Gio a crisp hundred-euro note after he set my luggage at my feet.

"Oh, no, it was only eighty."

"I know, but I really appreciate you making it such a pleasant trip. Keep it."

Gio returned my smile. "*Grazie mille, signore.* Enjoy your time in Italy."

"I will. *Grazie,* Gio." I waved goodbye as Gio peeled out in his Fiat and sped around the corner. When he was out of sight, I turned around and took in the building before me. I *really* hoped I wasn't going to be sorely disappointed when I walked through those doors. Then again, Italy had a way of hiding magnificent things in ordinary-looking places. I pulled the handle out of my luggage and rolled it up onto the small sidewalk in front of the hostel. Taking a deep breath, I opened the door and entered.

The interior of the building was warm but still significantly cooler than the air outside, quite refreshing after the long drive in Gio's hot car. Looking around, I knew I wouldn't be disappointed in the slightest. There was a dimly lit bar area off to the left where a pair of young Germans conversed over beaded bottles of beer. Straight ahead was a large, open-air courtyard with tables scattered throughout. High, yellow stucco walls enclosed the courtyard, and many tall windows opened into the guest rooms. Swimsuits and towels hung drying on the windowsills, and some windows had people sitting in them, conversing with other travelers across the way or in the courtyard below. Speakers mounted throughout the space projected upbeat European music that made me smile and certain I'd made the right choice.

"*Ciao!*" said a girl's voice off to my right.

Snapped out of the trance I had fallen into, I turned and smiled. "*Ciao.* I've got a reservation for the week under 'Wise.'"

The girl clicked her computer mouse a couple times and scanned the screen in front of her, muttering to herself in Italian. "Ah! Here you are." She stood on her tiptoes to reach into a cabinet behind the desk, pulling down a key attached to a bright red keychain with a large, white "7" in the middle of it. Handing me the key, she said, "Welcome to Seven Hostel, Mr. Wise. Let me show you to your room."

Chapter 13

Clara, the girl who ran the front desk and was now leading me to my room, told me they'd had a difficult guest who had demanded to stay in his private room one extra night. That room happened to be the one left that had been reserved for me.

"I hope it's alright that we placed you in a mixed dorm of six beds for tonight only. We're not able to waive the charge, but it is a lower rate, and I'd like to offer you a complimentary dinner in the hostel's restaurant as well as an extra welcome drink at the bar upstairs."

Clara was clearly a bit stressed at having to deliver this news, but, having spent nearly seven years in the hospitality industry with my share of difficult guests, I admired how confidently she pushed through and went for it. Smiling at her, I said, "Oh, it's alright, really. I appreciate the gesture. Besides, I could stand to meet some new people while I'm here." The subtle tension quickly left Clara's face.

"I'm glad you are satisfied. We do our best to make sure everyone enjoys their time here. But please, take these." She handed me vouchers for dinner and two drinks.

"*Grazie.*" I smiled to reassure her that I didn't feel at all inconvenienced.

"*Prego.*" She stopped at a door halfway down the hallway on the third floor. "Here we are." Clara put the key in the lock and opened the door. She knocked on the door before entering the room. "Anyone here?"

"Yes, come on in, Clara!" said a girl's voice with an Australian accent.

Clara led me down the short entry hallway into a high-ceilinged room with three sets of light-colored wooden bunk beds. The bedding alternated red and blue, and the walls were a clean, pale yellow. Each bed had a wooden shelf running adjacent to it with a small reading lamp at the headboard. Pulled away from the two windows in the room were pairs of heavy, bright-orange curtains. Three tall cupboards stood around the room, divided in two, one for each bed.

"Hi, Francesca. Did you guys have a good time in Positano?"

"We did, Clara, thank you. The bus ride knocked Laura on her arse, though. Now, who's this?" Francesca sat on one of the lower bunks, looking through pictures on a small point-and-shoot digital camera and drinking a beer. She was wearing a black bikini top and coral-pink shorts. Her wide, brown eyes stared pointedly at me, but with a friendly twinkle.

"This is Michael. He'll be staying with you guys just for tonight." Clara paused for a second. "*Derek* is in his room."

"Ah. *That* wanker. Say no more." Francesca smiled and swung her long, dark ponytail off her shoulder. "Consider yourself lucky, Mike. We're a fun group of gals. I hope you can handle it."

Laughing, I said, "I'll do my best to keep up." Then I nodded to the bunk above Francesca where a bare knee poked up into my view and a limp arm hung over the side of the bed. "I'm guessing that's Laura."

"Too right. Poor thing. She barely made it off the bus at the train station before she chundered *everywhere*. Can't blame her, though. It was bloody hot today, and she was a tad dehydrated. Fancy a beer,

Mike?"

"Please. Actually, that sounds perfect. It's been a long day." I gratefully took the cold bottle of German beer Francesca had pulled from the mini-fridge next to her bed. I popped the top off with my room keychain, which had turned out to be a bottle opener, and drank about a third of it in one swig.

Clara seemed pleased that Francesca and I were getting along so quickly. "There's one more girl and two guys in here, as well. I hope that's alright."

"That's fine, Clara. *Grazie mille.*"

"Your room should be ready by noon tomorrow; just come by the front desk when you're ready to move, and we'll get you all situated. Let me know if you need anything at all."

"That's great. Thank you again."

Clara left Francesca, Laura, and me alone, shutting the door behind her.

"So, what brings you here?" Francesca stood and moved in front of the mirror next to her nightstand to fix her makeup.

While it was a pretty standard question to be asked on a trip, I wasn't really sure at first how to answer it. *What can it hurt to be completely honest? I don't know her and I'll probably never see her again.*

"Life's been kind of stagnant lately, and one night I had too much whiskey and spent too much time looking at flights online. Sooo...here I am." I shrugged, pleased with my brevity.

"Brilliant. You picked a fine place to drunkenly buy a ticket to. Laura and I have been to this hostel several times. It's always a party and a half, and there are so many fun people to meet."

At that point, a pained groan floated from Laura's bunk, and a head with a messy, reddish-brown ponytail poked over the side.

"There she is! How're you feeling, darling?" Francesca handed a glass of water up to her friend.

"Bloody wonderful." Laura took a long drink of water.

"Laura, this is Michael. He's our roommate for the night."

"Hello. Pardon my appearance, won't you? I've had a rough afternoon."

"I don't judge. I haven't heard great things about that bus ride."

"That's good. Listen to those things. Goodnight." Laura set the half-full glass of water on the shelf next to her and flopped back down on her pillow.

"Don't let that be your lasting impression of her. She's brilliant. And radiant."

"I'm sure she is." I chuckled.

"You should join us for dinner later, downstairs. We're meeting some of our friends from another dorm at eight o'clock."

"That sounds great. Thank you."

"I'm going to get her a snack from the bar. Would you like anything?"

"No, thanks. I think I'll get settled in and rest a bit before dinner. It's been a long day. I'll see you guys at eight."

After Francesca had gone, I looked around the room, excited for my stay. It was probably a good thing I was stuck in a dorm for a night, actually, because I wasn't typically the kind to just go and meet random people, even in the comfort of my own town. This would force me out of my shell, something I knew I could use a little more often.

I looked out the window to see several smaller apartment buildings and houses scattered along the streets below, the hills of the Sorrentine Peninsula in the background. I still couldn't believe I was there. I didn't imagine that feeling of awe ever going away. I heard Laura groan from the bed behind me and laughed to myself.

My bed was the top bunk in the corner. I was grateful for the room's high ceiling—no chance of hitting my head if I sat up in the middle of the night. I found an unoccupied cupboard across the room from my bunk and lifted my suitcase into it, adjusting it until the door would close. I'd never been a fan of unpacking during a trip, even though most hotel rooms have dressers in them. It just creates more to do when it's time to leave, so I just live out of the suitcase. In this case, I'd have to move the next day to my private room anyway, so there was really no point in pulling my clothes out now. I climbed up to my bed and lay back with my hands behind my head. It wasn't the most comfortable mattress, and it was only a twin, but it felt amazing to relax, nonetheless. I closed my eyes and attempted to calm the excitement of travel that was burning in me so that I could get a little undisturbed sleep. It didn't work completely; I *did* fall asleep, but I dreamt heavily of Italian food, music, locales, and women.

Chapter 14

I woke to Francesca, Laura, and another girl talking and laughing. I sat up carefully, testing the headroom even though I knew there was plenty of space above me, and swung my legs over the side of the bed. I thought it best to make sure my roommates weren't in various stages of undress before making my presence known, hoping to avoid any awkward moments that might earn me the title of resident pervert.

"Hi, Michael!" Francesca waved me over to where the girls were sitting at the small table in the room. "Did you have a good nap?"

"Yeah, I did. I needed that." Nodding at Laura, I said, "You look like you're feeling better."

"I am, thank you. But what are you saying about how I looked before?" She looked at me curiously.

I hadn't seen that coming. I quickly stumbled around for words in my head, but fortunately, Francesca came to my rescue.

"Oh, stop it, Laura. He's nice."

Laura's curious look turned to a grin. "I know, I'm just taking the piss out of him."

I laughed, glad to have been boarded with a fun group of girls.

"Oh, how rude are we? Michael, this is Tricia. Short for Patricia. Tricia, this is Michael."

"Tricia, it's nice to meet you."

"You also." She shared my roommates' friendly, trusting demeanor.

Francesca asked, "Are you still joining us for dinner at eight?"

I looked at my watch; it was five o'clock. "Definitely. I think I'll reacquaint myself with the area a little before then. Sorrento is just down *Corso Italia* from here, right?"

"Yes. Just turn left out of the hostel, and that'll take you there. But, if you want to take your time and have a more enjoyable walk, I would suggest going straight out of the hostel instead and taking the back roads. There are a lot of pretty flowers there, and a lot of views of the sea."

"Then I'll take that way. Thanks." I stood and smiled at the three girls. "I'll see you at eight. Downstairs, you said?"

"That's right. See you then!"

I left the room and went downstairs to the ground floor. The pretty girl at the front desk smiled and told me to have a good evening. Out on the street, the humidity slapped me in the face, and I immediately felt my shirt sticking to me. I almost took a left for a quicker route to Sorrento but decided instead to stick with Francesca's advice and went straight ahead, hoping, at the very least, for a cool, coastal breeze. There was a small soccer field across the street, with a few Italian guys kicking a ball around. I stopped and watched through the chain-link enclosure for a few minutes before continuing on.

Francesca had certainly been right about the flowers. The streets were lined with fences and rock walls that protected residents' yards from straying passersby, and armies of flowers in countless varieties spread across the walls, seemingly on a mission to make them more beautiful. Some had short, spiky petals and looked like daisies while others had long petals that reached almost completely backward, opening their centers to the sun. They came in purples and reds and yellows, and their leaves were green and luscious and looked as though they'd been transplanted directly from the rainforest. My favorite were a vibrant peach color and looked like trumpets with four wide, rounded petals spread open, leading down into a long, deep perianth. They hung among the deep green leaves mostly in clumps, but several poked out on their own. All the flowers reminded me of Easter eggs nestled on an uncut lawn.

It was hot, but, despite the sweat dripping down my back, it didn't bother me. I'd heard Rome was experiencing its worst heat wave in a while, and I could only hope that it would subside by the time I got there. I fanned myself out a little with my damp shirt and continued past the old, grey, stone walls, peeking occasionally at the homes beyond them. A warm breeze picked up around me, and I realized, as the scent hit my nostrils, that most of these yards were completely full of lemon trees. Suddenly, I had a strong craving for *limoncello*. I'd never actually tried it before, but it just sounded so refreshing in the heat and in light of the aroma surrounding me. I decided I'd stop and have one at the first bar I saw once I got into the heart of Sorrento.

The road finally turned into a wide, vibrant view of the Bay of Naples and the Tyrrhenian Sea beyond. I stopped to take it all in on a bench under the shade of a large lemon tree, avoiding the urge to pull a plump, yellow lemon from its branches and hold it to my nose. As I was getting ready to move on, a friendly Swiss couple approached me, and we exchanged photography services and brief conversation about the view.

Sorrento was exactly how I remembered it: a bustling scene of tourists and locals taking in the sun, the sea, and the shopping. It was a largely retired crowd, but there were enough younger people wandering around that I didn't feel out of place. The main town square, *Piazza Tasso*, was full of people, many of them finding tables at one of the myriad bars surrounding the square so they could enjoy a cold aperitif. As I stood on the edge of the pedestrian flow on the sidewalk, I was reminded of the moment on my first trip to Italy when I became overwhelmingly aware of sundresses – a garment I'd never really noticed much back home that seemed to be worn by every other woman in any direction I looked in Italy. My appreciation for the countless colors, patterns, and the free-spirited way a sundress hangs from whoever is wearing it had stuck with me when I returned home, and sundresses remained one of my favorite parts about the arrival of warmer weather.

I wandered through the piazza toward the side streets where the limoncello might not cost me an arm and a leg. The shade of the surrounding buildings was also inviting and proved to be a few degrees cooler than the more open spaces.

I made my way quickly through the crowds, past all the shops, in search of an uncrowded *trattoria* or bar. There would be plenty of time to visit the shops later; for now, a cold drink took priority. Every watering hole I came across was filled to the door, but I finally turned a corner and saw a little hole in the wall with a few open tables outside and a handful of people inside. I imagined a golden aura and rays of light surrounding the door, an angelic aria beckoning from within. The host at the door noticed the relief on my face and gestured toward the nearest table along the outer wall, grabbing a menu from his podium.

"*Grazie,*" I said as I sat down. Holding up a finger, "*Un limoncello, per favore.*" I glanced quickly at the menu. Not wanting to ruin my appetite for my first dinner at the hostel, I added, "*E alcune olive, per favore.*"

"*Si, signore.*" The salt-and-pepper-haired host replaced the menu under his arm and went inside, returning mere minutes later with a small dish of olives, a bottle of still water with an empty glass, and a short, stemmed cordial glass filled to the edge with a bright-yellow, slightly translucent liquid. I could smell the lemon before I even touched the glass.

"*Grazie,*" I said. He nodded and went back to his post. I picked up the small glass and held it up in front of the sunlight, which caused the limoncello to glow. Then, I tipped it against my lips and took a small drink.

It was a sweet-and-sour kick in the face, and I loved it. Nothing could have prepared me for the strength of the flavor present in that quintessential Sorrentine liqueur. I puckered for a moment, but I immediately wanted more. I poured a glass of water and took a drink between sips of the limoncello to keep the kick slow and steady. I took an olive from the bowl and popped it into my mouth as I watched a moped make its way down the narrow alley in which I sat.

"Shit!" A sharp pain shot through my gums and teeth; I'd forgotten olives don't usually come pitted in Italy. Pulling the dangerous little seed from my mouth and placing it in the bowl, I ran my tongue around my teeth and gums to make sure nothing had chipped or been jarred loose. Most may attribute the un-pitted olives to cultural differences, but I was slightly suspicious that Italian restaurateurs and dentists might have some sort of unwritten agreement in place.

By the time I finished the bowl of olives, the waiter had brought two more glasses of limoncello, and I had finished the bottle of water. I left enough cash on the table to cover the check the host had brought over and thanked him as I passed the podium on my way out of the alley. It was nearly seven o'clock by my watch, so I decided to head back toward the hostel, taking the main roads this time. I glanced in shop windows as I passed, many of them now closed for the night. I chuckled at the never-ending rows of multi-colored motorini parked along the streets.

I followed the road back to the Corso Italia, hugging the wall as I made my way toward Sant'Agnello. Considering the number of pedestrians who walked that way, I couldn't understand why the sidewalk didn't continue along the entire stretch. More than once, I was convinced a side mirror had just brushed my elbow.

When I got back to Seven Hostel, I had just enough time to rinse off in the shower. No one was in the room, so I showered there rather than going down the hall to the communal men's shower area. I brushed my teeth and dressed in a light-blue button-down and khaki pants before heading down to the courtyard.

"Michael! Over here!" Francesca waved me over to the table where she and Laura sat with three guys who looked a little older than me.

"Hey, guys. How's it going?"

"Good, Michael! How was your walk?" Laura was in a much better mood now, her cheeks a faint shade of red from her share of the wine that had once occupied the three empty bottles on the table.

"It was just as amazing as I remember. I can't wait to spend some more time in town over the next few days."

"How rude of me!" Francesca chimed in. "Michael, this is John, Brent, and Rick. We just met them upstairs at the bar when we got here a couple of days ago. Michael is our dorm mate for the night."

"Nice t'meet ya, mate," said the one named Brent. All three shook my hand and gave friendly smiles. "How long y'here for?" Brent scratched his short, scraggly beard before taking a long drink of red wine.

"Just the week. Then, on to Montecatini and Rome."

"That's a good plan, mate. That's where we're headed at the end of the week, Rome. Meetin' up with some more of our pals who've been in Florence. We needed some quality time at the beach, though, so here we are."

The waiter came around the table, then, so we all ordered some food and more wine. Thankfully, the wine came quickly because the food certainly didn't. The tables in the courtyard were all full, so I knew it'd be a while.

The two bottles of wine were gone when the food finally came out, so the waiter brought two more. We drank and talked and laughed as we ate, and the *insalata Caprese* was as flawless as I imagined it would be. The tomatoes, basil, and mozzarella were all delightfully fresh. Even the olive oil tasted a hundred times better than any at home. The seafood linguine that followed wasn't half bad, either.

My acceptance of the girls' invitation to dinner was a significant step out of my comfort zone, largely driven, I think, by the fact that I was already sharing a room with them. Despite all the wine I drank with dinner, I found I was still reserved among the group and mostly just listened to what everyone else had to say. They all had plenty of interesting stories, so boredom was not a problem.

When our plates and the two new wine bottles were empty, Francesca insisted—to a chorus of dissent—on picking up the bill for the table. As we all arose to head to the bar on the roof, I promised myself I would be sure to buy her next drink at the very least.

The view from the lounge had been the biggest determining factor when I chose Seven Hostel, but none of the pictures on the website did it justice. The sun sat just above the horizon, casting a brilliant, orange glow across the towns sprawling around us and upon the hills surrounding the towns. The hills invoked a feeling in me that we were completely removed from the world in our own private paradise.

There were two seating areas, one at either end of the patio, each complete with a large umbrella, a table, two chairs, two couches, and a firepit in the middle. Near the small structure that housed the bar stood a handful of small, round tables that were just tall enough to comfortably lean on while standing. It was still relatively early, so the lounge wasn't packed. Our group decided to stake a claim on the seating area at the north end of the roof and go in two shifts to get drinks. The three Australians went first and came back a few minutes later with what looked like Vodka-Red Bulls. Once they had taken their seats to secure our spot, I stood and followed Francesca and Laura over to the bar.

As we got in line behind three other groups who had just come upstairs, Francesca turned to me and spoke in a hushed tone. "The bartender here is really quiet and *really* into his job. If your drink is shite, don't tell him; just order something different next time. I saw someone complain that their drink wasn't strong enough two nights ago, and he dumped it right out and refused to serve them for the rest of the night. But *I've* never had a bad drink from him, and I've stayed here at least two other times."

I looked ahead at the bartender in question and had to do a double take. He looked almost exactly like Colin Farrell, with short, black hair, thick eyebrows, and a tasteful five o'clock shadow. He also looked like he knew what he was doing, so my faith in him stood strong. He made each cocktail meticulously, treating each one as an individual art project, so the long wait to get to the counter didn't bother me. If a recipe required the juice or a wedge of citrus fruit, it was cut and squeezed only fresh and as needed. On the rare occasion he used a garnish, it was simple and classy. This wasn't a bartender who made pinwheels out of orange slices. He gave a girl a deadly glare when she requested an umbrella in her drink, but he obliged.

When we finally got to the bar, the girls both ordered some sort of elaborate, tropical drink from the specialty menu on the wall, the kind of drink that restaurant and bar owners love to sell but the bartenders hate to make. The look on the bartender's face, though subtle, said that he had *that* in common with other bartenders. As he made their drinks without a word, his eyes moved to me for my order.

"I'll have a Bombay Sapphire Tom Collins, *per favore.*"

His glowering eyes brightened ever so slightly, and there was a fleeting pause in his preparation of the girls' drinks. Then, he smiled and said, in a thick, Italian accent, "The American classic, huh?"

"One of," I said, returning his smile.

Francesca and Laura exchanged a surprised look as they pulled out some cash. "I've never seen him smile!" Laura whispered.

I smirked and shrugged. "I've got these," I said, waving my hand at them to put their money away.

"Thanks, Michael! That's sweet of you. We'll see you over there." I watched them make their way back to where the Australians were sitting and returned my attention to the bartender.

"Bombay Sapphire Tom Collins?" he confirmed as he pulled the squared, blue bottle of gin from the shelf behind him. He cracked several ice cubes in his palm with the back of a long bar spoon, dropping them into a tall, thin Collins glass. Then, he free-poured a shot of gin into a mixing tin and followed it with a teaspoon of sugar and the juice of half a lemon. Adding a small scoop of ice from the bin beneath the counter, he carefully stirred the concoction until the tin was frosty and poured it through a coiled cocktail strainer over the ice in the Collins glass. He shook the tin gently until no more liquid poured out and topped the drink off with a splash of club soda, garnishing it with a thin wedge cut from a fresh lemon. After he had pulled a small sample from the drink with his finger on the end of a straw, to ensure it was up to snuff, the bartender placed the glass on a cocktail napkin in front of me with a fresh straw in it and gestured for me to try it.

I gave the drink a quick stir with the straw, just enough to bring the heavier concoction of liquor, juice, and sugar up into the club soda, and took a sip directly from the glass.

"Oh my God..." I smiled at the bartender and said, "*Delizioso! It's perfect. Quanto costa?*" I gestured at my drink and back toward the girls.

Even the reserved bartender couldn't help but let a small, proud smile break through as he mentally calculated the total of the three drinks. "*Grazie mille, signore. Ventisei euro.*"

I pulled two twenty-euro notes from my folded wad and placed them on the counter. "The rest is for you."

He looked at it, confused, and said, "No, no. It's only twenty-six."

"I know, but this is the best Tom Collins I've ever had." I knew he was probably used to getting a euro or two at most for each drink, which is even generous given Europe's notoriously light tipping culture, but I wanted him to know how much I appreciated his work.

He put his hands together in front of him and nodded his head in gratitude.

I returned to the group just as Brent was telling the girls about the Australians' time spent in Morocco.

"We spent hours in the market in Marrakech. It's the biggest in Morocco, you know. It's heaven for a barterer. Handwoven clothing and carpets everywhere, spices and fruits and nuts of all kinds, outdated electronics, jewelry and leather goods—also handmade. I picked this up our first day in town." He held out his arm so we could all see the thick, brown leather cord wrapped around his forearm, with a hammered metal symbol secured between each end of the cord.

I pointed at the metal piece. "What's that mean?" It was the shape of a primitively drawn, though symmetrical, open hand with a large eye engraved in the middle of the palm. It almost appeared to have two thumbs rather than a thumb and a little finger. Other ornate designs were engraved up the fingers, though I couldn't really make sense of those either.

"It's called a *hamsa*." Brent pointed at each of the fingers. "These represent the five pillars of Islam. The symbol as a whole is supposed to be blessed with protective powers to guard the owner against the evil eye. A lot of people have them painted on their front doors or hanging as a doorknocker or other decoration on their stoops. If you ever go to Morocco, keep an eye out for them. It's very interesting to see the variety of designs they come in. Each one has its own special symbolism integrated into it."

"It's beautiful," Laura said, gently touching the amulet with her index finger. The group murmured agreement.

"But anyway, our last night in Marrakech, we were all drinking a few Flag Spéciales—that's the local beer of choice, for those who *do* drink—at this little café outside the city center, when this somewhat suspicious-looking old Jew came wandering by our table. 'You ought to be drinking better than that,' he told us. Then, he handed us an un-labeled bottle of some sort of clear liquor and said it was a gift."

Brent went on. "None of us was really in a place to use proper judgment by then, so we paid for the beers and wandered off into a less-lit part of town and passed the bottle of liquor around. It tasted strongly of figs and anise, and it punched us in the bloody faces. I still don't know what it was, but it was fantastic. Anyway, after a few passes of the bottle, John came up with a brilliant plan. 'People like Moroccan rugs, right? Well, we're obviously in the kingdom of car-pets right now. We could make a quick few quid off those when we get up north, couldn't we? Get them cheap here, and then sell them for a profit to some tourists who may not be making it to Morocco.'

"Well, that sounded completely logical to me and our mates, even the next morning as we fought our hangovers, so before we left town, we went to several different stalls at the market and bought up some carpets. We wound up with two carpets each, rolled up and strapped to our packs. They only cost us around a hundred and fifty euros each, which is a steal."

"That sounds like a good gig," I said. "My high school Econ teacher would've been proud. How much did you end up getting for them up here?"

"That's the best part," Brent said as he shot John an irritated sideways glance. "We've been up here for two months now, and we're *still* packing those things around! We haven't sold *one*. Turns out, tourists trust the integrity of a few dirty Aussie blokes about as much as they trust the gypsies in the Tuileries in Paris. We've even lowered our asking price to almost *no* profit, but still no takers."

"Shit, man. That's rough. I would've thought they'd sell like hotcakes."

"Yeah, I did too. Sorry, mates," John said sheepishly.

"No worries, John. If anything, it's given us all a good workout." Rick patted John on the shoulder.

Something Brent had said in his story sparked my curiosity. "You said you've been up here for two months now. How long have you guys been traveling?"

The guys looked at each other, trying to calculate the length of their trip thus far. Then, Brent spoke up.

"It's got to be going on five months now. Yeah, that sounds right. We were in Southeast Asia for a month or so, and then Africa for just under a month."

My jaw dropped. "Five months? That's crazy! How'd you get the time and money to travel for so long?"

"Well, it started out as just a month-long trip," Rick said, scratching his heavily stubbled neck. "We were all going to use our vacation time and spend it in Asia. Then, one night in Bangkok, we met this bloke who had just come from Africa and said we *had* to visit it. We all had a decent amount of savings, so we each called back home and told our bosses we wouldn't be back and could we have some extra time. They weren't exactly keen on the idea, so here we are. We figured we're young; there will always be other jobs to pick up when we get back home."

I nodded slowly as I took a long drink of my Tom Collins. I realized that these guys were doing exactly what I'd always wished I had the balls to do: quit working and travel until you can't any longer. Well, at that point I was halfway there, but I didn't exactly have the funds to finance an open-ended journey, or the carefree attitude it'd take to do it.

Rick must have read my mind because he said, "Mind you, it hasn't all been glamorous. We're staying in hostels everywhere, and none of them has been *anywhere* near as nice as this one. This is us splurging. We stayed in one where we shared a room with, like, twelve other people. The padlocks on the storage cubbies were shit, too. Our mate Geoff had his camera and passport stolen one night when we were downstairs for beers for maybe an hour. We never did find out who it was, but a couple of the guys in our dorm never showed up again while we were there. That was down in Johannesburg. We started running low on cash, though, after Marrakech. We thought we'd be recovering what we spent on the rugs, and then some, but when that didn't happen, we had to improvise."

"Yeah," said John. "My parents were able to send us a little money to help out, but I mean *a little*. We had to ration it pretty tightly between food and beds. We've had a few nights where we just found nooks and crannies to sleep in where local police wouldn't notice us. Since we've been in Europe, we've picked up a few odd jobs here and there to make some extra money. Simple stuff, ya know, under the table. Giving tours to English-speaking tourists, helping older folks transport their luggage, things like that." Then, he got a glimmer in his eye and looked at Rick. "Rick actually gave a rather kinky, and generous, middle-aged Japanese couple a tour of his favorite sex clubs in Amsterdam. Made us a thousand euros."

"The tour was easy," Rick said, chuckling. "But they insisted that I join them at one of the last spots we went to, and considering they were paying me so much, I figured I should go along with it. Let's just say I won't be drinking sake anytime soon."

"I don't even want to know," said Francesca as we all cringed and laughed. "Come on, Laura. My drink's out."

John and Brent followed the girls up to the bar, leaving Rick with his beer and me with my Tom Collins.

"So, what brings *you* here, Mike?"

"I just needed to get back here. I came here after high school on a trip with a few friends and completely fell in love with the place. I've never traveled on my own before, so I'm just revisiting the places we went then."

Rick eyed me as I talked, obviously sensing that maybe I wasn't sharing everything, but he simply smiled and looked out at the bay. "It's not a bad place to escape to."

"No, it's not…" I took another drink and stared out at the last traces of deep red-orange sky above the sea. "I really envy what *you* guys are doing, though. I'd love to just unplug from life for a bit and travel for a few months. Hell, even *one* month would be nice, but I'll be lucky to ever get that much time off."

"How many weeks of vacation do you get over there? We get four in Australia by government mandate."

"A lot of places start at one week, *maybe*. I was at my last job for nearly seven years and barely got two weeks there. You can earn it over time most places, but it'll take you years."

"Shit!" Rick's buzz was starting to show, as he'd slapped his hand to his red face in utter disbelief. "I just thought four weeks was stock as a rock anywhere. Some countries up here even get five or six weeks."

"Yeah, well, that's the American dream for ya. There's a reason we're rarely, if ever, on those lists of the happiest countries." I tipped my glass back and finished off the Tom Collins in one long gulp. "God *damn*, that was good!"

Rick chuckled, finished the rest of his beer and stood up to go join his buddies, who were talking to a group of girls they appeared to know already, patting me on the shoulder as he walked by. "Nice talkin', mate. We'll all have to go out on the town before we part ways."

"Sure thing, Rick. Have a good night." I stood and stretched my back before heading back to the bar for another Tom Collins. I didn't see Francesca or Laura anywhere.

The bartender had just sent a pair of girls, who were probably there on their high school graduation trip, away with pink cosmos when I stepped up to the counter.

"Another Bombay Sapphire Tom Collins, *per favore.*"

"Ah, it was good?"

"The best, really. *Molto bene.*"

"*Grazie, signore.* Coming right up." His face beamed as much as he would allow.

It's a sign of a good bartender when he makes a perfect drink the first time, and his process doesn't vary in the slightest the second time. This Italian was *definitely* a good bartender.

Again, he pulled a small taste with a straw before presenting me with the cocktail. Again, he approved of his work, and placed the glass in front of me on a cocktail napkin.

I handed him a ten-euro note and thanked him. Before I walked away, I asked, "*Come ti chiami?*"

"Daniele."

"Daniele, *mi chiamo* Michael." I reached out my hand to shake his. "*Con piacere.*"

Daniele wiped his hands on his bar towel and shook my hand. "It's my pleasure to meet you, also. I'm glad you enjoyed your Tom Collins."

"Daniele, I can honestly say you're the best bartender I've met. I'll be back plenty before I leave."

"*Grazie mille,* Michael. *Buona notte.*"

"*Buona notte,* Daniele." I took a sip of the drink, smiled pointedly at him, and turned to see if Francesca and Laura had reappeared. They hadn't, and the Australians had disappeared, too, so I walked over to the railing that faced the sea and looked out into the darkness. Breathing in the salt and citrus air, which enhanced the taste of my cocktail, I closed my eyes and thought about where I currently was and where I had been.

Gone were the feelings of hopelessness and despair that had inundated me over the last year or so. I stood at the edge of a three-story building and had no desire to climb over the edge and let go. While thoughts of my lack of direction in life and my general lack of happiness still meandered through my mind occasionally, I was finding it easier to push those thoughts away and enjoy the beautiful place I was visiting. I also realized I hadn't thought about Liz once since I'd flown out of PDX.

"Michael! What're you doing?"

I snapped out of my thoughts and turned around to see Francesca and Laura coming toward me, haphazardly carrying glasses of red wine.

"Hey, guys. I thought you'd left."

"No, no! We're up on the tanning deck over there." Laura pointed back in the direction from which they'd come. "Rick and the other guys are up there, too. C'mon!" She grabbed my hand and dragged me along with them past the bar and along the rail toward the solarium.

It was dark along the side of the building, so it caught all three of us off guard when two guys near my age came running around the corner and nearly knocked Francesca over.

"Sorry!" yelled the one wearing a baseball hat and an Abercrombie and Fitch T-shirt. His friend, slightly shorter and stockier and wearing a white button-down shirt, gave her a sheepish look before following the first one to the bar.

"Yeah? You bloody well better be sorry, you bloody wombat!" Her drunkenness showed as she waved a fist at the two passersby.

"C'mon, Francesca, forget about them." Laura grabbed her friend's shoulders and turned her around to lead her back in the direction we'd been going.

Amused, I chuckled and sipped my drink, following the girls as they stumbled up the short set of steps that led to the solarium. As I passed the door that led into the hostel, three girls walked out smiling and laughing.

"Jake! Jeremy! Wait up, guys!" one of them called. "Sorry about them," she said to me with a smile. "They're a little excited to be here. And to get drunk."

I returned her smile. "It's alright. Can't really blame them, can you?" My words were directed back at her, but it was one of her friends, the middle of the three, with whom I locked eyes.

Deep blue and wide with charisma, they stared quietly at me as I spoke briefly to her friend. Wavy, golden hair fell just past her shoulders, framing her tanned, smooth cheeks. Her soft-looking, pink lips curved into a small smile that made me immediately want to kiss her. I knew I'd be speechless if she unleashed a full smile.

"I suppose you're right. Some of us just contain it better than others," the first girl said cheerfully.

I'd completely forgotten the other two were there in what had likely been maybe three seconds of eye contact, and I looked back at the one who had spoken.

Apparently, the gaze I shared with her friend had been a little more obvious than I'd expected, because she looked from me to her friend and back again and smiled.

I took advantage of the break in what could barely be called conversation and took my leave. "You ladies enjoy your night. Don't let those guys have all the fun." I gave a slight wink, mostly directed at the blond girl.

"You too! Don't worry, we won't."

All three said "Goodbye" and started walking toward the bar area.

As I climbed the steps, I could've sworn I heard one of them say, "He was cute!" Granted, that's also most every guy's fantasy when he crosses paths with attractive girls, but when I glanced back toward them, I caught the girl in the middle looking at me before she quickly turned around and disappeared around the building with her friends. The image of her in that short, black cocktail dress immediately burned itself into my mind, and I was right: her wide, pearly smile left my jaw on the floor.

Chapter 15

Up at the solarium, the group had settled on a set of big couches and chairs at the far end of the long deck. Everyone was laughing and drinking and having a great time. John caught my eye over Francesca's shoulder and waved me over.

"Oy! Mike! Down here, mate!"

I smiled and nodded in his direction and pulled up a chair between Laura and Brent. Two other girls had joined the party; from what I heard in the chaos of several conversations going on at once, I guessed they were German. Brent had his laptop computer open on one of the tables, playing a lively mixture of music in the background.

It was so odd, so uncharacteristic, for me to be sitting with a group of people I hadn't known for more than twenty-four hours and having the time of my life. But I *was*, and far outside of my comfort zone. Since so many conversations were already going, I just sat and drank my cocktail and listened to the people around me as I had at dinner.

John and Brent entertained Francesca and Laura with a story that sounded, from the bits and pieces I heard clearly, like the tale of a rowdy night hanging around the pyramids of the Louvre that led to being chased on foot through the Tuileries by French police.

Rick seemed to be seeking self-affirmation from the German girls with a story of drinking three Englishmen under the table at their own pub. The girls were wide-eyed and appeared to be buying it, but as much faith as I had in Rick's drinking prowess, I had more in the pride and ale-swigging faculties of the English when challenged on their own turf.

"You're quiet, Michael." Laura had turned toward me and was sipping her glass of red wine with a curious look on her face. Her cheeks had reddened, but she was much mellower than her friend. "Are you having fun?"

"I really am, yeah. This is just so amazing. The hostel, this group of people I hardly know, just *being* in Italy."

"You've been before, though, right?"

"Yes, but I really feel like this excitement will never end. No matter how many times I come here, which I hope will be many more, it'll always just blow my mind."

"It *is* beautiful, isn't it? I suppose we take it for granted because we're so much closer and can travel like this quite often. I don't mean that I don't love it, because I do, but I think I've lost that childlike thrill that you seem to have. I love that."

"I'm jealous that you *do* live so close to travel here more often, but I still love how new it feels even the second time."

"I remember the first time I came here, to Sorrento. Francesca and I came with our families before she moved away. We were about thirteen, I think, and we wanted one last vacation together."

"I didn't realize you two had known each other for so long." I sipped my drink and waited for her to continue.

"Mmhmm. We grew up together, the best of mates, and then her father took a job with his company that required them to move to Australia. It was sad, but it was what was right for his family. It's worked out okay, though, because they're fairly well off and we're able to visit each other a couple of times a year."

"Oh wow, that would be really difficult, I'm sure. I can't imagine moving halfway around the world from any of my friends."

As Laura started to say something else, a loud *BOOM* cut her off, and the others in our group cheered and clapped at whatever had just happened.

I followed their lines of sight out toward the Bay of Naples just in time to see an enormous yellow burst of light in the sky, its remnants showering down on the water. Somewhere on the coastline, fireworks were being set off.

"Whooo!" Brent yelled. "Light another one!"

As if spurred on by his command, two more shells burst in the air over the water, this time silver and green, closely followed by three more in red, purple, and gold.

"Is there some sort of celebration going on around here?" I asked Laura.

"I'm not sure. Nothing that I'm aware of, but they do have a lot of those random types of things in Italy, and even the coast has some of its own. It looks like they're coming from around Meta."

"Hm. Well, whatever's going on, we picked the right night to come up here." I took another drink and sat back to watch the show, which had picked up pace and become a lot more complex.

Reminiscent of the Fourth of July picnic scene in *The Sandlot*, conversations had ceased as everyone's attention turned to the beautiful display. The only sounds were the stream of music coming from the laptop intermingling with the occasional "ooh" and "ahh" from our group. We could even hear them coming from the people down in the lounge.

And then there were the booms and crackles of the fireworks. Sorrento and Sant'Agnello are surrounded by hills and mountains that divide the Sorrentine Peninsula. Every explosion of the pyrotechnic shells reverberated across the mountains around us like chains of thunder. Each boom echoed into the next and the next. It was so powerful and so impressive that chills found their way down my spine, even in the warm, humid air.

At some point during the show, a familiar Disney song played on the computer and we all found ourselves singing along, arms around each other's shoulders:

"Hakuna matata! Ain't no passing craze... It means no worries for the rest of your days..."

This is officially the best night of my life, I thought, unable to stop an ecstatic grin from spreading across my face. We smiled at each other as we sang and drank and watched the fireworks light up the sky. We whooped and screamed and hollered. We were young and carefree on a rooftop in Italy.

"Hakuna Matata" eventually ended, and the group quieted down again to watch the grand finale. And grand it was. It put every display I'd ever seen at home to shame. Layer upon layer of every color imaginable lit up the sky all at once, raining sparks down as more shells burst to replace them. Several times, I caught myself wondering if magic had been used in creating the pyrotechnics. I'm not saying a dragon made of colorful sparks flew overhead, but some of the effects we saw certainly seemed impossible.

As all good things do, the show came to an end. The last of the sparks fell with nothing to follow, returning darkness to the sky, and we all sat there quiet and satisfied as if we had just eaten the greatest meal of our lives. After a few minutes, Brent paused the music and spoke up.

"So, what's everyone doing for the rest of the night?"

"There's a nightclub on the other side of the peninsula, Africana," said one of the Germans. "There's supposed to be a big party there tonight. Some friends of ours are taking us over there if you want to join."

"I heard about that! The waiter downstairs was telling me about it and invited us," said Francesca excitedly. "It's supposed to be in this enormous cave! I'm game if everyone else is." Everyone else said they were.

"Where on the other side of the peninsula?" I was having a good time with the group, and was still open to some more new experiences, but I knew the trip to the other side was not a short one, even cutting through the mountains instead of taking the road around, and I sensed that they were all quite a bit more of a nightclub crowd than I was. And it was already one in the morning.

"It's in Praiano, a little past Positano," said the German girl.

"Ah." That was all I needed to hear; it was probably an hour-long drive each way. One thing I never liked to be was dependent on someone else when I was somewhere that I may want to leave early, and I had no vehicle of my own in Italy. Not that I should be driving at that point, anyway.

"Let's go!" Francesca dragged Laura out of her chair and beckoned everyone to come with them.

The others stood, finished their drinks, and followed Francesca and Laura.

"Are you coming, Mike?" Rick asked as everyone started to file toward the staircase.

"Nah, man. You guys have fun. I think I'm gonna take it easy and have another drink here. I'm still pretty wiped out from the trip over."

"Alright, mate. We'll see you soon, I'm sure. Have a good night!" With that, he caught up to the group, put an arm around each of the German girls, and said something that made all three of them laugh in unison.

Once they'd all disappeared down the stairs and into the building and I could no longer hear the excited chatter, I finished the Tom Collins and went down to the bar for another. After I'd paid Daniele for what I decided would be my last drink for the night, I turned around and saw the blond girl from earlier sitting with her friends at the same table my group had been sitting at. I couldn't believe I'd forgotten about her, but I was glad I'd been able to stay present in such a revitalizing and uplifting moment. She was still there, though, and still as stunning as she had been the first time I saw her. Now that I was alone, I had no reason not to let her back into my mind.

I stood at one of the small round tables for a moment, tossing around the idea of going and talking to her, ultimately deciding against it. I tried to pretend it was to respect her time with her friends, since they seemed to be enthralled by a story the two guys in the group were telling. It *was* partially for this reason that I chose not to say anything. The other part, of course, was that I had no idea what the hell I would say to her. The social flaw that somehow always had a way of finding its way back into my daily routine reared its ugly head yet again.

As I picked up my drink from the table and resolved to go back to the solarium, I noticed one of the other two girls looking over at me and, with a smile, whispering in the blond girl's ear. A few seconds later, the blond girl turned slightly and made eye contact with me, showing off that smile of hers once more.

It may have been the amount of alcohol I'd consumed that evening, but when she smiled, my knees actually went weak, and I nearly stumbled as I smiled modestly back at her.

Her hand went to her mouth as she tried to suppress a giggle, and my face immediately felt bright red. I made a "yikes" face back to her to acknowledge the humor in what had just happened, raised my drink slightly in her direction, and gave her a wink and a smile before going back up to the solarium.

Fortunately, the upper deck was completely empty; I was ready for a few quiet moments to myself before heading to bed. I sat on one of the huge, round couches we'd just vacated, kicked off my flip-flops, and put my feet up on the low table. The noise from the lounge was just loud enough to let me know I wasn't alone, but not loud enough to be disruptive. Conversations and laughter and music made their way to my ears, reminding me of the memories we were all making. I drank that final Tom Collins slowly, my eyes closed, trying my damnedest to prolong the moment. Even though there were undoubtedly many more incredible moments to have while I was in Sorrento, I knew there would never be another exactly like that one.

Hearing a few excited yells coming from the street below, I decided to go take a look to see what was going on. As I stood up, I felt everything I'd had to drink that night hit me all at once, some of it for the first time and some for repeat business.

"Time for bed," I said aloud to myself. Leaning over the railing, I saw that there were still some young men playing soccer on the small field below across the street from the hostel. *This late? That's commitment,* I thought. Then, I made my way carefully down the short flight of stairs and to the bar to place my empty glass on the counter. I was at that point of drunkenness where I was so focused on my steps and my direct path that I didn't pay much attention to the people around me. My only concern at that point was getting down the last two sets of steps to the third floor of the hostel and down the hallway to my room.

When I was just about through the door from the patio to the interior of the building, I heard a pretty voice call from behind me: "Hey! Do you need a hand?"

Placing my hand on the door frame to hold myself up, I turned around—slowly, as the dreaded spins were kicking in—to see who was behind me.

It was the blond girl from the rooftop.

"Sorry?"

"I thought I'd see if you needed help to your room. Those stairs could be dangerous." Her smile was more amused than judgmental, for which I'd be grateful in the morning.

I looked toward the stairs and back to her. "I'd probably be an idiot if I said 'no,' huh?"

"You said it, not me." She winked.

"Then your assistance would be most welcome."

"I thought it might be." The girl pulled my arm over her shoulders and placed her own around my middle. She stepped down the stairs as slowly as I did, providing me with a surprising amount of support considering her small frame.

"Which way is your room?" she asked when we got to the third-floor landing.

I held a finger up in the air, moving it in a circle as if I were twirling some invisible person's mustache, as I tried to regain my bearings. "That way." I pointed to our left when I recognized one of the cheap-looking paintings on the wall.

"Are you sure? You're not getting me to help you break into someone else's room, are you?" She looked up at me with that smile to assure me that she was joking.

"I think I'm sure. We'll see soon enough if my key works or not. Aha!" I stopped at a tangerine-colored door. "Pretty sure this is it." Fumbling in my pocket, I pulled the key out and stuck it with some difficulty into the lock. It clicked and turned and the door popped open.

"Whew! I was worried for a minute." I smiled drunkenly at the girl, who clearly had been very entertained and was still holding onto me.

"Thank you for helping me back here. I didn't really feel like falling down some stairs tonight, or getting my ass kicked for going into the wrong room." I took her hand in mine and kissed the back of it lightly before directing my eyes up at hers. "You smell nice."

The girl giggled. "You're welcome, and thank you."

I smiled back at her again and then turned to go into my room.

"Goodnight!" she called as I shut the door. I could hear her laughter trail down the hallway as I made my way through the dark room, quietly so as not to disturb any of my roommates who hadn't been a part of our group and might be sleeping.

When my face hit the doors of the tall cabinets, I knew I was at the end of the room and that my bunk was to my right. I climbed carefully up the narrow ladder, hitting my head on the ceiling that I thought would never be a problem, and collapsed onto my bed. I couldn't have fallen asleep more suddenly if I had died.

Chapter 16

The next morning, my throbbing head woke me more effectively than any alarm. I sat up slowly and looked around. Laura and Francesca were the only roommates still there and in bed, so I climbed quietly down the ladder, grabbed some clean clothes and my shower things from the cabinet, and tiptoed out of the room. I'd heard the girls come in around five-thirty, and it was now only eight-thirty, so I didn't want to disturb what was likely a much-needed sleep.

The men's shower area was on the second floor, so I took one flight of stairs down and found it at the end of the hall. I was glad to hear only one other shower running; group showers had never been my favorite thing in the world. I placed my things on a bench next to one of the open shower stalls, went to the sink, and held my mouth open under the cold running water for a few seconds.

The hot, steamy shower drove the shitty feeling of too much alcohol from my body. Fortunately, the headache I had was manageable. Nausea would have been a different story and likely would have resulted in a day wasted in bed.

After I'd dried off, I brushed my teeth and got dressed quickly, dropped off my things in the room, and headed downstairs for some breakfast. I was excited and petrified to see the blond girl and her friends sitting at a table in the courtyard. She at least had her back to me.

I debated taking an alternate route to the breakfast buffet in the dining room just off the courtyard, but one of the other girls in her group had already made eye contact with me, smiled, and waved, so I knew it was pointless to avoid them. I walked up to their table, smiled, and nodded toward them in greeting.

"Good morning."

The blond girl smiled up at me. "Good morning, yourself."

"Hey, I just wanted to thank you again for the help last night. That was really nice of you."

"Well, you're welcome. It was my pleasure."

"I'm a little embarrassed how sloppy I was. I hope I didn't try anything. To be honest, I don't even remember if you told me your name, so I apologize if you did." My ears grew warm as my nerves kicked in.

The blond laughed. "Don't worry, you were a perfect gentleman. And I didn't tell you my name. I had a feeling you might not remember it this morning. I'm Emily."

I reached my hand out and shook hers. "Michael."

"This is Kasey, Jenna, Jake, and Jeremy."

I shook each of their hands as Emily indicated them, noticing that Jake's had an extra, firm squeeze in it, like he was trying to intimidate me. I brushed it off, figuring it was just his personality.

"It's great to meet you guys. Did you have a fun night?"

"We did!" It was Kasey who spoke this time; she was the one I had first spoken to the night before. "This place is so amazing. We can't wait to see the rest of the town."

"Oh, you'll love it. It's so beautiful here. And there are so many different things to see. Where else are you guys going?"

"Well, we're starting out here, and then going up to Florence, then

Venice, and then Rome." Kasey brushed her dirty-blond hair out of her face and ate a piece of pineapple.

"That's a solid plan. I don't really know you guys, but I think you'll like it a lot. It's damn near impossible not to."

"I think so, too," Emily said. From what I could tell, her gaze hadn't left me the entire time I'd been standing there.

Jake spoke up. "You were pretty trashed last night, huh?"

"Jake! Don't be a jerk." Kasey elbowed him in the shoulder and glared at him.

I laughed. "No, it's alright. I definitely had a lot to drink. It all kind of caught up with me at once. But I don't want to keep you from your breakfast. It was nice to meet you guys. I'm sure I'll see you around."

"Bye, Michael!" yelled Jenna between bites of food.

Jeremy smiled and nodded, but Jake just went back to the conversation with Jeremy and Jenna as if I hadn't been there.

Emily smiled and waved at me before leaning across the table and smacking Jake on the arm. As I walked away, I could hear her scolding him for being rude.

As I grabbed a plate and started piling it with food, Clara ran over from the front desk to let me know my private room was empty and had been cleaned. "It's ready for you anytime. It's just down the hall from where you're at now. And, please, take this as our apology for the delay." She handed me a bottle of red wine and the key to my new room.

"It was really no trouble at all, but thank you. I appreciate it."

She smiled and nodded. "Please just bring down the key to your current room when you leave for the day."

"I will. *Grazie.*" I set the bottle on the table while I finished filling my plate, and then took both up to the roof. The sun was already high in the sky, but the air still carried a pleasant morning breeze that kept the heat of the day at bay for a little longer. I ate quickly and headed to my room to grab my things. That way, I could make the transition to the other room as early as possible and enjoy the rest of my day.

Laura and Francesca were still fast asleep when I got to the dorm, and it looked like the other roommates had packed up and left, so I put my things quietly in my bag, wrote a quick note saying where I'd gone and that I was glad to have met and spent some time with them. I placed the note on the table and left the room, bags and bottle of wine in hand.

As I shut the door behind me, Emily came around the corner and stopped abruptly. The smile quickly fell from her face when she saw my luggage. "Are you leaving?"

"No, no. I had booked a private room, but they didn't quite have it ready, so I stayed in this dorm for the night. I'm actually moving..." I glanced at the new key and then to the numbers on the doors in the hallway. "...down there." I pointed to the door at the end of the hall that matched my key.

"Oh, well good! I was just coming up to apologize for Jake. He was an asshole earlier. But he's just protective of us, you know, when strange guys come around."

"Oh, I understand. You never know who you can trust, especially in a new place."

We smiled awkwardly at each other, neither of us sure what to say next. Finally, Emily spoke up.

"I should probably get back to them. We're getting ready to go into Sorrento."

"Alright. Take the road across the street from the hostel and stay right. It's a really pretty walk."

"Thank you, we will. Hopefully we'll see you again, Michael."

"I hope so, too."

With that, Emily walked back toward the stairs, smiling over her shoulder one last time before she turned the corner. She carried herself with such beautiful confidence. She wasn't tall but had a significant presence. I gazed at the deserted hall for a moment before remembering what I'd been doing. I let myself into the room at the end of the hall and set down my bags and the wine. The bed was larger and much farther from the ceiling, and I had a view of the sea from the window. It was going to be a relaxing stay for the rest of my time there. It would be nice having my own bathroom, too.

I opened the window to let the breeze in and took in the view for a few minutes. The water wasn't close, but I could still see a large span of it over a few rooftops. A brilliant, white cruise ship made its way toward the Port of Naples, its windows sparkling in the sun. I could barely make out hundreds of people, like ants, lining up along the rails to watch the ship dock and take in their new port of call. Some waved scarves or the flags of their home countries as people on the docks waved back in greeting. *How exciting would that be,* I thought, *sailing into a new place every day or so and having that as the hotel you get to go back to.*

In a window two buildings over, an older Italian woman waved laundry out the window and hung it from a line to dry. She looked toward me and half-smiled. It was the little details like that which made me love this country even more; line-drying laundry between buildings wasn't common back home. I still preferred a clothes dryer, but the visual novelty of it was pleasant. I smiled back and raised a hand in a brief wave, then went and flopped onto the bed. It was significantly more comfortable than the one in my last room. I knew it would be dangerous to stay there too long; I didn't want to waste a single minute of my time on the coast. Still, I decided that I would spend that day relaxing and recuperating from the long day before of travel and revelry.

Chapter 17

After a long, successful recovery day spent entirely at the hostel between bed and books and basking in the sun, I decided to get up early on Monday so that I could be sure to make a little more of my time on the coast.

Surprisingly refreshed when the alarm went off at seven, I had a quiet breakfast downstairs and decided to go to *Marina Piccola*, where the hydrofoils left to shuttle passengers from Sorrento to the isle of Capri. The quickest way I could remember was through *Piazza Tasso* and down the narrow staircase into the hairpin turn of *Via Luigi de Maio*, a vertiginous descent that would have a lot of people hanging onto the handrail. Fortunately, there weren't a lot of tourists on the staircase; it's not a fun place to be when lines of people are trying to go both ways, half of which have no sense for walking in crowds. At the bottom, I made my way out of the heavily shaded alcove through which the road turned and back out into the sunlight.

The smaller of Sorrento's two main ports, Marina Piccola doesn't really live up to its name in comparison to its counterpart, *Marina Grande*. It actually seems a bit larger as the port that dispatches and receives small yachts and hydrofoils, whereas Marina Grande is an older fishing port, filled with the smaller boats of the locals. High above Piccola, the Grand Hotel Excelsior Vittoria rises from a cliff in opulent, pink splendor and watches over the port below. Just off the road is a short promenade that runs around the ticket office and restaurants, shaded by a few scattered umbrella pines.

Several tour busses sat to the side of the road, allowing various tour groups to alight and stop traffic as they awkwardly made their way across the road to the ticket area. I stopped to observe the different groups and their respective dynamics. One Japanese group wore matching purple T-shirts and followed a guide raising a bright purple umbrella in the air; another mostly male group all wore white T-shirts with maps of Italy in neon green, orange, and pink across the chest and followed an exuberant guide who held a rainbow umbrella; and a group of high school students followed their exasperated teacher-chaperone and tour guide across the road, some of them engaging in horseplay that was better suited for a backyard or a park than the middle of a busy road. I chuckled, glad I was there on my own, and wandered along the far edge of the marina by the water.

At the end of the main dock where all the hydrofoils and ferries were moored, several entrepreneurs had set up tables or laid out blankets on the ground to display their wares. The wares consisted mostly of fake designer sunglasses, watches, and purses, still priced at an arm and a leg, but ultimately available for the cost of a little toe if you really felt like trying. A couple of the sellers, however, had arranged on their tables what looked like handcrafted jewelry and other decorative trinkets. One table in particular, manned by an old woman with dark, leathery skin and a missing ring finger, stood out to me with a plethora of handmade leather necklaces and bracelets exhibited on a dirty, white tablecloth, some with what looked like precious stones, metal tokens, or old coins woven into them. I'd kept my distance from the tables and blankets thus far, as the merchants weren't legally allowed to be there selling things, but I glanced around and did not see the usual authorities who periodically come through and clear them out, so I cautiously stepped up to her table.

"*Buongiorno,*" I said, smiling at her.

She simply smiled a semi-toothy grin and nodded her head. From a distance, I'd thought her extremely dirty, but up close I could tell she had just spent *a lot* of time in the sun.

My eyes scanned carefully over her creations, and I took care not to touch anything just in case she was out to scam people. I immediately thought back to Paris a few years earlier when a friend with whom I was traveling had made the mistake of extending his hand within arm's distance of a gypsy in the Tuileries. She immediately grabbed his hand and tied a bracelet of woven string to his wrist—like a "friendship bracelet" that a middle school student might swap with her best friend—and then tried to charge him twenty euros for it. At just the right moment, our teacher who had organized and was chaperoning the trip—Mr. Thomas—ran over and started yelling something in French at the woman. Whatever he had said worked because she waved us off and yelled something in what must have been her native language and spat at our feet. Fortunately, the woman in front of me now wasn't pushy, and I felt a little more comfortable. Still, I kept my hands in my pockets, just in case.

Most of her items were a little too gaudy for my tastes. It was rare that I wore any kind of jewelry, but I preferred it to be simple when I did. I'd always liked the idea of having something that I got on a trip that I could always have on me, and Brent's hamsa bracelet from Marrakech had been on my mind ever since he'd showed it to us. I almost gave up hope of finding anything when a flash of bright blue caught my eye. I pointed at the bracelet and looked at the woman with questioning eyes.

She gingerly picked up the bracelet, a proud smile on her face, and placed it in my hands as a king might present a knight with a sword.

It was woven of royal blue and black leather, with a basic clip fastener like the back of a necklace. I inspected it closely enough to tell that it was sturdy and would not come unraveled as soon as the euros were in her purse.

"*Quanto costa?*"

"*Quindici*," she replied, holding up her right index finger and all five fingers on her left hand.

I knew a lot of people who would barter and barter until they spent no more than two euros on something like this, but I had a great appreciation for the woman's craft and the pride she displayed, as well as the simple fact that she wasn't pushy like so many others that I'd come across, so I didn't want to disrespect her by talking her down. Besides, fifteen euros was a small price to pay for a token and reminder of this trip that I would keep for the rest of my life. The smallest note I had was a twenty, so I handed it to her with a smile and gestured for her to keep it all.

At first, she didn't seem to know what to do, and I gathered that no one had likely ever *over*paid her before. Then, she smiled wide again and put her hands together in gratitude. "*Grazie, grazie!*"

"No," I said. "*Grazie mille.*" I nodded and gestured toward her to let her know I was very pleased with my purchase. "*È bello!*"

She pulled my hand toward her and placed the bracelet around my wrist, ensured it was fastened securely, and waved me off happily.

As I walked past the other vendors, I admired the bracelet on my wrist, very glad to have found it. It had simple character, and it came from a place that made me happy. I went to the bar at the back of the port for some gelato.

Breaking with tradition, I chose a cup of lemon *sorbetto* over my favorite *stracciatella*. The sorbet was revitalizing in the mid-morning heat, light and crisp and just the right amount of tart. It also wasn't a gelato that would have me feeling full and lazy afterward. I ate it slowly with the small, flat spoon and walked toward the other end of the marina where rows of brightly colored umbrellas and cabanas marked the string of pay-beaches which charged way too much for something you could get for cheap or free just outside of town.

Each beach had its own jetty at the end of a long, elevated boardwalk. There were nice, enclosed swimming areas, but I was surprised that so many people paid to be out there. Proprietors stood at the entrance to a couple of the beaches, trying to convince tourists to come in, but I just smiled and continued along toward the staircase at the other end that would take me back up to town level. The long, back-and-forth ascent led me up the side of the cliff and came out at the *Villa Comunale*, a public garden that overlooks the gulf, filled with flower beds and tall shade-trees and benches. Bordering the garden, at the top of the stairs, was a restaurant and bar, the back of which shared a courtyard with the Church of St. Francis. I quickly claimed an open bench facing the sea and sat for a few minutes, watching all the other tourists take pictures of each other, before continuing past the church toward the center of town.

After having a sandwich for lunch and wandering around Sorrento for a few more hours, stopping for a nap in a shady park off *Via Correale* above Marina Piccola, I decided to head back to the hostel. On the way, I stopped at a small trattoria with a pretty outdoor dining area covered in grapevines and ate a decent plate of *gnocchi alla sorrentina* with a glass of crisp white wine that went nicely with the tomato sauce.

Back in my room, I took a cold shower and flopped naked onto my bed. It felt so good to have a private room with no one else to worry about; I had to take advantage of the freedom. It was too warm for clothes, anyway.

After becoming engrossed in a book for a couple of hours, I was startled when a quiet knock echoed through my room from the door. I marked my page and walked to the door. My hand was on the handle and about to turn it when I realized I still had no clothes on.

"Uh...hang on a second!" I ran and put on my swim shorts and a T-shirt before returning to open the door.

"Hi!"

"Hey, Emily." I couldn't contain the grin that spread across my face when I saw her standing in my doorway, wearing a white tank top and a pair of short, blue shorts. "What's up?"

"Can I dry my hair in your room?" She held up a hair dryer and made a faux-pouty face. "I forgot my plug adapter, and the dryer in our room barely blows any air."

"Ah." I laughed as she brushed her hands through her still-dripping hair. "And how do you know I have an adapter?"

"I don't. But you seem like the kind of guy who would come prepared. If not, I guess I'll just hang out here anyway and let it air-dry." She looked me directly in the eyes, daring me to turn her away.

Chapter 18

It had been my experience as a young man that a girl doesn't usually like to be bothered while she does her hair. I suppose the process of blowing it dry, brushing it out, and then styling it with myriad products—each with its own individual purpose of de-frizzing, softening, holding shape—or putting it into a braid or ponytail took a fair amount of concentration to reach the desired outcome. I eventually just quit asking questions and learned to appreciate my short hair and the simplicity of a little pomade. I wondered why more girls didn't choose to simplify their process more often and just throw it back in a ponytail. Hollywood often gives ponytails a bad rap, but I always thought they looked pretty.

I'd grown to enjoy watching the process, no matter how long it might take, no matter how late to the movie, concert, or dinner we might be. There's something inebriating about watching a girl do what makes her feel beautiful, and in wondering if, just maybe, she's doing it even a little bit for you. It's worth the wait to see her happy. A girl never looks more beautiful than when she is happy.

I sat on my bed with my back against the headboard and attempted to read while Emily sat cross-legged on the floor in front of the mirror, going through her routine of blowing her hair dry as she brushed out the knots.

As she performed her ritual, I couldn't help but admire her. Her features were pretty, yes, but much of her beauty lay in the way she gently ran her fingers through her hair as she dried it, the way she tilted her head to one side so that the hair all fell over one shoulder, the way she ever so slightly glanced at me in the mirror to see if I was watching. More than once, this resulted in a shared laugh, a blush, and her focusing again on her hair and I on my book.

It felt like an hour, but it probably only took Emily a few minutes to dry her hair. I had made it through a few paragraphs and was starting to remember what the book was about when I snapped out of my reading trance to the silence of a turned-off hair dryer and to Emily's captivatingly blue eyes staring at me in the mirror.

"Hey, you! You're quiet."

"I didn't want to interrupt and yell at you over the dryer." I smiled back at her.

"Oh, I wouldn't mind." Her eyes returned to the mirror and she ran her hands through her hair to check her work. "Ugh, it's still tangled in some places."

"Here…" I replaced my bookmark between the pages and scooted from the bed to the floor behind her. Picking up her hairbrush, I began to run it gently from her scalp down to the ends of her hair. I watched her in the mirror for any sign of brushing too hard.

"Mmm…" She closed her eyes as her lips spread into a relaxed smile.

As I brushed Emily's hair, she started humming a pretty tune I didn't recognize. After a few minutes, she asked, "So, where are you from?"

It shocked me to realize that I was just now exchanging such basic, introductory information with a girl I'd spoken to three times already and who was in my private room drying her hair. "Eugene, Oregon,"

I said, unintentionally quickly.

"Nuh-uh! We're all from Portland."

Crap. "Oh wow, small world, huh?" Her relative proximity to me suddenly made the thought of dating her so much more plausible. *Be careful,* I told myself.

"It is. What brings you here?"

Don't give her your life's story, Michael. "Just needed a vacation," I said. "Life has been so crazy lately, I thought it'd be a good idea to get away for a bit." *Not exactly a lie...*

"What'd you need to get away from?" She looked at me curiously. I half-laughed. "Can't slip one past you, can I?"

She smiled and shook her head, waiting for me to elaborate.

"I've just been in a very unhappy place the last several months," I said as I tried to work out in my head how much more to say. "I went through a rough breakup, which has been difficult to move past, and working at the same place for several years without anywhere to go has finally been taking its toll." *That's good, right? No need to be a downer.*

"I think we've all had those," she said without missing a beat. "It'll all work out how it's supposed to." She smiled in the mirror and reached a hand behind her, placing it on my knee. My heart began trying to break out of my chest as our eyes locked in the mirror. I was suddenly aware of how dry my lips were and quickly ran my tongue over them. My breath caught in my throat.

In an attempt to lighten the conversation, I added, "I'm also hoping to get some writing done while I'm here."

"You write? What kinda stuff?"

"Short stories mostly. I wrote a lot when I was younger, and I've just been getting back into it again. I figured there should be no shortage of inspiration in Italy, you know? I think it'd be cool to find an idea for a novel while I'm here."

"That's so awesome. I'd love t—" Two loud door-knocks echoed into the room.

"Emily!" Two more sharp knocks at the door, then the male voice again. "Emily! We're going out, but Jenna's staying in. Do you want to come?"

Emily noticed the confusion on my face as to how someone knew which room I was in. "I told them I was coming down here. You know, in case you tried to abduct me or something." She winked slyly to let me know she was joking as she went to open the door. "Geez, Jeremy, could you be any more rude? I'll pass tonight, I think."

"Okay, well, you're missing out! It's gonna be epic!" Quick, heavy footsteps signaled his excited departure.

"Don't have *too* much fun! I don't want to have to bail you out of an Italian jail!" Emily came back into the room, shaking her head. "He's crazy. I *should* probably go, though. I don't want to leave Jenna alone all night. We've got a bottle of wine in the room, so I think we'll take advantage of Jeremy, Jake, and Kasey being gone and have some girl talk. Kasey's not so good with that stuff, no matter how hard she tries."

"Yeah, you should take the chance while it's there. I can see how those guys could get in the way of that." I stood up, coiled the cord around Emily's hair dryer, and handed it to her.

"Thank you so much for letting me use your plug. You're a life-saver."

"Yeah, well, I don't usually invite strange girls into my room." I gave her a playful smile. "You never know what they could be capable of. So thank *you* for not strangling me with the cord."

"Oh, you're welcome." Then, Emily stepped toward me and wrapped her arms around my neck in a brief, tight hug and leaned up and kissed me quickly on the cheek. "Thanks again! You should come out with us tomorrow night. We're having drinks upstairs, and then maybe we'll go into town."

"Absolutely. That sounds really fun." I felt my face turning red.

"Great! I'll see you then." Emily smiled at me once more before walking out of the room and shutting the door quietly behind her.

"What the hell just happened?" I asked loudly and to no one but myself. I immediately began analyzing the last half hour or so of my life because nothing like that had ever happened to me. Never had a beautiful girl come to my room alone and asked to come in. Moreover, she could have easily asked to borrow my electrical adapter and brought it back later. But no. She chose to come in vulnerably and connect with me on some level that I didn't expect. Sure, the conversation had been minimal and cut short, but there was clearly a spark between us that was hard to ignore. Before I could start thinking about moving to Portland as soon as I returned to the States, I picked up my book again to distract myself.

I made it through maybe three pages in the next half hour, constantly realizing that I didn't know what I'd just read, before I finally gave up and put the book on the nightstand. I went to the small table by the window and picked up the bottle of red wine that Clara had given me, pulled the cork out, and poured a good amount of wine in the water glass from the bathroom.

As I drank the wine, I looked out my window at the small soccer pitch across the street. It was ten o'clock at night, but a group of twelve Italian men kicked a ball around, and several young boys ranging from about six to fifteen years old watched them. Eventually, the men allowed the boys to join in. By the time I'd poured a second glass of wine, I'd concluded that Italian children are probably taught simultaneously to walk and dribble a soccer ball.

I poured the rest of the bottle into my glass and lay down on the bed. Before I could finish it, I'd fallen into a heavy, dreamless sleep. I was grateful for it the next morning because I knew that, otherwise, Emily would have occupied my mind all night.

Chapter 19

My favorite Italian dish looks like testicles, I thought as a plate piled high with steaming gnocchi covered in freshly made pesto was placed in front of me, the scent of basil teasing my nose. Jake looked awkwardly from his plate of spaghetti to my plate and back.

"Those really look like balls, Mike."

"Thanks… You're really helping my appetite." I threw in a half-smile for good measure. I didn't mean to be rude, but I'd quickly learned over the last hour that Jake had no filter or sense of time and place. He shoveled forkfuls of long, thin noodles and tomato sauce into his mouth, simultaneously trying to ask me if I'd hook up with any of the girls that were currently dining in the hostel restaurant.

"There are some cute ones," I said as I speared two of the pesto-covered potato dumplings with my fork and popped them in my mouth, savoring the herby, garlicky flavor. There was only one girl on my mind, and she was up in her room getting ready for the evening.

I'd grown lost in thoughts of where the night might take us when I noticed that Jake was still blabbering, mouth full of food, about the girls sitting two tables away. While he powered through the inevitable difficulty of speaking both articulately and discreetly, anyone within earshot could only make out the worst possible parts of his sentences. Within five minutes, the table of girls was looking at us with disgust and with a clear intent of *not* going "boom-boom in Jake's room." Resting my chin on my hand, elbow on the table, I mouthed *"Sorry"* as they walked by.

"You're *sharing* a room with everyone else, man." I laughed. As the waiter passed, I ordered a Pernod. The small glass appeared quickly; he must have sensed my urgent need for a strong drink. I poured a few drops from my water into the Pernod and took a sip after it had clouded up the liquor, but Jake was still rambling on, so I tipped my head back and finished the rest. The strong licorice flavor of the imitation absinthe hit me fast. It's certainly not for the light drinker, nor should too many be had in one sitting unless you're drinking to forget.

My hunger fueled by the hard-hitting, pale-green liquid, I finished my gnocchi and sat back in my chair. There's nothing quite like a sated appetite. Jake had ordered a bowl of chocolate gelato, but I couldn't eat another bite. Besides, we were having drinks with the group soon; growing too full would be a disaster. I drank a glass of water while he inhaled the gelato. As we paid our bill and headed to the rooftop, I was flabbergasted that I'd just spent the last hour and a half palling around with the guy who had been so standoffish only a day before. Jake had shown up at my door a little before seven to see if I wanted to head downstairs for a drink and a bite to eat. Jeremy—his brother, it turned out—was taking a nap, and the three girls had eaten a little earlier so they'd have more time to get ready for the night. I'd been ready since six for a night scheduled to begin around eight, so I figured, *What the hell.* No point in wasting the balmy evening sitting in my room, dressed and hoping that a certain beautiful girl might realize she was attracted to me. It hadn't been half bad, either. Other than his sloppy manners and lack of an indoor voice, Jake seemed like a pretty cool guy, and he didn't seem to be overly wary of me anymore.

Emily and the other two girls were already lounging in the comfortable chairs drinking cocktails when we got there, so Jake and I went to the bar and waited for Daniele to finish making mojitos for the couple in front of us. They walked off, happily sipping the minty rum drinks, and we stepped up to the counter. Daniele looked at me with raised eyebrows, holding up a lemon and a bottle of Bombay Sapphire. I smiled and nodded. He cracked some ice for the glass and began cutting the fresh citrus, looking then at Jake for his order.

"I'll have a Vodka-Red Bull," Jake said. *"Per favore!"* he added quickly and with an exaggerated Italian inflection. Daniele gave me a sideways glance and a roll of the eyes so fleeting that Jake could not have noticed. The Italian bartender considered himself an artist; a Vodka-Red Bull was a slap in the face to him. I made sure to tip a little extra on my drink for the insult, for which he appeared grateful. We joined the girls in the lounge area. Jake looked around.

"Where's Jeremy?"

"Probably still sleeping," Kasey said with a laugh. Jeremy and Kasey had gotten up early that morning to take the *Circumvesuviana* train to Pompeii, and Jeremy was apparently exhausted by the time they returned mid-afternoon. "What did you guys do?" she asked.

"We took the ferry out to Capri," Emily said. "It was so pretty, and the water was *so* blue!" She had a huge smile on her face just thinking about it. She looked at Jake, and then at Jenna, who started to laugh. Jake looked up from his drink to see what was so funny. Then it hit him.

"No! No, Emily, you said you wouldn't tell them!"

"Ooh, tell us what?" Kasey asked, leaning forward with an excited look on her face. Jenna simply smiled and waited for Emily to tell the story.

"Sorry, Jake," Emily said with a giggle. "Jake got seasick on the ferry ride over. When we got to Capri, he had to lie down on the dock for a few minutes. A cute, old Italian couple came by and gave him a lollipop to help him feel better."

We all laughed until we felt awkward for disturbing the peace of the few other loungers on the rooftop. Jake's face had grown pink.

"Sounds like you're just a regular Captain Jack Sparrow, Jake," said a voice behind us.

We all turned around to see Jeremy standing there with a Peroni in his hand and a smile on his face.

"Well, look who's finally awake!" Jake punched his brother hard on the shoulder.

"I don't know how you didn't pass out for hours after that trip." He pointed at Kasey with his beer hand. "Cool place, but so damn hot!"

I nodded at the Peroni in his hand. "How do you drink that stuff? It tastes like shit." My palate had grown a bit spoiled as microbreweries popped up all over the Pacific Northwest in recent years. It was much less satisfying to drink the lighter, less flavorful lagers like Peroni.

"I know. The bartender gave it to me after I ordered a Vodka-Red Bull. Not sure why. Guess he doesn't understand much English, but it'll do, I suppose."

I smiled and glanced over at Daniele, who had no customers in line and a bitter look on his face. Draining the last of my Tom Collins and noticing the girls were also finished with their drinks, I told everyone I'd get the next round.

"Sex on the Beach for us, please!" said Kasey and Jenna, causing Jeremy and Jake to exchange a look, deciding if they should make a joke.

I leaned down to Emily, casually brushing her shoulder as I placed my hand on the back of her chair. "What're you having?"

"Clover Club, please." She smiled up at me.

"You got it." After meeting her gaze, I couldn't help but let mine stray to her smooth, crossed legs coming out of a very short dress. I promptly redirected my eyes to hers, where I found a sultry glimmer, and suddenly remembered why I was standing up in the first place.

"Hey! What about us?" called Jake as I walked toward the bar.

"Don't worry, I've got you covered." I threw a thumbs-up in the air over my shoulder.

Daniele was already making another Tom Collins when I stepped up to the bar. "You know, your friends have absolutely no appreciation for the art of bartending. All they want is Vodka-Red Bulls and Rum-and-Cokes and Arrivederci-Motherfuckers."

"I know, man, I know. And I'm sorry, because you're really gonna hate my next order. I need two of your bucket drinks. One Vodka-Red Bull and one Sex on the Beach. Well vodka is fine; they won't know the difference. And then I need a Clover Club. Bombay, like the Collins." I hated to be a pain in the ass but couldn't help chuckling at his frustration. He started pouring the bucket drinks, which were literally just that: liquor and mixer over ice in a small bucket. He put two long, colorful straws in each drink and I carried them over to the table. Kasey and Jenna giggled, their eyes wide with excitement. Jake and Jeremy fist-bumped each other.

"Thanks, Miiikey," the girls said cheerfully.

"Michael. You, sir, are a prince among men."

I laughed. "Thanks, Jeremy." As I walked back to the bar, I heard him asking the others how I had managed to get a bucketful of Vodka-Red Bull when he couldn't even get one glass.

Daniele was straining the rose-colored Clover Club into a cocktail glass. He handed it to me, and I took a sip, which left a small foamy mustache on my upper lip. The raspberry flavor of the Chambord was fresh and different.

"*Molto bene*, Daniele." Pulling out my cash, I added an extra twenty-euro note on top of the total, smiled, and thanked him.

"*Grazie*, Michael."

I handed Emily her cocktail.

"Thank you, darlin'." She smiled that enrapturing smile of hers and took a sip. "Mmm!"

"My pleasure."

I sat at the end of the couch nearest Emily, coated the rim of my glass with lemon juice, shoved the wedge into my drink with the straw, stirred it, and put the straw on the table. I took a long drink. It was refreshing in the Mediterranean evening air.

Jeremy was telling the group about the preserved dead bodies they had seen at Pompeii, using a reluctant Jake to mimic the poses in which the various people had died. He then moved on to describing what he had *hoped* to see. *They're definitely brothers,* I thought.

"I just kept waiting to come across a couple of people who had been doing it. You know, frozen in doggy-style or some shit. Those ancient Romans were freaky. Best way to go, I think."

Upon hearing "doggy-style," and likely fearing Jeremy's use of him as an example, Jake jumped over to the other couch next to Kasey and Jenna. Shaking my head at Jeremy's comments, I tried to stifle my laughter as I thought about how tragic the eruption of Vesuvius had truly been.

It turned out that Jeremy had completely missed the last train back to Sant'Agnello from Pompeii and had to find some other means.

"So, I'm standing there in complete disbelief, watching the tail of the train disappear around the bend in the distance. I could have sworn Kasey said it left at four o'clock, but apparently there's some sort of strike going on right now.

"Anyway, I walk back to the front of the station and sit on this bench that had bird crap and cigarette butts nearly covering it, wondering what the hell I'm gonna do. Then, this Italian chick walks up to a moped parked nearby and puts on a helmet. I yelled, 'Hey! Uh, *ciao!*' and waved my hands and ran toward her. I think she thought I was crazy because she got this look in her eye and I *swear* her hand went into her backpack to pull out a gun. But I smiled and slowed down, pointed from her to me to her moped, and she finally smiled and said, 'Oh, do you need a ride?' I was relieved that she even spoke any English and explained the situation to her. She handed me her helmet and told me to get on. Apparently, she lives in Meta, which is north of here, so she said she could take me the little extra distance to the hostel."

"How was that ride back?" I smirked, recalling the insane motorini-riders that had woven around my cab on the way to the hostel from Naples. There was no way I'd ever be caught dead on the back of one of those things.

"It was terrible! I pissed myself—just a little bit—when she shot between two trucks going opposite ways on a corner. Pretty sure she felt it, too, because she scooted *way* forward on the seat. Not sure why she didn't kick me off, really. I made a little small talk on the few occasions when we stopped in traffic, and she was very friendly. Then, as we're going slowly through Meta, we saw a couple with three babies in strollers, so I thought it was the perfect time to tell her about that time I saved a baby when that restaurant caught fire last year."

At that statement, the girls and I all put our faces in our hands and released heavy, exasperated sighs. Jake, however, was on the edge of his seat, his excitement ill-contained.

"Did she believe you? Did she take you back to her place and give you some sweet, Italian lovin'?"

"She immediately pulled over to the side of the road, told me to get off, and started off on this loud, English-Italian rant about how 'You Americans always think you can come over here and say your bullshit pick-up lines and expect us Italian girls to fall in love with you.' Then she burned out and drove off, and I had to walk the rest of the way."

After we'd all finally stopped laughing, Emily asked what everyone wanted to do for the rest of the evening. They all knew I'd been to Sorrento before, so they turned to me in the hope that I'd have an idea or two.

I laughed. "Sure, leave it to me. Um, well, there are a couple of pretty good bars in the main square of Sorrento that we could check out. And I think I've seen a club down the street from there."

Something told me that the bulk of the group was more interested, then, in the local nightlife over anything else I could suggest, so I left it at that.

"Sounds perfect," Kasey said, smiling. "Jenna and I were feeling like a night of dancing would be fun."

"Yeah, let's go get our grind on!" Jeremy looked half-insane with the glow of the firepit that sat in the center of our chairs dancing in his widened eyes.

Emily laughed at the sudden excitement in the air.

I looked at her. "Sound good to you?"

The look she gave me rendered the following "Yes" unnecessary. Her smile paralyzed me, and the flame in her eyes ignited something deep in my chest.

We finished our drinks—Jake and Jeremy took turns chugging straight from their bucket—and stood up to leave. I waved at Daniele, who gave a half-smile of appreciation as he placed three piña coladas on the counter for a trio of giggling girls. I led the way across the rooftop and opened the door to the stairs, allowing the group to pass through it. Jake patted me on the shoulder as he walked by.

Emily was the last to go through. My eyes ran up and down as I admired the alluring dress she was wearing. Strapless, it left her shoulders bare and fell just above her knees. Her tanned skin contrasted nicely against the pale-yellow fabric.

"That dress looks incredible on you," I told her quietly.

She smiled back and placed her hand on my chest before affectionately adjusting the collar of my shirt. "Thank you. You don't look too bad yourself."

I followed her through the door, and we caught up with the rest of the group at the bottom of the stairs in the courtyard.

"Lead the way, Michael!" Jake danced behind us all through the front door to the street in an awkward, twitchy motion to the music playing over the speakers mounted on the walls.

Chapter 20

I led the group south from Seven Hostel, past the small soccer field across the street, and along some of the back roads that kept the sea within view as we walked. Walking along the busy Corso Italia at that time of night seemed like a bad idea. The citrus-scented breeze put everyone in the highest of spirits.

"They're so lucky the air always smells this way," said Jenna. She took a deep breath as we passed by a fenced-in grove of lemon trees.

The sun had settled close to the horizon, but the air was still warm, making for a pleasant walk into Piazza Tasso. We walked quickly and made it in about half an hour. After weighing our options, we were seated at two adjacent tables right on the sidewalk at the Fauno Bar, an upscale-looking watering hole that was, as a good Italian restaurant should be, perfect for people-watching.

The tangerine tablecloths visually complemented the aroma of lemons and oranges that flirted in the air around us, and the tables were arranged just close enough that we could talk amongst ourselves without disturbing those around us without feeling too crowded together. A grey-haired waiter in a white dress shirt, black bowtie and vest, and a simple, black apron took our order almost immediately, and brought us our drinks just as swiftly. It was surprising for such a busy evening.

I decided to keep things simple with a Bombay and soda, but instead of my usual lime, I requested an orange wedge instead. It brought out a different taste in the gin that I'd never experienced before. We sat and sipped our drinks and watched all the people go by. After paying our bill, I said, "I want to show you guys something."

I took them across the street and down the steep, stone staircase to the hair-pinned road that led to Sorrento's main marina. When we reached the marina, the sun hovered inches above the edge of the world. It was one of those sunsets when you could clearly see the sun's movement. Pairs of lovers sat on benches and the retaining wall that ran along the edge of the walkway where the sea washed against the rocks. Other groups of people laughed amongst themselves at the bars situated in the marina.

It was a beautiful sunset, washing the sky with bright pinks and oranges and reminding me of the first time I'd visited Italy when my group had been photographed on that same wall during a sunset. We all watched the sun dip into the sea in a lovely silence until it was suddenly broken by Jake.

"Alright, this is pretty and all, but where the hell is this club you were talking about, Michael? I'm ready to dance!"

"Damn it, Jake! You always ruin nice moments like this," Jeremy said, feigning a pensive, longing stare across the water.

I laughed. "You ready to climb those stairs again?"

Jake and Jeremy looked at each other, dropped their jaws, and looked back to me. "You're kidding, right?" they said in unison.

"Of course I am. There's an elevator a little farther down the boardwalk."

The brothers breathed a sigh of relief, and we headed to the elevator. Once we reached the main town level, we wandered through the small side streets back to Piazza Tasso, and then turned down Corso

Italia toward a small nightclub I had been to very briefly on my last trip.

The front of the building was rather plain on its own, but its large windows afforded a clear view of the fun to be had inside. Strobes and multi-colored lights and lasers flashed in time to the loud, thumping music, which turned out to be primarily Euro-mixed American pop songs.

"This place looks great!" Jeremy ran inside, followed closely by his brother. Both pumped their fists in the air as they made their way toward the bar.

I chuckled and shrugged my shoulders. "After you, ladies." I gestured toward the open door, and Kasey and Jenna passed through. As I briefly touched my hand to Emily's lower back, she grabbed my hand and pulled me into the club behind her. We wormed our way through the sweaty, convulsing crowd and joined the others at the bar counter, where they had just ordered a round of tall, green shots, each with a small swirl of whipped cream on top.

"What the *hell* are those?" Emily asked, picking up her shot glass and looking apprehensively at its bright-green contents.

"Scooby Snacks! They're so good!" Kasey was beyond excitement. "The bartender made them double shots and added 151 to them."

"Oh, great." The last time I'd had Bacardi's high-proof rum, I spent the rest of the night clinging to my friend's questionably clean toilet.

Kasey raised her shot glass in the air between our group, and we all followed suit, clinking them together while being careful not to spill the contents.

"Here's to an awesome night in an awesome country with awesome friends!" Kasey said.

"Cheers!"

"This is gonna be so fun!"

"There aren't roofies in these, right?"

"Just take the shot, Jeremy."

I laughed at Jenna's exasperation and contributed a traditional Italian toast: "*Cin cin.*"

The six of us simultaneously—or nearly so, as Jeremy had taken a few sniffs first in a futile attempt to detect any signs of drugs—tipped our shot glasses back, emptying the contents into our thirsty mouths. After the initial sweetness of the whipped cream, the Bacardi 151 cut through like a knife, almost masking the flavors of the coconut rum, banana and melon liqueurs, and pineapple juice. The shot still tasted surprisingly good, and I gave my head a shake as the alcohol rushed to my head.

"Mmm! *So* good." Jenna licked her lips for any remnants of the sweet drink, and then laughed and pointed at Jake.

"What?"

"You've got a mustache."

Sure enough, Jake had a wide smear of whipped cream across his upper lip. It looked as though he'd completely missed getting the shot in his mouth the first time.

"I got it, bro!" Jeremy reached out with his thumb to wipe off the whipped cream, but Jake jumped away.

"I'll do it! Thanks, *Mom.*"

Once Jake was sure that he had gotten rid of his mustache, we set our empty shot glasses on the counter. Everyone ordered another drink to take with them to the dance floor; I decided to hold off for the time being, just in case the 151 decided to come back and kick me in the ass. A bouncy Kasey led us all toward the dance floor, weaving through all the people.

Kasey and Jenna jumped into the thick of the crowd and began dancing to the catchy, accordion-laced melody of a Eurodance song I recognized from the Top 40 radio station back home. The song had always made me think of Italy and conjured the image of riding a Vespa along the Amalfi Coast while erratically bobbing my head to music playing on my headphones.

A pair of young, Italian men had noticed the two girls and moved in to dance with them, to the chagrin of Jeremy and Jake, who began to look around for a new opportunity.

"What about them?" Jake pointed at two girls dancing a short distance from our circle. His eyes had glanced fleetingly in Emily's direction, but seeing how close she was standing to me, he had decided to go another route.

"Dibs on the blonde."

"Dude, I noticed them first, and the other one's a butterface. Not fair."

"If you're dancing behind her, why does it matter?"

"But what if I bring her back to the hostel? I'm not that drunk yet."

"Okay, one: we share a room at the hostel, so if you *do* bring her back, you can figure out another place to go. Two: I'm older. I get the blonde. Three: just drink more; you'll be fine." With his outstretched hand, he gave Jake a friendly, back-handed slap to the cheek.

"Bullshit!" Jake shoved his brother's hand away. "You have *got* to quit using the age card. Here, what about them?" Jake had noticed a group of five girls just past the two they had already been observing. All five were scantily clad and sloshing drinks all over as they gyrated against each other.

"I think the odds are in your favor over there," I said. Emily and I had been quietly following Jake and Jeremy's conversation, occasionally shooting each other an amused smile. I looked back at her and held out my hand.

"Would *you* like to dance?"

Her mouth spread into that smile and she took my hand, which I raised in the air, twirling her and allowing her to lead me to the dance floor.

"Good luck, guys." I gave the brothers a wink. As I followed Emily, Jake and Jeremy bumped fists and wandered over to the five girls. I found myself wondering what ridiculous lines they had in mind to sling at the unsuspecting group, especially considering they had no idea what language the girls might speak, but the thought evacuated my mind when Emily squeezed my hand and said, "Hey, you!"

She took both my hands in hers and backed slowly through the crowd, moving to the beat of the music, never breaking eye contact with me. Heat radiated from everyone around us as we joined them in what felt like a divergent, hedonistic line dance.

Emily and I began dancing with a couple of feet between us. As the beats got heavier, we moved closer together, and our movements synced with the music. I'd never been much of a dancer, but the few drinks I'd already had, paired with my attraction to Emily, made it easy to abandon that quality.

We continued to move as one through so many songs that I lost track of time. At some point, Emily turned around with her back to me and stepped as close into me as she could, continuing to rotate her hips, grinding her ass against me. She held my hand the entire time, constantly pulling me close to her. The smell of her perfume intoxicated me even more than the alcohol I'd had throughout the evening. Then, she turned her head and looked up at me. I took this as a very clear signal and leaned in to kiss her. The sweetness of her drink lingered on her lips.

After a few short kisses, Emily turned so she was facing me again and put her arms around my neck. My hands moved down her body, over her curves to her hips, pulling her into me, and I allowed my own body to move with hers. Our unwavering eye contact made the room seem ten times hotter than it was. Sweat dripped down my face from my temple, but I didn't care.

Emily ran her hands through my drenched hair; I felt it stay in awkward spikes, as if I had just gotten out of bed. "It's so hot in here!"

"Can I take you somewhere?"

A twinkle in her eyes, Emily said, "Yes, please!"

"Come on." I took her hand and led her through the crowd, my eyes searching out Jenna and Kasey, who had joined the two men they had been dancing with at a corner table with a mixed group of the men's friends. The situation appeared comfortable and harmless, so I then located Jeremy and Jake, who were awkwardly dancing around the group of drunken girls, essentially corralling them. The girls hadn't moved away from the brothers, but they didn't seem to be making much effort to dance *with* them either. I nodded toward Jake and Jeremy, who each flashed a conspicuous thumbs-up, and Emily laughed. We left the club and turned down the street back toward the center of town.

Chapter 21

Emily followed me down a narrow alley, past a group of tables outside a small trattoria where some Germans laughed over several empty pint glasses and an ashtray full of cigarette butts.

I stopped briefly at the counter of the trattoria and paid six euros for two Bacardi Breezers, a fruity alcopop that wasn't found, to my great disappointment, in the United States. When I turned around to offer Emily her choice of peach- or lime-flavored, she stood there with an amused smile on her face.

"*Breezers*, really?"

"Hey, they're good! And I'm on vacation. Now's the time to drink all the fruity drinks I can get." I gave her a playfully defiant glare.

"Ha, I know. I'm just giving you a hard time. I like them too." She took the peach drink from my hand and twisted the cap off.

I twisted my cap off as well, and we clinked the bottlenecks together before taking a long drink of the cold beverages. We walked along a couple more side streets and came out on *Via San Francesco*. Stopping for a moment to admire the 14th century monastery in front of us, illuminated by several well-placed lights, I put my arm around Emily's shoulders. She leaned into me and put one arm around my waist, rubbing one hand up and down my other arm, and took a drink of her Breezer.

"It's so pretty at night."

"Yeah, it is. You should see the courtyard. There are all sorts of flowers hanging from these beautiful archways. There was a wedding in there the last time I was here."

"It sounds like a perfect place for a wedding."

We walked past the monastery through the *Villa Comunale* to the lookout that provides a wide view of the Mediterranean Sea, Mount Vesuvius, and the Bay of Naples, as well as the beaches and the marina below. The moon was nearly full and cast a brilliant light across everything, reflected clearly in the water below. Off in the distance, a cluster of tiny lights moved slowly away from Naples, out of the gulf and into the sea beyond.

I leaned on my forearms against the railing. "I love to see cruise ships sailing at night," I said thoughtfully. "It's like when you're laying out under the stars, and you see a jet fly over, and, in that moment, *all* you want is to be going somewhere." I tipped the bottle back and drank the last of my Breezer, tossing the empty bottle in the trash can next to me. "I guess, this time, I *am* somewhere. But it's still an exhilarating thought."

"I love that feeling. The ship looks so pretty!" Emily leaned against the railing right next to me, and reached out and took my hand in hers, rubbing her thumb up and down my own. She turned and stood on her tiptoes to reach up and kiss the edge of my ear and then my neck. In my ear, she whispered, "I'm glad this is where you are."

I turned toward her, took her face gently in my hands, and kissed her long and slowly on the lips. She reached her arms around me and pulled me closer to her as she kissed back, teasing my lips with her tongue. Leaning against the railing, I moved my hands down to her ass and lifted her up as she wrapped her legs around me. Our breathing intensified, our chests heaving against each other. We kissed for what felt like hours before I finally lowered Emily to the ground. She giggled and adjusted her dress. I then remembered why we had come that way in the first place.

"Come on!" I took Emily's hand and walked quickly toward the long, stone staircase that led back and forth along the cliff down to the beach.

"Where are we going?"

"You'll see."

I led her down the staircase, through the small cave that housed part of the path, and along the boardwalk past the piers lined with cabanas and lounge chairs. Nestled between two of the pay-to-use swimming docks was a small, dark-sand beach with a few large rocks to sit on. Emily seemed to have gotten the same idea I'd had when deciding to bring her down there, because, when I turned around, she was lifting her dress over her head, revealing only a lacy, black thong. She tossed the dress on one of the rocks as she walked toward the water, turning her head to give me a come-hither smile.

Embarrassingly quickly, I unbuttoned my shirt the rest of the way and threw it aside. As she waded into the water, I hurried toward her, clumsily stepping out of my khaki pants. I put my watch in one of the pockets and kicked them to the side once I was finally free.

"Oh, my God! It's *so* warm!" Emily leaned forward into the water and did a short breaststroke for a few yards.

"When I was over here after high school, we went swimming here at, like, two in the morning. I'd never been in such warm water." I dove beneath the surface and swam out to where Emily had stopped swimming. Small waves lapped over our exposed shoulders; the water was shallow enough that we could still stand easily. She had a contemplative look on her face.

"What is it?"

"I'm so glad we met you at the hostel," she said, smiling.

"Me too. You've made this trip infinitely more interesting. I'm just glad I decided to come here first instead of the other way around."

"So am I. Who knows if we would have met otherwise." She ran her hand through her wet hair, pulling it back from her face, her longing eyes looking up at me. "Now you have something fun to write about," she whispered.

I reached under the water and pulled her into me. We kissed and swam back and forth for a while longer before walking back to the shore. As we emerged from the water, Emily shivered slightly. It wasn't cold out, but the slight breeze caused my wet body to break out in goose bumps, too. I looked around, realizing I hadn't considered a way to dry off at all. Then, a thought struck me.

"I'll be right back." I ran into the water and swam to a ladder at the end of one of the docks. Glancing around first to ensure no one was watching, I climbed up the ladder as stealthily as I could in my inebriated state and ran down the dock to one of the larger cabanas. Looking inside, I discovered just what I had hoped to find: a stack of clean, dry towels that were rented out to sunbathers during the day. I grabbed two of them and, gauging the height of the dock, jumped down onto the sand and walked over to the rock where Emily sat watching. She stood, and I wrapped one of the towels around her shoulders, watching her rub her petite, curvy body dry while I dried myself off.

This is not how I expected this trip to go, I thought to myself, pleasantly surprised by the events of the last few hours. I picked up Emily's dress and shook the sand from it. She smiled and raised her arms over her head, causing her small, perky breasts to push together slightly. I lowered the dress over her arms and head, and she adjusted it to her liking while I dressed myself.

"That was so much fun," Emily said as we began climbing the staircase back up to the level of the town. The elevator we had used earlier in the evening was closed for the night.

"I hoped you might enjoy it. I love swimming at night, especially when it's so warm."

"So do I." She reached down and took my hand as we walked past the monastery onto Via San Francesco.

Looking at my watch, I realized it was almost one in the morning. "You ready to head back?"

"Yeah, we probably should. I wish we could stay out all night, though. The others are probably staying out longer, but I'd rather walk back with you."

I smiled, happy that we agreed. We began the trek back to Seven Hostel, taking the scenic route once more so that we could still see the lights of Naples. We held hands the entire way and stopped to kiss whenever there was a secluded spot, as we weren't alone on the streets. There were still locals sitting and conversing at small bars and cafés at that point in the evening, and some wandering home. It was two o'clock by the time we reached the hostel.

We walked quietly through the lobby, said a brief "*buonanotte*" to the guy behind the front desk, and climbed upstairs to the third floor. We walked down the hallway, and I stopped in front of the door to the room that Emily was sharing with the other four. She hesitated to go in.

"I really don't want to deal with them tonight. They're going to ask so many questions. I'll never get to go to sleep." We both laughed.

"Do you want to stay in my room tonight? No roommates."

"Are you sure you don't mind?"

"Absolutely. I'd love the company. Do you need to leave a note or anything for them?"

She laughed that enchanting laugh I had enjoyed all evening. "No, they know I was with you. They trust you."

I led her down the hallway to my wing of the hostel and unlocked my door, allowing her to enter first. The room was pitch black except for the moonlight shining through the space in the curtains. I turned on the small lamp on the nightstand and took off my watch. The air was stuffy, so I opened the window to allow the breeze in.

"Do you mind if I take a quick shower? I want to rinse all that salt off so my skin doesn't get all dry."

"No, go for it," I said. "There are some fresh towels in the cupboard in the bathroom. You can use my shampoo and stuff if you'd like."

"Thank you," she said as she took off her dress, folded it, and placed it on the small table in the corner of the room. "Don't worry, I'll be quick." Her eyes twinkled at me as she turned away. My eyes followed her into the bathroom, where she left the door open. I watched her step out of her underwear and smile at me in the mirror. Then, she disappeared from view, and I heard the shower turn on. Steam began trickling into the room moments later. I grabbed the book I'd been reading and tried to pick up where I had left off, but found my mind wandering back to my current situation.

It was a new experience for me. I'd been an awkward, skinny adolescent but had eventually filled out a bit and gained much more confidence over the past few years, first noticing an improvement after my senior-year relationship and then again after Liz and I had broken up. Still, I'd never done much in the realm of casual dating, especially when my depression so heavily overshadowed my confidence. I'd had crushes here and there, some turning into more of an infatuation, but I'd never had a one-night stand, and I'd never even so much as made out with a random girl as so many of my other single friends had at parties or bars. *Come to think of it, I've never kissed anyone that I wasn't in a relationship with,* I thought. By no means was I embarrassed by that; it was just an odd realization to have. It had become clear to me that I needed a strong emotional connection to even entertain the physical.

But I felt a connection with Emily. I'd felt it ever since I met her three days earlier. I found everything about her beautiful, physically and otherwise, and her laugh was musical. We just seemed to mesh so well from the start. When I considered how much we'd both had to drink throughout the evening, I realized that I hadn't felt drunk at all, other than the time we spent dancing after taking the shots at the club and then trying to climb the ladder on the beach. My attraction to her was genuine, and, based on our interactions prior to any drinking, so was her attraction to me. I shook my head as if I'd dozed off behind the wheel of my car, telling myself that I didn't need to justify the night's events and to quit overthinking it. After Liz, I spent a fair amount of time trying to subscribe to the life-affirming cliché that everything happens for a reason. I thought it might give me a better feeling about the bad or confusing things that tend to happen in life, but it turned out to be more of a headache, constantly searching for the reason behind every little occurrence.

"Are you okay?"

I whipped my head toward the bathroom door, completely unaware that the water had turned off. Emily was leaning against the door frame, a towel wrapped around her middle and her damp hair pulled back over her shoulders. She had the same amused look on her face as when I bought the Bacardi Breezers.

"Huh? Oh, yeah. No, yeah, I'm fine. Just lost in thought."

"You're so eloquent at two-thirty in the morning," she teased.

I laughed and threw a pillow at her. "I'm gonna take a quick shower, too." I hung my shirt and pants on a chair near the window. Then, perhaps out of habit, or perhaps because the thought lingered in my head that I'd known Emily for three days and that no girl besides a girlfriend had ever seen me completely naked, I closed the bathroom door behind me, leaving it open just enough to allow steam to escape, before stepping out of my boxer-briefs. As the hot water poured over my head, I hoped Emily wasn't offended by my attempt at privacy, nor that she would think I might have thought less of *her* for completely ignoring privacy when she showered.

Quit overthinking things.

I shampooed my hair and washed my body quickly, rinsed off with cool water for a couple of minutes, dried off, and put on a clean pair of underwear before going back out to the room. Emily lay under the top sheet, smiling.

"Good shower?"

"Very."

I walked over to the cupboard where I stored my luggage and pulled out a couple of blankets for padding, an extra sheet, and a pillow.

"What are you doing?"

"I figured I'd let you have the bed. I can sleep on the floor tonight."

Emily laughed. "You're funny. That floor is so hard. Come on." She patted the empty space on the bed next to her.

I smiled. "If you're sure?"

"Of course I am. I didn't make out with you all night, go skinny-dipping with you, and then take shower in *your* room with the door open just to make you sleep on the floor. Get up here, silly."

I shrugged, dropped the extra bedding where I stood, and climbed ino bed under the sheet with Emily.

"Silly man," she said. "Thought I was gonna kick you out of your own bed."

I laughed and said, "I just didn't want to make any assumptions. I haven't been the best at reading girls in the past."

"I think you've read me pretty well so far."

I turned off the bedside lamp. "I hope so."

Emily turned with her back to me and scooted toward me until I felt her ass push up against me. I put my arm around her and held her close to me, locking my fingers with hers. I buried my nose in her shoulder and kissed it softly.

"I think my body wash smells better on you."

"I don't know about that."

I kissed her shoulder again.

She let out a soft moan. "Your scent kinda turns me on."

"I guess I can't complain about that." I moved my kissing up to her neck and then her ear, biting playfully at her ear lobe.

"So does that." Emily turned around and put her lips to mine, full force, her breasts pressing against me. She climbed on top of me and we kissed for a few minutes before I rolled over and propped myself above her. After kissing for a while longer, our bodies pressed together, I slowed down a bit, remembering that we'd barely just met. While the events of the evening had proven a mutual attraction, I didn't want to take it to a level where one or both of us might regret it the next morning. Not yet, anyway.

Emily seemed to sense that I had no intent to go any further and followed my lead in easing up on the kissing and groping. We lay facing each other again, both of us smiling and trying to catch our breath.

I kissed her again, softly, on the lips. Then, I turned onto my back and put my arm around her, and she laid her head on my shoulder, slowly running her fingers up and down my chest and stomach. My body twitched as her fingertips tickled my lower stomach.

Emily looked up at me with a tired smile on her face. "Goodnight, handsome."

I smiled, took her hand in mine, and kissed her on the forehead. "Goodnight, beautiful."

I don't remember what time I fell asleep for good that night, only that we woke up on two or three occasions and kissed for a few minutes before laughing and deciding again that we should probably get some sleep. The last thing I remember was thinking how lovely she looked in her deep slumber.

Chapter 22

I woke the next morning feeling better than I should have, considering all the alcohol and lack of sleep the night before. Turning over, I saw Emily still fast asleep, her blond hair fanned out on the pillow.

Taking care not to stir her, I went into the bathroom to relieve myself. I took a swig of mouthwash from my travel-sized bottle and swished it around for a few seconds before spitting into the sink. Pulling on a pair of shorts and a T-shirt, I left a note on the nightstand letting her know I was running downstairs to grab us some breakfast and slipped quietly out the door.

Down in the courtyard, a handful of people were scattered at the tables enjoying the hostel's complimentary breakfast. I took a plate from the stack on the buffet table and loaded it with a few pieces of fruit, two *cornetti*—the Italian version of a croissant—each with a spoonful of peach jelly, and two packets of butter. Before going back up to the room, I grabbed a small, plastic cup of delicious Italian orange juice I loved so much and sat at an empty table to enjoy it. I'd lost myself thinking about how I would spend my day when two small hands clasped themselves over my eyes. They pulled my head backward, and a soft, cool pair of lips met mine.

"Hey, you," said Emily. She came around me and sat down in the chair next to mine. Her hair was pulled back in a loose ponytail, and she was wearing a white bikini top with a pair of light-blue shorts. She looked just as happy as I had felt when I woke up next to her.

I smiled. "How'd you sleep?"

"*So* well. Your snoring was like a lullaby."

I bit my lip and smiled sheepishly. "Sorry, I didn't realize I snore."

Emily laughed and playfully pushed my shoulder. "I'm just joking. You didn't make a sound."

"Ha, okay, good. I'd hate to have kept you up all night."

"Well, you did keep me up, but in a good way." She leaned over and kissed me on the cheek before jumping out of the chair. "I'm going to go get some food for Jenna. I stopped by our room, and she's *so* hung over. Kasey's making her drink some water, and I said I'd bring back some food."

"That's nice of you." I smiled and watched as she half-skipped around the corner into the buffet room. Then, I forked a piece of honeydew melon into my mouth, and it was firm and sweet.

Emily came back with a plate piled high with fruit and cornetti and sat back down, taking a bite of one of the bread rolls.

"That should do the trick," I said. "What're your plans for the day?"

"We were talking about having a girls' day today. Jeremy and Jake are passed out, so we figured it'd be the perfect time to escape. That is, if Jenna feels better after she eats something. If not, then I'll probably stay around and help Kasey take care of her. What are you gonna do?"

"I'm not sure yet. I may try to find a beach to check out."

"You should see if the guys want to go. I'm sure they'd love to check out the talent once they're awake."

"Ha! I'm sure they would. Yeah, maybe I'll do that." *No chance in hell.* The brothers had grown on me a little the night before, but not enough to endure them without Emily present.

She wasn't convinced. Laughing, she said, "I wouldn't want to invite them either," and winked.

"Have you already made plans for tomorrow? We could take the bus to Positano."

"Let's! That would be nice."

"It'll be the perfect way to spend my last day here."

The smile fell from her face. I realized we hadn't talked about how much longer I'd be in Sant'Agnello.

"You're leaving already?"

"Yeah, I've got a hotel booked in Montecatini for a couple of nights before I go to Rome."

"Montecatini? Where's that?"

"In Tuscany, a little less than an hour from Florence by train. It's this little spa-resort town. The old town is on a hilltop that overlooks the valley. Absolutely *gorgeous*."

"It sounds amazing…" I could tell she was disappointed we'd be parting soon, and I was too, but it made me feel good to know that it seemed to matter so much to her.

She put the last piece of the *cornetto* in her mouth and chewed it slowly, avoiding eye contact with me. Then, she stood and said, "I should probably get this up to the girls. They get grumpy if they don't eat."

I'd have been really put off by her sudden exit if she hadn't turned and given me a smile that clearly said there were no hard feelings.

"I hope she feels better. You guys have a fun day, whatever you decide to do."

"You too. And tomorrow, it's you, me, and Positano."

"I look forward to it. I don't know what the bus schedule is like, but we should try to get an early start."

"Early sounds good to me."

I returned her smile and watched her until she disappeared around the corner on the staircase and then returned my attention to my food.

Tearing open one of the rolls—still slightly warm—I spread some of the jelly and butter across both halves. I felt half-starved but took my time eating the wonderful bread. In my limited travels, I'd found significant value in slowing down and appreciating even the simplest things, like eating breakfast. You never know what minute detail might stick with you for years, and taking things as they come and at a slower pace can greatly ease the inherent stress of travel. To worry about making the next train or getting to a particular restaurant before it closes is to put unnecessary strain on the trip. It can cause you to miss all the remarkable things an exciting, new place has to offer. The beauty of Italy is that there is *always* another train, and there are innumerable restaurants, probably cheaper and better than the one you were trying so hard to get to.

After breakfast, I returned to my room and lay back on the bed with my hands behind my head, contemplating how to spend my penultimate day on the coast. It didn't take long to circle back to the thought I'd voiced to Emily at breakfast: *I should go to the beach.*

It was only then I realized, other than the two night swims with Emily and my friends, I'd never actually been to a beach in Italy. I decided that would be a good way to spend the already-hot middle of the day. I changed into my swim shorts, folded a towel small enough to fit into my bag, made sure I had a notebook to write in and a book to read, filled my water bottle, and headed downstairs to find out where the nearest beach was.

The girl at the counter told me there was a reasonably priced beach if I followed Via Iommella Grande around the bend where it turned into *Via Ripa di Cassano*. Then, I should take the elevator down to sea level, and the beach was a short walk from there.

"Maybe about...*quindici minuti*," she said.

"*Grazie*."

I turned right outside the hostel and followed Iommella Grande as she had instructed, and, sure enough, after a short walk, I found a small building with a sign that clearly indicated an elevator could be found within. Flickering fluorescent lights lit the room housing the elevator, and the light blue paint on the walls had chipped away from years of neglect.

The elevator clunked to a stop in front of me after a few minutes, and I stepped inside—feeling a little apprehensive—and pushed the button next to a torn sticker with a simple drawing of waves and an umbrella on it. The descent was slow but less rickety than I had expected. I stepped out into a long, dark tunnel at the end of which sparkled the blue sea. I walked toward the sunlight at the end of the tunnel, passing a pair of larger Italian men who were pushing what looked like empty laundry carts toward the elevator. I guessed they were going up to the bed and breakfast that sat less than a block down the road from the elevator building.

Putting my sunglasses on so that I didn't burn out my corneas stepping back into the sun, I emerged from the tunnel and looked around. There was a small café nestled into the side of the cliff; one man sat at the bar with a beer, looking out at the sea, and another sat at a table with a tiny cup of espresso and an open newspaper. Directly in front of the café, a jetty jutted into the sea, and just past the jetty was a small beach with a short quay on the other side. Where the sidewalk met the sand, an umbrella shaded a makeshift desk where an old man charged beachgoers for the use of his chairs. Noticing that the beach was finely pebbled and had little actual sand, I opted to spend the eight euros for a chair, a small price to pay for a little comfort.

I took off my shirt and rubbed sunscreen in all the places I could reach before settling in a lounge chair a few yards from the water. The beach was filled with families, which meant a lot of kids splashing around in the water, so I didn't want to be in the middle of it all. Several yards from me, a group of young boys kicked a soccer ball around. Two more—a little older, maybe fifteen or so—sat on the edge of the jetty next to a girl who was probably in her early twenties. All three were smoking cigarettes.

The girl lay on her stomach, looking down at the gently waving water. One of the boys appeared to be flirting with her while the other watched with an annoyed look on his face. I guessed the latter was the girl's brother.

The brother nudged his friend, said something loudly in Italian, and jumped feet first into the water below. I imagined the other boy, the flirt, said something to the girl along the lines of "Watch this," because he stood up, took a running start, and twisted his body into a backflip before diving roughly into the water.

The girl looked unimpressed. In fact, she sat up, put her cigarette out on the rock next to her, and dangled her legs over the side of the jetty, looking down at those of us who sat on the beach. Even from a distance, I could see her head stop when her sunglass-covered eyes turned in my direction.

I whipped my head a little too quickly toward the boats berthed along the quay as I realized I'd been staring fixedly at her. She pulled her long, raven hair into a messy bun on top of her head, revealing an emerald bikini top that sparkled in the sunlight. As I started to imagine the way her sun-soaked skin might smell, I decided to pull out my book to distract myself.

I couldn't think of a better book to read on that trip than Bill Bryson's *Neither Here Nor There*, an account of his journey through

Europe in 1990, retracing steps he took as a younger man in the '70s. It was easy to relate to so many of Bryson's thoughts and anecdotes, especially when he described his own personal versions of the somewhat universal fantasy of a foreign romantic encounter. On top of that, the guy was funny as hell, making for some fun, light reading.

Just over halfway through the book, I decided to put my bookmark in at the chapter that covers Sorrento and the surrounding area. Placing the book back in my bag, I looked up and realized that the girl had disappeared. *Damn.* My eyes scanned the water, and I was delighted to find her floating on her back a few yards off the jetty. She flipped over and dove under the surface, her long legs sticking in the air for a split second before disappearing again, and came up just as quickly as she'd gone down, brushing her wet hair back out of her face with both hands. She moved into a breaststroke and swam until the water was shallow enough to stand in.

When she stood up, I fought to keep my jaw from hitting the ground. Her body glistened in the sunlight, and now that she was closer, I could tell just how much she embodied the American male vision of Italian women: tall, tan, and gracefully confident with slender curves. She was damn beautiful. The moment was reminiscent of the infamous scene in *Dr. No* in which Ursula Andress emerges from the surf. I'd never had such a hard time trying *not* to gawk like a twelve-year-old kid seeing boobs for the first time. But I did my best, reluctantly reclining the chair and closing my eyes behind my sunglasses, hands behind my head. My rest didn't last long. A few moments later, I heard the unmistakable sound of a ball connecting with someone's head, a scream, and then a child crying. My eyes shot open and in the direction of the sound.

The girl was kneeling on the ground next to one of the boys who had been playing soccer, giving him a hug and rubbing his back with the care of an older sister. He was crying, but it didn't seem as if there had been any real physical harm. The other boys who had been playing with him stood nearby, one of them holding the ball under his arm. The older boy who I had assumed to be her brother ran to the group from the water; he had been out at a small floating dock with his friend and another boy around their age.

Not wanting to appear intrusive, I pulled out my notebook and pen and began making notes of my thoughts on the foreign rendezvous fantasy, including elements of both the desire to find love and the mere satisfaction of lust. Then, I made a few notes about the beach and the road I took to get there, then closed my Moleskine and returned it to my bag. It felt good to get some words on paper. Using the bag as a pillow, I turned over on my stomach to get some sun on my back.

I dozed off and woke a half hour later to find an entirely new crowd of people at the beach. The girl and her brothers were nowhere to be seen. Feeling the heat from the sun deep in my skin, I decided it might be best to get out of the direct rays. I put my shirt on, thanked the old man for the use of the chair, and walked up to the small bar in the side of the cliff.

The beer selection was limited, so I held up a finger and said, "Peroni, *per favore.*" I remembered the thoughts on Peroni I'd voiced to Jeremy before and figured it couldn't hurt to give it another chance. Nothing sounded better than a cold, light beer, then, anyway.

"*Sì.*" The middle-aged man behind the counter set down the book he had been reading and popped the cap off a frosty bottle of Italian lager he'd pulled from the reach-in cooler under the counter. "*Vetro?*" He gestured toward a shelf of half-clean beer glasses.

"No, *grazie.*" I sat at the bar and turned the stool around to look back out at the beach and the boats. A new group of children kicked a new soccer ball around as their families watched them.

The bottle beaded up with condensation, causing the label to tear off in my hand. I drank the beer quickly and decided to head back to the hostel.

The return trip from somewhere always seems to take half as long as the initial journey. That was not the case this time. Maybe it was the heat and the fact that I'd been lounging in it for so long, but the walk back to Seven Hostel seemed to take an hour. When I finally reached its welcoming doors, I felt near collapse and was relieved to step into the cool lobby.

"Welcome back. How did you like the beach?" The girl who'd given me directions had her feet kicked up on the desk, and she was reading what looked like an Italian romance novel, judging by the shirtless muscle-head on the front cover.

"It was great. Thank you for the recommendation."

Back in my room, I fell onto my bed and looked at my watch. It was almost one o'clock. I was infinitely more tired than I was hungry by that point, so I decided a nap was in order. I laid my watch on the nightstand, pulled the curtains shut since the sun was shining directly into the window, and stripped off my clothes. I fell back to my bed and almost immediately passed out.

Chapter 23

Bright, orange light filtered through the curtains, landing on my face and rousing me from my sleep. The sun was significantly lower in the sky than it had been when I'd returned to my room. I looked at my watch and saw that I'd slept for six hours. I threw on a pair of khaki pants and a dark-blue button-down shirt, washed my face, and ran some cold water through my hair, drying it quickly with a towel.

There was a restaurant I'd seen a short walk away that I wanted to try for dinner, but, despite my lack of eating lunch earlier, I wasn't feeling very hungry. I decided to visit Daniele on the roof and whet my appetite with a cocktail.

"*Buonasera,* Michael."

"*Buonasera,* Daniele. *Come va?*"

"*Bene, bene. Grazie.* What would you like?" he asked, although he'd grabbed a lemon, anticipating my usual.

"Something different this time, I think. *Un aperitivo, per favore. Eh...un Negroni.* On the rocks, please."

"*Perfetto.*" He replaced the lemon in his basket and pulled out an orange and a rocks glass.

I watched as he poured equal parts of Bombay Sapphire gin, Campari bitters, and Italian sweet vermouth into a mixing tin over ice. He stirred the concoction slowly with the bar spoon, so as not to overdilute it with the ice. Then, he strained the red drink into the glass over freshly cracked ice.

Using a short knife, Daniele took a piece of the orange peel from the surface of the pungent fruit. Then, flicking a flame from a lighter in his other hand right next to the glass, he bent the peel in half. The oils from the rind shot through the flame, flaring over the drink. He finished by rubbing the peel around the rim of the glass and twisting it into the drink. He took a quick taste with a straw before placing the cocktail in front of me on a napkin. *"Ecco."*

After paying him for the drink, I smiled and swirled the glass under my nose, taking in the fresh orange aroma. "This smells fantastic, Daniele. *Grazie mille."*

"Prego."

I sipped carefully from the nearly overflowing glass as I turned to walk away. There were a few people occupying the couches in the area by the bar, so I decided to go to the other end of the rooftop to the solarium where it was typically less crowded. Upon climbing the handful of steps to the solarium, I had to chuckle.

Passed out on a couple of the couches to one side of the tanning deck were Brent, John, and Rick—the three Australians I'd met on my first night at the hostel. All three sported nasty sunburns that said they'd likely been there a few hours. Rick, the largest of the three, was sprawled completely over the smaller of the two couches, his arm drooping down to the ground as if he'd fallen asleep in the middle of reaching for the audio controls on Brent's laptop, which was open on the table and playing what sounded like Moroccan music, filled with plucky strings and the jingling zills of a tambourine. John and Brent were sharing a couch, each asleep on one of the couch's arms. Each of the three had a nearly empty bottle of wine loosely in hand, and several other wine and beer bottles littered the ground around the couches.

These guys really know how to live, I thought. Admittedly, I was jealous of the Australians' carefree attitudes and outlooks on life. Having experienced their drinking competence earlier in my stay, I imagined they would wake up that evening and, hung over or not, brush off the sunburns and say, simply, "What a fun time we had!" I wished I could worry so little. I decided there was a lot to be learned from Australians and that every uptight American should have a chance to spend some time around them.

As I sipped my cocktail, I made a few notes about the Aussies on a fresh page in my notebook. Then, I slid it back in my pocket, propped my feet on the table, and watched the sun sink low.

The Negroni did its job; by the end of it, I was hungry and ready to eat. I took my empty glass down to Daniele and descended the stairs to the courtyard, where I found Emily, Kasey, and Jenna having dinner at a table in the corner.

Emily's face brightened when she saw me. "Hey, you!"

I smiled. "Hey, girls. How's your day been?"

"We've been shopping *all* day."

"So, it's been great, huh?"

Emily laughed. "Very. Where are you headed?"

"I thought I'd try out that restaurant down the road on the cliffs. We passed it the other night on the way back from the beach."

"I can't say I noticed it."

At this comment, Jenna giggled, and Kasey choked on the food in her mouth. My eyes went to Emily's, saying, *I take it you* did *tell them?* Her eyes looked back, twinkling: *Sorry.* I just smiled at her. I really didn't care what she told her friends. I'd never been too concerned with that type of thing; I just strived to make sure only good things could be said.

"We're still on for tomorrow?"

"Of course," Emily said. "I can't wait to see Positano with you."

"Me neither." Our eyes lingered on each other before I said good-bye to the girls and headed out the front door in the direction of the restaurant.

The *ristorante* sat on the cliff overlooking Sorrento to the west, right where *Corso Marion Crawford* makes a hard left away from the sea toward the center of town. Some sort of crawling plant covered the front of the building, adding to its Italian charm. I was seated at a small table outside by the railing after a few minutes and asked the waiter what he'd recommend as he poured a glass of still water.

"The gnocchi alla Sorrentina is the favorite of Italians and tourists," he said proudly. "With a bottle of the house *bianco,* it is"—he clustered the fingertips of his free hand and kissed them before opening his hand as if to throw the kiss into the air—"*toccata da Dio.*"

It was a strong statement to say that the food was touched by God, but something in his eyes made me believe him. *"Si, per favore.* To both."

He left the bottle of water on the table. *"Subito, signore."* He walked quickly back toward the main restaurant with a satisfied look on his face. He returned a few minutes later with a bottle of wine and a short, stemless glass, pouring a bit of the wine before setting the bottle on the table.

"Grazie," I said, taking a drink as he gave a slight bow and walked away to another table. As I sipped the wine, I took in my surroundings. The restaurant wasn't nearly as busy as I'd expected it might be, and I was happy to have a quieter atmosphere. A golden glow stretched in a thin line over the horizon as the sun finished its descent into sleep for the night. The rest of the sky had turned midnight blue, and stars sparkled above as city lights twinkled along the coastline and across

the bay. Squinting across the water toward Naples, I could just make out the imposing, black cone of Vesuvius. In the other direction, colorful hotels and restaurants glowed along the cliffs all the way to Sorrento where boats floated quietly in the marina below. If I'd somehow forgotten I was in Italy, the crisp, cold wine and that view made it very clear. I couldn't help but smile broadly, feeling the childlike happiness I'd felt the first, second, and third times I'd gone to Disneyland.

A while after the waiter brought my food, which was as unbelievable as he'd hinted, a pretty voice with a thick, Italian accent spoke from a few feet away. "I saw you looking at me on the beach."

Swallowing the tomato sauce-covered dumpling I'd barely chewed, I turned in the direction of the voice. Approaching me in a flowing, peach-colored dress was, unmistakably, the girl from the jetty. The immediate eye contact I made with her surprised me, but my voice caught in my throat.

"Well, you're very pretty," I finally said, a little too quickly. With a smile, I added, more slowly, "I hope you don't mind me saying that."

She smiled and looked at her feet, then back up at me. "No, no, not at all. *Grazie mille.* Why are you eating alone?"

"I like to eat alone sometimes. It helps me clear everything out of my head," I said, although Emily wasn't far beneath the surface of my mind. I couldn't lie to myself; I wished she was there.

"I suppose it can be nice. Well, I won't keep you from it. I just recognized you and wanted to say *buonasera.*" She gestured toward what looked like her parents and her brothers, waiting back on the sidewalk along the road. "I'm walking into Sorrento with my family."

"It's a nice night for it. I'm glad you stopped…"

"Lucia."

"…Lucia. I'm glad you said hi. I'm Michael. *Piacere.*"

"*Piacere.*"

We shook hands gently.

"Enjoy your time here, Michael."

"*Grazie*, I will. You too."

I watched Lucia walk back to her family and disappear down the road. Then, I paid the waiter and thanked him for the suggestion. "*Toccata da Dio,*" I repeated, twisting the tip of my index finger in my cheek, hoping to God I remembered the correct gesture to signify that my meal was delicious.

"*Toccata da Dio!*" He grinned broadly and spread his arms as if to say, *I told you so!*

I thanked him again and headed off toward Sorrento, Emily at the forefront of my mind. I hadn't even thought twice about trying to pursue further conversation with Lucia. She was stunning, and seemed sweet, but my desire remained only for Emily.

After walking for a while, completely lost in thought, I realized I was at the same lookout point in Sorrento where Emily and I had watched the cruise ship the night before. Leaning forward on the railing, I looked out at the sea once more. Behind me, faint music flowed through the streets, I guessed from Piazza Tasso. Couples and families wandered happily along the streets. Children danced ahead of their parents, some twirling sparklers in the air, creating crackling pinwheels of light that reminded me of the Fourth of July. *Must be another one of those coastal festivals,* I thought.

The walk back to Seven Hostel was a lonely one. I wished I was with Emily, sipping cocktails on the rooftop, on the upper level away from everyone who danced by the bar. We would fall into each other on the couches, occasionally taking a few minutes to recover our breath and look at the stars that had taken the place of the sun high above.

Something about the citrus in the air would arouse us once more and we would return solely to one another's company. By the time any drunken couples from the bar made their way up to the secluded solarium, we would be long gone, hidden in my room under the white sheets of my bed.

The loud voices of some locals playing a late game of soccer across from the hostel snapped me back to reality. *How did I make it back already?*

In the off chance that Emily might be there, I went upstairs, first to the lounge and then the solarium. She was nowhere to be found. I looked at my watch; it was one in the morning. *She's probably sleeping,* I thought. *I should be, too.* I'd get to spend the entire next day with her, anyway. I went back downstairs to my room and climbed into bed. As excited as I was for my day with Emily, I fell asleep as soon as my head hit the pillow.

Chapter 24

I awoke the next morning to Emily pouncing on me. "Hey, you! Wake up!"

I pretended to be in a deep sleep, trying to contain the smile that ached to get out. The act didn't last long; I smelled the sweet scent of fresh fruit and warm bread, and my stomach growled. Sitting on my nightstand was a tray of breakfast food from the courtyard buffet. Smiling at her, I said, "You didn't have to do that. And how'd you get in?"

"You didn't lock your door last night, silly. You really should be more careful. Someone, *anyone*, could just come in here and take advantage of you or something." Her bright eyes told me she probably wished she'd have found the door unlocked last night.

"Yeah, we wouldn't want that, would we?" I winked as I picked up a cornetto and took a bite. "What time is it, anyway?"

"Seven-thirty. I know you said we should probably get an early start today, so I went to bed a little earlier last night. How was your evening? Was that restaurant good?"

"It was nice. The restaurant was great. They had *really* good gnocchi and a fantastic white wine. And the view was amazing, even in the dark. Then, I just wandered around Sorrento a little bit and took the long way back." I didn't mention Lucia. It was inconsequential, but I didn't want to risk setting Emily off.

"Something was missing, though." I leaned over and kissed her on the lips. "Mmm... Honeydew."

She simply pulled back and smiled.

God, that smile! Why is it that something as simple as a smile can make a man so damn weak?

"Hurry up! Finish eating and shower so we can go. I've been waiting two days for this!"

I laughed at Emily's excitement and ate a few more pieces of fruit and the rest of my cornetto, rinsing it all down with that orange juice I loved so much. Ten minutes later, I was ready to go.

"That was quick. I thought I'd at least get a nap in."

Laughing, I took her hand, pulled her up from the bed, and kissed her.

"You smell *good*." She wrapped her arms around me and buried her face in my chest, then my shoulder and neck, ruffling my hair with her hands.

"You don't smell too bad yourself." That was an understatement. I immediately recognized the scent she was wearing; I'd known other girls who used the same perfume, and it always won me over. "Let's go."

We walked quickly to the train station in Sorrento, stopping at a *supermercato* on the way for a couple of large bottles of water. It was still so early that the station was empty except for a few blue-collars and some other tourists with the same idea we had. I bought two roundtrip passes to Positano from the ticket window and led Emily out front. The bus arrived about fifteen minutes later, after a long line of tourists had gathered.

I surveyed the group, chuckling at several people who lived up to every stereotype you've ever heard about American tourists: cameras dangling around their necks, T-shirts and jackets emblazoned with the names and logos of their favorite NFL team or NASCAR racer, awkward-looking bucket hats like those worn by old fishermen, and—I shuddered when I noticed them—fanny packs. *Might as well just start handing their wallets and electronics to passing strangers,* I thought. *At least then they'd have nothing left for a pickpocket.*

As we started to board the bus, I couldn't take my eyes off Emily's sun-kissed legs coming out from under her flowy, seafoam-green sundress. I pointed to a couple of seats a few rows back on the right-hand side. "Grab those. That way we'll have a view of the water the whole time. Plus, they're by an open window, and it's already getting pretty warm today. The fresh air will be good."

We sat down—I gave Emily the window seat—and waited for the rest of the line to board and get seated. The last, a group of giggling, middle-aged tourists, made their way awkwardly between the rows toward the rear where no one else had wanted to sit. They all looked and sounded like they'd had three too many mimosas for breakfast that morning. As much as I love mimosas, I wasn't envious. The long, winding road ahead wouldn't make for a pleasant trip after a few drinks.

When the bus driver had finally talked the last tourists into their seats—*"Siediti! Siediti!"*— and threw out a slew of violent-looking gestures, the bus door folded closed, and we were on our way.

The driver took us out of Sorrento onto *Via Capo*, which would take us through the mountains and along the coastline to Positano. The road wound upwards, and soon we hit a curve that gave us a spectacular view over all of Sorrento and the Bay of Naples beyond. We'd gotten such an early start that a thin mist still hung over the rooftops, sparkling in the early morning sun.

Emily stared out the window in awe. "It's *so* pretty!"

"If you look carefully, you can see the roof of the hostel, *way* out there." I matched up my line of sight with hers as best I could and pointed in the direction of Seven Hostel.

"Ooh! I see it!" Emily smiled at me. We both knew it wasn't *actually* visible from where we were, but she seemed to appreciate my effort to get closer and scooted into me, put her head on my shoulder, and took my hand with both of hers in her lap. "Thank you for bringing me along."

"Thank *you* for joining me. I can't think of a better way to spend my last day here." I kissed her softly on the top of her head.

At my comment, Emily's body tensed up, and I could tell she wanted to say something. Rather than coaxing it out of her, I waited for her to decide whether or not she wanted to continue.

"I…I hate that you have to leave so soon. What if I never see you again?"

I smiled as she looked at me with concerned eyes. "What makes you think you won't? We live two hours away from each other. Besides, we're both going to Rome. Even though we're taking different routes there, we can still see each other then."

Her body relaxed once more, and she smiled up at me before kissing me on the cheek. "Thank you. I like you, Michael."

"I like you, too. Don't worry, we'll see each other again."

"Good." She settled back into me and looked out the window. I put my arm around her and rubbed her arm reassuringly.

The bus driver had started speaking over the bus's PA system as we drove through the small villages that dotted the peninsula. His English wasn't fantastic, so his commentary was heavily scattered with Italian. I could make out a few of the words, but for the most part, I wasn't really sure what he was trying to point out to us.

Most of the passengers didn't seem to be paying much attention, anyway, and had their faces pressed to the windows talking among themselves, some of them far too loudly. I wished they would be a little more respectful to our driver, whether they could understand him or not.

The Mimosa Club in the back of the bus was acting exactly as the "cool" kids did in school, talking loudly over each other, yelling at others they knew who were seated farther ahead. One of the men—an overweight, mustachioed cue ball—stood up, teetered for a minute, and then attempted to make his way up the aisle. He bumped several people as the bus tilted back and forth on the curves of the road until, finally, he reached the seat in which his friend was sitting, one in front of ours. He propped himself up between the seats, showing off the sweaty underarms of his T-shirt, and started talking even louder than before.

"Jim, how 'bout all them olive trees? They look all silvery. Great, huh?"

"Yeah, Harvey, they're gorgeous. Why don't you go sit back down? We'll chat when we get to Positano." Jim seemed to have missed the party and still had a level head; he glanced at us and rolled his eyes once Harvey had turned around.

The bus driver was clearly annoyed, too, because he started yelling at Harvey in the long mirror mounted above the windshield.

The surrounding passengers glared at Harvey as he made his return trip, roughly, between them.

I turned back around after I watched Harvey sit down. "What a jackass."

Emily laughed and said, "Oh, he's just having a good time."

"So are we, but we're not drunk and acting like that." But I left my comments at that; Emily had a way of calming me down, and I didn't want to ruin the trip for her with a bad mood. I leaned against the seat as she moved into me, and we both looked out the window at whatever the driver was describing.

The bus wound southwest of Sorrento through several different municipalities before cutting back across the tip of the peninsula to shorten the time to Positano. I found myself grateful the driver had made that decision. The day had grown very warm, and the small windows on the bus didn't allow for much airflow. Nausea had started to set in, causing my body to tense up and sweat beads to form on my forehead, and I stopped looking out the window to focus on the back of the seat in front of me. It was all trees and walls at that point anyway, and right then, I didn't care to see anything but the sea. The winding road didn't help one bit.

Emily noticed that I seemed anxious and began running her hand through my hair, massaging my scalp with her fingertips, which helped immensely. The nausea didn't cease entirely, but my nerves calmed, and I was able to relax. I looked over at Emily, who had a concerned look on her face, and smiled. "Thank you. That feels really nice."

That seemed to put her mind at ease because she just smiled back and continued what she was doing and watched out the window.

The last leg of the trip wasn't nearly as bad. We had gotten out of the center of the peninsula and back along the coastline. While the road was narrow and unnerving, I enjoyed seeing the azure sea again. The bus finally stopped along the side of the road in front of a small café with little blue tables and chairs outside, and the driver opened the door and looked at us all as if to say, *Time to get off.* Then, he stepped outside and lit a cigarette. We were still high above the water and the heart of Positano, a fact that did not go unnoticed by Harvey.

"Are you taking us down there after your smoke break? Hey, chief! When does the bus go down there?" He pointed emphatically with his fat fingers toward the main, sea-level part of Positano.

The man named Jim was now standing, and after looking at Emily and me and rolling his eyes again, he called back, "Harvey, the bus doesn't go down there. He's waiting for us to get off so others can board to go back to Sorrento. We've got to walk down."

"The *hell* we do! What did we pay them for, then?"

"Harvey, the tickets were ten euros. And *you* didn't even pay that. Gary bought your ticket!"

Harvey's red face froze; he finally had no words. "Well…it's just the principle of the matter. He should do what we pay him to do."

"Shut up, Harvey. Look at that road down there. Do you think *this* bus can make *those* curves? No. Now, grab your fuckin' fanny pack, and get your ass off the bus. I'm ready to see Positano." Jim winked at us before swinging his backpack over his shoulder and helping his wife out of the seat. "Let's go, honey. You're going to love it." Before walking off the bus, he leaned close to us and whispered, "There *is* another bus that goes down, if you're interested."

"Thanks," I said. "The walk sounds kind of nice, though."

"It is. It's steep, so take it slow, and have a good time." With that, Jim and his wife were off.

Harvey did shut up, and he did—with difficulty—put his fanny pack back around his waist, but he waited for everyone else to file off the bus before doing so himself. Apparently, his buzz had worn off enough for humility to set in.

If it wasn't hot enough *on* the bus, the air hit like a blow from Ali when we stepped out onto the street. But it felt good to stand again, and to at least have a cool sea breeze intermittently blowing by.

"Where do we go from here?" Emily asked.

I hadn't been to Positano before, either, so it was a mystery to me. People were dispersing every which way. The Mimosa Club was gathered around a map, trying to decipher the lines and the language, even though Jim, who had clearly been there before, was trying to direct them down a road marked with a sign depicting a swimming stick figure and the words "*la spiaggia.*"

"Well, I think that's the one *road* that goes all the way down. But I think there are staircases that go down, too, that are actually a nicer walk. That's the steep part he was talking about. You up for that?"

"Of course! Let's go!" She grabbed my hand and started off toward an alleyway that looked as if it might lead somewhere. Her instincts were correct; several others had already started making the trek downward ahead of us. A long series of small steps reached toward the town below, winding between houses and back-alley trattorias. Flowers and vines hung down the sides of buildings, and in a few places, the path was so narrow that both my shoulders nearly brushed the walls.

I wasn't prepared for the incline of the stairs we were descending. After ten minutes or so, I had finally accustomed my body to leaning back slightly as I walked, so as not to become front-heavy and topple forward. There were stretches where the pathway leveled out and had no steps, which Emily and I appreciated. There were even landings here and there on which we could rest and take a drink of water while enjoying the striking view before us.

Photos and paintings of Positano were in every Italian gift shop I'd ever been in, and in all kinds of books and magazines, but none do justice to the actual sight of it. The hillside is terraced with white and pastel-colored homes, most with olive trees, gardens, and arbors covered in grapevines and ivy and flowers. It all slopes downward, laced with one main road and several smaller roads and sidewalks that wind between shops and restaurants and apartments, culminating in a beautiful, beachfront promenade. From a landing, we could see the rows of red-and-yellow and blue-and-white umbrellas and lounge chairs that cover a good portion of the dark-grey sand.

"What I wouldn't give to be out on one of those right now." I pointed toward the twenty or thirty boats, mostly white, that were either sitting stationary or moving across the water.

"Mmhmm. That would be lovely." Emily put her arm around my waist and squeezed me before we continued on again. We'd made it about halfway.

She took off ahead of me, which I didn't mind. Her dress fluttered in the light breeze, hugging her body occasionally. The sunlight broke through the shadows of the buildings every so often, gilding her blond hair. I loved the way she moved between the buildings: curious, carefree, graceful. When she turned back to make sure I was still coming, her blue eyes sparkled in happy wonderment. It was illustrative of her entire personality, really. It was why I found myself falling for her.

When we finally reached the bottom, I looked up and around us in awe. It was all I could have imagined and then some. Music and scents of food, flowers, and the sea floated through the air. People spoke excitedly in languages from all over the world, likely about all the same things, but undoubtedly in varied idioms. Some people pulled rolling luggage, looking for their hotels. I hoped for their sake that they had taken a cab down the road rather than making the same trek we had.

Emily and I stood still for a few minutes, soaking in all that Positano's first impression had to offer and watching others do the same.

"It really *does* bite deep," I said quietly, recalling something I'd come across online after my first trip abroad, when I'd spent hours upon hours reading everything I could about the places I'd just been.

"What do you mean?"

"Steinbeck wrote an essay for Harper's Bazaar back in '53 about

Positano. He said, 'Positano bites deep. It is a dream place that isn't quite real when you are there and becomes beckoningly real after you have gone.'" I gave a quick nod in the direction of the sloping town above us. "He's not wrong."

"That's really cool. And *so* true; it does feel like a dream. I never want to leave."

"Neither do I." I took her hand in mine and gestured at the church in front of us. "You want to check it out?"

"Churches kind of give me the heebie-jeebies," she said, faking a shiver. "Besides, there are plenty to see in Rome. Let's just walk around."

I laughed. *My kind of girl.* "That sounds perfect to me."

We spent the next couple of hours wandering the labyrinth of Positano's artisan marketplace, glad to be in the shade of buildings and awnings. We explored souvenir shops, boutique jewelry and clothing shops, and antique shops. Emily bought a pair of white, leather sandals, which were handmade in front of us and fitted perfectly to her feet. At a liquor and wine store, I bought a bottle of limoncello to take home so I could fuel my memory long after the trip was over. Finally, with our travel budgets in mind, we decided to head down to the beach.

The promenade along the beach is lined with bars and restaurants, all providing some of the most enchanting seaside dining views you can imagine. Emily and I found a counter that sold gelato and bought two cones, and we grabbed the only open bench we could find along the sand. I had ventured away from my usual flavor again and chosen a peach gelato, which had small pieces of real peach mixed in. It was a nice change and tasted refreshing in the heat of the day. We swapped cones so I could try Emily's passionfruit, which was equally delicious.

We sat on our bench, holding hands and eating our ice cream and watching all the visitors with beach-chair dreams make their way down the small boardwalks jutting off the promenade across the sand. If I'd ever felt more at peace than in that moment, I couldn't remember it. The warm, salty breeze, the myriad languages intermingling in the background, the unbelievably blue sea dotted with pristine white boats, the impossible allure of Emily's sun-soaked skin. An unspoken excitement built between us as we uttered few words and simply enjoyed each other's company, and the occasional eye contact we shared told me she was just as ready to get back to the privacy of my room at Seven Hostel as I was.

Back on the main road, where we'd started our Positano adventure, we were relieved to catch a bus within a few minutes of finishing our exhausting ascent, which had been fueled mostly—at least in my case—by the anticipation of what seemed to lay ahead at the end of our return journey. The bus took a significantly quicker route than we had on the way to Positano, cutting almost directly across the peninsula and approaching Sorrento from the east. I paid too much for a cab back to the hostel, and we wasted no time going upstairs to my room. With the door locked behind us, we decided to rinse off the heat of the day's bus rides. We started the shower hot and stayed in it till the water cooled, at which point we found ourselves falling onto my bed, the bedding fresh and white and cool against our skin.

I woke several hours later to an intense, red glow coming through the window and Emily's leg across mine, her head on my shoulder. My head fell back onto my pillow, and a smile spread across my face wider than any in recent memory. I slowly wiggled and stretched my fingers to get blood flowing again and wrapped my arm around her bare shoulders, rubbing her skin with the backs of my fingers. My stomach growled as I grabbed my watch from the nightstand with my spare hand; it was eight o'clock—time to find a bite to eat. Emily stirred and I sensed her eyes blinking open. She ran her fingers up and down my chest and stomach.

"You want to get some dinner?" I asked, kissing the top of her head. Her hair smelled of sweat and sunlight. I breathed it in as my heart rate picked up speed again.

"I don't want to leave this bed. But I am *starving*. Where should we go?"

"Walk until we find somewhere?"

"Yes, please."

We took a quick, cooling shower and redressed, hitting the streets hand in hand. A few minutes' walk in the direction of the Corso Italia, we found ourselves in a small piazza at a *pizzeria* opposite the *Chiesa dei Santi Prisco ed Agnello*, a church that looked as if it were pulled off a wedding cake, frosted pale yellow and adorned with buttercream highlights. An identically decorated bell tower flanked the church, standing a story higher than its neighbor's façade.

"When do you leave tomorrow?" Emily asked as soon as the waiter had seated us and sauntered off to fulfill our order of a carafe of house white.

"Early. I have a train ticket out of Naples at nine. I need to leave here by, like, seven-fifteen, probably."

"Oh…" Her eyes lowered to her plate, and I nodded *Thanks* to the waiter when he brought a small jug of wine and two stemless juice glasses.

Pouring some into each glass, I said, "When are you going to be in Rome? I really would like to meet you there."

Her eyes lifted back to meet mine and she smiled. "I would like that, too. We're here for one more day and then going to Venice for a couple, then Rome. I would really like that, Michael."

"Me too. I'm glad." We smiled at each other, tapped the rims of our glasses together, and drank. I refilled from our carafe, and we ordered a *pizza Margherita* from the waiter.

"How long are you in Rome?" she asked, slightly cheerier, as she drank her wine.

"Five nights. No real plans, just seeing the city again, on my own terms this time. The tour was nice before, but restricting. We didn't have a whole lot of extra time."

"That will be nice. I'm looking forward to it, too. I really want to see the Colosseum."

"We did a quick walkthrough before. It's incredible, but I'll definitely go again, if you'd like me to wait for you."

"Yes, please. That would be a fun part of another nice day. If we leave the room, that is."

I laughed, feeling myself blush. "We may have to. I've got a room at another hostel, but it's a six-bed, all-male dorm room. Not sure how much privacy we'll get. In a room, anyway. I'm sure we can find some nooks and crannies around the city." I winked and took another drink of my wine. "This is delicious."

"Mmm, yes, it is. I like when we find nooks and crannies." She gave me a look that stirred everything in me. I felt a bare foot on top of mine that slowly made its way up my leg. I choked on the gulp of wine I'd just taken.

We finished our pizza and wine quickly and, though our minds were clearly in a more private place, decided to have drinks one last time on the rooftop, made by Daniele.

"*Buonasera,* Daniele," I said as we stepped up to the bar. "*Come va?*"

"*È molto lento,*" he replied, nodding behind us at the lounge area where a few people sat, drinking and laughing. "Not many people tonight."

"Must be a nice break for you. It's been crazy every time I've come up here."

"*Si*, the quiet is sometimes nice. A Tom Collins tonight?"

"*Per favore.*"

"And for *la bella signora*?"

"A Clover Club, please," said Emily, smiling up at me.

"*Arrivando.*"

Emily played with my hand as Daniele made our drinks with the same care he always did. As I paid for the drinks, I told him I was glad to have met him and that I hoped to come back to Seven Hostel for more of his impeccable drinks someday sooner rather than later.

"*Mi piacere,*" he said, placing his hand briefly on his heart, his ever-stoic face showing just a hint of pride. I reached out to shake his hand, and he accepted with a firm grip.

"*Arrivederci,*" I said with a nod.

Emily and I settled close to each other on a couch in the corner of the lounge and sipped our drinks as we looked out in the direction of the water.

"This place is perfect," I said after a few minutes. Memories of the last few days reeled through my head like pictures on a 1960s Kodak Carousel, beginning with the wild ride from Naples with Gio the cabbie and ending in the current moment.

"I'm glad we both found it."

"Me too," I said, putting my arm across the back of the couch. Emily leaned her head against my shoulder. The warm, Sorrentine breeze carried the scent of lemons and sea water over us, and I breathed it in as deeply as I could. I hoped that, somehow, I could keep it on call for whenever I missed that place. The lounge stayed pretty quiet, and we sat in happy silence as we drank our cocktails slowly, prolonging our time as much as possible and savoring every second.

Eventually, only small chips of mostly melted ice remained, and our eyes met with no intention of staying for another drink.

On our way to the elevator, we bumped into the rest of Emily's group.

"Hey, guys!" Jake threw an arm around each of us and gave a friendly squeeze. "Where are you going? We're just getting here!"

Emily glanced at me with a hint of a smile. "We're going for a walk. We'll come back up here when we get back."

"For sure," Kasey said. "You better. It's too nice out here tonight."

"We will," Emily promised.

We practically raced to my room and wasted no time at all undressing each other and climbing under the fresh sheets. We never made it back upstairs.

At some point, I made sure to set my alarm for six-thirty so I would have plenty of time to gather my things, check out, and get to the train station in Sorrento. Around one in the morning, we fell asleep spooning, my arms wrapped around her and holding her close, despite the combined heat of our exhausted bodies and the night air coming through the window. I kissed her shoulder and buried my face in her hair, committing another moment to memory as best I could.

A while later, I was roused from a deep sleep by movement in the room. I could feel that Emily was no longer next to me and opened one eye slowly, just enough to see her moving quietly around the room, gathering her things. I stayed still and quiet, and the next thing I knew, she opened the door and shut it behind her. I sleepily grabbed my watch from the nightstand: three-thirty. Exhausted as I was, confusion lingered in my mind for a few moments before I fell back asleep, watch still in hand.

Chapter 25

The alarm jarred me from a sleep that was apparently deep enough to leave me completely disoriented. I regained my bearings and noticed a folded piece of paper on the table by the window as I remembered Emily's odd, sudden exit in the middle of the night. I wiped the sleep from my eyes and got out of bed, stretching my arms and back before picking the note up from the table. It was on a page from the Seven Hostel-branded notepad that came with the room.

> *Michael,*
>
> *Sorry to just leave in the middle of the night like this. It was an incredible last night together, but I didn't want to wake up and have to say goodbye. I know we'll see each other in Rome, and I look so forward to it. Have fun in Montecatini, and I'll see you soon.*
>
> *XOXO – Emily*
>
> *P.S. My number is in your phone.*

The "i" in her name was dotted with a small heart, and the paper smelled of her perfume. I grabbed my phone and scrolled through the contacts until I found "Emily" with a red heart emoji next to it. She'd added a picture of herself, taken from the chest up, undressed but covering her breasts with one arm in front of the bathroom mirror. While I didn't fully understand why she'd left, the note and everything that came with it made me feel better about it. I took a quick, hot shower, dressed in khaki shorts and a T-shirt for comfort during the long day of train travel ahead, and packed my things, triple-checking the room to ensure I didn't forget anything.

I stopped outside Emily's room but quickly dispatched the idea of knocking to say goodbye. I wanted to respect what she'd said, telling myself I'd hold out just fine until Rome. Besides, her number was now in my phone; I could text or call her sometime later once I reached Montecatini. Down in the courtyard, I ate a quick breakfast of cornetti, fresh fruit, orange juice, and a cup of coffee before checking out at the front desk.

"I hope you enjoyed your stay, Mr. Wise," said Clara as she traded me a printout of the bill for my room key.

"It was incredible, Clara, thank you. And thank you again for the wine. This is my favorite place I've ever stayed. And for what it's worth, Daniele is the best bartender I've ever met."

Clara laughed. "I'm glad to hear that. He can take some getting used to, so I'm happy you got along with him. It has been our pleasure. We have a car if you'd like a ride to the train station."

I considered her offer for a moment but declined. "I think I'll take one last walk before I leave town. But *grazie mille.*"

"*Prego.* We hope to see you again very soon. *Ciao.*"

"*Ciao,* Clara."

I enjoyed the walk from Seven Hostel just as much as the first time I'd taken it. The morning air had a faint crispness to it, but I could tell it was going to heat up quickly, and I was glad for my shorts and T-shirt. I took extra care to store memories of the flowers climbing garden walls and the lemon trees on the other side of the walls, whose scent seemed to pop out to say *Arrivederci*. I noticed the places where Emily and I had stopped to kiss and looked forward to finding new places in Rome.

It didn't take nearly as long to reach the train station as I had expected, but I still cut it a little close for comfort to having to wait another half hour for a train going to the larger hub in Naples. I gave the man behind the ticket five euros for a ticket to the Garibaldi Station and sat on a bench outside for a couple of minutes before the train pulled in.

When everyone who was stopping in Sorrento had gotten off the train, I pushed my way through the slow-moving tourists who were trying to get on amid the throng of students already taking up most of the available space. I glanced left and right between people, searching for an open seat. Somehow, there was one in the corner at the far end of the train. But could I get there in time before someone else swiped it? I casually, but swiftly, made my way in that general direction so as not to draw unneeded attention to myself and cause a musical-chair swarm for the seat. When I got there, the seat was still empty, but before sitting down, I looked around me to see if there were any women—pregnant or otherwise—or elderly folks who might need the seat more than I did. Fortunately, there were not, so I set my bag next to the bench and sat carefully next to the older gentleman occupying the other half of the bench. He was reading an Italian newspaper and barely seemed to notice I was there.

The hour-long journey to Naples went by quickly, but, of course, the process to claim my ticket to Rome and Montecatini wasn't quick at all. I'd hoped that reserving a ticket online ahead of time would have saved the trouble and I'd just have to show my passport to get my boarding pass, but nothing is ever that efficient when traveling in Italy. The method of choice was to have those who had already paid for a ticket wait in the same line as those who were purchasing tickets that day. The counter dedicated to picking up pre-purchased tickets was closed for the day.

After waiting God knows how long for too many people to explain why they didn't have their passport or complain about the counter not accepting American currency, I finally received my ticket and rushed through the station, glancing at the departure screens to ensure I was heading for the correct terminal. I found my train and car and jumped on just as the large clock on the wall ticked leaving time. My seat was halfway down the car in a group of four. I wasn't fortunate enough to have the section to myself. As the train sat for another fifteen minutes, my three college-aged seatmates settled in for the four-hour journey ahead. After a half hour and not enough miles had passed, I could tell the trip would be a long one, as they hadn't stopped leaning back and forth to share videos on their cell phones with each other, laughing uncontrollably. I put my earphones in, turned up some instrumental music, and pulled out a book, hoping to distract myself for the better part of the ride.

The reading didn't last long. I fell asleep at some point and didn't remember a minute of the three-hour stretch between Naples and Florence, including the brief stop in Rome. And I might have kept sleeping if not for the clumsiness of the kid next to me. The quarters weren't so tight that he couldn't have made it out of the window seat and into the aisle without so much as brushing my leg, but he somehow managed to step on my foot, kick my knee, *and* knock my bag off my lap into the aisle, spilling everything that was in it. And then he followed his friends off the train without so much as a backward glance.

"Fuckin' asshole," I said under my breath as I gathered my things. But I had to thank him, I supposed, for not allowing me to miss switching trains, however inadvertently. That would have been worse than having my belongings briefly scattered. I checked my seat and the floor to make sure I had everything before leaving the train and heading through the station to the track where my connection to Montecatini Terme would be waiting.

It was an older, smaller train, and I had the distinct impression that the air conditioning was broken, as all the windows throughout the cars were open, and nearly every passenger was fanning himself with whatever would produce a breeze. What's more, every seat was full.

I walked back and forth through my car and the two adjacent cars twice in search of somewhere to sit, but to no avail. I ended up with two other passengers in the outer vestibule of my assigned car, where there was a small bench—already occupied—and limited other space. I picked a corner as far out of the way of either door as possible and strategically set my blocky luggage near the wall so I could sit on top of it and lean back. It turned out to be about as comfortable as if I'd just sat on the floor, though maybe a tad cleaner, but it would work for the short ride to Montecatini, scheduled to be only forty-five minutes.

After enough eye contact was made between me and my fellow displaced passengers, accompanied by curt nods to satisfy social expectations as minimally as possible, I pulled my boarding pass from my bag and looked it over once more. I'd expected to find some sort of assigned seat listed, but, as when I'd first boarded the car, there was nothing but a train and car number. I sighed resignedly and began fanning myself with my boarding pass.

The last leg of the trip ended up taking around an hour and twenty minutes due to an unexpected, and seemingly unnecessary, stop between stations. By the time we arrived at the Monsummano Station in Montecatini Terme, my T-shirt was soaked through. The only window that would open in that small area opened maybe three inches, and there was not another to create a flow of air. Since I was nearest the door, I grabbed my bags and hurried off the train as soon as we were allowed.

I'd run out of water about halfway to Montecatini since I hadn't planned on such a long journey on the final leg, so I trashed my empty bottle and bought another at a newsstand, drinking a third of it in a few swift gulps. Standing in front of a town map on the station wall, I pulled out the confirmation printout for my hotel to find out where I needed to go.

My hotel was on *Via Felice Cavalotti,* seven blocks down and four or five blocks up from where I was on *Piazzale Italia.* At that point, I would have paid just about anything for a quick ride to the hotel, so I glanced around for a taxi. There were none. I took one more long drink of water, pulled out the handle of my luggage, and started towing it down the street. I passed by all sorts of shops, restaurants, and hotels along the main road in town, none of which caught my eye except for the Ferrari dealership. Three different models in conspicuous Ferrari Red sitting just behind floor-to-ceiling plate glass windows have a way of drawing attention to themselves. I stopped for a moment to rest in the shade of the red and white-striped awning and admire the supercars' sleek curves, then continued in the heat.

What could have been a quick jaunt in cooler temperatures may have been the most draining experience I'd had in a while. I stopped several times for a few minutes at a time to rest my legs and rehydrate before I made it to the hotel. I couldn't decide if I'd been more relieved to arrive there or at Seven Hostel.

The Corallo was an unassuming, four-story hotel covered in pale-yellow stucco, which was complemented very prettily by Kelly green shutters in the windows of each room. A faded, yellow-and-green awning hung on the front of the building over a couple of small tables and several chairs that lined the sidewalk. Three small sets of arced double doors welcomed visitors in from the street to the lobby.

The high-ceilinged room was decorated with a hodgepodge of furniture styles, mostly in gold, black, and red. It reminded me of some of the small, local coffee shops and restaurants back home that decorated with whatever random furniture they'd been able to get their hands on; this was just a more upscale version. Several simple chandeliers hung from the ceiling, and a dark marble floor stood out clearly from the white-marble pillars and the matching staircase that wound upward to the second floor, fringed by a decorative wrought iron railing. At the base of the staircase sat a shiny, black baby grand piano. I imagined the space as a hotspot for evening cocktails at the right time of year, but that day, it was completely devoid of any signs of life. The lights were even off, causing me to wonder if the hotel was truly open for business.

Then, I heard a man's voice speaking quietly in Italian, coming from a room behind the small front desk. I walked over to the counter and tried to lean into his periphery. He saw me, gave a brief nod, and wrapped up his phone conversation.

"*Buonasera,*" he said. "Welcome to Golf Hotel Corallo."

"*Buonasera. Grazie.* I have a reservation under Michael Wise for two nights."

"Ah, yes, Mr. Wise. We're very glad to have you. You'll be on the third floor. Will that be alright?"

After the walk I'd had, if I hadn't seen the edge of an elevator door down a hallway off the lobby, I would have requested something lower, but I said that the third would be fine. *Closer to the pool on the roof, anyway,* I thought.

He checked me in quickly, verifying my credit card and passport information—taking a copy of the passport—before handing me a key. I gathered my things and headed for the single elevator in the dark hallway at the back of the lobby. After five minutes or so, the light on the wall lit up, the elevator chimed, and the doors opened slowly. It was as slow a ride upward as the elevator had been coming down. Once I reached my floor, I followed the numbers down the hallway until I reached the second-to-last door on the left, which corresponded to the number on my key. I stuck the key in the lock and jiggled it around a bit until the door finally opened.

The entryway barely had enough room to open the door all the way *and* fit my luggage and myself through at the same time. The closet-sized bathroom was immediately to the left. The first thing I noticed was that nothing separated the floor of the shower underneath the curtain from the floor of the rest of the bathroom, and the shower drain was no more than three inches in diameter.

The rest of the room was as small as I could've expected from my initial entrance, but it was only for a couple of nights alone, so it would do fine. Cheap-looking wood paneling covered the lower part of the walls, and the off-white walls above it looked as though they hadn't been thoroughly cleaned in years. In the corner of the room sat a small desk with two drawers. On the desk were two bottles of red wine and two dusty wine glasses. A small flat-screen TV hung above the closet opposite the bed, which was made up with shabby, blue bedding. The bed didn't look overly comfortable, but, again, it would do fine for two nights alone. Besides, after the train trip that day, some upcoming time in the sun by the pool, and the subsequent wine and dinner I planned to enjoy, there was no way I'd have trouble sleeping that night.

Two small lamps on nightstands flanking the bed were the room's only source of lighting other than the open window. *Not a problem*, I thought. *It's not like I'll be in here much except to sleep, anyway.* I placed my bags by the closet and immediately pulled out my swimming shorts, peeling off my sweaty T-shirt and khaki shorts. Nothing could keep me from taking a dip in the pool posthaste. Before I left my room, I refilled my water bottle, grabbed my messenger bag and a white towel from the bathroom, and headed to the short staircase in the hall that led up to the lounge and pool area.

There was a bar counter just inside the lounge area, along with a few tables, but no one manned it, and there were no patrons to serve, anyway. I put on my sunglasses and stepped out into the glaring, Tuscan sunlight to take in one of the most incredible views I'd ever seen.

The hotels and apartments and offices of Montecatini Terme rose around me in shades of white, yellow, and orange stucco, and beyond them sprawled the hills and countryside of Tuscany. To the northeast, I saw the real reason I had decided to spend some time there.

Montecatini Alto was the original town, built around a castle on a hill. What is now Montecatini Terme—the town at the base of the hill—wasn't established until the early 1900s, as tourists from all around Italy and beyond began coming there more heavily to visit the spas that had sprung up over the past couple of centuries to facilitate the use of the natural hot springs in the area. Hotels, restaurants, theaters, and a casino eventually sprouted, creating a hotspot for Italians and foreigners, celebrities, and average people alike. I'd visited both parts of Montecatini with the group on my graduation trip, and it stuck with me as a place I'd always want to come back to. The view from the hilltop alone was worth it. I decided I would just relax and find dinner that evening and take the *funicolare* to the top the next day, just before sunset.

After relishing the view, I walked across the blue, artificial turf-like flooring to the pool. The small swimming pool was bordered by wooden planks, and there were several pieces of blue-and-grey pool furniture. I pulled one of the padded cots close enough to the edge of the pool that I could dangle my foot or hand in the water while lying down. Then, I sat on the edge of the pool with my legs in the water, testing the temperature.

Sitting under the sun all day long, the water was the perfect temperature for swimming, floating, and lounging. I slid all the way under the surface, slowly blowing air out through my mouth, allowing my body to hang suspended above the bottom of the pool. All soreness and heat exhaustion I had felt from the day on the trains drifted from my body like a soul from its corpse. When I could hold my breath no longer, I pushed back to the top and broke through the surface into the warm air. I swam a couple of laps and floated around for a few minutes before climbing the small ladder at the end of the pool and lying on my stomach on the cot. I didn't bother to dry off—there was a pleasantly warm breeze that would do that in no time at all—but I did dry my hands so that I could read without soaking the pages of *The Sun Also Rises* completely through. I replaced my sunglasses on my face, drank a few gulps of water from my bottle, and opened my favorite book to read about Jake Barnes and Bill Gorton traveling to *Burguete* to fish in the Spanish countryside. I'd barely finished the chapter before a young, Italian couple came out to the rooftop for a swim. I marked my page, knowing I wasn't going to get much more reading done with their flirting and splashing in the pool, and folded my towel as a pillow so I could rest my eyes and soak up the sun. As it turned out, the occasional splashes cutting through the hot silence in the air was oddly soothing.

A half hour or so passed before I dove awkwardly into the water for a quick cool-down, gathered my things, smiled politely at the couple—who barely seemed to notice my presence—and headed back downstairs to my room. Seeing the couple had brought Emily back to the front of my mind, and I suddenly wished she was there. *Damn it. She'd love it here. I should have asked her to come with me.* I hadn't, consciously, because I didn't want to interfere in her plans with her friends. But maybe my subconscious was...afraid of something? There would have been no harm in asking her to come, I knew. Just a friendly invite. And based on all that had transpired between us, I was sure it'd have been a welcome invitation. But why hadn't I done it? *Who knows,* I thought, *but she's not here now, and that's all that matters.* I entered my room, stepped out of my damp shorts and hung them on the windowsill to dry in the sun. Then, I examined the bottles of wine on the desk and opened the Chianti, thoroughly cleaning one of the wine glasses in the bathroom sink before filling it halfway with the dry, Tuscan red. That glass was gone within minutes, and I refilled it. *This shouldn't bother me so much. I'll see her again in Rome.* The town was just so damn romantic, especially the hilltop. It seemed a waste not to share the experience with someone.

Leaning on the sill of the open window, I pushed open the green shutters and watched as people walked by on the street below. Across the street, I could see the pool areas of two adjacent hotels. A handful of people lounged around each of them, enjoying the warm afternoon as I had. I sat down on the bed and sipped my wine and thought about what I would do for the rest of the day since I was going to wait until the next day to go to the hilltop. I didn't really know what else Montecatini had to offer, but I had no doubt that it would be just as interesting as any other Italian town. Before I could think too much about it, I had placed my near-empty glass on the nightstand and fell onto the bed for a much-needed nap.

Chapter 26

Evening sunlight was splashed across the room through the open window when I woke. I yawned and stretched, stood up, and stretched again. I went over to the window and peered out, shielding my eyes from the sun with my hand. The people were gone from the pools across the street, but foot traffic had picked up on the sidewalks. Another yawn came, so I instinctively stretched again, my arms high in the air. I suddenly realized that I hadn't replaced my swim shorts with any sort of clothing before taking a nap, so I quickly stepped away from the window. Exhibitionism hadn't yet made it to my bucket list.

I picked up my watch from the desk; it was almost seven o'clock. *Jesus.* My stomach growled menacingly, reminding me I hadn't eaten since breakfast. Two glasses of wine hadn't done me any favors.

I went into the bathroom and turned the shower to a light, lukewarm spray. It felt good to let the water run over me, rinsing any lingering sweat and chlorine from my hair and body. Reminding myself of the joint structure of the shower and the rest of the bathroom floor, I quickly ran the small bar of soap all over me, rinsed off the suds, and shut the water off. Opening the curtain, I was pleased to see I had kept the flooding to a minimum. Still, it was annoying to brush my teeth while standing in a puddle, but I figured it was better to take care of everything I needed to in the bathroom all at once rather than tracking water back and forth into the rest of the room.

Back in the bedroom, I dried off and got dressed. I didn't know how long I'd be out on the town, so I put on a long-sleeved shirt just in case. I considered my messenger bag for a moment but decided to leave it and slipped my Moleskine and pen in my back pocket. Grabbing my key, I locked the door and made my way downstairs.

A few dim lights had been turned on in the lobby, and a couple of guests sat at one of the tables talking, but the place still didn't seem overly inviting. Out on the street, people sat at tables scattered in front of the hotels, buried deep in various conversations over *aperitivi*. A Negroni sounded perfect, but I needed food first. After taking a deep breath of the evening air, I turned left and walked toward the more crowded streets of Montecatini Terme to look for something to eat.

It turns out, when you're dining alone in an unfamiliar place with nothing specific in mind, it can be *very* difficult to decide on a place to eat. Every street I navigated had a handful of restaurants, but each one didn't appeal to me for one reason or another: *too busy—I don't want to be the only one in there eating alone*; *too empty—can I trust the food there?*; *too expensive—I'd like to eat for the rest of my trip, too*; *no gnocchi on the menu—enough said*.

It felt like I'd gone up and down every street in town, though it was probably only three or four blocks' worth, but I'd passed too many restaurants not to have found something to eat. I hadn't even taken in much of what I passed in the town because I had one focus. It was nearly eight o'clock, and I was getting hungrier and grumpier by the minute. Finally, the executive decision was made that the next place I found would be my restaurant for the night, no matter the menu, no matter the crowd or lack thereof. I was too hungry to care anymore.

Down a smaller side street, I saw the glowing opening of a

trattoria. It didn't look like anything special, but it was open, and there were a few available tables, so I went inside. The squat, old hostess gave me a rather pitiful look when I told her I needed a table for one, which I returned with my politest *Yes, I'm aware* face, but she grabbed a menu and seated me anyway. My table was against the wall, bordered on the other side by a white-haired English couple. The waitress poured me a glass of water from an old wine bottle, placed the bottle in front of me, and stood at the edge of the table, staring, waiting for my order.

I just sat down, I thought. "*Cinque minuti, per favore,*" I said. With a heavy sigh, she turned and walked away. She returned twenty minutes later to take my order.

"I'll have the gnocchi, *per favore.*" I handed her the menu, which she barely took before turning around and walking away again.

"Not the most service-oriented here, are they?"

"Hmm?" Then, I realized it was the old man next to me who had spoken. He was looking down his nose through his glasses at me with an amused look on his face. "Oh, sorry. No, they aren't. And I come from food service, so I notice that much more." I attempted to lighten my mood a little to be more polite.

"Ah, yes, that'll do it. Here, take our bread. Your food won't be here for another half hour." He handed the basket of sliced Italian bread over to me.

"Are you sure?"

"Oh, we've had plenty, dear," chimed in the man's wife. "And we already have our food. Take it, please."

"Well, thank you. I really appreciate that. I *am* hungry. Haven't eaten all day since leaving Sorrento, and I've been walking around trying to find a place to eat for over an hour." I poured some olive oil and balsamic vinegar onto a small saucer and dipped a piece of bread in it before taking a bite. "God, that's good."

The couple chuckled at my ravenousness and continued with their meal.

Realizing how rapidly I was stuffing my face, I put the third piece of bread down and took a drink of water.

I thought the man had to have been exaggerating that my food would take thirty minutes to come out, and I was right; it took twenty-eight minutes. The place was busy, but when I'd come in, nearly everyone seated had food in front of them already, so the wait was inexplicable. The server squinted suspiciously at me as she placed my plate in front of me, noticing the breadbasket that hadn't been there before.

"Excuse me?" The old man gestured to the server. "Could we please have some coffee with room for cream?"

"*Sí.*" The server walked away, presumably to bring coffee.

"Well, my dear, we should have that just in time to start our morning tomorrow," said the old man to his wife with a chortle, winking at me as he finished his glass of red wine.

I laughed, impressed that a man who I guessed to be in his early eighties still had such quick wit. I could tell his wife was impressed by it, too, by the rosiness that overtook her face as she smiled back at him. "Where are you folks from?"

"Surrey, but we've been on holiday for a couple of months now. We've just come from visiting friends in Provence."

"That sounds like a nice trip. Where to next?"

"Greece. In all our years of traveling, we've never quite made it there, so we figured now was as good a time as any."

I smiled as the couple continued to talk about the other places they'd gone in their lives, all over the world. I admired that they were seemingly in such good health that they could continue to travel as they pleased, that they still satiated their hunger for experiencing new things.

They eventually asked what I was doing there all alone, so I talked simply about my writing and the need to get away from things at home. I left out the darker pieces of my story, and their genuine interest in what I had to say found a way of bringing some peace to my mind.

I took a few minutes to eat more of my gnocchi while the couple drank their coffee, which had only taken a few minutes to arrive. The dumplings were nothing to write home about, but they satisfied the hunger that had built over the last part of the day.

"Oops!" The man pulled a pocket watch from his vest and spoke directly to his wife. "We're late." Then, to me, "I do apologize, but we must be going. We're meeting some friends for a nightcap in the hotel bar. It was a pleasure talking with you. Keep up your writing. You'll want to remember everything about this trip, and remembering doesn't always come as easily when you get to be our age." He tapped his temple and smiled.

I smiled back at them. "Thank you so much. I've enjoyed our conversation, too. It made dinner much less lonely. I hope you enjoy Greece." I shook the man's hand, and he placed three twenty-euro notes on the table, put on his tweed jacket, and followed his wife out the door.

I ate the last bite of gnocchi from my plate and followed his lead, placing a bill under my glass that I knew would cover my check. It would likely be another fifteen-minute wait if I paid with my debit card.

Despite the mediocre food and terrible service, my mission was accomplished: I was full, and even more tired than I had been post-swim. Knowing I had another full day in town killed any guilt I might have felt for not exploring more that night, so I decided to head back to the hotel. The walk back took longer than I would have liked, simply because I hadn't paid attention to how I got to the restaurant, and I didn't remember any of the street names except for the one my hotel was on. Therefore, I was forced to seek out landmarks I might recognize and work backward from there. Around 10:30, I walked through the dark lobby of the Corallo toward the elevator in the back, wiping my exhausted eyes, ready to fall into bed.

"*Mi scusa!* Mr. Wise!"

I stopped and looked back to see the man who had checked me in poking his head around the corner of the small office behind the front desk.

"Your other guest is here. She arrived about an hour ago. I hope it's okay, I gave her a key. And may I say, *bravo*, sir. Good for you."

"Huh? What other—?" I racked my tired brain, trying to figure out who would have been there looking for me. None of my friends at home would have spontaneously made the trip, and certainly none that would elicit a "*bravo*" from the man at the desk. *Unless...*

"Thank you. I appreciate it," I told the man, turning around and hurrying to the elevator. I didn't want to get my hopes up, but I couldn't think of any other possibility at that point.

Fumbling with my key in a combination of fatigue and nerves, I unlocked the door to my room and slowly pushed it open. Before I could even see into the rest of the room, the light scent of a familiar perfume in the air confirmed my suspicions. One of the table lamps was on, casting a dim glow over the bed and the gorgeous woman asleep in it, wearing nothing but lacy, black underwear and a white tank top. A half-drunk glass of red wine sat on the nightstand nearest her, and the TV showed a bad American comedy dubbed in Italian.

Shocked and elated that she had decided to make the trip, I brushed my teeth, stripped down to my boxers, turned off the TV, and climbed into bed next to Emily before turning off the light. I positioned myself behind her in big-spoon position, wrapped my arm around her, and kissed her on the shoulder.

Despite my intention not to wake her, Emily stirred slightly and turned her head toward me with a sleepy smile on her face. "Mmm... Hi... I wondered when you'd get here." She grabbed my hand with her tiny hand, kissed it, and held it close to her chest. "I wanted to surprise you."

I laughed. "Well, I'm surprised, and I'm glad you did." Emily's exhaustion seemed to match mine, so I didn't make any attempts to talk more or to get too amorous; there would be all day tomorrow for that. I simply kissed her on the cheek and twice more on the shoulder before we both settled our heads down to sleep.

Chapter 27

Birds chirping in cool, Italian morning air and the lingering scent and warmth of a beautiful woman made for the most incredible start to the next day. I felt like the happiest man alive when I woke up to the sputter of the shower starting, followed by a soft, familiar hum. On the street below, a few people were getting an early start to their day with coffee outside the hotels. I tossed my underwear next to my luggage in the bedroom and stepped into the shower behind Emily, pulled her close to me, and kissed her on the neck and shoulder.

She giggled. "Oops! I didn't mean to wake you. I was going to go bring back breakfast. I saw a cute little café around the corner on my way here."

I kissed her again. "We'll go together."

"That will be nice," she said as she turned and wrapped her arms around my neck.

I drew her closer, my hands on her lower back, feeling the small dimples at the base of her spine. Her tan skin was unbelievably soft. Add that to her glowing smile, penetrating gaze, and rousing scent, and I was a man with no chance, powerless to resist her.

We kissed heavily under the spray for a long while before deciding that we were hungry. Actually, *I* may have made the suggestion to go down to breakfast while it was still cooler outside; or maybe my subconscious made the decision. *What's my problem? What's stopping me right now?* I figured it was probably because I didn't want to rush things and run the risk of ruining things too early, or at all.

We took turns lathering each other up with soap and rinsing off before getting ready for the day. While Emily dried her hair, I wrote a few things down in my Moleskine—something about how much better it is to wake up with someone and know you have the entire day with them ahead of you. She came out wrapped in her towel, slipped on a pair of lacy, white panties, and pulled a beautiful, pale-blue sundress over her head. "Are you ready?"

"Mmhmm." I replaced my pen in the notebook and put it in the back pocket of my khakis before standing and pulling her into me for another kiss. "You look so damn sexy." Her face glowed as she took my hand and led me out of the room and down the hallway to the elevator.

We held hands and deeply breathed the cool air as we walked a few blocks south toward the café she had seen the day before. Our joint arms swung back and forth, and we looked at each other with quiet smiles. I couldn't remember the last time I'd felt so joyful, so happy to be alive. I felt unbelievably lucky to be spending that time with her, and the thought of continuing it even when we returned to our homes, only two hours from each other, made me that much happier.

"Here it is!" Emily pointed excitedly ahead at a casual-looking, robin egg-blue café that took up the entire street corner in front of us. A few rows of tables and chairs sat out front, and a white awning was rolled up against the building.

It didn't look like a bad place, but it looked like pretty much every other café I'd seen in town, so I wasn't quite sure what had drawn Emily to it. But then I read the sign above the door.

"*L'uovo o la gallina.*' Ah," I said, chuckling after I had quickly translated from my limited Italian vocabulary and recognized the joke. "The egg or the chicken? Nice."

"I thought it was cute," said Emily happily. "Come on!"

I love you. No, don't say that. Stop it, Michael. I smiled and followed Emily inside.

There was a decent crowd inside and out, but we were able to get seated at a table in the far corner of the patio, right along the sidewalk. We ordered mimosas and looked over the menu for a few minutes before both deciding on Eggs Benedict. The waiter brought out a bottle of champagne, a carafe of orange juice, and two glass flutes and proceeded to make our drinks for us. To our delight, he left the bottle and the carafe for our future utility.

"Emily, I'm really glad you came, but I feel bad that you left your friends to meet me. I don't want to get in the way of your trip."

She laughed. "Don't worry. I'm pretty sure they don't even care. They were so excited about taking gondola rides, and they could tell I missed you. They actually encouraged me to come down here, so I switched my ticket, and here I am. Jake might be a little upset, but whatever."

So he does *have a thing for her,* I thought. Although Jake had eventually grown friendly toward me in the short time we'd known each other, I still always got the feeling that my and Emily's flirtation bugged him, even if it wasn't blatant.

"I told them I'd meet up with them in Florence tomorrow. I just preferred to see you over Venice. Something about the idea of the city sinking kind of scares me, anyway. I don't want to be there for that!"

Her sense of humor charmed me even more. There was a twinkle in her eye that told me she had no actual fear of the city sinking. It felt nice to be wanted that way.

Emily took a sip of her mimosa. "Yummy! So, what have you been up to since you've been here?"

"Honestly, I was really exhausted after the train trip yesterday, so I went for a quick swim and hung out by the pool for a while. Then, I took a long nap and went and got dinner. I figured I have all day today to see the sights. And now I get to see them with you." I smiled at her and drank some of my own drink.

"Whoever came up with the mimosa is a genius," I said. "Coffee is barely a better way to start the day."

"I know! Can we go for a swim later, when it's warmer?"

"Of course. I think it's supposed to be another really hot day, so that will be good."

Finally, our food came out. The Eggs Benedict were made with slices of mozzarella, tomato, and a basil Hollandaise sauce over thin slices of prosciutto. Thick cuts from a loaf of Italian herb bread were used as the base instead of the usual English muffin.

"This is delicious! The basil is a nice touch."

I licked some of the sauce from my lower lip. "It is. I love it."

We were equally hungry and devoured our meals in no time, regularly refilling our mimosas in the process. But, as with a hamburger on a too-large bun, we had a good portion of our bread left with no topping, and an excess of sauce was left on our plates.

"*Fare la scarpetta*," I told Emily with a smile.

"Huh?" She looked from her plate to me, confused.

"*Fare la scarpetta*. It means 'make the little shoe.'"

I smiled at the increased confusion on her face. "It's when you use your bread to mop up the rest of your sauce." I glanced around at the other diners and then added, "It's not something you'd do at a fancy place, but I think we'll be alright here." Taking what was left of the bread, I pushed it around on my plate, collecting as much of the basil

Hollandaise as I could before taking a bite.

Emily smiled. "Scarpetta. I like that." She followed my lead, unknowingly leaving a spot of sauce on the corner of her mouth.

I leaned across the table, ran my fingers through her hair, kissed the sauce off before kissing her lips. "Mmm. It tastes even better on you," I joked.

"Nuh-uhhh. You're funny. Hey!" She reached across and playfully shoved my shoulder. "Have you written anything?"

"I've made a few notes about the trip. Not a whole lot, but enough to feel decent about."

"Can I read them?"

Her request caught me off guard. No one besides Ben, Marcus, and, more recently, Brian had asked to read my writing in a long time. And these were just notes, not even anything substantial. I wasn't about to tell Emily no, though, so I handed her my Moleskine, open to the page I'd started on the flight over. There wasn't anything incriminating that I could think of, so there was no harm in her reading it.

I sat back and drank my mimosa, watching her eyes scroll across the pages, giggling at funny things, intently rereading phrases or sentences that she liked, and smiling up at me when she read things that she could tell were about her. As a writer, it's nice to see people respond positively to your work, or to even show interest in it in the first place. As a *nobody* writer, it's either too easy or too difficult to believe anyone should be interested at all. Of course, you write for yourself first—if you're doing it right—but you also likely hope to write something that will impact at least one person in one way or another.

When Emily had finished reading my most recent notes, she closed the notebook and handed it back to me. "I *love* your writing! Even though they're mostly just notes, they're so good, so...relatable."

"Thank you," I said, sliding the notebook into my back pocket. "I'm glad to hear you say that."

"I want more," she said with an enticing grin.

I laughed. "More, huh? You'll have to give me a little time. I'm sure there will be more by this evening."

"I hope so."

"Are you ready to go?"

"Yes. Let's explore!"

"Sounds good to me. I don't know of much in this town besides the hilltop and this park near my hotel." I finished my mimosa, stood a little too fast, and placed some bills on the table to cover the check the waiter had left on the table.

As Emily stood up, she grabbed my arm and giggled as she straightened herself out and found her balance. "That was a lot of mimosa," she said.

We stopped at a small market around the corner and bought two big bottles of water to make peace with all the champagne we'd had and began our self-guided tour of Montecatini Terme.

As it's not one of the Italian towns that pops up in everyday conversation, Montecatini was, to me, a labyrinth of the unknown just waiting to be discovered. The thought of exploring a new Italian town with Emily, and without the commotion of world-renowned tourist traps at every turn, excited me. My friends and I had wandered around a little on my previous trip, but it had been several years, and we didn't have a lot of time then, so this would be like experiencing the town for the first time.

We spent the middle part of the day winding through the maze of characteristically Italian streets, past boutique hotels, trattorias, and cafés. There wasn't a place we didn't talk about coming back to, even though we knew our time was limited. The fact that we talked about doing anything in the future made me happy, even if it was just the mimosas inspiring the words. We found a public square, *Piazza del Popolo*, with a bell tower and a fountain, a church and several hotels around its edges. It wasn't nearly as magnificent as that by the same name in Rome, but it was still a gem within the maze, and we were glad to have found it. We came across a beautiful, two-story carousel capped with a green and white-striped canopy. The structure was covered in gold decorations, and the horses were some of the most colorful I'd ever seen. We stopped for a few minutes and watched families rotate their laughing children on and off the ride as the horses bounded up and down to the music, which sounded like John Philip Sousa with an Italian twist.

I wiped a bead of sweat from my forehead with the back of my hand. The heat of the day had suddenly come out swinging. "I think we're near the park," I said. "I see a gelato place down there. Want to get some and go find some shade?"

"That sounds nice. Let's go!" Emily took my hand, and we walked a couple of blocks farther down the street, bought a scoop each of stracciatella and butter pecan gelato, and made our way a few blocks over to *Parco delle Terme*. We followed one of the arterials through the park and found a lush space on the grass beneath one of many high-trunked trees that provided shade over much of the grounds. Emily sat between my legs and leaned against me while we finished our gelato and enjoyed the slightly cooler air. When the ice cream was gone, I lay back on the cold grass, and she followed suit, nestling her head in the crook of my shoulder.

After lying beneath the tall trees for a while, listening to the sounds of other people also enjoying the warm day, we decided to go back to the hotel for a swim and a nap. The heat of the day made us grateful that it was a short walk. Up in the room, we changed into our swimsuits and went to the roof.

"Oh, my God! This view is beautiful!" Emily ran to the railing and looked over the rooftops. "Is that where we're going?" She pointed at the nearby hill, where the bell tower of the *Chiesa di San Pietro* stood high above the other rooftops at the north end.

"Yep, but let's wait until later. It's a great place to watch the sunset. And there are some neat little restaurants where we can have dinner."

"I bet! Okay, I can't wait." Emily dropped her towel on one of the lounge chairs, dove smartly into the water with barely a splash, and swam underwater toward the other end of the pool.

I wished I could dive that smoothly, but it had never been my strength. To save my pride, I quickly threw myself headfirst into the water, arms outstretched, hoping to hit the water before Emily had resurfaced. *Success.* Swimming to the end after her, I came up for air right in front of where she had propped herself up on the edge with her elbows.

As I blindly wiped the water from my eyes, I felt Emily's hand tug at the front of the waistband of my shorts and pull me to her. Seconds later, her cool lips met mine, her small hand pulling my head close to hers.

Supporting myself with my hands on the pool's edge on either side of her, I pressed my body against hers as we kissed. The heat in the air was nothing to the heat between us; even the cooling water had no chance. We kissed with force, not angrily but out of desire and longing. Every little thing we might have thought or felt about each other since meeting in Sant'Agnello seemed to come together into one powerful eruption. Our chests heaved against each other, our breathing grew heavier, and our hands explored—

"Honey, I think the pool is out here!"

"Son of a bitch…" I said under my breath before whipping my head toward the poorly timed Midwestern voice, my chest still rising and falling against Emily's.

A middle-aged couple emerged through the door. Gobs of sunscreen visibly covered the man's nose and balding head, and the woman wore a large, straw sunhat that would look out of place even in the most fashion-conscious of company. Both were overweight and wore swimsuits that appeared a size too small. They placed their towels and sunscreen on the nearest chairs and looked around.

"Hello there!" The man waved in a naturally awkward manner when he saw us.

"How's it going?" I asked briefly.

"Oh, fantastic! It's just beautiful out here! We finally got some time away from our church group to relax a little bit. We've seen so much the past few days, you know, it's just time for some rejuvenation. God does some amazing things, but it sure takes a lot out of you, you know?"

"Right." I couldn't tell if the man *knew* he was interrupting or if he was just truly oblivious as to what he and his wife had walked in on, but I was irritated either way. "You came to the right place. The water is great."

"Where the *fuck* did they come from?" Emily whispered. "I haven't seen any sign of a goddamn church group at the hotel."

"I have no idea," I whispered back.

"It looks so inviting," said the man's wife, taking off her hat and dipping a toe in the water. "Ooh! Donald, it's just right!"

"Last one in's a rotten egg!" Donald kicked off his sandals and trotted past his wife, jumping out over the pool. "Cannonball!"

SPLASH!

The surface of the water undulated as much as could be expected after receiving a man of Donald's size, rolling out of the pool and across the floor.

"Oh, Donnie, you're too much!"

"C'mon in, Marie, the water's great!"

Donnie and Marie? Are you fucking kidding me?

Emily stifled a snort and caught my eye, biting her lip to keep from laughing.

As I wiped away the water that Donald had splashed in my face, I immediately reclosed my eyes as I saw Marie follow his lead, holding her nose as she created a slightly smaller splash that still sprayed me.

As the happy couple *ooh*ed and *ahh*ed at how great the water felt on such a hot day, Emily and I looked at each other, rolled our eyes, and got out of the pool, flopping down on two adjacent lounge chairs. As Donnie and Marie giggled and splashed around in the pool, we played with each other's hands, our eyes closed as we basked in the hot sun. After only a few minutes, Emily squeezed my hand pointedly. I opened my eyes and, after adjusting to the bright light, gave her a quizzical look.

I want you, she mouthed. Her eyes narrowed seductively, backing up every bit of that claim. She softly bit her lower lip.

Fuck this. I jumped up from my chair, grabbed both our towels and Emily's hand and pulled her up from the chair. We walked quickly toward the elevator.

"Bye!"

"See ya, Donnie," I said without a backward glance.

The second the hotel room door was closed, our swimsuits were on the floor. Emily jumped up and wrapped her legs around my waist and her arms around my neck. We kissed with such fervor, it was a miracle the lamps, pictures, and furniture remained unscathed.

We fell onto the bed, and I held her hands against the pillow next to her head, slowly kissing from her neck down to her belly button, all the while her hands massaging my head as she moaned softly. Moving back upward, I kissed her once more on the lips before pulling away for a second. Without a word, I looked into her beautiful, deep-blue eyes and waited for a word, a nod, or some other sign that I wasn't crazy, that this was actually happening.

"I want you," she whispered.

That was all I needed to hear.

Chapter 28

My eyes flickered open from a deep sleep that I didn't even realize I'd entered. My arms were wrapped tightly around Emily, our naked bodies pressed together with her back to me. The day had warmed the room significantly, and we were practically stuck together. Her skin smelled of the sun with hints of sweat and chlorine, an inexplicably appealing potpourri. I kissed her bare shoulder a couple of times and bit it playfully.

Slowly, she stirred. "Mmm... More?" She wiggled against me.

"How can I say no to that?" I turned her so she was facing me, and we started kissing again.

Afterward, as she lay with her head on my chest as it rose and fell, her fingers tracing indeterminable shapes on my stomach, I noticed through the window that the sun was much lower than it had been when we were in the pool.

"How long did we sleep?" I asked as I looked at my watch on the nightstand. "It's seven. We were out for hours."

"You wore me out. That was fun." Emily turned her head so that her chin rested on my chest and she could look at me.

Damn, I love her smile. I love her eyes. Everything. I tipped my head forward and kissed her on the forehead. "Yeah, it was. Both times."

"Mmhmm." She kissed my chest before resting her head again.

"Do you still want to see Montecatini Alto?"

"Yes! Let's get ready!"

Laughing, I followed Emily into the bathroom where we rinsed off under the cool water of the shower.

We walked out into the balmy Tuscan evening around eight o'clock – she in a flowy, white sundress that fell just below her knees and I in a white button-down and khaki pants.

"I like that shirt on you," she said as I took her hand in mine and led her in the direction of the funicular.

"Thank you. That dress looks beautiful on you, too."

We kissed as our clasped hands swung between us. We turned onto one of the roads leading to the park and found the carousel from earlier, all lit up, the two gilded levels of horses sparkling among the lights.

"It's *so* pretty!" Emily said.

After watching it go around for a couple of minutes, we continued down *Viale Giuseppe Verdi* where we could see the columned façade of the *Terme Tettucio*—one of the town's more stately and better-known spas—lit up spectacularly with several ground-mounted spotlights. The sidewalk took us past a rainbow row of Ferraris and Maseratis spanning generations, parked in front of the spa. Rich-looking men and women in tuxedos and gowns walked up and down the row, peering in the windows and snapping pictures in front of the cars before going through the front gates into an enclosed courtyard.

"I wouldn't mind being a valet there tonight," I said as my gaze swept across the shiny row of luxury and speed.

"You boys and your cars." Emily laughed. "But then you wouldn't be going up *there* with me."

"Good point." I squeezed her hand, and we continued past the spa.

Up ahead was the building that housed the ticket office and the end of the funicular track. I paid for two roundtrip tickets, and we sat on a bench to wait.

A small crowd had gathered by the time the car reached the station, more than would fit inside the small vehicle, so I made sure we were as near the entry gate as we could get so that we would be able to go up right away. Still, we had to wait nearly fifteen minutes to board after the car emptied out while the operator paced outside the ticket office. When he finally beckoned us forward, I picked a bench near the back of the car so we would have a good view of the valley through the windows as we ascended. Luckily, they didn't try to pack the car as tightly as possible, and we had the bench to ourselves.

Once all the doors had been locked from the outside, the operator got into the booth at the front of the car and we began our slow ascent to Montecatini Alto. It was a relaxing ride; the only sounds were the quieted passenger voices and the wheels squeaking on the track below us. The funicular traveled through a gauntlet of trees and bushes, eventually emerging to a 180-degree view of the Tuscan hills and towns around us. It was nothing short of breathtaking.

Tuscany rolled outward from where we sat, clusters of buildings situated between vineyards and hills and groves of trees. A warm breeze blew through the small windows on either side of us, carrying with it the sweet scent of the trees, their leaves hot from the day's sun. I closed my eyes and breathed it in. Emily tilted her head onto my shoulder and moved it around until she was comfortable.

At the top, the track attendant unlocked the doors, and we exited the car and left the station. Up a short set of steps, we followed the road to a low, stone wall that ran along the sidewalk. Stone benches were spaced out under the trees that lined the road. Couples and families and the occasional loner had started to gather along the wall to watch the sun go down, so I took Emily's hand and hurried over to the last free bench where we settled and got as comfortable as is possible on an old, stone seat. Emily burrowed herself against me and I wrapped my arm around her shoulders.

The sun cast the most vivid spread of colors across the sky. The burning orange that immediately surrounded the low-hanging star turned gradually into a hot pink, a combination that made what blue remained above seem bluer than any sky I'd ever seen. The range of colors glowed across the buildings and trees of the hilltop and the town below. The surrounding hills in the distance turned a deep, shadowy purple, silently watching over everything in the middle.

As those around us chatted quietly amongst themselves, taking pictures, *ooh*ing and *ahh*ing, Emily and I sat in happy silence, our hands clasped and resting in her lap. She had kicked off her sandals and began massaging the tops of my feet with hers. She let out a small gasp when the sun hit just behind the top of the hill next to Montecatini Alto and cast penetrating rays in every direction through the few wispy clouds that hung in the sky. As it set lower, the colors softened, a soothing, pastel end to an exhilarating day. A reassurance from the sun that said, *Don't worry, I'll be back tomorrow.* The blue sky high above grew darker and spread closer to the horizon as it tucked the sun into the earth. Stars made their appearance across the sky one at a time, twinkling at us in the twilight. It was at this point that the spectators gradually went their separate ways.

"That was really pretty," Emily said quietly, readjusting her head on my shoulder.

"Mm..." I couldn't say much more than that. Even as a writer—or maybe *especially* as a writer—the right words sometimes don't seem to exist to do a moment the proper justice. I simply squeezed her shoulder and held her close.

A few short minutes passed, and we were left alone by the low wall.

"You ready for dinner?"

"Starving!"

Her honesty made me laugh; her enthusiasm for food was another quality I found endearing. "Okay, let's go. I don't really know any of the restaurants here, so yell if something stands out."

"I will." This time, Emily was up first, putting her sandals back on and grabbing my hand to take me to find food. While I knew exactly how to get to the town's central piazza where there were at least three or four options, I let her lead the way. I enjoyed watching her virgin curiosity and excitement of seeing something for the first time, especially something like Montecatini Alto.

The road inclined just enough to feel like we were getting some good exercise as we strolled past the tiny cars parked along the narrow spaces between buildings. Shrubs hung deliberately off the walls and down the sides of houses, giving a neatly overgrown appearance to the neighborhood. Most of the buildings were stone and earth tones, rather than the pastel yellows and pinks and blues I'd seen along the coast. The windows all had shutters, most of which were open to the warm evening air.

Somewhere within the warren of alleys and side streets, a man sang loudly in a wonderful baritone. I imagined him perched in an open window with one leg dangling, inspired by the sunset that had just taken place, bellowing for all to hear, but intended purely for his own enjoyment. I guessed he felt a great sense of pride when his neighbors commended him for his talent but remained humble and continued to sing only for himself.

"That's so haunting," Emily said as she looked up around us in search of the source. "It's beautiful."

"I wonder if he has an accordion. He could walk around the town square past all the restaurants and serenade everyone."

Emily laughed. "That would be fun."

The streets eventually opened into the *Piazza Giuseppe Giusti*, lined on three sides with several different restaurants, all with the usual slew of chairs and umbrellas out front. At one end stood a statue of a woman holding a torch and laurels, erected in honor of the Italians who served and died in World War I.

"Let's go to that one!" Emily pointed at one of the restaurants in the middle of the row that was less crowded than the others, with plenty of seats available at the tables on the piazza.

A waiter seated us, took our orders, and delivered our drinks in a matter of minutes. We held hands and sipped our cold aperitifs and watched people walk past while we waited for our food to arrive. When it did, we ate quickly and ordered gelato to go.

We walked off our dinner and enjoyed the gelato on a scenic route back to the funicular station, which included a stop at the top of the hill by the church that afforded us an incredible view of Montecatini Terme. The valley beyond was now shrouded in the blanket of night. Lights from the town and houses scattered in the less populated areas shone brightly against the dark nooks of the landscape like streams of lava trickling through the hills. The road away from the church took us around the back side of the hill, where the valley was much darker, though still scattered with distant lights. As we came back around on the last stretch toward the station, a building much more modern than anything else we'd seen on the hilltop loomed above the road opposite the slope down to Montecatini Terme. Odder than the apparent youth of the structure relative to everything around it was the fact that it was completely devoid of light. No landscape lights, flood lights, or window lights illuminated any part of the building, and, through the darkness, many of the windows appeared to be broken or burned out. Considering that the building took up the better part of that section of the hillside, the darkness it cast over the bend in the road made it even more ominous. It seemed to have been abandoned before construction was even finished, although the creepy air it gave off left me with the distinct impression that someone might be watching from one of the dark windows.

"Let's go," I said, squeezing Emily's hand and moving to head down the road toward the funicular station. "That place is freaking me out." I threw in half a laugh to lighten my dead-serious tone.

"Me too. It's kinda creepy," she said with a knowing smile.

By the time the funicular reached the bottom of the hill, Emily and I both were the sort of quiet one becomes when there is no energy left, no second wind to be had. It had been a long, hot day and we'd done a lot of walking around town; even the nap we'd taken earlier couldn't ward off the sleepiness. We took the quickest route that we knew back to the hotel, our pace sluggish, our moods relaxed and happy. Emily rested her head on my shoulder most of the way.

In the elevator at the hotel, she wrapped her arms around my stomach and leaned against me with her sleepy head on my chest, and I kissed the top of her head, my nose lingering in her hair as I wrapped my arms around her and held her.

Back in the room, we stripped down to our underwear, brushed our teeth, and climbed into the bed facing each other, pulling only the top sheet over us. Propped up on one elbow, I tucked a strand of hair behind her ear and wrapped my arm around her, tracing random shapes lightly on her back and shoulders with my fingertips. Without realizing I was doing it at first, I found myself softly humming the song I'd heard her hum the first night she had been in my room back in Sant'Agnello, what pieces of it I could remember, anyway.

Emily's eyes had closed as she dozed off, but a small smile appeared on her face as she heard what I was humming. She ran her fingers up and down my chest and stomach.

I returned her smile, kissed her on the forehead, and slowly faded out my humming. I was still curious what song it was, but I didn't want to keep her awake when she was so tired, so I let the mystery remain. I closed my eyes to attempt sleep myself, continuing to run my fingers gently across her back and trying to avoid the thought of saying goodbye to her tomorrow. I must have fallen asleep at some point, because, a while later, I was stirred from some depth of unconsciousness by Emily's soft lips brushing against mine.

"Michael?" she whispered.

I slowly blinked my eyes open to find hers aimed downward in uncertainty. "Hmm?"

"When does your train leave tomorrow?"

"Not until around ten. Why?"

"Oh. Mine leaves at seven-thirty."

"I'll walk you to the station in the morning."

"I'd like that." She kissed me again and closed her eyes.

Even though we'd meet up in Rome, I didn't want to part ways with Emily at all. Such a connection had formed between us over the few days we'd known each other that it didn't feel right to be apart again so soon. The way she had moved closer to me after she closed her eyes told me she felt the same way. That was a nice feeling.

Chapter 29

I'd set the alarm on the nightstand to go off at six-thirty the next morning, but when its obnoxious buzz jolted me from my sleep, it said eight o'clock.

"What the hell!" Then, I realized that I was alone in the bed. "Emily?" Nothing. She wasn't in the bathroom, and her bag was gone. A note was folded on top of my Moleskine on the desk across from the bed. *Again?*

> *Good morning Michael,*
>
> *I'm sorry I left again. It's just so hard to say goodbye, even when I know I'll see you again soon. I thought you could use the extra sleep anyway. I've loved the time we've spent together so far, and I can't wait to see you again in Rome. Text me when you're on the train and headed there. I'll be thinking about you.*
>
> *XOXO - Emily*

As with her last note, a small heart dotted her "i", and her perfume wafted from the piece of paper.

Somehow, I wasn't angry that she'd left that way again. I understood completely, and she was right: I *did* appreciate the extra sleep. Besides, I knew we'd meet up in Rome in just a couple of days. Still, I wished I'd have been able to kiss her one more time before then.

Rather than lying around and putting off packing my things until the very last minute as was my norm, I got up and showered and readied myself for the day's trip as quickly as possible. I was ready to get to Rome and, eventually, to see Emily again.

Before lugging my bags out of the room, I ran up to the roof to say good morning to the rooftops of the town and goodbye to the view. A low, thin layer of mist hung over the buildings, reminding me of the view of Sorrento as our bus took us through the hills toward Positano. If I had been going home from Montecatini, it might have been a more melancholy goodbye, but I knew what lay ahead for me in Rome, and I couldn't wait to experience its majesty all over again. I checked my room thoroughly before locking it behind me, bags in hand, and heading downstairs to check out. It was quick and simple, which I appreciated that morning.

"Did you enjoy your stay, sir?"

"Very much so, *si. Grazie mille.* And thank you for making sure my friend found me. It was good to see her."

The man behind the desk gave me a knowing smile. "*Prego.* Here is your final bill; it has all been charged to your credit card. Enjoy the rest of your trip, and thank you for staying with us."

"I'll be back someday, that's for sure. Thanks again." I folded the computer printout in thirds, slipped it into my messenger bag, and headed out the door toward the train station.

On the way, I figured I should grab something to eat so that I wasn't traveling on an empty stomach. I found a corner market a couple of blocks from the station and bought a breakfast sandwich of prosciutto and Havarti on a long Italian bread roll, a bottle of orange juice, and a cup of fresh fruit. I added the paper bag of breakfast to my bag and continued to the train station. I wanted to get there and make sure everything was in order before taking time to eat.

The older man at the ticket counter looked at my boarding pass, then at his watch and his computer, handed the pass back to me, and nodded. *Yes, sir, your train is on time. We have our shit together here; don't doubt us so.* I imagined that's what he would have said, anyway, if he had any sort of inclination toward customer service. I had even asked him in Italian, trying to garner a little mutual respect: *"Il treno è in orario?"* But no. He didn't feel like giving more than a nod, and I wouldn't let that ruin my day.

I thanked the man and found a bench near where my train was to pull into the station. Taking advantage of the spare time, I devoured the sandwich, guzzled the orange juice, and then took my time with the fruit cup.

Lo and behold, the train arrived *early*, and boarding was quick and not delayed until the last minute. I found the seat listed on my boarding pass near the end of the car and placed my bag in the seat next to it, hoping the train wasn't completely booked and that I would be able to enjoy the trip in solitude. Naturally, the railroad employee who was checking tickets asked me to move my bag as he walked by, but when the train started moving out of the station, the seat was still empty. A grin spread across my face, which I quickly stifled to avoid odd looks from nearby passengers. I pulled out my cell phone and texted Emily to let her know I was on the train and ready to go, watching the screen for several minutes in hopes of a quick reply. When none came, I slipped the phone back in my pocket and pulled out my notebook to write some more about my time in Montecatini. I hit a good zone, filling page after page, glancing up occasionally to watch the Tuscan countryside roll by.

My day of good luck had not yet come to an end by the time I arrived at the Termini Station in Rome. The train had reached Florence in just under an hour, departed that station right on time, and arrived in Rome *before* it was supposed to. I hoped it was a sign that things were going to continue going well for the rest of the trip.

I gathered my things from the seat and the overhead storage cupboard and followed my fellow passengers off the train into Rome's central station. The throng moved along the platform to the main part of the station with its shops and restaurants, many joining up with friends ànd family who were there to meet them. I continued through the station and onto *Via Marsala*, one of two main roads that flank the station. My hostel was a five-minute walk from Termini.

Situated around the corner from the station, my accommodations certainly weren't on the same level as Seven Hostel, but they would do for a few days. My room was four floors up and had a tall window that opened to a view of the street below. If I leaned out just slightly over the rickety, wrought-iron railing, I could see across a huge slice of Rome, a view dotted with a few of the hundreds of church rotundas in the city. In the distance, the snow-white *Monumento Nazionale a Vittorio Emanuele II* stood out above the sea of terra cotta roofs. I took a few minutes to settle in, unpacked a few of my clothes so they could air out, and left the room with my messenger bag fully loaded with a Moleskine and pen, *The Sun Also Rises,* and a map of Rome—just in case. I left the window open so the air could refresh the room while I was out, hoping that Rome's pigeons wouldn't take it as an invitation.

I hit the streets heading west toward *Piazza della Repubblica*, a large, semi-circular crossroads on the doorstep of the Basilica of St. Mary of the Angels and the Martyrs, housed within the ruins of the Baths of Diocletian. Two tall, bronze doors welcomed me to the church, each decorated with a haunting sculpture: to the left, a naked male body with a cross imprinted deeply in his torso, and to the right, an angel with broken wings flying above a crouching woman. The figures resembled ghosts passing through the doors. I debated going inside but decided that I would rather spend the day making my way around the city before choosing which places I wanted to delve into further.

I crossed the street to look at the Fountain of the Naiads in the center of the piazza. Streams of water arc from a ring of spouts toward a statue of Glaucus, the fisherman-turned-god of Greek mythology, at the center of the fountain. Glaucus is frozen in battle with a large fish, which sprays its own water high in the air from its mouth. Four statues of water nymphs—the eponymous naiads—sit around the fountain, each facing a different direction. From the southwest side of the fountain, I looked down the long *Via Nazionale*, which leads to the *Piazza Venezia*. On such a clear day, I could make out the bright, white top of the Vittorio Emmanuel monument against the blue sky way down at the end of the street. I decided that would be my next stop.

The monument is commonly referred to as the *Vittoriano,* and also as the *Altare della Patria*, though that nickname refers specifically to an altar within the structure. The Vittoriano was built to honor the first king of unified Italy and looks not unlike a giant wedding cake. Romans have also nicknamed it—not out of endearment—after a set of dentures and a typewriter. While the Corinthian columns and statues of kings and horse-drawn chariots in bronze and marble are very Roman, a widely held opinion among locals is that the Vittoriano is too flashy and does not fit in with the more subdued tone of the rest of the city's architecture. Its construction also came at the expense of several Roman ruins and medieval churches that once stood on the Capitoline Hill where the monument stands now, which didn't sit well with many who valued Rome's long history.

I stood on the sidewalk in front of the Vittoriano for a few minutes in awe of its pristine enormity. Two different groups of people asked if I would take photos of them in front of it, so I obliged and then hurried off before anyone else decided I was a photog-for-hire.

Via dei Fori Imperiali runs straight from the piazza to the Forum and the Colosseum. Along the street, vendors set up tables, blankets, or stands to display their wares, most of which include the same small replicas of Roman statues that are found all over the city. What caught my eye, however, was a small cart loaded with a rainbow of fresh fruits covered in a dewy mist that sprayed from small hoses running along the top. You could buy the fruits individually or in pre-cut fruit cups, but what I really wanted was the coconut.

On my first trip to Rome, I had found fresh coconut to be a rejuvenating snack in the heat. A three-tiered cake stand displayed wedges of coconut in three different sizes for one, two, or three euros. I picked two of the largest pieces, paid the proprietor, and continued toward the Colosseum. As I ate, I realized it wasn't nearly as hot outside as I'd expected. It seemed the heat wave had subsided, and for that I was grateful.

The street runs parallel to the Forum, so you can view the remains of temples, monuments, and statues from the sidewalk. It's impressive to know you're looking at fragments that have survived for centuries, some crumbled and some still standing. Like many other visitors, no doubt, I couldn't help but imagine the daily hustle and bustle of the ancient citizens visiting the market and viewing processions, speeches, trials, and matches between gladiators. I found myself deaf to everything around me for a moment as I stopped and surveyed the expansive ruins, trying to place myself in the middle of the Forum at the prime of its life. It would have been rather freeing to walk around in a toga all day, every day, a nice breeze keeping me cool in the summer heat. But, alas, I was here now and in shorts, and it just wasn't quite the same.

The Colosseum loomed ahead, drawing me to its immensity. I walked the short remaining distance to the ancient amphitheater and looked up. Three levels of arcades still stand along the north half, the original exterior wall. The rest of the current exterior, two levels of arcades, is actually what was once the interior walling. I compared in my mind the excitement of walking to Autzen Stadium on the day of an Oregon Duck football game back in Eugene to what it might have been like to approach the Colosseum in its heyday, coming to see the gladiators, a mock naval battle, or a classical drama. It would have been an incredible adrenaline rush, I thought, but I was happy avoiding the spectacle of brutal, bloody death, and instead enjoying a few hours of football.

I introduced myself to a nearby couple who I'd heard speaking English and asked if they would mind taking my picture in front of the arena. I held my hands up in front of me to form an "O" with my fingertips touching, the common sign made by Duck fans at home. After they snapped a few photos with my phone and gave it back to me, the man asked, "Are you from Oregon?"

"The 'O' makes it obvious, I guess, huh?" We both laughed.

"Our son went to high school with one of their wide receivers," the woman explained.

"Oh, okay. Yeah, I live in Eugene. Where are you from?"

"Tampa."

"How long have you been in Rome?"

"A week. This is our last day, though. We're headed up to Florence and then Lake Como. What about you?"

"I just got here, but I've been in Italy for a week."

"It's a beautiful country. Well, listen, it was nice to meet you, Michael. We need to be heading back to the hotel to start packing. Just wanted to see this beaut one more time. Have you been in yet?"

"Not on this trip. I'm meeting someone in Rome, so I thought I'd wait for her to see it again." I shook the man's hand. "It was good to meet you, too..."

"Mark. And my wife, Rita."

"...Mark and Rita. Thanks for the picture. Enjoy the rest of your trip."

We waved goodbye, and they headed up the road.

I looked down at my phone and the pictures they'd taken, which had turned out well. However, I hadn't noticed the thick, dark clouds that had rolled in, showing up clearly behind me in the photos. Then, I felt that the air had changed, too. I pulled out my map to determine the quickest route back to my hostel, found the road, and walked quickly in that direction. A light, invigorating rain began to fall.

The walk back was quicker than I'd expected, and I made a quick stop at a market on the way for a bottle of Bombay Sapphire, some limes, and a few small bottles of club soda. Thunder growled deep and low overhead, and it seemed likely that I might be confined to my room for the rest of the night, so I wanted to be prepared. Realizing I had no way to cut the limes, I also grabbed a cheap corkscrew with a small, fold-out foil blade. The corkscrew would also come in handy later when Emily and I inevitably found ourselves somewhere in the city with a bottle of wine. The steady rain gained weight just as I reached the front door of the hostel. Back in my room, I was pleased to find no feathery or shitty signs that pigeons had taken the open window as an invitation. The room temperature was pleasant, and a light breeze accompanied the sound of raindrops pattering on the sidewalk below, so I left it open for ambiance. Sitting on the bed, I took my shoes off and rubbed my feet for a minute. *So much walking,* I thought. *And I've only been here a couple of hours.* I still had no messages from Emily, so I decided—heart pounding—to send a quick text: *Made it to Rome safe and sound. It's beautiful and stormy here. Can't wait to see you.*

Her response was almost immediate: *Can't wait to see you either. Soon!* She followed with a winking, kissing emoji. That made me feel a little better, so I left my phone on the nightstand and vowed to myself not to contact her again until she let me know she was in Rome and ready to see me.

I made a strong drink with the gin and soda and a couple of roughly cut wedges of lime. It was just what I needed after a quick jaunt around part of Rome, despite the lack of ice. I hadn't seen an ice machine anywhere in the hostel. I grabbed my notebook from my bag, pulled the chair from the small desk in the corner over to the window, and propped my feet on the sill, sipping the gin and soda as I watched the rain come down outside before attempting to get some more words on paper. It was barely five o'clock, but the sky was near black. Heavy drops of rain pounded on every surface outside, and between the sounds of traffic, I heard another long, low rumble in the distance.

Chapter 30

Hunger hit me like a city bus, but it was the sudden slowdown of the rain that snapped me back to reality from my writing. Watching outside for a few minutes until I felt that the lull in the storm might last, I decided that getting out for some food would be a smart idea. I glanced over the few pages I'd written, making sure I didn't still have any lingering thoughts that needed to be recorded, and placed my notebook on the desk. I pulled my lightweight jacket from my luggage, closed the window most of the way, and headed downstairs.

The front desk attendant directed me two blocks down and a block over to a place with, according to him, the best *doner kebabs* in Rome. I thanked him for his recommendation and walked that way. I wouldn't have known it was so early in the night by the sky outside, but the black clouds yielded no rain until I got to what I assumed to be the place, and, even then, only a sprinkle.

For a place that supposedly had *"il migliore"* doner kebabs in town, it wasn't very busy. Two middle-aged Italian men at one table, four younger Australian men at another. It didn't look welcoming from the outside, either, and there was no mention of their renowned status posted on signage anywhere. *Maybe they're just really modest,* I thought. But if I'd learned anything from watching hours of Anthony Bourdain's travels around the world, the best food rarely came from a place that looked like it could pass a health inspection.

I stepped up to the counter where a thin, older man stood in a white apron covered in meat juice and sauces, waiting quietly for my order.

"*Un kebab, per favore,*" I said, holding up a finger.

The proprietor immediately turned around and sliced open a ciabatta roll and placed it just inside an open oven on the brick to toast for a moment, then went to the enormous cone of lamb that sat spinning slowly on a vertical rotisserie and began shaving thin strips off with a large knife. He pulled the roll from the oven and piled on shredded lettuce, tomato, cucumber, and onions, tonged a surprising amount of lamb on top and drizzled some kind of white sauce over the whole thing before wrapping it in wax paper and handing it to me.

I paid for the kebab and a Peroni from the cooler near the counter and sat at a small table by the window. The kebab was huge; it took both hands to hold it together and keep everything from falling out. It was one of the most delicious things I'd ever eaten. I had taken a couple of bites and was wiping sauce from the corner of my mouth when I realized the Australians were trying to catch my attention.

"Oy! Come over here, mate. No one should dine alone."

After glancing around just to make sure it was actually me they were talking to, I picked up my things and joined them. "Thanks, guys. That's really nice of you. How's the night going?"

"Just startin'," one of them said, his mouth full of his own kebab. He took a quick swig of beer before saying, "We're going to check out some bars down around *Piazza Navona*. You're welcome to join if you'd like."

"Thanks. I may just do that." *Famous last words*, I thought. I didn't want to make it too crazy a night after the long train ride and with so much to see the next day, but I now knew how quickly an easy night could turn into a riot with some lively Australians involved.

I *did* go out with them—Brice, Kevin, James, and Will were their names—but I was somehow able to keep my beer count to a reasonable number that wouldn't leave me debilitated the next morning. The night was a blur as they took us from bar to bar in a whirlwind, usually downing a couple of quick beers at each, making passes at some attractive women who they thought had been making eyes at them, and then moving "on to the next," as they put it. The fifth and final bar we went to, some dive near the Pantheon, yielded better returns.

A pair of girls sat in the corner of the room, wearing dresses that were suited for a much nicer establishment. They appeared deep in conversation, but their eyes constantly darted in our direction, followed by quiet laughter. After a repartee of eye contact that lasted for several minutes, Kevin finally waved them over to our table. They looked at each other for a moment before grabbing their purses and walking over to us.

"Hi," one of them said coyly. The other stayed silent but batted her long eyelashes at one of the Australians. Or maybe all of them, I wasn't too sure.

"Hey there," Kevin answered. "What are you lovely ladies doing in a place like this at this time of night?"

"Getting into trouble. What are *you* doing in a place like this at this time of night?"

"Oh-ho!" Kevin looked back and forth at us, as amused as I was by her quick wit. "So that's how it goes, eh? I'm sorry, I've been rude." He introduced us all to the girls who, in turn, introduced themselves as Marie and Julia from Chicago. Brice pulled up two more chairs, and we all scooted closer around the table to fit the girls in.

Two rounds of sambuca shots later—the second of which I stealthily avoided by sliding it in front of Will and convincing him it was his—our table was a raucous centerpiece in the bar. There weren't many other people there at that point, but we were certainly the loudest. We finally left the bar, and the Australians informed the girls that there was more beer back at the hostel if they were game. They were. I told them I probably wouldn't join them but would walk with them since it was near my own hostel.

Rain had begun to fall lightly again while we were in the last bar, so we tried to pick a quick route back to our part of the city. Thunder purred beyond the city center, and, when we were out of the cover of some of the taller buildings, we saw lightning illuminate the sky every so often. Our pace quickened; a downpour was imminent.

Finally, when we were only a couple of blocks from Termini, it hit. There was barely a breath between light, pleasant rain and forgetting what it felt like to be dry. We could scarcely see each other between the sheets of rain emptying from the clouds. We made a run for it, laughing and bumping into each other as we splashed through puddles that now lined the gutters. Two of the Australians—I couldn't tell which—grappled with each other, each trying to push the other into the biggest puddles. One of them succeeded, and we all laughed as we looked back at the other struggling to get up. At one point, there was a question as to which way we needed to go, but between the buildings we could just make out the area where busses picked up and dropped off passengers outside the train station.

As we came up to the station on the side farthest from our hostels, I could see a small group of people under the cover of the extended roof at the front of the station, waving at us and shouting something over the din. We all shared glances back and forth before wordlessly agreeing that, even though we were close, it'd be good to get some shelter for a moment. Now nearer, we could see that they were four younger men, maybe in their early twenties. They stood against the wall, smoking cigarettes and joking back and forth as they watched us. One of them walked toward us and said something in Italian.

"*Non parliamo Italiano,* mate," Kevin said.

The Italian said something back, again in Italian, holding out his pack of cigarettes to us. His friends also walked over.

Kevin waved the cigarettes away. "I'm sorry, I don't understand. Do you speak English?"

Two of them were easily over six feet tall, but all four were slightly built. Something about them didn't sit well with me. I could tell Brice, James, and Will felt the same because they had taken subtle steps toward the girls. Heavy tension hung in the air; our eyes remained locked on the young men who we had originally thought to be our guides to safe haven.

As Kevin tried to communicate with the leader, the other three seemed to close the gap between us. My heart skipped a beat as a fleeting glint of steel caught my eye. I discreetly nudged Will, who was closest to me, and directed a quick glance and a nod toward the second smallest of the four Italians. He followed my line of sight to the guy's left hand, which held an open pocketknife at his side, its five-inch blade catching what little light it could in the stormy night.

Will nudged James, who nudged Brice, who wisely did not say a word to Marie and Julia, who had remained quiet in the tension, aside from a few nervous whimpers. James took a step forward to be nearer to Kevin, and the rest of us moved closer together to put more of a barrier between the Italians and the girls. I was glad they took the front line; I'd never been in a fight before, and my heart was making every effort to escape my chest. James and Kevin were the largest of our group, both built like lean bulls, so it seemed like this move would diffuse anything that was about to happen.

The Italians exchanged brief comments amongst themselves, and then the leader tried to take a step past Kevin. Kevin put a muscular arm out, his enormous hand flat on the guy's chest. The Italian looked at Kevin for a moment, then pushed his arm down and threw a quick right hook across Kevin's face. All hell broke loose.

Will ran forward and shoved the leader back, leaving Brice and I with the girls. Kevin simply seemed amused that the guy had even hit him in the first place. Two of the others—the ones without a knife—ran in and began swinging and shoving and groping. James, Will, and Kevin landed a few punches, but the Italians were quick, so nothing settled too hard or directly. Marie and Julia screamed at everyone to stop, but to no avail. At some point, it became James and I who were shielding them, and it was then that the knife-wielding Italian—who had somehow stayed out of the fray and off the radar—came toward us. James was a big guy, but even he looked scared, which, in turn, scared the shit out of me. Nevertheless, we stood our ground and pushed the girls farther behind us. I did my best to keep the fear I felt from manifesting in my eyes as we stared the Italian down, clenching my fists to suppress the shaking.

Brandishing his knife, the coward pointed at Marie and then at his own neck. He then made a gesture that said, *Give it to me.* Trembling, Marie stepped forward and placed her necklace in his outstretched hand before moving back behind us. As she did, the Italian glanced at James and me with arrogant, taunting eyes, daring us to stop him. Knife still at the ready, he held the necklace up in the light to inspect it.

As soon as the Italian closed his hand over his loot, James said, "Fuck this," cocked his fist, and laid a strong, smooth jab across the mugger's face. To this day, I'm still unsure if the crack we heard at that instant was another clap of thunder or the guy's jaw. Either way, he dropped to the ground and didn't move.

The others stopped brawling and looked over at us. As James

reached down to pick up the necklace, the other assailants began shouting in Italian, broke their grapples with the Australians, and ran over to check on their fallen comrade.

"Come on!" Kevin yelled, motioning for us to run with them. We followed and didn't stop running until we reached their hostel. Up in their room, which was a dorm similar to mine in Sant'Agnello, the Australians compared their damage. Shirts were torn, knuckles bloody, lips and eyebrows cut, but they laughed about it. It had been a dangerous situation, but they'd somehow enjoyed themselves. Brice grabbed some beers from the mini fridge and passed them around. I figured the least I could do was stay and have one to celebrate.

I found myself zoning out a bit, still present and enjoying the moment, but receded from the conversations. As Will theatrically recounted every punch, every grapple, and James's final pummel, I found myself genuinely grateful for the time I'd spent with them that evening, starting with a simple invitation to dine with them.

At one point earlier in the night, I'd asked Kevin if all Australians were as friendly and welcoming as they were. I talked about the Aussies I'd met in Sant'Agnello who had the same attitude. He said he couldn't speak for *all* Australians, because, "of course, you do get the arseholes."

"But I'd say majorly, yes. It comes from how things are done down there, though. I'm sure the other blokes you met talked about this, but a lot of it is in the wages we earn, the amount of paid vacation we get, and, of course, all the bloody sun. We don't wake up every day thinking 'I don't want to go to work' and complaining about everything. We're mostly happy people, so that translates to how we see and treat others. That's not to say we don't cross paths with tossers who get on our nerves, but we just don't have a lot of reason to treat most people poorly. Why *not* make them feel welcome, y'know?"

I had then told Kevin that I felt like Australians might be the wisest people I'd ever met. He laughed and didn't say anything, but he knew I was probably right.

When I finished my beer, I took advantage of a sudden break in the conversation and said my farewells. I thanked them for the exciting evening and their companionship. We said maybe we'd see each other around Rome in the next few days, and I left and headed around the corner to my hostel to crash. Rome had so much to see, and I didn't want to waste a minute of my remaining time there. On the short walk back, I started making mental notes of all the places I wanted to see with Emily when she arrived.

Chapter 31

My first morning in Rome began with a staggering sunrise into a clear, blue sky—quite different from the menacing storm clouds the night before. After showering and dressing for a warm day, I made sure my notebook, map, and a book were in my bag and headed to a quaint café just around the corner from my hostel. As I enjoyed a glass of orange juice, a macchiato, and a cornetto at a table outside, I pulled out the map and my notebook and started marking all the places on the map that I wanted to visit while I was in Rome. Then, I drew a line connecting them all in a path that would be easy for me to follow over the next few days. I paid for my breakfast and a bottle of water, packed up, and headed toward *Piazza Barberini*.

The first stop on my map was a church near the piazza on *Via Vittorio Veneto*, one of Rome's most expensive and elegant streets. From what I'd read about the place, Via Veneto was a somewhat peculiar location for it. I hadn't heard of the church of *Santa Maria della Concezione dei Cappuccini* when I visited Rome the first time. In the years since, it had popped up somewhere in my internet searches and became a place I absolutely had to visit.

Standing in the already-welcome shade of the tall trees lining Via Veneto, I looked up at the façade of the church before passing through the small, wrought-iron gate and up one of the two half-turn staircases leading to the entrance. The interior of the church was beautiful and crowned with high, intricately painted, vaulted ceilings and several chapels recessed on either side. I wandered quietly up one side of the church and down the other, peeking in at the artwork contained within each chapel. Then, I found the museum and stood in line to buy a ticket to the crypts. Over the centuries, somewhere around 4,000 Capuchin friars had been exhumed from their graves, their skeletons disassembled, and every bone used in some way to decorate several small chapels below the church. I'd looked at dozens of pictures of the crypts online before my trip, unable to fathom the sheer volume of skeletons that would surround me should I choose to enter. The Crypt of Skulls seemed especially disturbing, given all the hollow eyes staring out from the walls. As I progressed in line, my excitement grew and then was replaced by the thought that Emily might like to see it too when she arrived. When it was my turn to pay the six euros to get in, I had decided to wait to share the new experience with her.

"Uh… I'll be back…*tardi*," I said to the man at the counter. "*Mi dispiace.*" The apathetic stare over his glasses rendered my apology unnecessary, and I left the church. Outside, I found *Via Sistina* and followed it in in the direction of *Piazza di Spagna*.

The *Trinita dei Monti* stands sentry at the top of the Spanish Steps, which lead to the Piazza di Spagna below. The façade stood out from the others I'd seen in the city, with two identical bell towers at either end of the roof. One of Rome's many obelisks stands just off the street in front of the church; I read later that it was a slightly smaller reproduction of the obelisk in *Piazza del Popolo*. I chose not to visit the church that morning but made a mental note to come back later in the week if I had time.

The famous staircase was already filled from top to bottom with people out enjoying the sun. It would have been a task to find enough space on any step to sit comfortably and take in the view, so I leaned on the stone railing at the top for a few minutes and enjoyed it from there. Around and beyond the Steps spread innumerable pink and tan and white stucco buildings, capped with brown and red tile roofs. My gaze wound back and forth across the steps, down to the piazza, and beyond that along the long, straight *Via dei Condotti,* which changes into a couple of other streets before running into the *Lungoteveres* along the Tiber River. Reeling my focus back, I scanned the rooftops picking out as many rotundas as I could. I counted at least six, and I appreciated every single one of them for the effect they had on the cityscape. I was always impressed by the works created in the name of religion, despite having no particular inclination myself.

As I made my way down to the piazza, my ears were filled, as in Positano, with a mixture of languages. I smiled at the thought of everyone around me saying relatively similar things about the view, the atmosphere, the architecture, but in ways unique to where they were from. Then, my mind moved on to Emily, and my smile remained, though I wished she were there with me to enjoy it. I glanced hopefully around me at the various faces, but to no avail. She was probably still in Florence, I knew, and I knew I'd see her soon. I fought the urge to send her a picture of the Steps from my phone and continued down to the *Fontana della Barcaccia* at the bottom to refill my water bottle, which I'd quickly emptied in the morning heat.

As I stood in a short line of tourists waiting to refill their own vessels at one of the fountain's spouts, I admired Bernini's sunken boat sculpture that was the focal point of the fountain and flowed with water from one of the ancient aqueducts that still supplies Rome with pure drinking water. When it was my turn, I stepped out on the stone platform that juts into the main base of the fountain and filled my bottle partway, taking two long drinks before filling it to the top. With one last look back up the crowded Spanish Steps and a long drink of water, I regained my bearings and headed down *Via del Babuino* in the direction of Piazza del Popolo. Amid the row of stores that included Dolce & Gabanna, Chanel, and other equally expensive brands whose names I didn't recognize, I found a *gelateria* and bought a small cup of lemon sorbetto. I wondered if it was too early for gelato until I saw an old Italian man walk by with two scoops on a cone. As I ate and walked, I glanced in the windows of the high-end shops as mannequins in various gaudy outfits caught my eye. I accepted that I didn't understand the world of high fashion then, and I likely never would. Beyond the mannequins, the shops were filled with people who were wealthy enough to buy or who wished they were.

The buzz of motorini echoed down every narrow side street, reminding me to stay as close to the building side of the sidewalk as I could to avoid getting clipped by a careless rider or the side mirror of a tiny Fiat. Italian drivers weren't afraid to push their way through the crowds of pedestrians who obliviously meandered back and forth to the myriad storefronts. The roadway itself was narrow and made of worn, dark cobblestones that had seen, quite possibly, centuries of traffic, and sidewalks ran parallel on either side. Up ahead, I could see where the road opened to my destination. Dead in the center stood another of Rome's obelisks, that which was the inspiration for the monolith at the top of the Spanish Steps.

I'd forgotten how expansive the square is, though it's shaped more like a high school track than a square. The entire thing is paved with the same cobblestones as the road, which itself encircles the whole piazza and connects with two or three roads that shoot off in other directions. Fountains are built into the walls at either end of the piazza, and the Pincian Hill rises above the wall to the east. The focal point, however, is the obelisk in the center and the platform on which it stands. Several steps lead up to the base of the obelisk, and on each of the four corners is a tiered pedestal that supports a resting lion statue. All four lions spout healthy streams of water from their mouths into small, round pools below.

As I admired the plinth and the obelisk above it, I saw a group of students vacate a space next to one of the lion statues. I seized the opportunity and walked quickly over to stake my claim. It would be a relief to rest my feet and rehydrate while I observed what was going on around me. I pulled out my notebook and pen and propped my bag against the step behind me as a backrest. Leaning back against the bag, I stretched my legs out in the sun and finished my gelato. Ahead of me was the road I'd come in on, and to the right of that were two churches that looked damn near identical. My last visit to Piazza del Popolo had been very brief, and I didn't remember seeing them. They appeared to be mirror images of each other, each topped with a large tile dome, a bell tower, and a triangular pediment capping six Corinthian columns along the front of the church. Reaching deep into whatever remained of the artistic ability I'd had as a child, I turned my notebook sideways and to a fresh page and began sketching the churches in front of me as best I could.

It was hard as hell. *I really shouldn't have quit drawing,* I thought as my eyes flicked from the page to the churches and back, over and over again. While I'd always been interesting in writing, drawing was how I spent a good chunk of my childhood, even into middle school, and I was good at it. Seventh grade, however, was the year my focus shifted to words. Despite an ongoing struggle to help me develop a basic system of organization for my class binder, my English teacher that year also helped me to develop the ability to write strong sentences. As a seventh grader, that seemed like a means to an end—a powerful book report and an A in class—but as I grew older, I appreciated her for working so hard to teach me what I've learned isn't such a simple skill. What began as a class lesson evolved into a tool that I could use in conjunction with the passion for storytelling I'd had since I was about five years old. As I finally began working on the second church, a kind voice yanked me back to reality from the memories I'd been swimming in.

"You know the story behind those?"

I set my pen in the crease of my notebook and looked around. When I turned around, I noticed an older gentleman sitting on the base of the obelisk. He raised a hand in greeting and smiled from under his wide-brimmed Panama hat.

Returning his smile, I asked, "What was that?"

He nodded ahead of us at the churches and looked back down at me. "Those. Do you know their story?"

"I can't say that I do. I figured there must be one, though. Are they as identical as they look?"

"Not quite." He gestured at the space next to him, so I grabbed my bag and water bottle and walked over to the open seat.

Now that I was closer, I could see his kind eyes and cheerfully rosy face in the shade of his hat, accented by the forgiving wrinkles of a graceful aging. Wisps of straight, white hair were combed neatly behind his ears, giving the strong indication that there was nothing left on top under the hat.

"They were commissioned by Pope Alexander VII and financed by Cardinal Gastaldi, with a set of identical circular plans drawn up by Carlo Rainaldi. Rainaldi began working on the first one—the one on the left, the *Basilica di Santa Maria in Montesanto*—and at some point along the way, Bernini helped out. You know Bernini?"

"Mostly thanks to Dan Brown, yes."

The old man chuckled and continued. "Work stopped for several years after Alexander VII died. The next pope just wasn't as interested in it. But construction eventually resumed, and at some point, the project was taken over by Carlo Fontana, who ultimately finished the churches. It was *Bernini*, however, who altered the plans for the first church such that it would be elliptical rather than circular. Consensus for his reasoning is that the site of that church is narrower than the other. The other church—the *Chiesa di Santa Maria dei Miracoli*—was finished a few years after the other. And the domes are slightly different: the one on the left has twelve sides, and the other only has eight."

"Huh. That's really interesting. I like hearing the history behind these churches. It's always unique."

"There are plenty of them to hear about, certainly, and the history is almost never as straightforward as one might expect. Now, since I told you the story, will you show me your sketch?"

"Ha… I was hoping you wouldn't ask, but sure." I handed over my notebook.

"This is quite good." He handed it back. "Do you do a lot of sketching?"

I felt a hint of pride cross my face. "Thank you. I used to all the time. Over the past several years, though, I write."

"Ah. From one medium to another. It's good to be multitalented. Makes it that much harder to get bored in life." He suddenly gasped and raised his eyebrows. "I've been rude. My name is Jack Porter." He extended his hand.

"Michael Wise."

His gently firm handshake suited his age and demeanor. "It's good to meet you, Michael."

"You too. And thank you for the story."

"I'm glad to have shared it. I don't want to take up more of your time, but I appreciate you sitting here for a few minutes. What else do you have planned for your time here?"

I pulled out my map and opened it for him to see, pointing out all the places I'd marked to visit. "I met a girl in Sorrento who should be here in the next day or two, so I'm hoping to spend some time with her seeing a lot of this stuff."

"A beautiful girl has a way of making even the most remarkable things a little better." He gestured across the map at all my waypoints. "You've got your work cut out for you. You better get on your way. But if you decide you're interested in some more conversation, I'm here around this time most days." He patted my shoulder and shook my hand, the warm smile never leaving his face. "Assuming, that is, that this girl doesn't confine you to your hotel room when she gets here." He winked slyly.

I laughed. "I'll keep that in mind. Thanks, Jack. I really enjoyed this, too. I'll be sure to come back by here." He stood up with me, shook my hand one more time, and briefly touched the brim of his hat.

"Enjoy the sun, Michael. You came to Rome at a good time."

"It sure seems like it. See you soon, I hope."

I left the piazza through the west end on a road that led to the Tiber. As I walked, I couldn't fight the feeling that I wanted to stay and talk with Jack as long as I could that day. After two blocks, I was almost at the river, but I'd made the decision that I could still see all I wanted to see in Rome in the next couple of days. I turned around and headed back to the piazza.

Jack was nowhere to be seen. After finding his seat at the obelisk vacant, I surveyed the area and wandered around for a few minutes, but I couldn't find him. A knot formed in the pit of my stomach, though I couldn't explain why. "Guess I'll have to take his word for it," I said to myself, resolving to be at the fountains slightly earlier the following morning. Back on my previous path, I hit the *Lungote-veres*—the roads that line both sides of the Tiber River—and wandered south along the river in the shade of the plane trees that are so plentiful in Rome.

I didn't know how long I'd been walking when I sat down on the low wall overlooking the river, but I had found myself lost in thoughts of Jack Porter. What was his story? He obviously wasn't a tourist if he spent as much time as he said he did at the piazza. His face was happy, but there was a loneliness buried in his eyes. I was glad that our brief conversation seemed to have meant something to him as I was learning it had to me. My stomach grumbled as I watched the murky, green water flow lazily by. It was one o'clock, so I figured I should probably get some lunch. I found a hole in the wall near *Ponte Garibaldi* that sold pizza and had a decent number of customers, so I hopped in line and ordered a crispy piece of Margherita and a Coke. Back on the *Lungotevere de' Cenci*, I found some steps to sit on and eat, right where the Tiber splits into two channels around the *Isola Tiberina,* a narrow island in the river occupied by a hospital, a small basilica, a bank, and a restaurant, all surrounding a small piazza. The food and shade did me good, but the heat of the day had already taken a toll, so I pulled out my map to find the quickest route back to my hostel for a rest.

The quickest route, which passed by the Vittorio Emanuel monument, still took forty-five minutes in my exhausted state, and I fell onto my bed the second the door to my room was shut behind me. I pulled my phone from my pocket and glanced at the screen—nothing from Emily—before dropping it on the bed next to me and closing my eyes. Three hours later, I woke up sweaty and disoriented, but ultimately relaxed and refreshed. I decided not to explore much else on my mapped-out route that evening, but showered, changed, and wandered out to find a decent place to have dinner on the way to the Trevi Fountain.

The balmy air somehow rejuvenated me even more, despite the exhaust fumes and cigarette smoke that mingled with the smells of all sorts of food. I loved the energy exuded by all the people out and about for the evening as the blue sky grew darker and the orange glow above the rooftops sank lower. While I felt in a very good place, I also found myself envious of every man who had a beautiful woman on his arm, laughing at his jokes and looking at him with admiring eyes. My hand twitched toward the phone in my pocket—*Where the hell is Emily?*— but I left it there. *She'll get in touch when she's here, don't worry. Maybe her phone is dead.*

Seated at a table along the sidewalk at a trattoria near the Quirinal Palace, I ordered a bottle of white wine recommended by the waiter, which was crisp and perfectly dry, and a plate of *cacio e pepe*. The simplicity of the pasta dressed with black pepper and Pecorino Romano turned out to be exactly what I needed—along with the wine, of course—to get to a happy baseline for the rest of the evening. I paid my check and headed off toward the Trevi, full, satisfied, and pleasantly buzzed.

The area around the fountain wasn't nearly as crowded as I had expected for that early in the evening, and I was able to move between people, without feeling like I was groping them, to a space on one of the low walls that encircles the fountain. I sat down and marveled for the second time at the enormous, Travertine piece carved against the *Palazzo Poli*. The wide pool at its base shimmered a crystalline blue in the accent lights scattered around the fountain, and the water spilling into the pool trickled loudly between the chattering voices, creating an enchanting ambiance. After I'd sat for a moment, I gave up my fortuitous seat and found a street vendor selling cold drinks among those hawking replica Gucci and Prada accessories. Bacardi Breezers were on the menu, so I bought a bright-green lime Breezer and found a spot at street level overlooking the fountain to lean and sip my cold beverage. It made me wish more than ever that Emily was there with me, and the bottle of wine urged me to text her. So I did.

Hey, you. Hope you'll be here soon, I miss you like crazy.

I held the bottle in front of the fountain and took a picture with my phone, attached it to the message, and sent it. The wine had gotten its way, but I still had enough of my wits to put my phone back in my pocket rather than stare at the screen, waiting for the icon of three dots to appear, signifying that she was texting back. I finished the Breezer slowly, had another—mango this time—and decided to go back to the hostel and relax for the rest of the night. I wanted to be sure to get up at a decent time so I could hopefully meet Jack Porter again, and I knew staying out at that point might produce different results.

Back in the hostel, I made another Bombay and soda with lime and sat in the chair in front of the window. The air coming in was much drier and more relaxing than the night before, and I didn't even try to write. I sat with the lights off and sipped and watched the stars twinkle as bright as they could above the city lights and listened to the cars and people buzzing along the streets below. I was quite drunk at that point, and I felt lonely and happy at the same time. A glance at the bed made me long for Emily even more, so I set the half-consumed drink on the nightstand, stripped naked, and climbed under the top sheet. At some point later in the night, I awoke to a buzz from my phone on the bed next to me. The brightness of the screen shocked my sleepy eyes, and I squinted to see what the text message said.

Mmmmm Breezers! That looks so beautiful!

I passed out again before I could reply, and it wasn't until the next morning that I realized there was no reciprocity in Emily's text.

Chapter 32

I was back on the streets of Rome once more by eight-thirty the next day, having a quick espresso and a cornetto from the café near my hostel. The air had a refreshing chill to it that hadn't been there since I'd arrived, but I could tell there was plenty of heat ahead. Piazza del Popolo was still quiet when I got there; only a few tourists milled around taking pictures, and Jack did not appear to be there yet. I sat on the steps of the plinth in the center and decided to read while the air was peaceful. After about twenty minutes, I glanced up and saw Jack walking across the cobblestones from the direction of the Spanish Steps. His khaki pants were neatly pressed, and he was ready for the day in a crisp, white bowling shirt and the same wide-brimmed, straw Panama hat he'd been wearing the day before.

"Good morning, Jack!" I waved as he approached.

"Well, good morning, Michael. You're here bright and early." His rosy smile seemed to be an ever-present fixture. Gesturing at the step next to me, he asked, "May I?"

"Of course." I marked the page in my book and moved my bag to the other side of me. "How are you this morning?"

"You know, Michael, it's the best day of my life. The air is fresh, the sun is out, and I'm still kicking."

I chuckled. "Those are all reasons to feel good, I'd say."

"That they are. What's on your list of sights to see today?"

"Thought I'd go check out St. Peter's. We were sort of rushed through last time I was here, and we spent more time in the Vatican Museum than anything. It was interesting, but I'd like to see more of the basilica. What do you have going on? Do you want to come with?"

"You won't believe this, Michael, but I'm not doing *shit* today. Excuse my French. That said, yes, I'll come along."

I laughed at his bluntness and told him he'd quickly learn that swearing wasn't offensive to me.

"Why don't I buy us some coffee, and we'll find our way to the Vatican."

"I can't say no to that."

Jack led the way out of the piazza and across the river to a small coffee shop and bar with a beautiful assortment of pastries in one sparkling glass case and a colorful array of gelato in another. He caught my eye with a sideways glance as we stepped up to the bar. "You feeling Irish today?"

I smirked and nodded.

He leaned on the high, green marble countertop. "*Buongiorno, Stefano. Due caffè irlandesi, per favore,*" he said to the well-dressed man behind the bar. "*Portare via.*" He gestured out the door with his thumb.

"Coming right up, Jack." With a smile under his dark-grey mustache, Stefano tapped the side of his nose with his index finger and went off to make our coffees.

"It's good to know people, Michael. Stefano and I go back a long time, and he knows just how to make coffee the way I like it."

"Huh." I smiled at Jack's pride in a connection that made such a simple thing in life special. Just as I began wondering how he and Stefano had met and what their story was, Stefano returned with two twelve-ounce paper cups and placed them on the counter in front of us. Jack handed him a colorful note and gestured at him to keep whatever change was left from it.

"*Grazie mille, Stefano. Arrivederci.*"

"*Arrivederci,* Jack. Enjoy this beautiful day." He smiled and nodded at me.

"*Grazie,*" I said as I followed Jack out onto the sidewalk.

Steam rose out of our cups as the cool air hit the surface of the coffee. We each took a long, careful sip.

"That's *strong*," I said. "But delicious."

"Mind you, that's not my usual coffee order, but it sounded nice this morning, and Stefano pours it just right."

The Bailey's cut the Jameson on the next sip, and the strength of the coffee came through. It was good, rich coffee. We walked back to the river and turned south onto the *Lungotevere del Mellini*. We kept a leisurely pace and sipped our coffees in pleasant silence.

"Stefano was my wife's brother." Noticing the somewhat surprised look on my face at his out-of-the-blue comment, he said, "I could tell you were wondering."

"Oh, well…you didn't have to tell me. I didn't want to pry."

Jack chuckled. "You can feel free to ask anything."

"I *did* wonder what the story was. He seemed very friendly, but he didn't say much."

"It's difficult, sometimes, for us to see each other, but it's always nice to at the same time."

"I bet. So, your wife—"

"Marcella passed away almost five years ago." He took a drink of his coffee and held it in his mouth for a moment. "Heart failure," he added, anticipating the next question I was too afraid to ask.

"Ah. I'm really sorry to hear that, Jack."

"Thank you, but don't be. We lived a good, long life together. She was taken far too soon, but we made more of our time together than a lot of folks."

We had rounded a bend in the river and were coming up on the colossal Palace of Justice, which houses Italy's supreme court. Just beyond that rose the cylindrical tomb of Hadrian: *Castel Sant'Angelo*. The statue of St. Michael at the top appeared tiny from a distance, his sword pointed downward into the center of the castle. Jack followed my gaze to the mausoleum.

"Have you been in?"

"No," I said. "Every time I see something else in this city, I realize what a whirlwind my last trip was."

"Why don't we go see it?"

"That sounds great."

We dropped our empty coffee cups in a nearby trash can and paid a few euros to get into Castel Sant'Angelo. The coffee's Irish influence had given me a light buzz and I felt very relaxed and happy as we explored the ancient halls of the mausoleum built by the emperor Hadrian for himself and his family.

Outside the mausoleum, on the *Ponte Sant'Angelo*, we looked down at the Tiber and farther ahead, down *Via della Conciliazione* where St. Peter's Basilica stood at the end. After a few minutes, Jack broke the silence.

"Marci loved this bridge. She always said she felt like she was protected by all the angels when she walked across. Now, I never did believe in all that shit—no disrespect to her—but I loved that *she* did. I think it was part of the reason she had so much grace."

"How did you two work so well, her being so strongly Catholic and you—"

"—me not believing in a damn thing?"

I chuckled awkwardly. "I wasn't going to say that, but I didn't want to assume what you *do* believe in, or don't believe in, one way or the other. I find it hard to believe in anything myself. Nothing makes any real sense to me, and most of the time I feel like it doesn't really matter anyway, so I don't bother."

"Right there with you, Michael. You might expect me to say that being with Marcella changed me and that I found God, but I never did, and I never wanted to. She never tried to force it on me, either. I respected her beliefs and she respected my lack thereof. Of course she changed me; she made me a better man. And maybe it was her fervent beliefs that helped her do that, but in my opinion, it was all up to her no matter what. What I believe in are people, however they may be personally influenced.

"Anyway, Marci felt that faith is a very personal thing and should be kept as such. Sure, she went to Mass every Sunday, and when we were younger, we had big, post-Mass lunches with her family, but beyond that, she cultivated her faith on her own, in private. I think she was happier doing it that way, rather than feeling like she was being judged by everyone around her. She only went to Mass to satisfy her family, and it eventually turned into more of a nostalgic ritual for her than anything. After her parents died, she would meet me after Mass for our own Sunday lunch. We always had reservations at the same trattoria near our apartment."

Jack gazed downriver in the direction of the next bridge, a tranquil smile on his face, his cheerful countenance enhanced by the whiskey and Irish cream. I admired the peace he'd made with his wife's death. Though it had been five years since Marcella had died, I imagined I'd be a wreck for the rest of my life if I lost the love of it. Jack was clearly happy with the life he'd lived with his wife and didn't seem to have any unsettled regrets.

"Now that we've established that neither of us believes in God, on to the Vatican?"

Smiling, I said, "Absolutely." I appreciated that Jack was so open to following along on my wandering, even acting as a tour guide. And his candor during it all was refreshing, considering we were so newly acquainted. I suppose there is more risk in opening up to someone you're familiar with than to someone you've just met.

Only a few yards from the Bridge of Angels, *Lungotevere Castello* ends at *Piazza Pia*, and Via della Conciliazione begins. Mussolini designed the thoroughfare as a means of symbolically connecting the heart of Rome with Vatican City, and it certainly had the grandiose effect he intended. Obelisk-like lampposts line both sides of the road, which culminates at *Piazza Papa Pio XII,* just beyond which is the much larger *Piazza San Pietro*. The elliptical St. Peter's Square was one of the most awe-inspiring public spaces I'd ever seen, protected on both sides by Bernini's Doric colonnades, which the architect appropriately referred to as "the maternal arms of Mother Church." An obelisk and two flanking fountains are all that occupy the space inside the colonnades, which makes the square more than capable of handling the crowds that gather when the Pope speaks. Those crowds even spill down into Via della Conciliazione, as I'd seen on my first visit to the city. The magnitude of seeing the pope speaking from the balcony of his apartments, high above tens of thousands of Catholics all directing their attention at him, had been lost on me at the time, but now, to see the space empty in comparison was almost soul-shaking.

We waited only about twenty minutes in line to get through security and into the basilica. Jack suggested we buy tickets to go to the top of the dome, assuming correctly that I hadn't been up there before. In fact, I didn't know until he mentioned it that you *could* go to the top. I made him promise me that his heart and body were up to the task, and he responded by making me promise the same thing. I was less sure of myself, then, than I was of him.

At Jack's recommendation, we took an elevator up to the roof level with several other visitors—"The stairs around the dome will give us plenty of exercise"—and followed the crowd down a long hallway covered in yellowed subway-style tiles to the interior of the dome. All words caught in my throat as we took the last few steps up a short set of stairs and entered the space of the dome. Only a tall, black grated fence stood between us and the vast expanse of the basilica below, spanning most of the circumference of the dome to the other side.

"Wow..." I breathed, looking up and around me before gazing down at the basilica visitors on the marble floors far below.

"Beautiful, isn't it?"

"You weren't kidding."

"And this is just the beginning. Wait until we get to the top."

We walked slowly around the edge of the dome, taking in everything around us. The wall to our left caught my attention, which then slowly rose all the way to the top.

"This is *mosaic*?" I ran my hand lightly across a small section of the millions—or billions?—of tiny pieces of glass and tile that made up the images covering the entirety of the dome.

"Damn near all of it." Jack cracked an amused smile at my discovery as he watched my eyes dart all over, trying to make out the minute details of what I previously thought to be a fully painted ceiling.

"That's incredible. I don't know which I'd hate to do more: paint the whole damn thing or take the time to put all these together."

"It's a chunk of time either way," Jack said.

When we'd seen all we wanted of the dome's interior, we followed the hallway toward the staircase that would take us up and around to the cupola at the top. It started off as a steep, corkscrew staircase, the walls covered in the same yellowed subway tiles running vertically from floor to ceiling. At the top of the corkscrew, the staircase narrowed to a one person-wide path up equally steep stairs along a slower curve. This was the outer edge of the dome.

Windows had been placed every so often along the dimly lit corridor, helping to ease any claustrophobia that may set in during the ascent. The tight space didn't bother me, but as the dome became more prominent, the walls on both sides tilted inward, making walking straight a little more challenging. I stopped at one of the windows to catch my breath for a minute and take in the view of Rome. After letting a couple of larger groups of people pass, we continued on. A few yards farther, the path turned into a tightly zigzagging, metal staircase lined with bright-red handrails. At the end of that section, we ducked through a small archway into another tight corkscrew. This one was so confined that a knotted rope hung all the way down from the ceiling high above for additional support. At the top, natural light and fresh air flooded my senses and I took a deep breath to clear my lungs.

A series of thick pillars encircled the dome, and beyond those, a fence of iron bars enclosed the whole thing to prevent visitors from falling—or jumping—over the rail. Just below us at the front end of the roof atop the façade of the basilica, Maderno's statues of Christ, John the Baptist, and all the Apostles except for St. Peter watched over St. Peter's Square, looking regal with its curving colonnades on either side and the obelisk in the center. Beyond *that*, Rome was sprawled out before us in all its ancient glory. My eyes slowly scanned the city for familiar structures. The Vittoriano, of course, stood out clearly, gleaming as white as ever in the late morning sun. Just past it was the Colosseum.

"There's the Pantheon!" I pointed in the church's direction more excitedly than I had intended. Its dome is flatter than the others in Rome, so it stood out from the other lower buildings.

"Did you know that dome is actually bigger than this one? Not in height, but in diameter. It's about four feet wider."

"No way. I never thought about it, but it *is* enormous inside."

"Over there is the *Villa Borghese*." Jack pointed in the direction of a sprawling, forested area to the northeast of Castel Sant'Angelo. "Have you been?"

"I haven't. I hear it's beautiful, though."

"It is *very* beautiful. Marci and I used to rent a rowboat there occasionally, when the weather was warm, and have a picnic on the lake. She loved being on the water. You should go there if you have time."

We spent a few more minutes on top of the dome, Jack pointing out several other landmarks that I hadn't noticed, before we decided to head back down. At the roof level, we walked out toward the front overlooking the piazza below, where we got within yards of the statues along the top of the façade. I hadn't realized before how tall they actually were—from my new vantage point, I guessed about twenty feet.

The elevator returned us to the main floor of the basilica, where we walked slowly and quietly through its aisles and bays. Once again, I found myself astonished at the cavernous nave, where whispers echoed slowly into nothing in the ceiling high above only to be replaced by new whispers. We found the bronze statue of St. Peter, crowned with a halo and holding the keys to heaven, the toes of his right foot worn down from centuries of pilgrims touching and kissing the foot.

Directly under the dome we had just climbed, Bernini's *baldacchino* caught my eye. The enormous, bronze canopy over the high altar is supported by four ornately cast columns that appear snakelike from a distance. I opted not to follow the staircases to the Vatican

Grottoes beneath the basilica, thinking it might be fun to bring Emily when we finally connected again. My hand brushed the shape of my phone in my pocket, but I decided to wait until Jack and I had parted ways to check for any word from her.

"Thinking about your lady friend?"

I glanced at Jack, who had a knowing smile on his face and nodded toward my pocket.

"Hear from her yet?"

"Not yet. Soon though, hopefully." I was starting to wonder, though, and if Jack had any skepticism about it, he didn't let on. *She'll text you. Or call you. Or something,* I told myself.

Stealing a look at my watch, I realized it was after noon and I was starving. "I should probably get going," I told Jack. "I want to get something to eat and relax in my room for a bit before I see some more of the city this evening."

"Good idea. And you can clean yourself up for your girl when she gets here." He winked and gave me an encouraging pat on the shoulder. "Why don't you walk with me back to the Piazza del Popolo and leave me there for a bit."

I did. We were quieter on the walk back than we had been all day, but I could tell Jack sensed that I was trying to work some things out in my head and was leaving me alone to do so. Back at the piazza, we shook hands and I thanked him for the tour and the conversation.

"I really enjoyed it," I told him. "Sorry I've been quiet, just looking forward to exploring the city with Emily, too."

"I don't blame you, Michael. I'm sure she's much prettier than me. But listen, why don't I leave you alone tomorrow, and we can have coffee the next morning? You can bring Emily with you. I'd love to meet her and show her around, too."

"That sounds great, Jack. Nine o'clock here, that morning?"

"Perfect. See you then, Michael. Knock her dead."

"Ha, I'll do my best. Thanks, Jack. See you in a couple of days."

Before I was out of the piazza, I looked back in the direction of the obelisk. Jack sat on the steps contentedly, his hands clasped in his lap, observing the activity in the square around him. When his gaze found me, he smiled and touched the brim of his hat. I raised my hand in a still wave and headed back down Via del Babuino toward the hostel.

I ate the sandwich I'd bought on the way back—tomato, basil, and mozzarella on a crusty ciabatta roll—in front of the open window in my room. Then, I decided to take a nap, still striving to remain positive that I would hear from Emily that afternoon and that we'd have a romantic dinner and walk through Rome that evening, ending in my room with fewer clothes on than we'd gone out in. I took my shirt and shorts off and lay on my back on the bed, looking at our short text message thread on my phone again. Still nothing. I went into my photos and opened to the photo she'd left for me in Sant'Agnello. *God, she's sexy.* I felt a pang of longing for her in my chest and put my phone on the bed next to me. With the sounds of the city coming in the window, there was no reason to set an alarm, and I closed my eyes to rest.

A couple of hours later, my eyes blinked open. Against my usual form, I didn't seem to have moved at all in my sleep and was still flat on my back. I felt rested after spending the morning hours of the day in the Roman heat, but my mood had darkened. Why hadn't I heard from her? Sure, she'd texted me back the night before, but it had been *long* after I'd texted her and with no allusion to any real interest in seeing me again. That had nagged at me all day, but my time with Jack had kept my mood afloat for the most part.

Now, back in the confines of my room and my mind, it was eating at me again. I wanted so badly to talk to her and to know when she'd be arriving, but I didn't want to appear desperate, even if that was the direction I was headed. Past experiences had taught me to consciously avoid coming on too strong. I just wanted to spend more time with her, and I wanted to tell her that. But I didn't.

Instead, I stayed in my boxers in my room and read in front of the window for the rest of the afternoon, a seemingly bottomless gin and soda sitting on the sill next to my propped-up feet.

Around six-thirty, I'd finished one book and started another but found myself staring mindlessly out the window with a glaze over my eyes. It was time to eat, but I really didn't feel up to wandering too far. That went for the evening sightseeing I'd planned on, as well. My mood had dimmed beyond repair at that point, and I felt a familiar sunken feeling that hadn't been around in a while. I put my clothes on and decided to eat a quick dinner at the restaurant on the ground floor of the hostel. It was busy enough that I figured the food couldn't be that bad.

A heaping plate of fettucine and two beers did nothing to quell the storm that raged in my head as I went back upstairs. I'd hoped I might feel like exploring the city a little more after a meal, but I just wanted to be asleep and away from my thoughts. *Emily will be in Rome tomorrow. You'll hear from her, just be patient.* I told myself this over and over again while I stripped back down for bed. Leaning against the wall next to the window, I stared out at the dusk-soaked city, shaking off the spins and willing belief to take hold.

Chapter 33

No hangover plagued me the next day when I woke before the sun. Fortunately, I was clear enough of mind at that early hour to know that I shouldn't waste a miracle like that. So, despite deeply present thoughts of Emily and the lack of any overnight messages, I urged myself to get in the shower, get dressed, and get out to see more of Italy's capital.

Few things stimulate me so much as walking the streets of an unfamiliar city in the morning hours free of the commotion of crowds, the air fresh and cool and clear of overwhelming exhaust fumes and cigarette smoke. Instead, the early morning brings the smells of freshly baked bread. Many of the streets are hosed off and sidewalks cleaned up to prepare for the various shopkeepers to display fresh fruits, vegetables, and other wares, and birds chirp symphonies from every tree. There is rarely anything more pleasant than all of this gently stirred together and poured freely over the senses.

I didn't have any real plan for the day, but I thought it might be best to avoid Piazza del Popolo. Today was the day. Emily would be here, and while I enjoyed my time with Jack, I'd prefer to stay available. Sure, I could probably run into Jack anywhere—come to think of it, I didn't even know where he lived—but so far, that piazza seemed to be his common area. I found a café just down the street from the Colosseum and had a couple of espressos, a cornetto, and some fresh fruit at a table outside, where I could see the sun commanding the ancient arena out of the dusty blue of the early morning. After I paid, I decided simply to wander. I didn't pull my map from my bag, I didn't seek out any site in particular, I didn't try to keep track of where I was at. I just walked and took in as much as I possibly could, stopping occasionally to rest my feet or write a random thought in my Moleskine. When I sat at a trattoria on a quiet piazza in *Trastevere* for lunch, I realized I'd made several pages of notes that day alone and, even better, that there was a strong story developing within my notes. I spent my lunch going back and forth between eating, writing, and drinking a small carafe of cold white wine. When I took up my wandering once more, my head felt clear and my focus had shifted completely to hashing out the story.

I spent a portion of the afternoon checking out some of the smaller and lower-profile churches I came across, in the interest of both getting out of the heat and seeing some new places. It was early evening before I made it back to my hostel to take a quick shower and change into some fresh clothes. Then, I decided to go sit at the Spanish Steps before finding a place for dinner. The evening chatter rippling across the crowds gathered at the Steps set a nice mood for watching the sun set. After it'd gone completely down, I went off to find a restaurant.

After a long, slow meal of gnocchi that was well worth the wait at a busy restaurant near the Trevi Fountain, I paid the most I'd paid for a meal so far and headed out into the night again. I still hadn't heard from Emily, so I decided to go and check out a couple of different bars for drinks. I walked to Piazza Navona first to see one of my favorite spots in Rome.

The *Fontana dei Quattro Fiumi* might be even more incredible at night than it is during the day, but that goes for all of Rome's fountains, I think. Another of Rome's famous pieces designed by Bernini, the Fountain of the Four Rivers is made up of four travertine sculptures of river gods representing the Danube, the Ganges, the Nile, and the *Rio de la Plata,* four major rivers on the continents where papal influence had spread when the fountain was created in 1651. From the center of the marble base rises another of Rome's granite Egyptian obelisks. The entire piece is situated in the middle of a low, turquoise pool. Underwater lamps shine upward from the edge of the pool creating an otherworldly glow around the sculpture in the middle of the long, rectangular piazza surrounding it.

I stopped for a drink at a table outside one of the restaurants bordering Piazza Navona. While I sipped my Negroni, I wrote down some observations of the fountain, the piazza, and my walk to get there. My thoughts had re-centered on Emily, I realized as I kept glancing at my phone. I knew I could send her a message rather than wait, but I reminded myself not to be overeager and potentially push her away. She said she'd get in touch when she got to Rome; I had to let *her* keep to that plan.

When I'd paid for and finished my drink, I walked a couple of blocks over and had another outside at the little place across *Piazza della Rotonda* from the Pantheon. The ancient, domed church stood ominously beyond the fountain in the center of the square, its columned portico capped by a triangular pediment standing sentinel in front of the large, bronze doors.

I had a second drink in Piazza della Rotonda and decided to move on to the next place. They'd been strong drinks so far, so I was starting to feel them, but I was also getting some decent writing done despite my wondering about Emily. It made sense at that point to keep going, even though it was nearly eleven o'clock.

I wandered a few blocks south toward the Tiber and found myself in *Campo de' Fiori*. When I realized where I was, I decided I'd better find a different area to have a drink. The reputation it had gained for assaults and rowdy college students had killed any draw it might have had for me, and, walking alone, I didn't feel as safe as I would have liked. It was there that Marcus and his friend had been drugged and mugged. As I made my way quickly past the bars and restaurants scattered around the square's edges, I heard a familiar voice talking loudly nearby. Glancing over, I saw Jeremy sitting at a table outside one of them—a pulsing, laser-and-strobe dance club—smoking a cigarette with a group of people I didn't recognize. I walked in his direction.

"Michael!" he said when he saw me coming. "How the hell are ya?" He stood up with some drunken difficulty and gave me an equally drunken hug, a cigarette in one hand and a near-empty glass of beer in the other.

"I'm good, man. So you guys are here. Where's everyone else?" I suddenly felt incredibly curious why Emily hadn't let me know, and I realized an anxious knot was forming in my stomach.

"Yeah, dude! We got into town last night. They're all inside. You should go say hi! I'll come with." He reached down to the ashtray on the table to put out what was left of the cigarette.

"Nah, Jeremy, go ahead and stay here. I feel like you could use the sit-down."

"Good idea! I'll be here." He turned his attention back to the group he was sitting with, who all looked either amused or annoyed by their new friend.

"That's my friend, Michael..." I heard him say as I headed into the club, the knot tightening in my stomach. Inside, I scanned the darkness for any of the rest of Jeremy's group. Between the wall of gyrating people and the flashing, multi-colored lights, I couldn't make out a thing, so I moved around the edge of the crowd, trying to get a better angle rather than having to hack my way through.

Near the DJ booth in the back, I finally saw Kasey and Jenna, dancing away with a couple of overly tanned guys with spiked hair, white tank-tops, and gold chains who looked like they'd come straight from the Jersey shore, but no Emily. As my eyes flicked across sweaty, drunken faces, a small group of people near me stopped their movements and made their way toward the door, likely for a cigarette and a cooldown. It was then that my heart stopped for a moment before it began pounding out of my chest.

In a small space beyond where the group had been were Emily and Jake, squeezed up against each other, lips locked, grinding to the vibrations of the music. Nothing about the scene was anything different from the way she and I had been in the club in Sorrento a few days earlier. Emily's hands ran across Jake's head; his found their way up and down her curves, going so far as reaching up her short, black dress to grab her ass.

I stood motionless, unable to break my gaze, even as people pushed their way past me, sloshing drinks on my shirt and feet. I couldn't believe what I was seeing, kept telling myself it couldn't be them and I was imagining things. It was a couple of minutes before I realized that my hands were clenched in fists and I was shaking from head to toe. Finally, I shoved my way between several people to the neon blue-lit bar near the back of the room.

I hated ordering drinks at places like that, where the bartenders focused only on the hottest women with the fewest clothes, and a guy had to damn near grab them by the shirt to even get a greeting. I found a space between two people at the counter and stepped in sideways. The bartender actually made eye contact and raised his eyebrows. Glancing at the people next to me, I saw several dangerous-looking shots he'd just poured and lit on fire. I nodded at the shots and held up two fingers. He nodded and began pouring. I wasn't in the mood for anything but a strong hit right then. I handed him enough in euro notes to pay for the drinks and blew the first flame out, tipping the shot back. Whatever was in it burned and kicked me in the head. As I held the other shot glass in my hand, allowing the first one to settle, I cycled through memories of my brief time with Emily, wondering what the hell had happened.

She had seemed as interested in me as I was in her. She'd put so much effort into spending time with me, even going as far out of her way as to surprise me in Montecatini. And now she was out on the dance floor, as good as *fucking* Jake. I realized I was shaking again and took the other shot before my jittery hand spilled it all over the place. Then, a pair of familiar shoulders covered by sweaty, blond hair appeared at the bar in front of me. But Emily didn't even realize I was standing right next to her. Her eyes were pointed in front of her, a twenty-euro note in her outstretched hand, as she tried to attract the bartender's attention.

Part of me considered just walking out, but I was drunk and furious enough that I couldn't leave it alone and walk away and leave her behind me. I leaned down to her ear and said, loudly enough for her to hear me over the music, "Glad to see you guys made it safely!"

Surprised by the sudden voice in her ear, she jerked and looked up at me with a drunken look of recognition.

"Michael! You're here!" She smiled sloppily at me and reached up to give me a tight hug.

I stood with my arms at my sides, not returning it. Staring back at her, I felt a hatred in my eyes not unlike that which I'd directed at Liz when I'd dropped her things off at her house. "How was the trip?" I yelled over the din.

"*So* good! Venice was beautiful! I'm so glad you're here!"

I cocked my head slightly and narrowed my eyes. "Are you?"

"What do you mean?"

"What the hell were you doing with me?"

"What do you mean?"

"You know fucking well what I mean! Does he know about us?"

"No, it's fine!"

"'It's *fine*'? What the hell does that even mean?" My throat was parched from all the alcohol without any water to balance it out, so the screaming back and forth over the music agitated the hell out of it.

At that point, Jake stumbled between several people behind us and appeared at my side.

"Mike, my man, there you are! We've been looking all over for you!" He patted me merrily on the back.

In that moment, I felt something snap. I'm still not sure if it was residual emotion from Liz mixed in with whatever I was feeling from this new situation—though it seems likely—and I'm not sure how I did what I did next. In a flash of movement distorted by strobes and lasers, my right hand flew to Jake's throat, I hooked my right heel behind his ankles, and, with all my weight into it, I threw him backward to the disgusting, liquor-soaked floor.

"Michael! Stop it!" Emily screamed, standing still and unsure what to do. Her screams faded into the irregular beats of the music that shook the room.

I suddenly realized I was kneeling with one knee on Jake's chest and my right arm was cocked back, hand curled into a tight fist. Blood dripped from a fresh cut on Jake's left cheekbone, which was already swelling, but the look on his face was more confused than pained or afraid.

Two rough hands grabbed me under the arms and pulled me upward and away from Jake, then shoved me in the back in the opposite direction. Turning around, I saw that it had been a bulky, buzzcut Marine with an Eagle, Globe, and Anchor tattoo on his bicep just below the sleeve of his tight, black T-shirt. He didn't come at me, but he stood his ground in front of Jake, who was still on the floor, the confused expression lingering heavily on his face. Kasey and Jenna were making their way through the crowd behind him, and I saw their eyes dart from Jake to me, back to Jake, and then to Emily, who was fully hidden from my view by Jake's savior.

I stared dumbly down at Jake, unable to fully grasp what had just happened. Then, my focus widened, and I was aware of all the people immediately around me, staring, on edge, and unsure of what else to expect from the crazy guy who'd just thrown some other guy to the ground. My eyes found their way back to Jake and then to Kasey and Jenna. Emily was still eclipsed by the Marine. My mouth opened slowly, but no words came out. My lip quivered, so I shut my mouth. My jaw clenched, and an anxious current surged through my body. Then, I turned and wove my way quickly through the mass toward the front door. I glanced back just as the crowd went back to their dancing and as the Marine conveniently leaned down to help Jake off the floor, allowing a direct view of Emily. She stared at me with a look on her face that I never did fully comprehend.

I started running as soon as I was outside the club. No one seemed to be following me out, since I'd left of my own volition, but I didn't want to take that chance. I needed to get away from there.

"See ya, Michael!" I heard Jeremy call from the same table where I'd left him a short time before. He had no idea what had just happened, but I'm sure once he did, he'd want to see me again for different reasons. Drunken cheers from Jeremy and his companions sent me off into the night.

I ran through some narrow, less-crowded side streets and across a bridge, which I later realized was *Ponte Sisto*, into Trastevere. Slowing down, I breathed heavily, my entire body shaking from a combination of anxiety, adrenaline, and poor physical fitness. Two teetering Germans ambled past me, engrossed in an enthusiastic argument. I headed in the direction from which they'd come and found a bar in a small piazza not far off the Lungotevere.

At a table outside, I ordered a Jameson on the rocks and slouched in my chair as the adrenaline wore off. A dull pain made itself known as I gripped my glass. I switched the glass to my left hand and inspected the knuckles of my right. They'd already swollen a bit, and blood had dried dark along the edges of the broken skin. I sipped the whiskey and then held the condensation-covered glass against my knuckles, letting out a long, slow breathe in relief. Staring at the small church across the street, its façade dimly lit in the flood lights of the square, I replayed the last half hour over and over in my head.

I clenched and unclenched my fist as I realized my hand was shaking. The image of Emily's final stare lingered vividly in my head. My eyes grew wet, and I quickly wiped it away. I ordered another whiskey and fought the feeling of hatred that had tightened my chest.

My phone buzzed in my pocket; it was a text message from Emily. *Where are you, Michael? Will you call me plz?*

I stared at the message on the screen until I was looking through the phone and blinked my eyes back into focus. I tapped the button to reply and began typing out a message, deleted it, and started over. Two more times, the same thing. Eventually, I simply texted, *Tell Jake I'm sorry.* Nothing else I could type out was worth saying. I set my phone on the table and stared at it until the screen went dark. Then, I finished my whiskey and paid the waiter, who seemed eager for his last customer to leave.

I set off at a quick pace toward my hostel, giving Campo de' Fiori a wide berth and ignoring the occasional buzz from the phone in my pocket. It was just after one o'clock when I got into my room, and my head throbbed with a persisting headache from the music. I stumbled to the bed, fell onto it, and was out before I could think back on that disaster of a night.

Chapter 34

I woke at ten the next morning, an hour after I was supposed to meet Jack. "Shit! Fuckfuckfuckfuckfuck!" I jumped out of bed, too hastily as my head was pounding worse than it had been the night before. I ran into the bathroom, took a quick shower, and brushed my teeth before throwing some clothes on and hurrying out the door. The sun shone brightly in the cloudless sky, so I put my sunglasses on to try to dull the headache.

"Shit, Jack, I'm so sorry," I said as I walked up to him where he sat on the steps of the fountain in the piazza.

He smiled at me without an ounce of irritation on his face and gestured at the space next to him. "You look like hell, Michael. What happened?"

"You know Emily, the girl I've been waiting on?"

"Yes, sir."

"Not waiting on her anymore." When his brow furrowed, I delved right into the story of the previous night, Jack listening intently and without interruption. By the end of it, my blood was simmering again, and the shakes were back. I'd done all I could the night before to put things behind me, but there's *always* the next day, when you're hungover and forced to revisit the reasons you feel so shitty. I leaned forward with my elbows on my knees and my head in my hands, trying to slow my breathing a little.

Jack patted me on the back. "Take it easy, Michael. You'll be fine.

I promise you that much. Here, let's go get some coffee. You look like hell."

My mood lightened a little, and I chuckled. "So I've heard. Alright, let's go."

Jack stood up and watched to make sure I could stand alright. Then, we walked out of the piazza and headed to his brother-in-law's café across the river. This time, we sat at a small table outside along the sidewalk.

"I'm really sorry again, for being late," I said as I took a sip of my tiny macchiato. "That's not like me."

"I know it's not. I've known you all of three days, but I know that much, at least. This young lady sounds like she really worked you over, so I can't blame you."

"She definitely did…" Realizing I still had the picture Emily had left on my phone, I pulled it up, zoomed in on her face to keep the rest private, and showed it to Jack.

"Holy shit! She can work me over as much as she'd like," he said.

"Yeah. As you can see, it didn't take much effort on her part." As I closed the photo app, I noticed I had two missed calls and four unread text messages. I ignored them and returned my phone to my pocket.

Jack suddenly grew a little more serious. "We all have at least one girl like that who tests our mettle, who crosses our path and makes us feel like there's nothing more we need from this life. We're lucky if there's only one. Frankly, we've all probably done the same thing to at least one girl in our lives, too. Or will. Even if we don't know it and have the best of intentions. It's how we become who we are and how we become who we need to be for the right person when they come along."

We had a second espresso, and Jack let me vent and talk my way through everything that happened with Emily, as I was wont to do in situations like that. He didn't try to tell me how I should feel or handle it, which I appreciated.

"You ever have a girl like that in your life?"

"Like *that*?" He pointed at the phone in my pocket. "Shit, no!" I laughed.

"Ohhh, yes, I had a couple like that, actually. One of 'em, though…she was a stone-cold *bitch*, and I don't use that term lightly." He paused and insisted on ordering me a cornetto and a small glass of orange juice.

"Her name was Ellen. I met her at the flea market two weeks before I was set to leave for boot camp, and she was hot-*to*-trot. Wasn't a bitch when I met her. Or maybe she was, but it didn't come out until later."

"What happened?"

"We spent those two weeks doing all the things two stupid kids do. Spent every day together, drank too much, stayed up all night. That's a lot of time to fill, mind you." Jack chuckled and smiled to himself as a pleasant memory passed through his mind. "She was an all star with my friends, too. Fit right in; they loved her. We made plans to see Italy when I was done, ironically. I'm glad we didn't, because maybe I wouldn't have met Marcella.

"Anyway, three weeks into training, I get a letter from my best friend back home saying he'd been hearing rumors around town, and finally, one night, he'd seen her in a steamy car by the river with this asshole we'd grown up with. I never heard from her while I was at boot camp, and I made no effort to reconnect when I got back. Found out later she'd also slept with a friend of mine who had been at the flea market when we left. Last thing I heard—oh…twenty, twenty-five years ago—she wound up with three babies from three dads and not a picket fence to show for it. Life is a conniving bitch, herself, I'll say that much."

"Jesus, Jack, that's terrible. I'm sorry."

"Don't be. Like I said, maybe I wouldn't have met Marci if Ellen and I had eventually made it over here. I much prefer the outcome I got." His face stretched into his rosy-cheeked, coffee-stained grin.

We sat in silence for a few minutes, watching the late-morning crowd meander past the café.

Jack glanced at his watch. "I had intended to ask if you wanted to have lunch with me today, but I've got a better idea now. Why don't you spend the better part of the day relaxing and taking care of yourself, and then come by for dinner this evening? I think a slow evening with a home-cooked meal and some salty, old company would do you some good."

It took seconds for me to realize I no longer had unspoken, tentative plans for my remaining days and evenings in Rome, and both of his ideas sounded better than anything I'd probably have chosen to do on my own, given the circumstances.

"That sounds great. Where do you live?"

"Do you have your notebook?"

I handed it to him from my back pocket, and he wrote the address on a page and handed it back to me.

"Piazza di Spagna?"

Jack smiled. "Look for the big green door. Five o'clock? I used to enjoy the long, late dinners, but these days, I'm an early bird."

"Perfect," I said. "I'll be there. Can I bring anything?"

"Stop by Gino's wine shop near the top of the Steps. You can't miss it if you look for all the grapevines. He has the best wine for the best prices, but the trick is to bring your own bottle. Buy one of those big, plastic bottles of water from a market on your way back to the hostel. Drink it, refill it and drink it again, then take the empty bottle with you to Gino and tell him you're meeting me." He met my amused smile with a wink that I'd come to learn was characteristic of Jack.

I thanked him for coffee and breakfast and said goodbye, found a market, and bought two large bottles of water at less than a euro each. My afternoon was spent lying in my bed, first sleeping with my head buried under the pillow, then reading, then trying to write, then sleeping again—anything to get Emily off my mind. It worked on and off.

Spending the bulk of the day on a water diet *did* clean up my mind and my system, and it left me famished by the time I needed to clean myself up and get ready for dinner at Jack's. Around three-thirty, I did a few stretches in front of the window and hopped in the shower. I spent some extra time under the cool stream of water, willing the shit to completely leave my body and my mind. Out of the shower, I shook out my light-blue button-down as much as I could, trying to work out the wrinkles that had accumulated. When I was half-satisfied, I did the same to my khaki pants. Dressed, I neatly folded the sleeves of my shirt to just below my elbows and stood in front of the mirror. I felt presentable. As much as I could be without any real on-the-road clothing maintenance, anyway. With my notebook in my back pocket and my empty water bottles in hand, I locked the door and headed downstairs to find Gino's *enoteca*.

Jack was right: it wasn't difficult to find. There were so many grapevines hanging over the edge of the roof above the door, the door itself was nearly hidden. The interior of the shop itself was small but opened to a large patio area shaded by a canopy of latticed grapevines. There was no question I was in the right place – the balding proprietor behind the counter was very clearly Gino. When the handful of customers ahead of me had paid for their bottles filled from taps behind the counter, I stepped up and stuttered around between Italian and English, trying to tell Gino that I was sent there by Jack Porter. I awkwardly set my bottles on the counter, and he simply smiled and nodded knowingly. He scratched his thick, greying mustache with two fingers while glancing around to see if anyone was watching, then walked to a section of the counter with no wine taps and, after glancing around again, pushed a framed painting of what looked like one of the northern Italian lakes to the side to reveal a stray tap. He carefully filled both bottles almost to the top with a deep, garnet-red wine and recapped them.

"*Cinque euro,*" he said as he placed them in front of me. "Jack has *spettacolare* taste in wine, you won't be disappointed." He tapped the side of his nose in a manner that reminded me of Redford and Newman in *The Sting.*

"Here you go." I handed Gino a five-euro note, shocked at the low cost for about three total liters of wine and slightly skeptical of the quality. "I look forward to trying it. *Grazie mille.*"

"Enjoy. And please tell Jack I say hello."

"I will. *Buonasera.*"

As I came down the Spanish Steps, the green door Jack had mentioned was quite conspicuous, even though it was opened into the depths of the entry hallway of the building, which just happened to be right across the piazza from the Steps. The entryway was tucked between Dior-emblazoned windows. I was perplexed at how I'd never seen Jack in the times I'd passed that square over the past few days. I found Jack's name on the tenant register on the wall next to the door and pressed the button.

A few seconds later: "Michael, is that you?"

"Hi, Jack."

"Come on up, the door will be open. Hold onto the rail in the elevator. It's a rickety ride."

He wasn't wrong. The building was old, and the elevator likely not much younger. I hadn't counted windows outside to know how many floors the building had, but I was on my way to number six, though the elevator moved so slowly I might have been going twice that high.

The elevator opened to a small, windowless landing which housed only two doors, one on either side. I walked up to the one with Jack's address on it and knocked. He opened quickly.

"Hi, Michael! Come in, come in." Jack's cheeks were rosier than normal, and I suspected he'd already had a glass of wine. He wore a black apron over his uniform of white bowling shirt and khaki pants. When he opened the door fully to wave me in, I saw the apron sported the iconic cutout image of Marlon Brando with a red rose corsage. In the space just below Jack's shoulder, a cutout of a hand held a control bar that dangled the words "*il padrino*" on its strings.

"Nice apron," I said.

He smiled and clicked the barbeque tongs he held in his hand. "'Revenge is a dish that tastes best when it is cold,' but filet mignon is not. Let me find some glasses, and you can pour that delicious wine. The steaks are ready to go on."

Fully expecting to see a smoking cast-iron skillet on the stove, I was surprised to smell grill smoke coming through the open door at the end of what Jack had called an apartment, where he had just gone out to just as impressive a patio.

"Jack, this seems more like a penthouse to me!" I called through the apartment as I poured the delicious-smelling red into the two short, simple juice glasses he'd left on the counter.

As I joined him on the patio, which I discovered was on the roof of the building and lined with planters full of beautiful flowers, he said, "Marci's parents were rather generous with their money. I never could get used to it, but I learned to accept it. And I couldn't leave the place after Marci passed." A somber dullness flashed across his typically bright, blue eyes, so quickly I almost didn't catch it.

"They *gave* you this?"

"Sure did," he said as he flipped the two juicy steaks on the grill, his eyes following my gaze as it drew back and forth across the rooftop patio complete with two comfy chairs, a table, and the most spectacular view I'd ever seen from an apartment. Over the tops of the flowers, I had a perfect view of the Spanish Steps, from whence the cacophony of languages floated.

"This place is incredible, Jack. I'd never leave either." Turning to him, I asked, "Is there anything I can do?"

"Try the wine. Then, grab the plates from the table over there and pull the baked potatoes out of the oven. They should be ready."

I took a long drink of the wine that I hadn't touched in my preoccupation with the view in front of me. "Oh my God," I said. "I don't drink a lot of red wine, but this is perfect. Just sweet enough. What kind is it?"

"If Gino ever tells me, I'll let you know." He laughed and took another drink from his glass. "All I know is it's made from '*un'uva speciale*'"—he used a friendly mocking voice and made air quotes with his fingers—"from his family's small, private vineyard near *Fioranello* to the south. I've been badgering him about it for years, and that *bastardo* still keeps it locked tight, even after we're both a bottle of wine in. Some family secret, I'll tell ya."

"It sure is." I couldn't tell you anything about the nose or the body or the tannins, but I could tell you that wine was no slouch. I took the plates inside and carefully pulled the two large, foil-wrapped russets from the oven, balancing them on the plates as I took them back out to Jack.

He carefully positioned a filet and some grilled rounds of zucchini and yellow squash on each plate and carried them over to the table, gesturing at me to join him. "I wasn't kidding when I said home-cooked," he said. "I figure you've probably been having a lot of delightful Italian fare, but it seemed like some comfort food might hit the spot right now."

"You're not wrong. I've never pictured people grilling in Italy, but this is a nice surprise." I carefully cut into the filet mignon in front of me. It was just the right amount of pink and melted like butter the second it was in my mouth.

"Oh, they certainly grill, but it's nothing like Memorial Day weekend or the 4th of July in the States. I keep this as sort of a reminder of home, and I still try to cook out here on those days. Marci loved all the American-style grilling I did."

"Well, if everything else you grill is as perfect as this steak, I can't say I blame her."

"You're too kind. It took years of grilling for me to make a steak like this." His face lit up as he took his first bite. "That *is* good, isn't it?"

The clatter of forks and knives blended into the background with the voices below us as Jack regaled me with his favorite grilling stories, including one about the first time he grilled for Marci's family.

"Beer brats, Michael, beer brats! Only Stefano was supposed to come over, and we were going to watch the SS Lazio match on television. I decided to introduce him to beer brats—soaked in Peroni, of course. Well, when the son of a bitch showed up, who was with him but Mom and Dad."

Chuckling over a sip of wine, I asked, "How'd that go over?"

"They *loved* the damn things! After the way Marci and Stefano had always spoken of their parents, I expected the brats to go in the trash and a migration to be initiated to one of the nicer restaurants in the neighborhood. But no, it's a damn good thing I made so many. No one left hungry *or* disappointed. I always joked with Marci that my beer brats were the reason they gifted us this place." He looked around at the living quarters he was so fortunate to enjoy, memories flashing across his eyes as he took a long drink of wine.

"So"—I swallowed a bite of buttery potato— "if you don't mind me asking, why *did* they give this place to you? It's quite the gift."

"They just wanted to take care of us. Her father had done very well for himself at a large shipping company, and their home life was rather modest, despite their means. So, when Marcella and I decided to get married, this was our wedding gift." Anticipating my next question, he added, "Don't worry, Stefano didn't get left out. His flat is on the Janiculum and he can see all of Rome."

"That sounds incredible," I said as my mind traveled across the Tiber and through Trastevere to the *Gianicolo* Hill above it. "I'd take this any day, though. I love that you're just in the middle of it all."

"It's a nice place to be. I walk a lot, and it's a short walk anywhere from here. Some people don't like the noise of the crowds, but it reminds me how alive this city still is."

I admired Jack. He was a widower and he was up there in years— I guessed seventy, give or take—but life hadn't taken an obvious toll as with so many others his age or even younger. He carried the wisdom and wrinkles of his years, but he radiated the youth of a far younger man. For a man who'd been through as much as I'd guessed he had, based on the time in the military he had mentioned, his constant state of joy was stunning.

We chatted a little more as we finished our meal and one of the bottles of wine, and I helped Jack clean up the kitchen. As he finished drying the last plate—we handwashed everything—he looked at his watch and said, "Michael, do you have time to take a walk with me?"

"I've got nowhere to be. That sounds like a good idea."

"Perfect. Then now is the time." Jack hung his apron on a hook next to the refrigerator and ushered me out the door, locking it behind us.

The Spanish Steps had filled up even more in the evening sunlight. Finding an unobstructed path to the top seemed nearly impossible, so I was glad when Jack headed in the opposite direction toward the Tiber. Upon meeting the river, we followed the pathway south at a leisurely pace.

As we walked in silence for a few minutes, I realized our actions mimicked each other. We both took in as much as we could of our surroundings, our focus not lingering for too long on any one thing or person. It seemed like everyone was out doing the same thing in one fashion or another. We passed couples of all ages, groups of younger people sitting on the low walls and laughing amongst themselves, occasional loners doing what I'd have been doing if not for Jack's invitation. The thing I noticed about all of them, and about Jack and myself, is that everyone seemed simply at peace. The evening was warm, but the shade from the trees lining the river brought the temperature to a comfortable level. The sun had sunk below most of the buildings by then, casting a pacifying orange glow over the entire city.

"Marci and I used to walk this route almost every night."

"Every night? That's quite the commitment. I bet it kept you guys in great shape."

Jack chuckled and patted the small gut that likely came from spending years with an Italian wife who loved to cook. "For a while anyway. It took a lot for us to miss it. Rain, shine, snow, or sleet, we were out here. Not that we get a lot of snow or sleet in Rome, but you get the idea. It doesn't get overly cold here in the winter, but there were some days we'd go out when it was colder than a well-digger's ass, so right back inside we went for a hot toddy."

"Doesn't sound like a half-bad plan B."

"Not at all. So, we'll follow the river all the way down to *Ponte Testaccio* near the south end of Trastevere, cross, and head back up-river. And we'll stop—Marci and I always did—for a cocktail at one of a handful of places we really enjoyed. If you've got the time, of course."

I nodded, honored that Jack would so eagerly include me on what seemed to be such a sacred *passeggiata*. "I've got nowhere to be."

Chapter 35

Jack pointed out some of the places he and Marcella had stopped for drinks or a meal and the churches they had explored. Rome's endless supply of churches never ceased to amaze me. Some were crammed into spaces so unlikely, you'd miss them if you blinked. It wasn't until we crossed Ponte Testaccio and turned north along the *Lungotevere Portuense* that I noticed the sidewalk was becoming home to a few leaves. Sure enough, I looked up at the London planes overhead and saw several leaves falling here and there, floating smoothly down to their final resting place on the sidewalk. Autumn was coming.

For a few seconds, I was transported home to where the leaves were likely falling in the same way, slowly turning from green to the same oranges and yellows and reds that were beginning to spatter the plane trees. It would be hard to leave Italy the next day, but there was some light at the State-side end of the tunnel because fall was my favorite season. I looked forward to the crisp mornings, warm days, and the crunchy footsteps that came with autumn in Oregon. I looked forward to wearing a comfy sweatshirt and jeans again, and I longed for the smell of chimney smoke on cold evening walks. Just as quickly as I found myself in Eugene, I was back along the Tiber with Jack, and I didn't want to go anywhere for the moment.

We came around the bend in the river where we could see Castel Sant'Angelo basking in the evening light. Farther around the bend, the

Bridge of Angels came into view, its occupants appearing golden on their pedestals. Jack led us away from the Lungotevere and down a couple of side streets to Via della Conciliazione, where we were seated at a table along the sidewalk at the Caffé San Pietro.

"*Due* Bombay Sapphires, *per favore,*" Jack said when the waiter came around. "*Con ghiaccio.*" The waiter nodded and left to place the order. "Ice is okay, I hope? I like my gin on the rocks with nothing else."

"That sounds perfect to me."

"Good. Before Gino, I wasn't much of a wine-drinker, much to Marci's chagrin. 'What Italian woman marries a man who doesn't drink wine? *Una donna sciocca!*' she always yelled to the sky. We could always agree on a nice, long pour of Bombay Sapphire, though. I think we ended up drinking more of that than wine, eventually."

"I'm the only person I know who even *likes* gin."

"It's an acquired taste. I think you're just older than your birth certificate says you are." Jack chuckled and leaned back from the table as the waiter placed our drinks on cocktail napkins in front of us.

"*Grazie,*" we both said. The waiter gave a slight bow and went to serve another table.

"To new friends, pleasant memories, and the women who ruin us," Jack said as he lifted his glass toward me. "*Cin cin.*"

"*Cin cin,*" I said, touching the rim of my glass to his.

Clink, said the glasses happily.

We drank two more Bombay Sapphires each as we sat facing the street that leads to St. Peter's Basilica, watching the myriad groups of people enjoying their own *passeggiatas.* It wasn't a weekend night, but even the locals seemed to be out in full force, meeting their friends, shooting the shit, and simply enjoying the fact that the heat wave was finally over. The ritualistic evening stroll was one of my favorite

Italian traditions I'd come across, and one I wanted to try to propagate amongst my friends back home.

"So, Michael, what do your folks think of you traveling around Italy on your own? You're young enough that I imagine they must be somewhat concerned."

I forced a smile and took a long drink of the third Bombay the waiter had just brought. "If they even knew I was over here, they *might* be concerned, but that's probably a long shot."

A question mark crossed Jack's face, so I elaborated, searching for the right words. "They...didn't really ever want to be parents, I think. They were always good to me, but they were very focused on their careers all the time, and any real time spent as a family was at church on Sundays. When I graduated high school, they helped me find an apartment and moved to Arizona the second my last box was out of the house."

"Do you talk to them much?"

"We exchange Christmas and birthday cards, usually with gift cards inside. I don't remember the last time we spoke on the phone, and I haven't seen them since they left."

"That's difficult, Michael, I'm very sorry."

"It's alright, I make it work. I was always closer with some of my friends' families around home anyway, so I usually have somewhere to go for Thanksgiving and Christmas."

"That's good to hear, but it still hurts my heart. No child deserves that from their parents."

"It could've been worse, though."

"That is very true."

We sat and sipped our gin in a few moments of silence and watched people walk by, gasping in delight at the way the basilica looked in the evening light.

"Marci and I got a little too drunk here more than once," Jack said, as we neared the end of our third round.

"I think I'm a little too drunk *now*." I laughed, having just realized how much the wine and liquor had caught up to me. "Not spinning yet, but this should probably be my last one. I've got a longer walk back than you, and I fly out tomorrow evening."

"Leaving already? We're just getting started!" Jack's face was rosier than usual, and while his typical cheer was still very present, I sensed a true hint of disappointment behind it.

"I know, I really wish I was staying longer. But I'm running out of travel money, and I've got no job to go to when I get back." I laughed, but it was in that moment that the reality of returning home hit me. *You don't have a job, and your savings will only last so long. What are you gonna do?*

We finished the last drops from our glasses, and Jack paid our tab before I could even think about pulling out my wallet.

"I mean I have enough money to pay for *drinks,*" I said. "But thank you, Jack. I appreciate it."

"Hey, I owe you, kid. It's been nice spending this time getting to know you over the last few days." His demeanor saddened as we began the walk back to his apartment. "I don't hear much from my daughters anymore. As a matter of fact, I don't think we've spoken since just after their mother's funeral."

"I didn't know you had daughters, Jack. The way you've talked about life here with Marci, I guess I never thought to ask. Jesus, I'm really sorry to hear that."

"Yes, Mia and Isabella. It's alright. They do send Christmas and birthday cards every year with pictures of their kids. They each have two of their own that're growing so fast. I'll show you when we get back to the apartment."

"I'd like that."

Sensing what I'd left unasked, he added, "I wouldn't move back to the States after Marci died. They really wanted me to, said there was no point in me staying a lonely, old man in a city 6,000 miles away from home. I told them this *was* my home and that I'd love for them to keep visiting as they had. They both married well and made plenty of money that had them taking vacations several times a year. Some years, they'd get over here to visit us *twice*. But even the once-a-year visits stopped after I told them I was staying. So did the phone calls."

"That's terrible, Jack. They can't expect you to just uproot things at this point in life."

"I suppose not. I make sure to send surprises for all their birthdays and Christmas, but I never know if the kids like them or not. I like to think that they do."

I grew very annoyed, and I'd never even met his daughters. Fortunately, I also felt suddenly sober and had my wits enough about me not to fuel the fire. I simply said, "I'm really sorry, Jack. I've known you less than a week, but I don't understand how they could shut you out so much. You seem like you care. I've appreciated our time the last few days, and I've *really* appreciated you letting me vent about all my shit."

He smiled for the first time in several minutes. "I'm glad you decided to forego whatever hot rebound you might have found somewhere in the city to spend more time with an old asshole like me. Letting you vent is the least I could do. You've just got to remember to roll up your pantlegs sometimes because the shit can get very deep. It doesn't do any good to just sit down in it and hope it passes on its own. Occasionally it might, but more often than not, you need to shovel your way through. It doesn't matter if the direction you're going is agreeable to other people or not. If it's where *you* need to go, then it's the right direction."

His advice put a smile on my face, and I realized how many times in the past couple of years I had just sat and hoped. Like sending thoughts and prayers to my own disasters. It never did me any good, not when I was in a place to truly *do something*. It was just a matter of figuring out what I needed to do.

Jack spent the rest of the walk talking about his grandkids: Eric, 12; Ellie, 8; Bryson, 4; and Daniel, 2. Despite having little contact with them over their lives, and no contact whatsoever with the younger two, he was so proud and seemed to remember every single detail Mia and Isabella had ever chosen to share about his grandchildren. It pained me to know that they made no real effort to bring the kids and Jack together.

"I've floated the idea of me flying out to visit. They live in Madison and Chicago, so it wouldn't be too difficult to see them both. But they always have reasons why it's not a good time—prior commitments, work functions, bullshit like that. So, I keep sending cards and gifts and occasionally throwing the idea out there again, just in case."

The Spanish Steps were just as full as they had been when we left the apartment, and the surrounding streets were even more lively. We took the elevator up, and Jack unlocked the door.

"I'll show you the grandkids real quick so you can get back to your room and get some rest." He grabbed a couple of frames from the bookshelf in the far corner and brought them over.

Both families smiled happily at the camera, but I felt bad that the kids would likely never get a good opportunity to know their grandpa. The oldest, Eric, even looked like what I imagined Jack to look like at that age. I hoped—but doubted—that the girls at least told the kids many stories about their grandma and grandpa. Their memory didn't deserve to be lost to a stale, selfish grudge.

"That's a good-looking family you've got, Jack. I'm sure they'll come around soon. They've got to. Kids need to know their grandparents. I never did, but they died when I was a baby. A year or so apart."

"Thank you. I hope they do. It's been far too long."

"Hey, I don't fly out until around six tomorrow evening, and I don't need to be out of my room until eleven. I was going to just take the train out to the airport and hang out there for a few hours, but do you have time to get coffee in the morning?"

Jack's cloud lifted, and his eyes lit up. "I'd like that. What time?"

"How's eight-thirty? I want to leave a little time for a long walk back to the hostel afterward."

"Eight-thirty is just fine. I'll see you then, at the piazza?"

"Perfect. See you then, Jack. Have a good night, and thank you for the drinks and for taking me on your little tour of Rome."

"I enjoyed it very much, Michael. See you in the morning."

I took a long walk back to the hostel that night, too. I wanted to see Rome after dark one last time before heading back to Oregon. Every city has its own kind of magic when the sun goes down, and Rome's is a timeless magic that is damn near painful to leave. Strolling past the churches, the fountains, and the Colosseum, all mysteriously glowing amber or turquoise in their accent lights, I found myself impossibly full of gratitude for this trip bringing Jack into my life. My limited relationship with my parents had left me wandering aimlessly through the current stage of my life. I realized as I overlooked the luminous Trevi that what I'd needed, what I'd been subconsciously searching for, was someone to help me up, dust me off, and remind me in their way that I was being a fucking idiot. Jack was that person, and he couldn't have come along at a better time.

I was back in my room a little after ten-thirty. I got ready for bed and flopped on top of the covers, setting the alarm on my phone for seven the next morning so I'd be sure to have time to get packed before meeting Jack.

My eyes seemed to open as quickly as they'd closed, but my watch said two and a half hours had passed. I was oddly alert and inundated with thoughts for the book idea I'd been conceiving. In the chair in front of the open window, I propped my feet on the sill and closed my eyes as the first true autumn breeze blew through my hair, bringing with it just a hint of the smell of the trees down the street. Then, I opened to a fresh page and started writing.

Chapter 36

My alarm went off in the morning, but I had stopped writing only to watch light flood the city as the sun came up. I flipped through my notebook with a painfully cramped hand, staring in astonishment at the ink-filled pages.

What the hell did I do? I asked myself, flipping through the Moleskine again. I'd never had a writing session like that in my life, and I wasn't entirely certain what I was seeing was even real considering I hadn't slept after waking up the first time. After rereading several of the pages and finding myself pleasantly surprised at what I'd written, I realized my alarm was still going off and hit the button to stop it. Morning light came through the window, illuminating the small, black notebook sitting on the sill. I gazed at it for a moment with heavy eyelids, still not sure how I'd done what I appeared to have done overnight.

Eventually, I took a quick shower and put on a T-shirt and pants in anticipation of a cool morning and the long flight ahead, then packed my luggage and set it at the end of the bed. With my notebook in my back pocket, I locked the door and walked to Piazza del Popolo.

Jack was already on the steps beneath the obelisk when I arrived, and he stood and gave me a smile and a kind handshake. His usual rosy joy had fully returned to his face.

"Morning, Jack," I said, following with a lion-like yawn. I pulled my sunglasses off and rubbed my eyes.

"Michael, you look like hell." He chuckled and stared at me for a moment. "But you seem...happy. What happened?"

I pulled the Moleskine from my pocket and held it out to him. "This."

Jack took the notebook and, after an approving nod from me, opened it and flipped through the pages. After stopping to read a sentence here and there, he handed it back. "Good work, Michael. There's a lot of you in there, I don't doubt. The real question is: did you sleep *at all?*"

"Less than three hours. And not since I started writing."

"Oh boy, that won't do with the long day you've got ahead of you. Let's go get you some caffeine."

At a sidewalk table outside a café near one of the churches, we ordered two espressos and some cornetti and enjoyed our view of the entire piazza.

"I proposed to Marcella here," he said after sipping his coffee. At my caught-off-guard look, he said, "I realized I never told you."

"Here? At the café?"

"The piazza. Over there by the lion at the east corner of the obelisk." He pointed toward the center of the square.

"Ah." I nodded, finally having an answer as to why he seemed to spend so much time there, though I realized I'd never really explored the question.

In the spirit of his uncanny ability to read my mind, Jack added, "I come here damn near every day, even for just a few minutes. I feel her everywhere, you know, but never more than here. I proposed here because it's where I first saw her, forty-eight years ago. More beautiful than any woman I'd ever imagined winding up with, at the beginning and at the end."

Wow, I thought. *And I thought I was a hopeless romantic.* "You loved her so much."

"*Love* her so much." He winked and ordered two more espressos.

Over the next hour, Jack prompted me through a recap of the finer points of my trip, strategically switching directions when I neared the lower points.

Wise old bastard, I know what you're doing. But I was grateful that he did his damnedest to send me home with the best possible impression of my time there. It was an impression that, even then, I knew would be deep and lasting.

"Michael, it's okay to cherish the time you spent with Emily, you know. Those are pleasant memories to have, no matter what followed. Some people in life are temporary, and some are lasting. Appreciate both, but when you have to make a choice, spend your energy on the ones who last."

I hadn't thought about it that way before, but he made a good point. The time with her in Sant'Agnello and Montecatini had been extraordinary. I knew I'd never forget it, so there was no point in tarnishing it by holding onto the bitterness I'd felt following the events in Campo de' Fiori, nor in trying to force myself toward the wrong thing.

As we finished the Irish coffees Jack had ordered after the second espressos, he pulled my notebook back across the table and flipped through again. "Keep this up," he said firmly, holding it between us pointedly like a scolding Sunday school teacher might wave a Bible at a disobedient kid. "I've only read a few words, but I know you've got something good to say. So say it."

"Thank you, Jack. I will. It's a long flight so"—I saw his eyebrows raise—"*after* I get some sleep, I'll get back to it. I've got a fresh notebook ready to go in my bag. Hopefully I need it."

"You will. Especially after you sleep a little."

I drew my wallet quicker when the waiter came around and insisted on paying our tab. Jack lost graciously and thanked me.

"Are you going back home now?" I asked as we walked slowly across the piazza.

"Not yet. I think I'll go see Stefano and maybe take a little walk in the Villa Borghese."

We sat on the steps next to each other and stared across the square at the two churches and the long avenue between them. Jack broke the silence with more stories of his and Marci's younger years together. After about twenty minutes, a middle-aged photographer who'd been wandering around the piazza approached us.

"May I take your picture?" he asked in a thick, Dutch accent.

Jack and I glanced at each other, and I asked, "How much?"

"Oh, no, please. You've misunderstood. I just like to take pictures for people. No charge at all. I can even send them to you by email if you'd like."

I looked at Jack again, and we both shrugged. "Sure, that'd be great," I said.

The photographer told us to continue our conversation as if he wasn't even there, and we obliged. He snapped several photos and, reviewing them on his camera screen, said, "That is beautiful!" He leaned over to show us the photos.

"Those are fantastic. Thank you so much," I said. I wrote my email address on a page in my notebook, tore it out, and handed it to him.

"I'll send to you soon. Thank you for letting me take your photo. It is a joy of mine to capture moments for people. Enjoy your day." And with that he was off.

"Well, he was interesting," said Jack as we watched the

photographer wander toward the edge of the piazza.

"Nice of him, too."

We sat in silence for a few more minutes, breathing in the morning air.

"Alright, well..." This was that awkward moment of goodbyes I always hated, and it was especially difficult to say goodbye to Jack. I extended my hand. "Thank you...for everything, Jack. I'm really glad you spoke up that first day. These days in Rome wouldn't have been the same."

"No, but you still would have found a way to enjoy them on your own." We shook hands, and then he pulled me in for a warm, paternal hug. With two firm pats on the back, he said, "Take care of yourself, Michael. You've got a lot to offer a lot of people, don't forget that. Write me sometime. You have my address. Please send me a print of that photo, too. I don't use email." He chuckled.

I felt tears welling in my eyes and tried to blink them away before stepping back from Jack. "I will, Jack. I promise I will." I'd made a lot of in-the-moment promises to people in my young adulthood that I never kept, but this was not going to be one of those.

"Go say goodbye to the city, kid. And write well of it."

I returned his warm smile. "There's no other way to write of it. Bye, Jack." And I left him sitting in his usual spot at the base of Piazza del Popolo's obelisk, just feet away from where he first viewed his wife-to-be, and where he later asked her to marry him. At the edge of the piazza, I took a deep breath and turned around one last time. Even from a distance, I could see that warm smile spread across Jack Porter's rosy face under his Panama hat as he lifted a hand in farewell. I raised my hand back and smiled as best I could, turning back to the street ahead of me as a single tear trickled down my cheek.

My walk back to the hostel was brisk but scenic. I made a wide loop that took me past Castel Sant'Angelo, St. Peter's, the Pantheon, the Trevi Fountain, Piazza Navona, the Vittoriano, the Forum, and the Colosseum. As I walked, I breathed in the fresh air of the emerging Roman autumn and appreciated the sunlight splashed across the buildings, monuments, and fountains. My chest was tight as I tried to accept that I was going home.

As I stopped for a last piece of fresh coconut from the vendor near the Forum, my phone buzzed in my pocket. It was a text message from Emily, her pretty eyes staring up at me from the tiny picture next to her name.

Are you still in Rome?

I thought for a split second about what I might say and if I had time to try to see her, but instead deleted the message, her photo, and her phone number, and returned my phone to my pocket.

Check-out was quick once I had given my room a last look for anything I might have left out of my luggage, and I had an unimpeded walk to Termini. I bought a ticket for a few euros and waited about twenty minutes for the next train to leave for FCO. I spent the half-hour train ride staring out the window, avoiding social contact with anyone around me. At the airport, after checking in for my first flight to Atlanta and receiving my boarding pass, I found a quiet corner near a food court and staked my claim. I needed to sleep, and I knew it'd be difficult once I was in the air. It always was.

My flight wasn't for another five and a half hours, so I set an alarm for four hours and lay down on the bench with my messenger bag under my head, the shoulder strap looped through the handle of my luggage. I was out cold in minutes.

The alarm chimed and I sat upright after rubbing the sleep from my eyes. My stomach growled because I hadn't eaten any lunch beyond the piece of coconut, so I grabbed a sandwich and a bottle of water at a nearby market. Then, I found my terminal and pulled out my notebook to figure out where I'd left off. I reread and took more notes all the way until my seating group was called to board.

Chapter 37

As the tires hit the tarmac at PDX, I felt a deeper sense of purpose than I'd ever felt before. Waiting for the pilot to give permission to leave our seats, I flipped through the fresh notebook I'd damn near filled in the eighteen hours since flying out of Leonardo da Vinci-Fiumicino. As soon as we'd settled into the flight, I'd pulled out the spare Moleskine I'd brought along and tore off the plastic wrap and the orange label, writing my name, cell phone number, and promise of a twenty-dollar reward on the lines of the first page as I did with all my notebooks. At the top of the next page, I wrote *In the Piazza* and underlined it. *That could use some work*, I thought. Then, the words had poured out.

I'd stopped writing only twice that I could remember: first, when my hand cramped up after a few hours and I decided to watch an in-flight movie to give it a break; and second, during an hour-long layover in Atlanta when I found a Sam Adams brewpub right across the concourse from my next gate.

Any cold beer sounded perfect, but what really drew me in was the poster of an enormous, frosty mug of Octoberfest, their autumnal release that had become a favorite of mine the previous year. I ordered one at the counter and found a stool at a long, high table where a businessman and two older couples sat. The 22-ounce mug was made of such thick glass that my forearm strained just to bring it to drinking level. I breathed in the mildly spiced aroma as I tipped back the glass and the burnt copper-colored elixir hit my tongue, flooding me with everything I loved about fall. Warm sun, crisp air, the smell and sound of leaves crunching with each step. I was almost home, and I was happy about it.

When the pilot gave the go-ahead, I hurried off the plane as quick as the flow of people would allow. The sight of the iconic teal carpet was welcome as I found my way downstairs to the baggage claim. When my luggage finally came around, I pulled it off the conveyor belt, gave it a quick once-over, and headed toward the coffee shop where Marcus said he'd meet me when we'd texted briefly prior to my flight out of Atlanta. Sitting at a table sipping an iced coffee, he wasn't hard to find. He waved me over and stood to give me a hug.

"Welcome back, man." He handed me a second iced coffee he'd bought.

"You too. Thanks, I need this."

"I thought you might. How was it?"

"Unbelievable. It was so tough to leave, but I'm ready to be home for a bit."

"I feel ya. New York was too short, but it was a good time."

As we made our way to find his car in the multi-level parking garage in front of the airport, he told me about his trip to New York. His girlfriend was happily surprised to see him, and they'd had a wonderful time exploring the city.

"But enough about me. Did you get any writing done? I'm sure you spent some time at a café or two."

We got in the car, and I pulled out my notebook. "I did a little. Look at this." I held the notebook open in front of Marcus and flipped through the pages. "I think I got a book out of it."

"Holy shit!" He grabbed the notebook from my hand and riffled through slowly. "You did some work. You did all this while you were over there?"

"That's just from the flight *back*. I filled up my other notebook with notes before I left Rome. I can't feel my hand."

Marcus laughed and handed the Moleskine back. "Jesus, dude, I would guess not. I bet you're exhausted between the traveling, the flying, and all this writing."

"I am, but I've also never been more motivated. I think I'm gonna hit my bed as soon as I'm home, then get up early and start back at it."

"I'm glad to hear that. I know you've been struggling with it for a while, so it must be nice to have something driving you like this."

"You have no idea. For once, it's something I *know* I need to do."

We spent a good portion of the two-hour drive home talking about my trip. Marcus had been there during and after Liz, so he understood how bad the whole Emily thing had been for me and why it had sent me to such an incensed place.

"You did good, deleting her number and not responding to her texts. Old Michael wouldn't have done that."

"I had some guidance," I said, transitioning the conversation to the old man who'd approached me in Piazza del Popolo.

Marcus dropped me off at my place a little after ten, and, after I'd thanked him for picking me up and said goodbye, I did exactly as I said I would. Without bothering to unpack, I dropped my luggage in the living room, went into my bedroom, and collapsed on my bed. It felt better than anything I could think of after two weeks of sleeping on foreign mattresses. I didn't set the alarm on my phone but opened the blinds and closed my eyes. I had an unusual level of faith that I'd wake up the next morning at a decent time, ready to get at the page again.

Chapter 38

I spent the next month doing exactly that. After transferring everything from my notebook to a Microsoft Word document, I kept going on my laptop. Without a job to worry about, it was refreshingly easy to get into a habit of waking up at seven and taking a short walk in the morning with coffee before sitting down to write with more coffee. Sometimes, I'd make a late breakfast, and lunch was usually pretty simple, but I always took my time making dinner. After a longer walk and some reading in the evening, I felt ready for bed at a decent hour and usually fell asleep quickly. I wanted to be sure I wasn't burning myself out on the writing itself, and the consistency helped me feel good about my days. It was a marathon I'd never thought I could do, but at the end of it I had a 300-page first draft. At that point, I really didn't know what to do with it. My first instinct was to get in touch with Brian, but then I remembered my promise to write to Jack, and I did.

Dear Jack,

It's finished. I don't know how, but it's finished. There are 300 pages, and I think they're mostly decent. I'm excited for you to read it, but you're going to have to wait until it's been edited by someone. I want to be sure you get the best possible version of it.

It's been difficult, revisiting things with Emily as I've had to in order to write this thing. A lot of nights, she kept me up. I realized at one point that I could probably remember her phone number and damn near tried texting her before ultimately leaving my phone in the other room and getting back to work. It hurts that it didn't turn into anything more, but I'm happy I can still appreciate it for what it was – I have you to thank for that. I don't know how the rest of my trip would have gone if you and I hadn't met.

But enough about me. How the hell have you been, Jack? Tell me what's going on in Rome right now. I hope you're doing well and still getting some quality time at your favorite places. I'd really like to make it back there to see you again soon.

Very sincerely,

Michael Wise

Once I'd reread the letter, I sealed it in an envelope and placed it by my front door so I would remember to take it out. Then, I emailed Brian. He responded much more quickly than I had expected, and we met for beers a couple of nights later.

"Funny that you emailed me, Michael. I'd been meaning to get in touch with you, too. What's been going on? How was your trip?"

I took a long drink of my beer as I opened my bag and pulled out my printed manuscript, setting it carefully on the table in front of him.

Brian set his beer back on the coaster and leaned over the pages. "*In the Piazza...*" His eyes went quickly from the stack of pages to me to the stack to me again. "You wrote this?"

"Mmm-hm. Wrote nonstop on the flight home, and I've been working on it for the past month that I've been back. I think it might be alright, and I want you to read it. Don't judge it by the title, though. Still not sure how I feel about that."

Brian was already flipping through the pages, taking the time to read a paragraph here and there. "I *want* to read it. Can I take this copy?"

"Sure, I have another one at home."

"Great. I should be able to knock this out in the next couple of days."

"I look forward to hearing what you think. What were you wanting to get in touch with me about?"

"Huh?" Brian looked up from the page he was reading and took a sip of his beer. "Oh, yeah, I just wanted to hear about Italy. I know it took a lot for you to quit the restaurant like you did, so I hope no panic from that hung around and ruined your trip at all."

"It popped into my head a couple of times, but overall, the trip was great. Best time of my life, actually. I figure I'll be able to find *something* now that I'm back. I've got enough saved, still, to pay rent and bills for another month or so."

The next hour flew by as Brian asked questions and listened intently to my answers about the goings-on of my two weeks in Italy. The whole time he seemed very involved in what I was saying, but he also seemed to be deep in thought.

"That sounds like a solid trip," he said when I ended with getting back to Eugene and writing the rest of the draft. "And even though it's the *in*tangible benefits that people like you and me travel for, you

wound up getting something tangible out of it." He held up the manuscript, the pages flopping into a fan.

I couldn't help but smile at the sight of what I'd completed in
what, after the fact, felt like no time at all. One of the most beautiful
moments in writing is when a chink in the dam bursts into a goddamn
flood.

A few nights later, on Saturday evening, I took advantage of the un-
characteristically warm November air and sat on my patio with a
Jameson on the rocks. It was early in the night, so a lot of the college
kids who lived in the complex were just showing up to various apartments to pregame before heading to a bar or a house party on campus.
Carrie walked by, her short, black dress causing me to choke on a sip
of my whiskey.

"Hi, Michael! You going out tonight?"

"No, I don't think so. Think I'll just relax at home. You look nice."
There's some confidence you never had before, Michael.

"Aww, thanks! Well, have a good evening then. If you change
your mind, look for me downtown!" She waved and casually flipped
her hair, which seemed to emit a golden glow in the night.

"I will. Have fun!" I returned her smile and waved goodbye. That
was when my phone buzzed on the glass table beside me. My chest
tightened when I looked at the caller ID on the screen. I pushed the
button to answer.

"Hey, Brian. How's it going?"

"Not bad, Michael. What're you up to?"

"Sitting outside my apartment with a glass of whiskey. It's a nice
night." I watched as several more attractive girls walked by, dressed
for a night out. "*Really* nice."

"Good to hear that you're sitting down."

Curiosity inflated inside me. "Why…?"

"It's phenomenal, Michael. I finished it in a day in a half. I rescheduled two meetings to finish it."

Pride shoved the ballooned curiosity aside. "Seriously? You liked it that much?" I set my glass down on the table when I noticed my hand quivering. Brian was only one person, and a person who I didn't know *that* well, but he was someone whose opinion I knew I respected.

"I'll say it again. *Phenomenal.* And there's something else."

I had no idea what else there could be, so I didn't say anything, instead picking my glass up for a quick drink to try to calm my nerves.

"I hope you don't mind, but I showed it to someone. A friend of mine who's visiting from Portland."

Rather than getting upset at Brian for showing someone my manuscript without asking me, I followed my curiosity. "And?"

"He read the first three chapters and loved it."

Whew. "Well, good. That's two people who like it at least." That thought alone was enough to bring a smile to my face.

"More than two people are gonna love it, Michael. My friend works for a small press up in Portland. He wants to *publish it.*"

All the breath I had left my body, and the pounding of my heart drowned out the chatter of passersby. I was thankful I'd placed my glass back on the table.

"Michael?"

I took a deep breath. "Yeah, yeah, I'm here. You're fuckin' with me, right?" I knew he wouldn't be, but I had to make sure.

Brian laughed. "Of course I'm not. It's *good*, Michael. He even figured you might already have a publisher from *your previous books.*"

"Ha! It's not *that* good."

"It is. Accept it."

"I'm trying, but that's a lot to take in. Can I call you back tomorrow?"

"Sure thing. I didn't want to take up much of your night, but I thought you might want to hear the news."

"Well, you were right about that. Thank you, Brian. I appreciate you reading it. And sharing it."

"No problem, man. I'm excited for you. We'll talk tomorrow."

"Sounds good. Goodnight." I ended the call and set my phone back down on the table, picking up my whiskey once more. Holding the glass up against the light shining from one of the poles along the path, I took in its beautiful amber color before tipping the rim against my lips.

Chapter 39

Brian and I talked again the next day after I'd woken up early and gone for a walk along the river path. The night before, I had poured one more glass of whiskey to celebrate my news, drank it slowly outside, and then went to bed at a decent time. Despite my excitement, I managed to fall asleep quickly.

We decided to meet for coffee at a newer place downtown, across Willamette Street from Kesey Square. There were some small picnic tables outside, and the streets were pleasantly quiet, even by ten o'clock. The coffee menu was simple and limited, something I unexpectedly appreciated. I ordered a cortado. Brian, a latte. The barista served them within a few minutes, and mine came with a small glass of soda water.

Outside in the chilly air, Brian slid a sturdy business card across the table to me as we each took a long sip of our coffee to warm our bones. I rubbed the charcoal-colored card between my fingers, feeling its weight and admiring the quality. On one side, in simple, cerulean text:

Both Ends Press
Brooks Leighton, Talent Curator

His contact information was below that, along with the company web address.

"Brooks Leighton, huh? How do you know the guy?"

"We had a few classes together in college. I've done some work for him and some of the writers in his stable." Brian had pulled his laptop out of his bag and was navigating with the touchpad.

"Hm." I flipped the card over to find a simple logo: a candle of the same blue color as the text on the other side, laying horizontally with an orange flame burning from a wick at each end. "Fancy card. How 'small' is this press?"

"It's not huge, don't get the wrong idea. Brooks just believes in a strong image. Who's going to publish with someone who doesn't take the work as seriously as the writer does? But it's big enough. He's got a lot of great connections, so they've got some decent distribution channels across the country. Here, look."

I took his laptop from him and adjusted the screen to decrease the glare from the sun. I was looking at an elegantly clean homepage that featured an animated version of the candle graphic from the business card, flames flickering away, and the name of the press. Below that were photos of three featured authors who had recently released books. I clicked around the various pages and discovered that Both Ends had, to date, published twenty-eight books by eighteen different authors and had several of them in Barnes and Noble, Powell's, and various smaller bookstores in thirty-five states. The most refreshing thing I noticed when reading author bios, different from a lot of smaller publishers I'd heard of, was that around two thirds of the authors on the roster were relative nobodies. That is, they weren't known academics or journalists or anyone of any renown of any kind. They, like me, were just people writing something they felt needed to be written, who found an opportunity to share it with a lot of people.

"Seems legit," I said, clicking around the site a little more before turning Brian's laptop back toward him.

"They are. And they want to publish *your* book, Michael. They *really* want to publish it."

Taking another sip of my coffee, I gazed thoughtfully at the table between us before redirecting my eyes at Brian. "Any chance you can set up a meeting? How long is he in town?"

Brian clapped his hands together and grinned at me. "Come on," he said as he repacked his laptop in his bag and picked up his coffee. "Brooks is inside."

"Pretty confident I'd be interested, huh?"

Brian shrugged. "I didn't want to waste an opportunity since he was already down here."

I followed Brian inside the coffee shop, which also had a full bar and a unique vintage camping vibe, and followed him over to a guy who had been sitting in the corner. He stood and shook Brian's hand, patting his back in a half-hug.

"Brooks, this is Michael Wise. Michael, Brooks Leighton."

We shook hands and said, "Good to meet you." Brooks screamed *Portland* in his black-and-red flannel shirt and grey knit beanie, which was pulled over dark hair that fell just below his stubbled jawline. Brian and I pulled out chairs and sat opposite Brooks on the bench in the corner.

"So, Michael," Brooks said, taking a sip of his steaming cup of tea, "tell me more about this book."

I left Brian and Brooks at the coffee shop around one o'clock rather elated, overcaffeinated, and slightly buzzed. Brooks had ordered us more coffees as I told him about the rest of the book. Upon shaking hands at a gentleman's agreement, witnessed by Brian, to publish my novel solely with Both Ends in exchange for a $5,000 advance followed by forty-percent royalties, Brooks had insisted we all take a shot of Jameson to celebrate. While the whiskey still burned my throat, he'd ordered a round of Irish coffees, which I can't say was unwelcome on such a cold day.

Before heading back to my apartment, I stopped at a nearby teahouse more for a handwarmer than for something to drink. On the long, cold, sunny walk home, I felt like skipping and clicking my heels. Had that just happened? Had I just been offered $5,000-plus for something I'd written? I looked around me for something unfamiliar, something alien or out of place, anything to tell me I was in a dream. *Nope.* I passed all the same businesses, the same apartment buildings. The river and the park were still the same, and Autzen Stadium's enormous "O" was still bright yellow.

Back inside my apartment, I chided myself for not turning on the heat before I left, and grabbed a blanket and my laptop and huddled up in front of my wall heater. I opened my novel file and started reading from the beginning. I still liked the writing, but even more so now that I knew it wasn't all in my head. After reading a few pages I shut my laptop and texted Ben. I'd texted him here and there about my book since I'd been back from Italy, but we hadn't gotten together yet because I was so focused on finishing the manuscript.

Dude, I sold my book. Some indie pub in PDX that Brian knows. $5K up front!

I set my phone on the carpet next to me and pulled a throw pillow off the couch, lying back on it with my feet on the wall above the heater, the blanket forming a cozy sort of tent. Nothing had made me so happy in a long, long time. It still felt too good to be true, and the realist in me accepted that, somehow, Brooks could pull out of the agreement, even if Brian had been there to witness it. Gentleman's agreements seemed to be a thing of the past; now, signatures were king. I quickly pushed those thoughts out of my head; it'd do no good to dwell on the what-ifs of the situation. Brian trusted Brooks, and that was good enough for me. *Just let it happen*, I told myself. My stomach grumbled in response, and I decided I should probably eat something.

My phone buzzed twice while I was making a sandwich. One was a text from Ben:

Sweet! U'll have to tell me bout it over beers soon, ur buying, rich boy.

I rolled my eyes before texting back that we should meet up sometime later in the week. The second text was from a number I didn't recognize, but I guessed correctly who it was by the 503 area code.

Michael, it's Brooks. So great to meet you and hear more about your book. I want you to know I really am very excited about this opportunity for you, I think it's a great one for both of us. Wanted you to have my cell in case you have any questions. Just text or call anytime. I'll be in touch very soon. Can you email me a copy of the manuscript?

Maybe too quickly, I responded: *Sure thing, Brooks. Great to meet you too. I'm very grateful for your interest in the book. I'll send a copy to the email address on your business card. Talk to you soon!*

Back on the floor in front of the wall heater, I ate my sandwich happily and enjoyed the warmth and the fact that I had no desire to go curl up in my bed and sleep the rest of the day away.

Chapter 40

The next few months passed in a blink of an eye. Aside from eating and sleeping, nearly all I did was sit at my desk and edit my manuscript. Occasionally, I'd go for a walk to stretch my legs and get some fresh air because I knew staying cooped up in my apartment for so long could lead to craziness. Jack and I exchanged a few letters. He had settled into Roman winter and was doing well, still getting his walks in every day that he could.

Eventually, Ben and Marcus stopped by unannounced and commandeered an afternoon or two, coaxing me out into the world with the promise of beer. They were proud of what was happening for me, but they didn't want me to burn myself out, either. I was grateful they reached out that way. It was nice to retain some level of normalcy when the process I was going through with my book was far away from any normal I'd ever known.

A couple of weeks after our first meeting, Brooks had sent me a lengthy email that outlined the next steps for us to move forward, along with some more significant bullet points regarding the meat of my novel. He attached a copy of the manuscript that had been marked up by Both Ends' in-house editor, along with a contract for me to sign. Trudging through the legalese, little of which made much sense to me, I made sure that the advance and royalty numbers we'd agreed upon were still intact. Sure enough, I'd be paid $2,500 once Brooks received my executed contract and $2,500 when we hit "publish" on the final version. When—"not *if*," as Brooks had enthusiastically noted in his email—the book sold enough copies to earn out my advance, I'd be making forty-percent royalties, paid to me quarterly.

I printed out the contract, signed, dated, and initialed where I needed to, and filled out the form Brooks had attached to set up my payments to be deposited directly to my bank account. Finding an envelope in the back of my desk drawer, I put on my coat and drove to the old post office on Willamette Street to buy a stamp, make copies of the pages, and mail the documents back to Brooks. My heart pounded out of my chest as I dropped the envelope through the slot in the wall.

The most stressful part of those months might have been the realization that a lot of what I'd written – overnight, on the plane, when I returned home – was complete shit. Sentences that sounded good at three in the morning were nearly incoherent, and areas where I'd gotten a little loose with the rules of writing stood out like an awkward sore thumb. I felt like an idiot as I re-read it all, but the editor, Brad, was nothing but constructive. He provided candid feedback and knowledgeable guidance that came from ten years of experience as an English teacher followed by five years with one of the Big Five. I quickly learned to take nothing personally. We were, after all, there as a team to turn my book into the best possible product it could be. Jack's encouragement through his letters over those months made him an indispensable, remote member of the team. Without Jack's eloquent prods, I don't know that I would have made it past the point where Brad suggested that I completely scrap one of the subplots I'd most enjoyed weaving into the story.

Use it somewhere else, Jack wrote. *I hope to God this isn't the only thing you're ever going to write.*

I knew I'd never forget the day I hit "Send" on the email that included what was to be the final draft of my novel. Nearly nothing felt better than closing up three months of staring at my monitor, reworking and tidying the parts marked up by the editor, and sending the document back only to receive another copy with more notes within a few days. There had been significantly more than the plot holes and continuity issues I'd expected, but at the end of it all, I knew that working with Brad had only made the work stronger and cleaner. I was thrilled to read through it and realize how much better it sounded.

Amid all the back and forth of the editing process, I was also in contact with a designer the company contracted with, whose work had stood out to me when Brooks had sent a list of possible cover artists. Janie was exceedingly talented, and she'd done several distinctive covers for authors in the Both Ends lineup. However, as she sent me various mock-ups, nothing stood out as the right one. Nothing quite hit that chord in my heart that said *I want this to represent my work.* They weren't bad ideas, but they just didn't fit.

One day, Brooks called me.

"Michael, Janie is getting a little stressed with this design process. What's wrong?"

Stressed? More like pissed off is my guess. "I know, Brooks. I feel bad turning down everything she's thrown at me, but none of it feels right."

"I get that, man, I do, but we're damn near through this, and our printer is primed and ready to go. If we don't have a cover, what do we do? You've gotta give her something."

"I know, I will."

"Thanks, Michael. Talk to you soon."

As I'd gotten up from my chair and paced around the room while we were on the phone, I went and sat back at my desk, leaning back in my chair and scrolling through the ideas Janie had sent me so far. Nothing even jumped out at me from the screen as being on the right path to what I wanted. But what the hell did I want? I decided it might be a good idea to get outside for a walk and maybe a hit of inspiration. I closed out of all my windows and clicked the button to turn off my computer, figuring it could use a break from such constant use. As I watched it go through the process of shutting down, it hit me. I knew exactly what I wanted my cover to be.

I reversed what I'd just done and hit the power button to start my system back up again. When it was all ready to go, I opened a folder on my desktop and scrolled through several files until I found the one I wanted. Then, I opened my browser, navigated to my email account, and opened a new email. I typed Janie's email address in the "To:" line, carbon-copied Brooks, and typed "Cover" as the subject. After dragging the file from my desktop folder to the attachment box on the email window, I typed two words into the body of the email:

Use this.

Twenty minutes later, I sat on a bench on the Autzen footbridge staring into the fog that hovered above the river. In the silence of the cold day, my phone chirped with a new email. Opening the email app, I saw it was from Janie.

It's perfect! I can work with this.

Chapter 41

Two days later, Janie emailed Brooks and me a mock-up of what she'd done with the file I sent her.

That's fantastic! What do you think, Michael? Brooks replied before I had even seen it.

I think it's exactly what the book needs. Thank you, Janie. Sorry I was such a pain in the ass!

No problem, I'm glad we finally found something. :)

Brooks followed up to tell me that the last revised draft I'd sent back was, if I was comfortable with it, the final draft. My heart flinched. I told him I was happy with it. He said he'd send everything over to their printer and have it expedited; he wanted it on shelves *quick*. Working as closely with him as I had over the last few months, I trusted Brooks that expedition didn't mean a half-assed product.

Almost two weeks later, after silence from Brooks and anyone else at Both Ends, my phone rang with Brooks's number on the screen.

"Hi Brooks."

"Hey, Michael. Listen, can you make it up to Portland sometime this afternoon? I need to go over a couple of things with you." His tone was somber and difficult to decipher.

"Uh…yeah, sure, Brooks. Everything alright?"

"Oh, yeah, just some last-minute things we should discuss. Can you make it to the office at four?"

I looked at my watch; it was a little after one o'clock. "Yeah, that should work."

"Cool, I'll see you then, man. Drive safe."

The next half hour dragged by, despite my taking time for a quick shower and change of clothes to refresh myself for the nearly two-hour drive north. I left just before two o'clock to allow a little extra time for traffic.

Alone in my car on the long, boring stretch of I-5 north, I couldn't help but feel a little anxious. I really didn't like the way Brooks's voice had sounded on the phone. Did something go wrong with the printing? Did they find more edits that needed made? I knew it did no good to dwell on it, so I turned up the country music station and tried to relax. *Country music is good for the soul,* a friend had once told me. Time and time again, I'd found so much truth in that. Before I knew it, I was making my way across the Burnside Bridge toward Northeast Portland, where the office of Both Ends Press was nestled amid several of Portland's unique historic homes.

I found a parking space across the street and noticed, as I walked up to the brick building, that the lights all seemed to be off. It wasn't quite four yet, but no one seemed to be there, and the door was locked. I called Brooks, who said he was in the back and would come up and let me in.

Shaking my hand, he said, "Glad you could make it up on such short notice. Come on in."

I followed him inside before he relocked the door.

"Where is everyone? It's not even four o'clock."

"Oh, I sent them all home a little early so we could have the office." He gestured for me to follow him through the dimly lit lobby and down the hallway toward the conference room.

"Why do we need the office?" At this point, my curiosity was reworking itself into irritation. Brooks had never been so opaque about anything to do with my book. My heart pounded. "What's going on, Brooks?"

"Just come into the conference room and sit down." He opened the door and went in to find the light switch. I followed.

As soon as I stepped into the room, the lights flashed on and a yell of "Congratulations!" rang out. Around twenty people, most of whom I recognized as employees of Both Ends, stood around the table smiling and clapping. Brian was also there, standing next to Brooks with a grin on his face. Then I noticed, in the middle of the long, espresso-colored conference table, a large poster of my book cover displayed on a tabletop easel, flanked by a copy of the book on a smaller display and two small stacks of additional copies. Next to the display sat a few bottles of champagne, several rows of champagne flutes, and an enormous sheet cake with the book cover superimposed on the surface. I managed a wide grin amid slight trembling caused first by my anxiety and irritation and then by the shock of a room full of people yelling at me.

When the clapping ceased, I turned to Brooks. "Not gonna lie, Brooks, I was getting kind of pissed at you before we came in here." Everyone laughed.

"I don't blame you. I'm sorry for being so mysterious, and possibly worrisome. I wanted to be sure you weren't expecting this. By the look on your face, I did my job. So, what do you think?"

Still shaking, I stepped up to the table and picked up a copy of the book from one of the stacks and held it carefully with both hands, my eyes examining the cover. It was *real*. I turned the book over to read the description on the back. *Perfect,* I thought. My heart raced; I was afraid to open it, afraid that I'd find something wrong with the final product. I pushed past the fear and opened the front cover. Flipping through the pages, I inspected all the front matter, the chapters, and finally the acknowledgments and my short bio in the back. Then, I closed it and stared at the front cover once more.

"Everything is perfect..."

Brooks didn't say anything but continued to watch me look over my finished work.

Flipping the pages again, I couldn't help myself and stuck my nose in it.

Everyone chuckled, and Brooks said, "It'll be a few years before that smell shows up, but I have no doubt many people will be sniffing your pages in no time."

I laughed at the thought and suddenly realized my eyes were wet and dripping slowly down my face. I quickly ran my sleeve across it.

"Well, shit, why aren't the bottles open yet?" Brooks yelled. A couple of the employees stepped forward to start pouring champagne while another pair began to cut and serve the cake. Corks popped and bubbles fizzed over. Someone who had been taking pictures since I walked in the room came over and directed me, then Brooks and me, then Brian and me to stand in front of the display and smile for the camera. It didn't take much effort, and I felt like I'd never produced a more genuine smile for a photo.

Over the next couple of hours and a few glasses of champagne, I received a series of congratulations and pats on the back from the various staff in the room. I even got simultaneous kisses on the cheek from one of the other editors, Carly, and from Janie, the designer whose life I'd made a living hell over the past few weeks. As they both pulled away, I locked eyes with the photographer to confirm he got a good picture; he gave me a thumbs-up.

Turning to Janie, I said, "You did a great job, Janie. Thank you. I couldn't have asked for a better cover." I reached my arm around her shoulders in a brief hug.

"You're welcome, Michael. It was worth the strife." She winked and kissed me again on the cheek. "Congratulations," she said before going to get a piece of cake.

"You've been eyeing this like an ex-con fresh out of prison since you saw it," Brian said as he walked up and handed me a huge piece of cake on a plate.

I was ravenous and took an enormous bite. "Oh my god..." It was white cake with a marionberry filling and buttercream frosting, and it was more delicious than I had imagined.

"Congratulations, man. I knew when I read that first chapter that you'd written something amazing. I think this"—he waved his hand across the room—"proves it."

"Sales and reviews will prove it," I joked.

"I mean, *technically* you're right, but this group of people wouldn't be here—this book wouldn't be on that table right now—if they didn't think it was something great. Just wait, you'll see."

Brooks joined us, holding three fresh glasses of champagne and handing one each to Brian and me. "Cheers, boys."

We all clinked the rims of the glasses together and took long drinks of the crisp bubbly.

"Did you give it to him yet?" Brooks asked Brian.

"Not yet." Brian began fumbling in his pockets. Finally, he produced what looked like a gift card and handed it to me.

The face of the card said "The Nines" on it; it was a keycard to a hotel room.

"We got you a hooker," Brooks said.

The three of us laughed before Brian said, "Not a hooker—the suite was expensive enough—but there is another surprise up there for you. And you've got it for two nights. I hope you don't have anything to do back home for a couple of days."

Staring in amazement at the card in my hand, I sipped my champagne again. "Nothing that can't wait."

Chapter 42

The town car Brooks had hired dropped me off right in front of The Nines on SW Morrison. I thanked him, and he congratulated me; Brooks must have told him of the special occasion. At the front desk, the concierge directed me to the twelfth floor—the Club Level—and asked if I had any bags to be brought up. I told him no, that I was there spontaneously, and he smiled and wished me a good evening. The elevator took me up quickly.

The view across the Willamette River, Portland's bridges, and Southeast Portland toward Mount Hood was nothing to shake a finger at. The lights of Downtown's buildings sparkled across the river's surface. Brooks hadn't scrimped on the accommodations. I'd never stayed in a hotel room anywhere close to as nice as that one, and it added significantly to my feeling of accomplishment. I looked down at the copy of my book I still held and smiled. A glint of glass from the desk next to the window caught my eye. Sitting next to a folded piece of heavy stationery was a beautiful, green bottle of Jameson 18-Year Limited Reserve. The note was from Brian, congratulating me on the publishing of my book and inviting me to dinner the next night with the promise of another surprise. I couldn't imagine what more there could be, but somehow the thought didn't linger.

I stood at the window for what seemed like an eternity before finally glancing at my watch. It was only eight o'clock and, while I didn't feel hungry, a celebratory drink in my own company sounded appealing. But I wanted to save the gifted Jameson for another time. I grabbed my coat, wallet, and the keycard to the room and shut the door behind me.

The Nines is largely known for its rooftop restaurant and bar, Departure. While it was late winter, the night was clear, and I wanted to take in the city as much as possible. Stepping off the elevator, I turned down a long hallway with squishy chairs and couches along one side, dimly lit with a fuchsia glow. I couldn't help but smile at the various groups of people occupying the furniture as I passed, though I knew they'd have no idea why.

A small bar was situated at the end of the hallway just before the two doors that led out to the open-air lounge. I waited behind a threesome of women all wearing black cocktail dresses while they paid the bartender for their cocktails, then stepped up to the counter.

"What'll you have?"

"Jameson on the rocks, please. The twelve-year."

"You got it."

I traded a twenty for a brittle rocks glass with a heavy base, occupied by a single large ice cube and a couple of fingers of good Irish whiskey.

"Keep the change," I told him.

Outside, I found an open spot along the railing next to a tall, saucer-shaped space heater and looked over the edge. It was a long drop to the street below. The sounds of the evening traffic floated up to the lounge, a medley of car horns, screeching brakes, revving engines, yelling, and laughter. No sight had been more beautiful, no sound more pleasing, with the exception of all I'd seen a few months earlier in Italy. Except now I had a significant accomplishment under my belt, and it felt like a golden aura glowed around me. I wanted to tell everyone around me, not to brag but because I finally felt truly happy about something. I imagined myself in a movie scene set in, say, Grand Central Station, where the main character stands up on a bench and professes his love to a woman in front of hundreds of passersby, except in my case, I'd be holding my book in the air and saying, "I did this!" Everyone would applaud and wish congratulations on my happiness and success and the credits would roll to a happy song. In reality, I knew no one would care, all would keep on walking, and it might wind up as a viral video of a "crazy guy getting thrown out by security" shot from someone's cell phone.

Snapping back to the moment, I glanced down at the book in my hand, oblivious until then that I had even brought it with me, and took another sip from my glass. The whiskey combatted the cold February air all the way down my throat to my stomach, and I smiled.

"You picked a noisy spot to read."

"Huh?" I turned in the direction of the voice. A middle-aged couple stood next to me at the railing, dressed in black suit and evening gown. "Oh, this? I didn't come here to read. I didn't even realize I'd brought it with me."

"What book is it?" The man reached his hand out, and I handed over the book. He and his wife glanced over the cover, turned it over, opened to the first page, and closed it again. Looking back up to me with a knowing smile on his face, he handed it back to me. "Is this you?"

At that moment, I had no doubt I was beaming, and I tried immediately to tone it down. "Yeah, it is. Brand new today, actually. I really didn't mean to bring it with me, though. It's not like I'm here trying to show it off." I chuckled awkwardly.

The pair laughed. "You should be," said the woman. "That's quite the achievement. How old are you?"

"Twenty-four."

"That's very impressive. Good for you"—she looked at the cover again—"Michael. Let us buy you a drink."

By that point in my life, I'd learned better than to turn down both a kind gesture and free alcohol, so I told them what I was drinking, and they returned a couple of minutes later with another Jameson and a fresh round for themselves. He said a short toast, we clinked glasses, and they said they'd leave me to my evening and that they would look for my book at Powell's soon. I thanked them and said goodnight before they went back inside to the warmer lounge area. Looking back out at the city lights, I felt infinitely prouder than I had a few moments before, and that was saying something. I couldn't wait to tell Jack and to send him a copy.

The next day, I woke at eight and called room service for a French press of dark roast coffee. It came quickly while I was standing at the window, looking out at the city. I drank a couple of cups of coffee while I showered and dressed for the day. Down in the lobby, the concierge recommended a place around the corner where I could get a hearty breakfast sandwich.

He wasn't wrong, and I left the shop with a thick sandwich of bacon, ham, and a fried egg between two halves of a toasted bagel, dripping with melted cheese, all wrapped in a piece of wax paper. I ate my sandwich as I zigzagged a few blocks north in the clear, cold air, passing the city block bordered on all sides by food trucks. Most were closed, but a few exuded delicious smells of various breakfast food cooking for Saturday's early risers. At Burnside, while I waited for the signal to turn, I looked across the street at the low, understated storefront of Powell's City of Books. It was still unbelievable that something I'd written was about to be sitting on a shelf or display somewhere in that infamous haven for bookworms, the self-proclaimed largest independent bookstore in the world. I couldn't imagine a bigger bookstore; the City of Books took up a full city block.

Powell's truly is a city within Portland. Towers of books create a labyrinth that any bibliophile would happily get lost in. Every time I'd been there, I'd wished I had thousands of dollars to spend, and a U-Haul to transport my loot back home. Then the question of shelf space would come into play, and that's a whole other issue. As a kid, one of my favorite movie scenes was the library scene in Disney's *Beauty and the Beast*. I longed for a high-ceilinged room with wall to wall shelves of books to read whenever I wanted. I wandered the aisles for an hour or so, stopping every so often to read the back of a book with an attractive cover or by a writer whose other work I'd read.

Miraculously, I made it out of the store with less than $100 worth of books. It was almost eleven, so I decided to walk down to the Tom McCall Waterfront Park along the river before I'd hail a cab to take me back to my Jeep at the Both Ends office, where Brooks had assured me it would be safe as long as I needed to leave it there. The park was busy with pedestrians, cyclists, and joggers all enjoying the sunny winter day. Every few minutes, I stopped along the railing to watch the water flow by sluggishly before continuing south. It didn't take long to flag down a cab, and I hopped in the warm back seat, which smelled of cigarette smoke and incense.

My Jeep appeared untouched as we pulled up in front of the office, and I paid and thanked the driver before getting out. I stayed parked for a few minutes while the engine and my seat heated up, finally taking the time to text Brian to thank him for the whiskey and to ask where and when dinner would be.

A few minutes later, he replied that he'd meet me in the lobby of

The Nines at seven and we'd go from there, but he didn't say where. I agreed and drove off back to the hotel to rest for a bit. Suddenly, I couldn't shake the curiosity of what surprise he might have in store for me.

Back in the hotel room, I hung up my coat, kicked off my Clarks, and fell back onto the clouds that were my bed. I stared at the ceiling, unable to wipe the smile from my face. I still couldn't believe that I was there, or *why* I was there for that matter. I'd never thought that I would write anything that someone would have some kind of faith in, but Brooks and Brian had it from day one. They'd pushed me every step of the way, through the constant doubt that what I was doing was actually worth something. Despite the doubt, I'd surprised myself that I had been so nose-to-the-grindstone the whole time when, even a few months earlier, I would have just as easily put things off until another day. Their faith in me had been instrumental in that change.

I closed my eyes for about an hour, although I'm not sure how much of that was spent in sleep. Feeling refreshed, I made a cup of coffee with the in-room coffeemaker and sat by the window to read one of the books I'd purchased at Powell's. Before I knew it, I'd made a dent in the book, and dark had settled over the city, bringing with it a modest layer of fog. It was only five o'clock, so I decided to take a hot shower and go up to Departure for a pre-dinner drink.

I broke from tradition and ordered a bourbon distilled outside of Portland, served neat. It wasn't disappointing. I sipped it slowly to prolong its warmth in the cold fog that enveloped the rooftop. It wasn't such a thick fog that I could no longer see the buildings around me, but it added a hint of magic to the lights twinkling from all the windows and the streets below. At five till, I tipped back the last couple of drops of whiskey and headed to the elevator, leaving my empty glass on the bar as I passed. Brian was already downstairs in the lobby, reading a newspaper on the couch.

"I hope you weren't waiting long. I just had a quick drink up on the roof."

"Only about five minutes. You ready?" He wrapped a green Portland Timbers scarf around his neck and led the way out into the night. We headed up 5th Avenue in the direction of the Burnside Bridge.

"Where are we going?"

"There's a Brazilian food truck I've been wanting to try up near the Roseland. Brooks said they have an incredible take on a Philly cheesesteak."

"Say no more. That sounds great tonight. The whiskey whet my appetite nicely."

A short walk took us to a small pod of food trucks off Couch Street, and ten minutes later, we had steaming, toasted sandwiches of shredded steak, melted mozzarella, caramelized onions, and sliced tomatoes doused in a healthy serving of jalapeno chimichurri.

"Ohmagod," I said between too-big bites. "Brooks was right."

Brian nodded as he wiped a glob of cheese off his chin with a finger and ate it. "Let's walk down by the river. I'll cut to the chase."

I took another bite of my cheesesteak, waiting for the chase, still completely unsure of what to expect.

"You're still not working, are you? I mean, I know you've been *working*, but you're not, like, gainfully employed right now?"

I chuckled. "Nope, and I've been thinking about that over the last couple of days. I feel like I need to start looking for something. This advance isn't gonna last forever."

"Don't look. Work for me. Or, rather, work for *Intangible*." We stopped by the railing along the waterfront path, and he watched me for a response.

"What's *Intangible*?"

"Remember I talked to you about my idea for a travel magazine, back before you went to Italy?"

"Yeah."

"*Intangible* is it."

Something sparked in my chest, something similar to the moment I realized I was going to Italy, and then the moment I realized I was writing a novel. My heartbeat quickened.

"You're making it happen? Or it's already happened and you're just now telling me?"

"It's already happening. I mean, I've got the whole team together—pending you—and we've got the first issue pretty much put together, along with a lot of great digital content on the website. I would've said something sooner, but I didn't want to distract you from your book."

Chuckling, I said, "You know me too well. So, what do you want me to do for the magazine?"

"Write, edit, whatever you want, Michael. I think those are your strong points, but I want your eye on as many things as possible. What do you think?"

My mind raced in a thousand directions, caught between anxiety of taking such a risk and the excitement of writing for a travel magazine.

"Michael, I was there when we were having beers at 5th Street. Barring maybe last night, I've never seen you happier than when you were simply *talking* about travel and writing. I'm not going to tell you what to do with your life, but I'm also not going to hide that I think this is it."

I smiled; he was right. Nothing made me feel more alive than traveling. "I think I want to work for *Intangible*." One small reservation lingered at the front of my mind.

"I'm glad, and I can tell you"—he pulled a folded slip of paper from his pocket and handed it to me— "you'll be compensated fairly."

I glanced at the paper and my eyebrows raised quickly. I'm not sure what I expected to be able to make working at a start-up magazine, but it wasn't what was written on the paper.

"This is a lot, especially for a new magazine. It's well over what I was making at the restaurant in good months."

"I know, and I don't want you to worry, I've got a couple of investors who really wanted to make this happen, and I made it clear that we need to pay our people what they're worth from the get-go. They barely questioned it. Of course, if the magazine doesn't do well in the first couple of years, the plug may be pulled, but I don't see that happening. Brooks has helped me acquire some talent and has used his resources to build some preliminary buzz. And he's giving us access to his distribution channels, so we will already have a reach.

"And, who knows, even if the quarterly print edition doesn't take off—which, of course, I hope it does—the digital content should do just fine. We've got some good ad space sold already, and a lot more interest coming in."

Looking from Brian back to the slip of paper in my hand, I took a deep breath. It seemed too good to be true, but I trusted Brian and that he wouldn't ask me to put so many eggs in this basket if it wasn't a viable path to take. He'd been right about Brooks, as far as I could tell.

We threw our trash in a nearby can and headed back toward the hotel. At the front entrance, Brian said, "I'm really glad you're on board, Michael. Of course, if you decide it's not right for you, don't feel obligated, but I really think it'll be a good thing for you and for all of us. And trust me, you'll be earning that salary, especially over the first year. There's still a lot of legwork to be done."

"Ha! I have no doubt, but I'm willing to do as much as I need to and then some."

"I knew you would be." He reached out and shook my hand. "I'll send you more information in the next few days, and you can let me know when you're ready to start working. I still want you to focus on your book release, but I don't know how long you have before you'll need a steady paycheck again." He winked and waved goodbye.

"Thanks again, Brian. I'll talk to you soon. Have a good night." I walked through the lobby to the elevators and took a lift up to my floor. I felt much higher than twelve floors that night.

I spent Sunday morning lounging in the warmth of my bed with the book I'd started reading and another French press brought up by room service. Around eleven, I checked out of the hotel and thanked the front desk staff for the exceptional stay. Then, I grabbed one more sandwich from the place around the corner and drove up to Hoyt Arboretum for a walk through the tall evergreens.

As I walked between the sentinels on the trail damp from settled mist, I savored the silence that didn't exist in the city below. Just one more reminder of why I was happy to call the Northwest home. A fifteen-minute drive ago, I was in the middle of it all, surrounded by tall buildings and the honks and whirs of traffic. Now, the only sounds were of birds and the occasional unseen mammal in the underbrush. Not even the wind came through, and the fog hovering above the canopy acted as a shield from anything outside the forest. I was glad to cross paths with only a few other people but returned greetings when I did. About a half hour in, my phone buzzed with a text message in my pocket. It was from Brooks.

You still in town? The front desk said you already checked out.

Yep, up at Hoyt Arboretum right now, I replied.

Can you make it by the office for a few on your way out of town?
Want to touch base on a couple of things.

Sure thing. See you in about an hour?

That works. See you then.

I drove back into the city feeling rejuvenated in every way. It had been a cold walk in the woods, but it had cleansed me. There hadn't been a lot of destructive stress in my life the past few months, but it still felt good to leave what stress there *had* been behind.

At the Both Ends office, I called Brooks and he came to the door to let me in.

"Good walk?"

"Beautiful. It was damn near silent on the trails."

"I love it up there. Don't get up there as much as I'd like but love it when I do. Come on into my office."

I followed him and sat down in a chair across his desk from him. "What's up?"

He pulled a Both Ends-branded folder out of a drawer and slid it across the desk to me, opening it to a few papers that were neatly stacked inside.

Pulling out the first one, he said, "This is a schedule of some events we have coming up. By 'events' I mean signings and readings. We'll need you for all of these, but I tried not to overbook you. It can be overwhelming for some, so if you're not feeling up to it at any point, let me know ahead of time and we can work something out."

Running my finger down the list, I was a little surprised to see both Powell's in Portland and Barnes and Noble in Eugene on the list. The rest seemed to be independent bookstores anywhere from Portland to Eugene, and there was even a book club listed.

"That'll be interesting," I said, pointing to the book club.

Turning his head to see what I was looking at, Brooks said, "Oh, yeah! I thought you might like that one. No pressure or anything, but it's a group of people I know who are *very* selective about the books they read in the club, and I was able to get them to put yours on the agenda. They're reading it as we speak."

"Hm, I'll try not to worry about that too much," I joked. "These all look good to me, and it's spread over a couple of months, so it shouldn't be too bad. Thank you for everything, Brooks. I really appreciate all you've been doing."

"And I'll keep doing it. You're welcome, Michael, but it's been *my* pleasure. I've been doing this for a while now, and I don't push anything through if I don't love it, but yours is far beyond that. There was no other decision to be made, and I'm glad I made the one I did. I think this is going to go incredibly well, and I think people will be better for reading your book. Just be ready for demands for a second book, even a sequel." We both laughed.

"Oh! One other thing…" He turned around in his chair and grabbed a small box from a shelf next to the window, then turned back around and placed it in front of me. "It's a few copies of the book for you to give to who you will, free of charge. If you want anymore, you'll have to buy them—at cost, of course—but we at least wanted to give you a few.

"The rest of that"—he gestured at the folder—"is just information about where your book is available, some general information about the post-publishing process we give to our authors, and a list of the bloggers and other people we've sent copies to for a review. You can read it all whenever you feel like it. For now, you should get back to Eugene and celebrate with your friends and family."

We stood, and he walked me to the front door.

"It sounds like you've got a pretty good opportunity with Brian's magazine, too. I'll do my best to make sure I schedule everything around that once you get started with them. I think you'll do very well there. Brian's a smart guy. He'll help make it happen for you, too."

"Yeah, he is. Thanks again, Brooks. For everything." I held the box of books under my arm and we shook hands.

"Sure, Michael. Have a safe drive, and I'll see you later this week at your first signing." He winked and waved before pulling the door shut and locking it.

With the folder and box of books on my passenger seat, I took off for the freeway toward Eugene. I sang nearly every song on the radio during the drive home.

Back in my apartment, I placed the things from Brooks on the counter and pulled a copy of the book from the box. At my desk, I opened the front cover and began writing.

Jack,

This book wouldn't exist if I hadn't met you, nor would the perspective on life that I have now. For both of those, I am eternally grateful. More than anything, I'm happy to have you in my life. Thank you for lighting a torch to help me out of my darkness. I'll try to visit soon.

Sincerely yours,

Michael

On my way to meet Ben and Marcus for a beer, I stopped at the UPS store and purchased a padded envelope and the quickest shipping option, filling out the shipping label with Jack's address from my notebook. Unworried about the cost, I wanted Jack to have it as soon as possible.

"Take good care of that, please," I told the woman at the counter, knowing it was completely out of her control once the package left the building.

She seemed to sense the emotion behind my request because she replied simply, but warmly, "I will."

I returned her smile before leaving the store and heading to the sports bar to fill Ben and Marcus in on all that had happened over the last few days.

Chapter 43

My first event as a published author came the following weekend with an afternoon signing at the Eugene Barnes & Noble. I felt oddly calm on the days leading up to it, but the morning of, I woke up feeling clammy and jittery. I drank too much coffee and got clammier and more jittery, and Ben, when I called him, insisted on buying me late breakfast at IHOP to help get my head in the game.

"How the hell am I supposed to talk about my book to all these people?" I asked with a mouthful of Denver omelet.

"I mean, there probably won't be that many people there."

I flipped him off. "You know what I mean. Still, I hope you're right."

"Just imagine everyone naked."

"That what they taught you in your acting classes?" I glared at him. "That'll probably just make it worse."

Ben shrugged and finished the last of his bacon in one bite. After we finished and paid our check, he said, "Alright man, go home and try to get out of your head. You've got a couple hours before you need to be there."

"Yeah, I'm going to flip through and try to figure out what passages I might want to read. Brooks said he didn't put it on the official docket, but he said people may request that I read a section."

"Ugh, I don't envy you on that. Well, good luck man. Get

prepared, and I'll see you in a bit. I'll do my best not to make faces."

"Fuckin' better. See you later."

Back at my apartment, I pulled out the already worn copy of my book that I had flipped through over and over again—the first copy I'd picked up at the launch party. I folded the top corners of pages down at spots I thought I might want to read from, in hopes that no one would ask me to read anything and I could just answer a few questions and sign some books. I took another shower and changed into the clothes I'd decided I wanted to wear: a charcoal V-neck shirt, my black blazer, and a nice pair of dark-washed jeans. Comfortable, but put-together. Finally, it was time to go. I gave myself one last look in the mirror to make sure nothing was off, then headed out the door to my Jeep with my copy of the book in hand.

I arrived at the bookstore a half hour before the event was scheduled to begin. The store was as busy as it always was on a Saturday, but I could get no feel for how many were there for me. The table was already set up with a display similar to the one at Both Ends, minus the champagne and sheet cake. People milled around but looked more curious as to what was going on than looking around for the author they'd come to see.

"'An Afternoon with Michael Wise?'" I asked Brooks, reading the caption on the poster board next to the display table, when he broke away from the store manager.

"Ha! Is that too cheesy? I thought it had a nice ring to it."

I stared at the display for a moment. "You know, I don't hate it."

"Good. You ready for this? You look good."

"Thanks. I think I am. As ready as I'll ever be, anyway. I was a nervous wreck this morning, though."

"I'm not surprised. These things aren't easy, especially if you're not used to being in the spotlight. Now, I don't think you need to worry about speaking for two hundred people or anything like that, but I expect we'll see a reasonable crowd. I got you in the paper, on the radio, and in a local news spot, too. People know this is happening."

"I appreciate all your work on this, Brooks. I don't necessarily get it, but I appreciate it."

"Get it. You wrote a *fucking* good book, Michael. The story you put into those pages is something that people need to read, something they want to read, even if they don't realize it yet."

"Thanks, man. It helps to hear that, oddly. No pressure on me or anything." We laughed.

Brooks looked at his watch. "Getting close to game time, Michael. Head back there through the door at the end of this row. The manager said you could hang out in the breakroom for a few minutes until it's time to come out. Plan on being out here, waiting in the shadows, in fifteen minutes. I want you to make an entrance."

"You got it." I found the door and went through to find, to my relief, no one else in the breakroom. I bought a bottled water from the vending machine and drank a little, keeping a close eye on the time. I sipped it slowly but made sure to use the restroom within five minutes of being out there to avoid any additional discomfort once I was at the table. My fifteen minutes flew by, and when it was time to go, I took a few deep breaths and let them out slowly. Then, I walked through the door and waited where Brooks had indicated. I could hear him speaking clearly.

"Ladies and gentlemen, it is with sincere honor and excitement that I present this book and this writer to you today. I think you'll all come away from reading this novel with a much stronger understanding of yourselves and what's important to you in life. I sure as hell have, and it gives me great pleasure to finally introduce you to the guy who made it happen: Mr. Michael Wise!"

I only had to read my short first chapter to the group of nearly fifty people who had shown up for the event, and I felt oddly calm as I did so. The group watched with genuine interest as I introduced myself and shared a little of my background before diving into the beginning of the book.

Ben and Marcus were there together, and Beanie was on the other side of the group. Brian lingered in the back. A handful of other friends were there, too, but the group was made up mostly of strangers. It flattered me to know that so many people who didn't know me had taken the time out of their weekend to be there for *me*.

When I'd wrapped up my reading to a quiet, contented applause, Brooks then took the reins and opened the floor to questions. A surprising amount of people raised their hands, and he took to calling on them one at a time.

They asked questions about how I came up with this and where I got the idea for that. I spoke candidly, telling them that it's quite easy to write from experience—this sparked a few concerned glances and murmurs back and forth, considering the dark tones my novel carried at times—and that after meeting Jack Porter, the real-life inspiration for the book's sage, "Walter Harris," the book practically started and wrote itself.

I answered a few more inquiries of this general nature, along with the inevitable "Are you working on your next book?" before I heard a matter-of-fact female voice call out, "The thirteenth statue is John the Baptist."

I was confused, both by the lack of a question and because I couldn't tell who had spoken. "Sorry?"

"In answering a previous question, you referred to the thirteen statues on the façade of St. Peter's as Christ and the twelve Apostles. Only eleven of the Apostles are up there. Peter is down below, next to the stairs, and John the Baptist is on the façade." As the girl finished speaking, she stepped out from behind a couple of taller men who had been obstructing her view. Instead of looking like she had just won an argument, she wore a soft, genuine smile, framed by silky, half-curled, brown hair.

I smiled back at her. "It's a common misconception, and I was being lazy. Thank you for keeping me honest."

She shrugged. "I've taken a few art history classes in college. Don't worry, you got it right in the book." Her subsequent wink made my heart skip a beat. I saw Ben and Marcus exchange glances, and Beanie's face slowly donned an "Aha!" expression of realization.

Not wanting to create an awkward moment for everyone in attendance, I quickly thanked the group for coming and for their support and proceeded to sign copies of my book for them for about twenty minutes. Ben, Marcus, and Beanie had quickly left the building when they saw the brown-haired girl get in line. She was the last to come to the table, holding her copy with gentle security against her chest, just as she'd held her coffee when I first met her.

"Hi."

"Hi." She was as charming as I remembered. "What are the odds that I'd run into you again?"

She laughed. "I don't know, but I saw your face in the newspaper when they printed that piece about your book last month and had to come and say hi at least."

Still astonished at this ridiculously serendipitous moment, I quickly asked, "What's your name? I can't believe I never asked you that night."

"Ha, it's okay. I didn't get yours either. My name is Joy."

"Michael," I said awkwardly, pointing my thumb at the poster of my book cover, causing her to smile. "I'm really glad to see you again, Joy." I couldn't shake the feeling that I had a goofy grin on my face, and it was certainly bright red, but I didn't care. "What are you doing this afternoon?"

"Whatever you're doing, if that's alright with you." Her caramel eyes twinkled.

"Let me help them get this all taken down, and then I know a really good coffee shop downtown."

"That sounds great." She handed me the book. "Will you sign mine, please?"

"I'd be happy to."

For Joy,

Here's to missed opportunities coming back around.

Michael Wise

I folded down the table and helped the bookstore staff replace a few of the unsold copies of my book on the shelf. Inspired by something I'd seen one of my favorite new authors do, I signed one of the copies and placed it amongst the others.

"Get out of here," Brooks told me, grabbing the table out of my hands before I could help with anything further. "You definitely don't want to keep *her* waiting." He nodded toward where Joy was sitting at the in-house Starbucks. "She hasn't taken her eyes off you."

"Seriously?" I looked over at Joy, who smiled patiently, then back at Brooks. "God, she's beautiful. You're sure you don't need help with anything else?"

"Go! We've got this, man. I'll talk to you tomorrow."

"Thanks again for everything, Brooks. I could probably do another one or two of these."

"You'll need to do a few more than that, but we'll talk about that later. Have a good time and relax. You did it." He shook my hand and pulled me in for a hug.

I walked over to Joy, still unable to wipe the grin off my face. "Shall we?" I asked, gesturing toward the door.

"We shall."

She stood and put her copy of my book snuggly into her purse, and I followed her out of the bookstore into the warm, spring sunlight.

Chapter 44

Eight months later…

"Thank you again, I appreciate you calling. Okay, you too. Bye." I ended the call and stared down at my phone in my hand, held so loosely it was likely to fall to the floor. With a grimace, I gripped the phone tightly and flung it across the living room against the wall. Shattered pieces flew every which way, and I went to the kitchen, poured some whiskey in a glass, downed it in one swift gulp, and refilled.

"Michael? What the hell was that?"

I looked down the hallway to see Joy cautiously making her way toward me, rubbing the sleep from her eyes.

"Michael, it's seven-thirty in the morning. What are you doing?" Her voice was concerned, not scolding, as she eyed the glass in my hand.

I took another long drink before saying anything. Looking into the glass rather than at her, I said, "Jack died."

Joy's hand moved slowly to her mouth as she breathed a small gasp and her eyes softened. "Oh, my God… Baby, I'm so sorry." She rushed to me and took the glass from my hand, set it on the counter behind me, and threw her arms around my neck, pulling my forehead to hers. I wrapped my arms around her as tightly as I could and held her close to me.

"What happened?" she asked.

"That was his daughter, Mia. Apparently, it happened three weeks ago, but they couldn't figure out how to get in touch with me. Then, they found my book in his apartment and called Both Ends and talked to Brooks." I paused, my voice stuck in my throat. "He was walking home from the piazza in the afternoon and had a stroke. There were plenty of people around to call for help, but he didn't make it to the hospital. The funeral was a week after."

Finally, I was unable to hold back any longer, and I buried my face in her neck and broke down. Tears poured from my eyes, soaking her hair and shoulder as she gently ran her fingers across my scalp.

"I'm sorry, Michael. I know Jack meant the world to you. I'm so sorry it happened like this."

We stood there for a few minutes before she took my hand and led me back to bed, where I lay for hours into the afternoon, curled up in blankets with my head under a pillow. I tried to let myself fall asleep, where my thoughts just *might* stray to something besides Jack Porter, but it was difficult amid the helpless sobs.

Joy lay with me for a while, rubbing my back, holding my hand, and giving soft, comforting kisses. At one point, after I'd dozed off for a bit, I woke to her voice speaking quietly to someone outside our bedroom. I didn't hear the other voice, so I guessed she was on the phone.

"No, he's not ignoring you. He got some bad news this morning, so he's without a phone right now."

Pause.

"Is there anything you want me to tell him for you?"

Pause.

"Okay, well I'll have him give you a call when he can. Call me again if you need to get in touch with him."

Pause.

"Alright, I'll tell him. Okay, bye."

Once I felt her weight settle next to me, I pulled my head from under the pillow and rested it on her chest, where she resumed running her fingers through my hair.

It had always been difficult for me to allow myself to be broken and vulnerable in front of people, to remove the armor with which I protected myself—or tried to—and let them see me at my weakest. But Joy made it possible because I knew she wouldn't judge and that she would be there as long as I needed her because she *wanted* to be. She knew what Jack had meant to me, so she would be there however I needed her to be.

I woke suddenly in a sweat from a nightmare that would plague me over the next few weeks. I was in a church in Rome, staring down at Jack's pale face in a deep-walnut casket. I tucked a photo into his folded hands and turned to leave the church. On the way out, I silently acknowledged his family, who I'd only ever seen photos of, and then his favorite wine shop owner, Gino, and his brother-in-law, Stefano. Stepping out of the church, I was shocked at how cold it was in Rome and drank some whiskey from my flask to cut the pain. Back in my apartment, I realized Joy was rubbing my back and staring at me with sad and curious eyes, but she said nothing. I lay back down and closed my eyes again.

I woke again later to Joy gently rubbing and squeezing my arm. She had brought in a tray with a bowl of soup and a cup of tea, something easy for me since I hadn't eaten or moved all day. I smiled weakly and sat up against the headboard.

She placed the tray on my lap and sat next to me. "How're you feeling?"

"This looks delicious, babe, thank you. I'm okay." I softly blew at the thick, yellow soup on my spoon and sipped it cautiously. It was broccoli and cheddar with chicken, one of my favorites. The warmth was so soothing and nourishing as it traveled down my throat to my empty stomach. "I just can't believe he's gone... And I can't believe I wasn't there. When I woke up earlier, I dreamt that I was there, at his funeral. It was so small and so cold. I couldn't speak, I couldn't feel my footsteps, but when I left the church, I could feel the cold air biting at me. I can't believe I wasn't there."

Joy took the tray from me before I could fling it against the wall like I had my phone.

"You should take some time off," she said.

"I can't. We've got deadlines coming up for December, and there are still some things I need to finish up.

"They'll be fine, Michael. Do you want me to call Brian?"

"No, I don't want to bother him."

"Michael, he'll understand! More than almost anyone, don't you think?"

"I know you're right. I just hate not being there when we're close to print."

"I know you do, but you need some time, baby. Brian will understand."

We locked eyes, her stern, caring resolve coercing my reluctant acceptance.

"Okay."

"Okay what?"

"Okay, I'll ask Brian if he minds me taking a few days."

"Good." She pulled her phone out of her pocket and held it toward me.

"He's probably in the office. I'll just go down there. I could use some fresh air, anyway."

"That'll be good. Finish your soup first."

I mustered a small smile. I'd never be able to tell her how much I appreciated her, but I always tried.

Joy watched me finish the soup and tea and took the tray into the kitchen to clean up.

It was nearing two o'clock, so I decided I should probably shower before running down to talk to Brian. I climbed out of bed and stretched out my arms and back, loosening the muscles that had tightened from hours spent in the fetal position. I stepped out of my pajama pants and boxers and wandered into the bathroom. Joy was watching TV in the living room, so I closed the bathroom door to muffle the noise from the shower.

The water heated quickly, filling the bathroom with steam you could cut with a knife. Stepping into the shower and pulling the curtain shut, I leaned with my palms against the wall, tilted my head down, and let the hot water cascade over me. I tried so hard to let the burn of the water numb the pain I felt, to cleanse my mind, but it was easier said than done. My chest tightened and I felt the sobs coming before I heard them. I just couldn't believe Jack was gone, that I hadn't had a chance to say goodbye.

It was times like this, with the death of a loved one, that made me wish, however fleetingly, that I had some sort of religious faith. I always felt like that was the one true downfall of not believing in anything: when someone dies, they're completely gone to you. There isn't Heaven or Hell to reunite you someday when you die, too. It's why death can often be so much harder on those, like me, without faith. "Goodbye" is "Goodbye," not "See you later."

With a burst of cold air, the shower curtain slid open briefly and closed again, and I felt Joy's presence before she stepped up behind me and wrapped her arms around me. An overwhelming sense of calm surged through me as she pressed her body against mine and kissed my back and shoulders, her hands lovingly rubbing my chest. It wasn't the kind of calm like nothing is wrong anymore, but the type that says everything will be alright, and that was the kind of calm I needed. I clasped my fingers with hers and let my body loosen up even more between the heat and her touch.

There's something so uniquely intimate about being naked with someone in a nonsexual situation. You're both completely bared and vulnerable, free of any restraint or protection. All you can do is trust the other not to let go. I turned into Joy and pulled her into me, my hands gripping her waist and lower back. I tilted my head down, our foreheads meeting and resting against each other, and repositioned us so she could share the warmth and comfort of the water.

She scrubbed shampoo into my hair and rubbed body wash all over me, massaging my tense muscles as she did so. Then, while I rinsed it all off, she dried herself and grabbed the hot towel that she had put in the dryer before joining me. She was waiting for me with a reassuring smile on her face as I stepped out, and she wrapped the towel around me.

"I love you," I said, kissing her softly on the lips.

"I love you, too, Michael. Do you want me to drive you down to the office? I need to run to the store, anyway."

"No, thanks, babe. I could use the walk today, I think."

"Okay, be safe, baby."

"Mmhmm."

She looked up at me, concern still glistening in her eyes. Then, she kissed me again and went to get dressed.

The shower had revived me, so I quickly brushed my teeth, got dressed and pulled on my Clarks before saying goodbye to Joy and heading out into the foggy afternoon. I was glad I'd layered my sweatshirt under my wool overcoat, pulling my hood up over my head as the air clawed at my face.

I decided to walk through the park and over the bridge to our office. It was cold, but I needed the time and the exercise. I pulled the collar of my coat up around my hood and the placket across my chest, making my way out of the complex and across the street to the bike path.

The trees had shed most of their leaves by that point in the year, and the moisture in the air matted them down to the sidewalk, creating a beautiful mosaic of dull reds and yellows for me to walk on. I took care not to slip on the small piles of leaves on the path as I had probably too many times in the past. What few leaves remained on the branches of the oaks and maples around me stood out through the thick fog that hung around them, occasionally breaking free in the cold and fluttering to join their fallen comrades below. The timing was appropriate. I'd first met Jack Porter in the early stages of a Roman autumn when the leaves had just begun to fall. Now, Jack was gone, and that same season along with him.

Autzen Stadium loomed behind the curtains of fog; only the bright yellow "O" on the south side broke through clearly. A handful of people watched their dogs run around and sniff each other at the dog park across the street from the stadium, intervening only when their dogs would get too rough with each other. The usual stream of students flowed across the bridge, making their way to and from the library on campus, and cyclists and joggers weaved in and out of those of us who were in less of a hurry. It was one of those days where you nodded and forced a smile if you accidentally made eye contact, but for the most part people were heads-down, focused only on getting out of the cold.

Pausing for a moment to look down at the river below, I was reminded how lucky I was to have Joy in my life. Despite the incredible pain I felt then, it was nothing like what I'd been dealing with not too long before her. My thoughts while standing on the bridge were completely different than the thoughts I used to have in the exact same place. I smiled to myself and continued across the bridge and along the river toward Downtown.

As I'd expected, the light in Brian's office was on, the only one in the row of offices above 5th Street, across from the Public Market. As in every quarter around that time, he was burning oil at all hours of the day, trying to plan and perfect every detail of the next issue. I waved my key fob in front of the infrared sensor by the door and, when the lock clicked, retreated into the warmth of the building and pulled my hood off my head.

Upstairs, I used the fob once more to get into our office, which was dark except for the lamp and computer screen in Brian's office. The blinding bank of fog outside made the office appear even darker than it was, and my eyes took a moment to adjust. Brian was on the phone but caught my eye and held up a finger. I nodded and gestured toward my office to let him know I'd be in when he was done. There was no doubt that Brian would tell me to take all the time I needed, whether he felt it would put a strain on him and the rest of the team or not, so I figured I should set an out-of-office message on my email account.

In my office, I flopped down in my desk chair with a heavy sigh and flipped up my laptop screen, waited as the computer came out of hibernation, entered my password, and waited some more for the operating system to load. Of course, it decided it needed to finish installing some updates, so the process was a little longer than normal. Leaning back in the chair, my eyes moved up the wall to the 18-by-24 canvas above my two widescreen monitors. It was the photo the Dutch photographer had taken of Jack and I sitting on the steps of the fountain in the Piazza del Popolo. He had followed through and emailed it to me a week or so after I returned from Italy. His face animated, Jack was telling me the story of when he and Marci had snuck into one of Rome's smaller churches one night to seek shelter from a massive rainstorm and wound up running from a priest who caught them half-naked in the confessional. I smiled at him as he gestured wildly at the finer points of the story. It was one of my favorite photos, a representation of wisdom and knowledge and life being passed from an old man to a younger man. It was also the cover of my book, and I had a framed print of it on my desk at home. That photo had quickly become one of my most prized possessions, now even more so.

My gaze snapped back to my screen as I realized the updates had finished. Opening my email program, I quickly set an auto-reply message that would redirect any incoming emails to Brian for the next week. Just as I saved the settings, a couple of raps came through the wall. *Brian's infamous summons,* I said to myself as I shut the computer down since I wouldn't be there for a few days.

"Hey, Brian." I poked my head in the open door of his office.

"Michael!" He whipped around from his computer screen, at which he'd been staring intently. "Come on in."

I sat down at one of the two chairs in front of his L-shaped desk. "What're you working on?"

"Oh, just finishing up some formatting for the December issue. That was Sam on the phone, explaining to me that he doesn't want to trim his piece on skiing in Vail. But let's talk about you, man. What's going on? Joy said you got some bad news."

I hesitated for a minute and took a deep breath. "Jack Porter died." My voice quivered, but I held myself together. I knew Brian wouldn't judge me, but I was tired of crying.

"Shit, Michael…" Brian leaned forward on his desk with his elbows. "I mean, he was getting up there, but I didn't expect you to say that. The way you've talked about Jack, I kind of figured he'd live forever. Well, I'm sorry. Is there anything you need, anything I can do for you?"

"Thanks, Brian. I appreciate it. Joy's insisting I take some time o—"

"Do it. You've done so much on this issue. The others can tie up any loose ends."

"Are you sure?"

"Of course I'm sure." Brian had turned back to his computer and was quickly typing something and then scrolling down the screen.

"What're you doing?" I tried to see what was on the monitor, but to no avail. For such an open and transparent person, I'd always been surprised that Brian used privacy screens.

Click, click-click. Click. Then the printer started whirring. He walked over and pulled a paper off the tray and handed it to me.

"Consider it a thank-you for all you do around here."

Looking down at the printout, I saw it was a confirmation of a two-night reservation at the Sylvia Beach Hotel in Newport. The hotel itself was named for the original proprietor of the Shakespeare & Co. bookstore in Paris, and each room was decorated after a different author of note. He'd booked me the Shakespeare room. "Shit. Brian, you always show plenty of appreciation."

"Well, you keep earning it."

"Seriously, you don't need to do this."

"I know, but I want to. What kind of boss would I be if I didn't make sure you were taking care of yourself?"

I could tell there was no swaying him. "Well, thank you, I really appreciate it… You're too good to me. But I'm coming in as soon as I'm back to help out with any last-minute details."

Brian appraised me with a hint of amusement on his face. This time, he knew he couldn't sway *me*, so he just smiled, nodded, and said, "You're too good to us, too, Michael."

"It's gotta go both ways. It's the least I can do."

Brian clicked a few things on his screen and shut off the monitor. "Feel like a beer?"

"Two."

We locked up the office and headed downstairs to the taproom on the first floor of our building. There was a decent crowd but not so large that we couldn't find a table in the corner where we could hear each other and observe everyone else. Over several beers and at Brian's request, I recounted the story of how I met Jack and stories of our time together and stories he'd told me about his life with Marcella. Brian had heard them all before, but he urged me to carry on. I'd told them plenty of times to various other people, but the stories never got old. Not for ego but for nostalgia, I could read my book over and over again and feel like I was meeting Jack for the first time with each read.

Six o'clock came around, and Brian's cell phone buzzed on the table between six empty glasses and two more half-drunk pints.

"It's Joy," he said, looking at the screen and handing me the phone.

I swiped my finger across the screen to answer the call and held the phone to my ear. "Hi, babe."

"How're you doing, hun?"

"Really good, actually. Brian and I are at the tap house by the office. We've been having a few beers and talking about Jack."

"Do you want me to pick you up? It's dark out and a lot colder now."

"That would probably be a good idea. That's a long walk in my condition, and there's no telling if I might accidentally fall down an embankment." I glanced up and saw Brian snicker.

Joy laughed. "Okay, I'll be there in a few minutes. I love you."

"I love you, too." I ended the call and handed Brian his phone.

"That's a great image," he said, "you tumbling down the slope into the river."

"Ha, yeah. And not entirely improbable at this point."

"You've got yourself a good one in Joy. Don't let her get away."

"I really do. I'm trying."

Brian went up to the counter and closed out our tab, and we grabbed our coats and went outside to wait for Joy. She pulled up within a few minutes.

She leaned across the seat and opened the passenger door. "Do you need a ride, Brian?"

"No, thank you, Joy. It's a short walk, and I've been in the office all day. Appreciate the offer."

"Of course. It's the least I can do to repay you for taking care of this guy for a while." She looked up at me with a gleam in her eye and blew me a kiss.

"Thanks again, Brian. For the talk, the hotel, everything."

"Hey, you've got it, Michael. Take it easy this week, and I'll see you when you're back in the office."

"Sounds good." We shook hands, and I got in the car and shut the door.

Joy leaned over and kissed me before driving off. "Maybe it's just the beer, but you seem to be in a better place than earlier."

I laughed, reaching my hand behind her on the car seat and playing with her soft hair as she drove. "It's partially the beer. But I'm glad I got out of the house for a bit. The cold air was refreshing, and I got a lot of good time to think about things. I'm really just happy that I had the time with Jack that I did, and happy that I have you to share things with, good or bad."

"I'm glad, baby. I was really worried about you. I know the places you've been in the past, the darkness you've felt, and I'm just afraid something will send you back there. If anything would, I feel like it's this. And if that happens, I'm afraid I won't know what to do and that I won't be enough to bring you back."

"Pull over."

"What? We're almost ho—"

"Just pull over."

She did.

I took her hand in mine and kissed the top of it, looking her dead in the eye. "Joy, I'm not going back there. I won't lie and say there haven't been struggles over the last year, but since I met Jack, I haven't gone anywhere near the places I used to live. And since you, well, since you... Don't even worry about not being enough to bring me back, because you're more than enough to keep me away from all that. I've never been happier, and I've never felt more at peace with everything in my life. The pain of losing Jack won't just go away, I know that, but what I had with him, and what I have with you...it's what keeps me going every day."

A tear streamed down Joy's face, shimmering in the streetlight's glow. "I believe you."

I could tell she did. Joy had been burned in the past, and trust wasn't something that came easily for her. At the time we had started, it didn't for me either. I think that's what had brought us closer; we understood each other well enough to recognize the veracity within each other.

I took her face in my hands and kissed her, brushing the tear away with my thumb. When we pulled away, she smiled.

"*Now* you can drive," I said, smiling back.

When we got back to our apartment, I turned on the electric

fireplace in the living room and the wall heater in our bedroom. When I came back to the kitchen to make some tea and see what sounded good for dinner, Joy was sitting on the counter. She reached out and grabbed my hand, pulling me over so that I was standing between her legs against the counter. She started kissing me, differently than she had been earlier in the day.

I chuckled and looked at her between kisses. "Are you taking advantage of me?"

She gave me an enticing look. "I'm taking *care* of you." With that, she pulled my shirt off over my head and pulled me closer.

Chapter 45

Eleven months later...

The sun warmed my face in the brisk mid-autumn air. I squeezed Joy's hand, smiled at her, and led her down the Lungotevere Prati along the Tiber. Castel Sant'Angelo and the Bridge of Angels stood fifty yards ahead of us; Saint Peter's Basilica peeked majestically over the buildings in the distance.

Colorful leaves crunched underfoot, mingling with the voices of all the tourists and locals enjoying a similar afternoon walk. We stopped for a moment and looked over the edge of the bridge at the murky water below. Then, I quickly put my finger to my lips.

"Shh..."

Joy looked confused. "What is it?"

"Listen."

She looked upward as if she were trying to see whatever sound I was hearing. I grinned when a soft smile spread across her face as the sounds of distant church bells floated through the air to her ears.

"They're so pretty!"

"Aren't they? I remember the first time I heard those. I felt like I shouldn't move until they stopped."

We continued down the street, past the castle with its statue of Saint Michael looking down at us, pointing his sword toward the center of the keep. Crossing the Piazza Pia onto Via della Conciliazione, we walked into Saint Peter's Square. Pigeons wandered around and cooed, flying away as people meandered near them, oblivious of the birds and lost in awe of the pillared colonnade that flanked both sides of the square, crowned with statues of the saints. My eyes followed the colonnade on the right up to the basilica. The grandiose house of worship took my breath away, as it had every time I'd seen it. I smiled at the astonished look on Joy's face as she took it all in for the first time.

"It's so much more beautiful than I ever imagined! I can't believe people get to just look at this every day if they want to."

"They're damn lucky." I couldn't imagine how anyone could take something so awe-inspiring for granted.

"Excuse me," I said, catching the attention of another younger couple that was walking near us and who I'd heard speaking English. "Would you mind taking a picture for us?"

"Not at all," said the guy, who looked like he was a couple of years older than me. He took my cell phone, and Joy and I positioned ourselves with the basilica at our backs. I put my arm around her shoulders; she wrapped hers around my waist and leaned her head on my shoulder.

"Say '*formaggio!*'"

Joy and I obliged and smiled for the camera. After the flash, I said, "Thank you so much. I'm Michael, and this is my girlfriend, Joy." I shook the guy's hand.

"Greg. And this is Gina. It's nice to meet you. Where are you guys from?"

"Eugene, Oregon. You?"

"Oh, wow! Small world. We're from Salem."

"No kidding? What're the odds?"

We all laughed, I thanked them again, and we parted ways.

"They were nice," Joy said happily.

"Mmhmm."

We reviewed the photo Greg had taken of us, which had turned out well. Of course, Joy looked beautiful in it. "I'll have to get that one printed and framed when we get home," I said.

A cold breeze blew past, causing Joy to shiver and rub her arms up and down. I put my arm around her shoulders and pulled her close to me. We walked toward the basilica, our eyes rising to the top of the façade, where the statues of Christ, eleven of the Apostles, and John the Baptist stood, looking over the visitors of their domain.

We stood in the short line of people, all bundled up on the chilly October day, to get into the basilica. After passing through the metal detectors, I led Joy through the enormous bronze doors from the outer narthex and into what I still considered to be the most stunning piece of architecture I'd ever seen.

The "Wow" whispered from Joy's lips told me our thoughts were in sync.

"I—it's—wow."

I smiled at her uncharacteristic ineloquence. "Beautiful, right?"

"Beyond words!"

"I've accepted the fact that I'll probably never get over the enormity of it all, no matter how many times I see it."

"I don't think I will either." Joy meandered directly to the right toward Michelangelo's famed *Pieta*, a piece representing Mary cradling Christ's body after the Crucifixion.

"Such a beautiful sculpture," she said as I stepped up beside her. "I hate that it has to be behind that glass." The glass she referred to was an acrylic glass panel in front of the sculpture that was installed after a crazed Australian geologist had attacked the statue with a hammer back in the '70s.

"I can't believe someone would do that. I'm surprised he didn't burst into flame right after."

Joy nodded, her face showing a genuine sadness for the tragedy.

We continued walking slowly down the right side of the basilica, stopping to look at each of the chapels and statues carved to honor various popes and saints. Joy stopped to look longer than I would have had I been there by myself. While I appreciated the talent of the artists behind all the wonders of St. Peter's, Joy had developed a true passion for this type of art and the period in which it was created.

We reached the Chapel of the Blessed Sacrament, one of the larger chapels, built by Bernini and guarded by a sign: *Only those who wish to pray may enter.* Joy followed a small group in, resting on her knees at one of the prayer kneelers and turning to look at me with a sly smile. I knew full well she had no intention of praying but that she would fake it in order to get a better look at the chapel. I loved that about her. I laughed and gave her a subtle thumbs-up.

"Hey! You alright?"

"Huh?" I snapped back into St. Peter's where Joy had just rejoined me after "praying" in the chapel.

"You were staring at something *very* intently. Are you getting religion?" We both laughed.

"No, no. I was just thinking about when we met. Officially, I mean."

"I love that day. I was so proud of you for publishing your book. And I loved that coffee shop you took me to, where we sat under the eaves on the big porch, watching the spring rain come down. What was that called again?"

"Vero. I can't believe we haven't gone back since then."

"I know! It was so good, and it's such a neat place. We'll go when we get back home."

"That sounds great." I took her hand and we continued to walk through the church.

Once Joy had seen all she wanted to for the day, we walked back to our hotel and took a long, late-afternoon nap. We left the windows open a bit and held each other close to keep warm.

Around six o'clock, we showered and changed our clothes for the evening, before walking out into the cold, late-October evening air. Fortunately, there was no breeze, and it was a clear, dry night.

We found a nice, warm ristorante with gnocchi on the menu and were seated after a few minutes. After two bottles of wine and a long, delicious meal, Joy whispered in my ear. "You have an early morning tomorrow. We should head back and get to bed early." She kissed my earlobe, sending an excited current through me.

"I suppose you're right. I love you so goddamn much." I paid the bill and we hurried back to the warmth of our room.

I'd set the alarm on my cell phone for seven o'clock the next morning, and at a lower volume, so that it wouldn't wake Joy as I knew the in-room alarm clock would. As the chime went off, I kissed Joy's bare shoulder and slowly slid out from under the fluffy, white bedding. I made my way to the bathroom, guided only by the yellowed light coming through the crack in the curtains from the streetlights.

As the hot water poured over me, I took a few moments to collect my thoughts. It was about to be a day that could be full of emotions, and, even though I knew I couldn't—and shouldn't—hold them back, I wanted to prepare myself. It had been almost a full year since Jack had died, and I'd held myself together for the most part. But that didn't mean there weren't times that I found myself breaking down over a glass of Bombay Sapphire on the rocks. I tried to save *those* times for when I was drinking at home rather than at a bar.

When I came out of the bathroom, Joy's soft voice floated over from the bed. "Hi."

"Hey, you. Sorry, I was trying not to wake you. I know it's early for vacation."

"I wanted to be up to see you off. I know it's a big day for you." She sat up with the sheet wrapped around her shoulders.

"I appreciate that, babe. And we get to do it together tomorrow, and I'm looking very forward to that." I stood in front of her as she sat on the edge of the bed and took her face in my hands, tilted it up at me, and leaned down to kiss her. "You know I love you, right? Like, generally, but I also love you for doing all of this."

"I know you do, and I love you, too. I'm really glad we could make it work."

"Me too." I pulled a T-shirt over my head and put a button-down over that, but Joy gently pushed my hands out of the way and began buttoning it for me. When she was done, I grabbed my jeans from the desk chair and put them on, then some wool socks and my Clarks. Back over at the bed, I pushed Joy back so her head was on the pillow and propped myself above her with a hand on either side of her head.

"Go back to sleep, sweetheart," I said, kissing her several times. "I appreciate you sending me off, but you also need your rest."

"I do. I'm so sleepy. I love you, Michael. Have fun today, and I'll talk to you a little later and see you tonight." She closed her eyes with a sleepy smile on her face.

"I love you, too." I pulled the bedding up around her and kissed her forehead. Then, her lips, her ear, her neck. Her eyes shot open.

She playfully pushed me away. "Later!" she said with a sly look in her eyes before she closed them again.

I laughed. "Later it is. Bye, baby." I pulled on my wool coat and shut the door behind me.

Downstairs at the front desk, as I ordered breakfast to be delivered to Joy in a couple of hours, I thought again about how lucky I was to have her in my life. About six months after Jack died, I'd come home from the office to find two plane tickets to Rome on the counter, along with a note:

This is birthday and Christmas for the next two years.

Love, Joy

"I think it's time for you to go back," Joy had said after she'd come out of the bedroom and wrapped her arms around me from behind. "And I want to come with, if it's alright."

I turned around and wrapped my arms around her waist, pulling her close. "Of course I want you to go with." I brushed a tear from my eye. "You're the best, Joy. I don't know what I did to deserve you."

The next few months were a whirlwind as we planned the rest of our late-October trip, nearly a week of which would be spent in Rome. Joy wanted the main focus to be revisiting my time with Jack, but I made sure she told me where else she wanted to go so that we could scratch her art history itch. She settled on Florence, Siena, and Venice, so we planned for a couple of nights in each.

Once I had confirmed the order for Joy's breakfast in bed, I made my way to the café on the edge of Piazza del Popolo. There, I sat outside under the awning for about an hour with a cornetto and a couple of espressos, watching other early birds pass by. After paying my check, I walked to the plinth in the middle of the piazza. Jack's seat at the base of the obelisk was vacant. For a moment, I stood staring at the steps, somewhat ceremoniously. I almost felt unworthy of sitting in the seat he'd so often occupied. Finally, I took a deep breath and sat down, leaning forward with my elbows on my knees and my hands clasped, watching as tourists and locals made their way through and around the square, filling the cafés at its edges, taking pictures of the fountains and statues and churches, entering the churches to pay respects or find solace.

As I sat there, I thought about Joy and the magazine and how different my life was from the way it had been only two years before. I thought about Jack and how glad I was that, in the midst of all of Rome's history and glory, I'd taken the time to talk to the old man who sat in the same place nearly every day, honoring his wife, forever madly in love with her. Something he had said as we sipped our gin that last night resonated in my head like the fireworks over the bay in Sant'Agnello: *Life-changing things don't come along every day, but when you see an opportunity that gives you that feeling, don't ask questions. Take it, and hold onto it like your life depends on it.* I smiled to myself as I thought of Joy back in the hotel room, waking anytime to a knock from room service. With a last look around the piazza, I headed off toward Stefano's coffee shop to get an Irish coffee and take a long walk along the Tiber.

Acknowledgments

Thank you, first and foremost, to Sean Kelly – my good friend, business partner, and fellow storyteller. You've been closely involved for this entire ride and have provided insight at damn near every turn I've made in this book.

Thank you especially to Sharlyn Anderson. Ten years ago, over cold Sierra Nevada Pale Ales, you listened to me describe with uncertainty the idea I had for a novel. Then, you told me to "just write it." Your advice was invaluable, and I've never looked back.

Thank you to Jarrett Thompson – my longtime friend and former high school newspaper editor. Not only did you read my first draft within 48 hours, you spent time picking through it with your finely tuned editor's eye and gave me notes that proved integral to what this turned out to be and taught me so much about myself as a writer.

Thank you to Laura Chappele and Francesca Delo for drawing me out of my shell in Sant'Agnello. Those memories are some of my best.

I am truly grateful to all my friends and family who have stuck with me on this over the past decade, who have kept asking: "How's your book coming?" and "When do I get to read your book?" and "You done yet?" and "Oh, you're still writing that?" Your support has been vital to my endurance on *Catalyst*, and I'm happy you now get to read it.

Stay in touch with Dustin and see what he's up to on Instagram @dustinmynotebook and at www.dustinmynotebook.com!

Check out these other releases from Emerald Inkwell:

The Drive Home
by Sean Kelly

For a Ghost-Free Time, Call
Episodes 1-5
by Sean Kelly

Watch for more great stories from EI in the future!

www.emeraldinkwell.com

Made in the USA
Columbia, SC
30 October 2020